FIT Guys

Volume One

By Kim Dare

FIT Guys Volume One © Kim Dare 2015
ISBN # 978-1-910081-08-2

Worth Waiting For Copyright © Kim Dare 2013
Worth a Shot © Copyright Kim Dare 2014

Published by Kim Dare
Edited by Christine Allen-Riley and Shannon Leeper
Cover Art by Kris Norris

First Print Edition – June 2015

This is a work of fiction. All characters, places and events are from the author's imagination and should not be confused with fact. Any resemblance to persons, living or dead, events or places is purely coincidental.

Please note that this book contains sexually explicit content and is not suitable for anyone under the age of eighteen.

Contents

Worth Waiting For

Chapter One

Three years ago

Colby Landon stared intently through the window, but he didn't see anything that happened in the street below him. The living room of the fourth floor flat had a perfect view into the dance studio on the third floor of the building opposite, and his gaze never wavered from it.

Behind him, Colby heard his older brother, Tony, wandering around the room, collecting all the things he'd want ready for training the following morning. Colby's attention remained fixed on the view through the window.

"What time are you heading out tomorrow?" Tony asked.

Colby still didn't glance in his brother's direction. "Coach Walters wants us in the pool by five-thirty, so I guess I'll be out of here at about five."

"So, shouldn't you be in bed by now?"

"Yeah, but so should you," Colby said, vaguely. There was no sign of movement in the dance studio, but Colby had no doubt the dance instructor was still there, tucked away in one of the more private rooms at the back of the studio. Colby had been watching the building for hours; the guy couldn't have left without him noticing. And, since the dancer never went to sleep without switching off the lights in the studio, that meant—

"You know you're turning into a stalker, right?" Tony asked.

"Yeah, okay. Goodnight. I'll see you tomorrow evening," Colby said, automatically. "I think I should be home at about six."

Tony laughed and ruffled Colby's hair on his way past. "Don't stay up all night watching your crush, kiddo. And don't blame me when your coach busts your balls for falling asleep in the pool tomorrow morning."

Colby heard Tony's bedroom door click shut. A few minutes later, a complete hush settled over their flat.

His crush, as Tony had been so nice to label him, was bound to come back into the studio's main room soon — even if it was just to switch off the lights. There was still a good chance Colby would be able to get a final glimpse of him before he went to bed.

Half an hour later, one of the doors on the back wall of the studio space finally swung open. The bright lights above the dance floor made it easy to see every detail of the dancer's appearance as he strode through the room. Colby leaned closer to the window. Damn, but the guy was stunning. Dark brown hair that begged to be touched and a body that would make any gay man whimper.

Tonight, the dancer was obviously going out, because no one would wear leather trousers that tight if he was planning to stay in. Colby watched the dancer leave the studio. He'd seen him through the window more than often enough to know what would happen next. In an hour or two's time, the guy would return wrapped around some apparently random stranger, and they'd both disappear through the door leading into a private space at the rear of the studio.

Colby sighed. If he was the one who was lucky enough to go home with the dancer, it would be different. If he was there, they'd fall asleep curled up together in the same bed — Colby wouldn't walk out the moment he zipped up, the way every other man seemed to. And Colby wouldn't just visit the studio once, either, he'd go back every chance he got. Hell, if he ever managed to get into the dance studio, he'd never want to leave at all…

One moment Colby was staring out of the window, the

same way he had dozens of times before, the next moment he'd made his decision and was already halfway across the living room. He probably had an extra two flights of stairs to catch up by now, but the dancer hadn't been walking that fast. It might be possible.

He raced to the flat's front door, only to stop short with his fingers wrapped around the handle.

"Damn!" Rushing into the kitchen he scrawled *gone out* on the note pad hanging on the fridge. It wasn't that much of a heads up for his brother if Tony went looking for him, but there was no time to worry about that now. Tony's wallet lay on the kitchen counter, along with his keys, his i-pod, and everything else he intended to take to training the following morning.

Colby patted his pockets and tried to remember where he'd put his own wallet. No time for that either. He slipped Tony's wallet into his pocket and headed for the door once more.

Colby threw himself down the stairs three at a time. He reached the door out of his building just in time to see the guy from the dance studio turn the corner at the end of the street. Tucking his hands into his pockets and striding out, doing his best not to look like he was stalking anyone, Colby headed after him.

Three corners later, he'd caught up enough to be less than ten yards behind the dancer. Then, for the first time since he left the flat, Colby hesitated. He watched the dancer stride confidently past the line of men outside a nightclub. A quick smile and the bouncer waved him inside.

The queue stretched halfway along the building and didn't seem to be moving at all. Colby looked along the row of men, sighed, and joined the end of the line.

A few minutes passed, and he spotted one of the club's bouncers walking down the row of men waiting to get in. Every so often the bouncer stopped to speak to someone. Some guys were sent to the front of the queue and invited to go straight in. Others were sent out of the line altogether.

Stepping closer to the wall, Colby did his best to look inconspicuous—it wasn't easy. Everyone around him was dressed for clubbing. He was still in worn-out jeans and a long sleeve T-shirt advertising his attendance at the Falconer Institute of Training. He stared down at his trainers, pushed his hands deeper into his pockets, and tried not to look nervous.

"ID?"

Colby blinked up at the bouncer.

"ID?" the man repeated.

They weren't that close to a streetlight. People always said he looked a lot like his brother. Colby took Tony's wallet out of his pocket and handed over his brother's driving licence.

The bouncer looked from him, to the ID and back again. "You're nineteen?"

Colby nodded. He was six foot three compared to Tony's six foot four. They had the same blond hair and blue eyes. Hours of swimming every day had given him more muscle than most guys his age. He could pull this off if he didn't say something stupid.

The bouncer handed Tony's ID back to Colby and motioned him out of the line. Colby felt his cheeks turn red. He was just about to head home with his tail tucked between his legs when the bouncer pointed him toward the front of the queue.

Was he supposed to tip him? Before he had a chance to work out the right answer, the bouncer had moved on to those who'd joined the queue after Colby. Trying not to feel too guilty about all the people who should be going in ahead of him, Colby walked to the front of the line. A second bouncer looked him up and down.

Colby smiled hopefully. The bouncer smiled back and waved him in.

The instant Colby stepped into the club, music

surrounded him. It pounded through the whole building, seeming to pump up between the floor boards and seep straight into his feet.

Nudging people out of the way as politely as possible, he worked his way deeper inside. His height advantage over most of the men there didn't help much in the gloom.

Half an hour later, he was in the thickest part of the crowd and —

There! The man from the dance studio! Relief rushed through Colby.

The guy was on the dance floor, moving to the beat as if the music was part of his soul, but he didn't seem to be dancing with a specific partner. The men around him seemed more of an annoyance than an attraction.

As Colby watched from the edge of the dance floor, a whole succession of men approached the dancer, rubbing themselves up against him in what Colby considered to be a quite unnecessarily intimate way, but the dancer never allowed one man to keep his attention for too long. He soon moved away, letting the music reclaim him.

Colby stared, completely enchanted. It was so different from watching him at the studio. The simple fact that Colby could hear what the guy was dancing to made it a hundred times more intense. Several yards still separated them, but there were no window panes or streets to keep them apart. He'd never been closer to everything he'd ever wanted in his life.

Then, suddenly, the dancer was moving away. Colby instinctively stepped forward, desperately trying to keep him in sight. Past the other side of the dance floor, Colby saw the dancer join a group at the bar. From the way he spoke to them, the other men were all friends of his, but there was still no one man he focused on.

Colby took a deep breath and walked up to the group. He stopped a foot or two behind the dancer.

"Can I buy you a drink?"

The guy turned toward him, so did everyone else in the group, but Colby kept all his attention on the dancer.

"He's pretty," one of the other men observed. "Why don't you let me buy you a drink instead, honey?" He stepped up alongside the dancer, reached out and put a friendly hand on Colby's arm.

"No, thank you." Colby never looked away from the dancer. This close he could make out the colour of his eyes for the first time. They were deep blue and damn near hypnotic.

"Oh, come on," the dancer's friend began.

The dancer frowned. "Leave him be, Kevin."

"Why?" Kevin asked.

"Because he needed a fake ID to get in here," the dancer said, with complete conviction.

"What?" Kevin said.

Even while he spoke to his friend, the dancer kept his attention on Colby. "He's underage. Let him be."

Colby felt the heat race to his cheeks and prayed that the lighting was low enough that no one would spot his blush.

"He looks like he's old enough to know what he wants to me, Noah," Kevin said. He slid his hand higher up Colby's arm.

Noah—at least Colby knew the dancer's name, now. It wasn't much, but he was willing to be thankful for it. "I am old enough to know what I want, and I don't want your hand on my arm, thank you." He looked pointedly at the way Kevin's fingertips caressed his upper arm.

Kevin chuckled, seeming completely unrepentant, but he also let go of Colby's arm.

Colby turned his attention back to Noah.

Noah looked him up and down, still frowning slightly. "You don't belong here, kid. Go home."

The dismissal cut deep, but Colby held back a flinch through sheer force of will. "I'm not a child."

Noah's eyes turned slightly sad. "Yeah, right, and I bet you believe you actually know what you're doing, too. Don't you?"

Colby didn't know what to say to that. All he knew was that he could feel the dancer slipping away from him even while they stood there. "I'm nineteen," he rushed out.

Noah held out his hand. "I can spot a fake ID from the other side of the room."

"No problem." Colby fished out Tony's wallet and handed over his ID. "It's genuine."

Noah studied it for what felt like hours, tilting it toward what little light there was. "You're right," he finally admitted. "It's genuine."

Colby smiled.

Noah didn't. "There's a good family resemblance, too. I'm guessing Anthony Landon is your brother, or maybe a cousin?"

Colby automatically took the ID back when Noah offered it to him. "Brother," he muttered.

"And how old are you really...?" He left a gap inviting Colby to fill it with a name.

Colby considered lying, but a quick glance at Noah's expression and he thought better of it. "Colby. Fifteen," he admitted.

"And what the hell are you doing in a club like this?"

"I wanted to talk to you."

"To me?"

Colby nodded.

For the first time, Noah looked confused. "Why?"

Colby's blush deepened. He hadn't actually thought about how to explain himself past that point.

Noah grabbed his arm. His grip couldn't have felt more different than Kevin's. When Noah walked away from the bar, Colby willingly went with him. Hell, it wasn't much, but the hand on his arm was at least physical contact of a sort.

He didn't pay too much attention to where they were going until Noah led him out through a side door. The alley was quiet compared to the club. A nearby security light meant it was actually brighter out there than it had been inside.

"I don't know you," Noah said. "I'm good with faces. I'd remember it if we'd met before."

"I live in the building opposite you."

Noah just stared at him for a few seconds. "You followed me here?"

Colby nodded. "I'm not stalking you, I swear, I just... You're a really amazing dancer."

Noah half smiled at that. "You're some sort of unlikely fan of modern dance?"

"Our flat looks down into the dance studio."

That earned him a full smile. "So you're spying on me as well as stalking me?"

"No! I mean—"

"Don't worry about it, kid. Come on." Noah turned on his heel and strode toward the end of the alley.

Colby hurried to catch up. "Where are we going?"

"I'm taking you home."

Colby stopped walking. "To your place?" It couldn't be that easy, could it?

"No, to your place." Noah retraced his steps and took hold of Colby's arm again. He led him out of the alley, into the street. "Come on. You're way too young for this sort of club."

"I'm fifteen."

"Yeah, and I spent enough time in these clubs when I was your age to know that you shouldn't be within five miles of them."

As they passed under a street lamp, Colby brought them to a halt. He looked down into Noah's eyes and saw the regret in his expression. Suddenly, everything he'd been about to say seemed stupid.

"If you want to get laid you should find someone your own age," Noah informed him. "Or even better—wait until you can get into the club with your own ID."

Colby reached out and stroked his fingers down Noah's cheek, hating the sadness in his eyes.

Noah turned his head away sharply and strode off toward their street. "Do your parents know you sneaked out?"

"I don't live with them. I'm staying with my brother."

Noah slowed his pace slightly, making it easier for Colby to catch up. "My parents weren't thrilled when they found out I was gay either."

Colby shook his head. "It's not like that."

Noah cast him a glance out of the corner of his eye but he kept walking.

"I got a swimming scholarship to the Falconer Institute of Training. My folks didn't want to drag my younger brothers and sisters down here. Tony was already here on an athletics scholarship. It was easier for me to just move in with him."

Colby chewed on his bottom lip as he waited for Noah to say something, but it seemed like Noah was more than happy to walk in silence.

"Your parents freaked out when you told them you're gay?" Colby finally asked.

"Yeah, something like that," Noah muttered. His pace sped up again.

Colby easily matched his stride. "I'm sorry."

Noah shrugged. "Shit happens. No big deal."

Colby couldn't let silence descend again. They were already less than two street lengths away from his building. He couldn't let his chance to talk to Noah just slip away. "How old were you when you came out?"

"Your age," Noah said. "Do you always ask this many questions?"

"Only when I'm trying to get to know someone."

Noah stopped. He looked Colby up and down. "You're actually like this, aren't you? You know you've got no chance of getting laid, but you're still this genuinely bloody *nice*."

"What else would I be?"

Noah shook his head. "Well, you're too damn innocent to have a crush on someone like me, that's for sure."

They turned onto their street. "What do you mean 'someone like you'?"

"I mean you should be chasing after boys who are more like you—nice—all clean cut and white picket fences, not someone who left nice behind when you were still in primary school."

Colby stopped. Noah kept walking for a few paces, then he turned back to face him. "Try to keep up, kid."

"I don't like the way you talk about yourself."

"So don't listen." Noah shrugged and started walking again.

Colby stood his ground.

Noah looked over his shoulder, sighed and walked back to him. "How did you think tonight was going to turn out?"

Colby shrugged. "I thought I'd buy you a drink. We'd talk. Maybe we'd get to know each other a bit better."

Noah shook his head, but he smiled too. "You're cute, and you're obviously incredibly sweet, but..." He considered him for a few moments. "I'll tell you what—come back when you're eighteen, and I'll take you up on that."

"That's three years!"

Noah chuckled. "Eighteen minus fifteen is three? Well, I was never that good at maths, but I'll take your word for it."

Their slow stroll brought them to the door leading into Colby's building all too soon. Colby hesitated. "You're going back to the club now, aren't you?"

Noah shook his head. "No, I'm calling it a night."

Colby rocked back and forth on his heels.

Noah touched his cheek very lightly with the tips of his fingers. Going up onto his toes to bridge their height difference, Noah pressed a chaste kiss against Colby's other cheek. Turning away, he headed for the building opposite.

"Did you mean it?" Colby called after him.

Halfway across the deserted street, Noah turned back to him. "Mean what?"

"About when I'm eighteen?"

Noah laughed. "Of course I did. Let me know when you turn eighteen, and we'll have some fun."

Colby stood on the doorstep and watched Noah disappear into his building. When he was out of sight, Colby took the elevator up to the fourth floor and let himself back into the flat as quietly as possible.

Heading straight into the kitchen, he tore off the top sheet of note paper, where he'd scrawled his message to his brother.

Underneath his note was another note, in Tony's hand writing. *Wake me when you get in.*

Busted! Rolling his eyes, Colby went to Tony's bedroom door and tapped against it.

A muffled curse and, a moment later, Tony opened the door, flattening down sleep spiked hair. "Nice note," he said. "Very informative."

"Yeah," Colby agreed.

Tony sighed and led the way into the living room. "Where did you go?"

"A nightclub."

Tony paused mid-step. "A real club? Did you get in?"

Colby took Tony's wallet out of his pocket and tossed it across to him. "I borrowed your ID. All the money's still there."

"Slick," Tony said, with a surprised yet appreciative little nod. "Which club was it?"

Colby tried to remember seeing any sort of sign outside it and failed. "I didn't notice the name." His feet automatically led him to the window.

Noah stood in the window opposite. For a moment, it looked like he was staring straight back at Colby. Then his attention moved away, and it was obvious he was just looking at the block of flats in general.

"Does this have something to do with him?" Tony asked, stepping forward to stand next to Colby.

"His name's Noah."

"What?"

Colby glanced at Tony out of the corner of his eye. Suddenly, Tony seemed to be wide awake and tense as hell.

"Noah," Colby repeated, more calmly than he felt. "That's his name."

"You met him?"

Colby nodded. "I followed him to the club."

"And you didn't think this was something you should tell me about?"

Colby watched as Noah turned away from the window, switched out the lights, and headed toward one of the rooms at the back of the studio. "It was a spur of the moment thing."

Tony pushed a hand through his hair. "What happened?"

Colby shrugged.

"Colby..." Tony warned.

Colby glanced at him again. "Nothing happened." Heat flooded his cheeks.

"Then why are you blushing?"

Colby forced a twisted smile. "Because nothing happened."

"Oh. You struck out with him." There was obvious relief mixed in with the sympathy in his voice.

"He told me to come back when I could get in using my own ID," Colby admitted.

"Ouch."

Colby shook his head. "It wasn't like that. He was nice about it, but he just thinks I'm some stupid kid."

"You are a stupid kid."

Colby bit his tongue, knowing it was useless to argue that point.

Tony turned and leaned back against the window sill. "He's about nineteen, twenty, right? About my age?"

Colby nodded.

"If I hooked up with a fifteen year old girl, what would

12

you think of me?" Tony asked.

"That would be different. I can look after myself."

"Of course you can."

Colby glared at him, but Tony just laughed. "It sounds like he's a good guy."

Colby couldn't hold on to his annoyance then. "He is a good guy." Colby smiled, just a little sadly.

"But?" Tony prompted.

"Don't do that," Colby protested.

"What?"

"Don't do the parental mind reading thing. It's bad enough when Mum does it — don't you start, as well."

"Point taken," Tony allowed. "But I still want to know."

"I think his parents threw him out when they found out he was gay."

"That's rough."

Colby nodded. The thought of Noah back then, what it had to have been like for him, made Colby feel like he'd been kicked in the stomach. "He said he'd been going to clubs since he was fifteen. That's about the same time he came out to his family."

"So now you're wondering how he survived on the streets when he was that age, what he was doing when he hit the clubs?"

"He doesn't have anyone," Colby whispered.

"And you want to change that?"

Colby took a deep breath. "He said I should try again when I'm eighteen."

Tony whistled under his breath. "That's a long way off."

Colby frowned. "Do you think he'll be okay?"

Tony ruffled his hair as he turned away from the window. "If you stick to your current schedule, I don't think much can happen to him without you seeing it from here."

Colby sighed. It didn't seem like anywhere near

enough.

Tony chuckled. "Damn, you've got it bad for him, haven't you?"

Colby glanced at him out of the corner of his eye once more. "If you say one word about puppy love I'm going to have to take a swing at you. I know I'll be the one who ends up getting whipped, but I'll still have to take a shot at it."

Tony held up his hands in mock surrender. "I didn't say a word. Hell, who am I to judge—I've never had the puppy version or the real thing. Anyway, the way I see it, if it's puppy love you'll grow out of it without my saying anything. If it's the real thing, nothing I can say will make a damn bit of difference. Either way, I might as well save my breath. And, on that note, I'm going to bed. Try to stay in the flat for at least a few minutes after I close my bedroom door, okay?"

Colby nodded.

"Seriously, kiddo," Tony said. "If you want to take another nocturnal jaunt, I want to know about it—in advance."

Colby nodded again. He looked back to the window. The lights were off opposite, the whole building was in darkness.

"Three years!" He leaned his forehead on the glass. "Three years…"

Chapter Two

Two years ago

"I don't think Dad would have been so quick to buy you that telescope if he knew you'd be using it to study biology rather than astronomy."

It wasn't anything Colby hadn't heard several times before. He didn't even bother to take his eye away from the view finder.

"A year ago, this crush was mildly amusing, now you're starting to freak me out," Tony said from somewhere behind him.

"Your life's so amazing you have nothing better to do than hang around and harass me?" Colby asked. Through the telescope he was able to see every detail of Noah's expression. He currently stood at the front of a beginners' class and had his I'm-going-to-be-patient-if-it-kills-me smile pinned to his lips.

"Mum phoned up to check on you while you were at training," Tony said. "I'm being your responsible adult of record—and harassing you over your crush is far more fun than checking your report card."

"There's nothing wrong with my report card," Colby protested.

"Exactly! Apart from your obsession with your dancer, you're freakily like a Stepford child. Your coach says you never miss a practice and are way ahead on every training regime he concocts for you. Your teachers all think you have a little halo floating over your head. I thought I'd have lots of opportunities to shout at you when you moved in with me—

I'm very disappointed."

"Is your date running late or something?" Colby guessed, adjusting the focus slightly and zooming out so he could watch Noah demonstrate a particular move to his class.

Tony chuckled. "She bailed on me at the last moment. I'm all yours for the evening—but I'll be damned if I'm going to spend the whole time watching you watch your crush get it on."

"I don't do that."

Tony sighed. "Yeah, I know. The rules."

"I just watch him dance. Watching him with another guy would be creepy."

"And you'd get jealous," Tony added, helpfully.

Colby said nothing. It was damn hard to argue with the truth.

Footsteps warned him Tony was approaching the window. Right on cue, Tony's hands landed on his shoulders and tugged him away from the telescope. "Come on. How does pizza sound?"

Colby studied Tony's expression for a moment. He had that stubborn look in his eye. Colby cast a regretful glance at his telescope, but he knew when he was beat. He grabbed his coat and followed his brother out of the flat.

It was no big deal really. It was Thursday—Noah would be teaching beginners classes until nine. Colby would have to wait until everyone else left to see Noah really dance. He wouldn't miss much in the meantime.

On the street outside their building, Colby fell in step beside his brother. There was a comforting kind of familiarity about those occasions when Tony decided that he had to take his position as Colby's "responsible adult of record" seriously.

Sitting at a quiet table near the back of Colby's favourite pizza place, Tony dutifully ticked off all the main points before they'd even finished the first half of the pizza. School—good. Swimming—great. Any problems—no. Anything you want to talk about—no.

16

Colby took a swig of his Coke and relaxed back in his seat. The conversation during the second half of the pizza was usually a lot more fun, and a lot less like talking to both his parents rolled into one, slightly sarcastic, package.

Tony reached for another slice. "There's a new guy that's just joined the athletics programme—a long distance runner."

"Yeah?" Colby asked, taking up another slice of pizza.

"Nice guy," Tony said. "Seventeen. Blond. Pretty. Gay."

Colby nodded automatically and waited for the amusing anecdote.

Nothing.

Colby looked over his shoulder, wondering if some girl had caught Tony's attention. There was no one he imagined being Tony's type within view.

Colby frowned as he mentally ran over Tony's description of the runner. He grinned around his slice of pizza. "Are you trying to set me up with one of your friends?"

"No. Well, maybe." Tony shrugged. "You need to get a life."

"I have a life."

"You need a *social* life."

Colby rolled his eyes. "You're right. I'll be sure to fit it in between doing school, forty odd miles per week in the pool, strength training, physio and everything else."

"You find plenty of time to watch Noah," Tony observed.

Colby put down his slice of pizza. "Yeah, I do."

"It's not healthy."

Colby sighed. One of the benefits of knowing that a particular conversation was building for a long time was the chance to get all his answers worked out well in advance. "I'm not under any illusions. I spoke to him once for five minutes over a year ago. He probably doesn't even remember me. I'm not as stupid or as clueless as you think I am, Tony. I don't think he's my boyfriend or anything like that, and I don't expect anything other than a nice view in return for my time."

Colby was quite proud of that little speech, especially his ability to get through it without blushing, stammering, or wilting under Tony's less than impressed gaze.

"Don't you ever think about just going out and meeting a real guy?"

"Sure I do, but I'm realistic. I spend all my days either studying or in the pool. I don't have time for anything serious, and I don't think I want anything casual." Colby shrugged. "The way coach pushes us, most of the other swimmers just crash in front of the TV when they get home. I crash in front of a telescope instead. It's not so different."

Tony leaned back in his seat with his arms folded across his chest, apparently resigned to his fate. "So you're just going to wait until you're eighteen and throw yourself at the guy from the building opposite?"

Colby picked up another slice of pizza and smiled across the table at his brother. "Sounds like a bloody good plan to me."

"You know that's another two years?"

Colby's smile turned wry. "Yeah, I know…"

Chapter Three

One year ago

Colby sighed and took his eye away from the telescope's view finder. Another night and yet another random man arriving home with Noah—another guy that wasn't him.

Leaning back in the armchair he'd positioned in front of the window, Colby stared up at the ceiling. Watching Noah walk through the studio all wrapped around another guy wasn't only creepy, it was also very depressing.

Maybe Tony was right—he needed to spend more time out of the house. He should get on with his life and stop obsessing about Noah. Even as he made the decision and stood up, Colby couldn't help but glance across the street one more time.

Telescope or no telescope, it was still easy to lock onto the right window in the building opposite and focus in on Noah and his date.

No.

Colby dropped back into the chair by the telescope. That wasn't right.

The two guys were no longer entwined and stumbling toward the back rooms of the studio together. Noah now stood in the middle of the studio several metres away from his date. As Colby watched through the telescope, Noah took another step away. He said something to the guy. The other man waved his arms around and shouted something back at Noah.

With no possible way of making out the words, Colby

could only do his best to interpret their body language and gestures. Noah shook his head. The guy closed the gap between them and grabbed Noah's arm before Noah had a chance to retreat out of range.

He was bigger than Noah, taller and far more heavily built. Noah yanked his arm out of the guy's grip and tried to back away. The guy lurched forward and grabbed him again. This time he had hold of both Noah's shoulders. He shook him hard enough that Noah's head snapped back and forth with the force of the movement.

Frozen in place, Colby couldn't do anything but watch as Noah pushed against the guy's chest, wrenched himself free and stumbled backwards. Noah pointed at the door. The other man yelled something. Noah made some sort of reply and stood his ground, refusing to back away or even drop his gaze when the other man strode toward him.

The back of the guy's hand slammed into the side of Noah's face. Noah tumbled down onto the floor.

Colby jerked away from the telescope. He tripped over the chair as he turned to rush out of the room. One final glance back at the window, and he saw Noah's date storm out of the studio.

Colby hesitated. He watched Noah pull himself to his feet and rush across to the door. For a horrible moment, Colby thought Noah was going to follow the other man, but he just locked the door in his date's wake. Colby shifted his weight from one foot to another, unsure what to do.

As Noah leant against the studio door, Colby righted the chair he'd knocked over and turned the telescope toward him.

The other guy was gone. What the hell could Colby actually say if he raced across the street at this point? *Hi, I saw you getting assaulted while I was spying on you and your date, are you okay?*

Through the magnifying lens Colby saw Noah close his eyes and rest his head against the studio door. There was already a slight mark blossoming across his cheekbone.

Colby pulled away from the telescope and looked at the real sized view for a moment. Noah looked so small, so alone. Right underneath the studio's main window was a large banner advertising the dance classes. It had a telephone number printed on it in a big red font.

Colby had been fascinated by those numbers since the banner first went up, but he'd never actually given in to the temptation to call, never found the courage to take that big a risk. Not giving himself time to think better of it now, he pulled his mobile out of his pocket and dialled the number on the banner.

As it rang, Noah straightened up and turned toward the phone hanging on the wall nearby. He rechecked that the door was locked before he answered it.

"Hello. Michelson's Dance Academy. Noah speaking."

Colby's mind went blank. Just hearing Noah's voice again scattered every thought in his head.

"Hello?" Noah repeated. He looked suspiciously at the phone. "Sam, if that's you—"

"No, I'm not Sam. I'm sorry, I... I think I have the wrong number," Colby blurted out.

"Okay, no problem." Noah moved to hang up.

Colby sprang forward, until he was on the very edge of his seat. "Wait!"

Noah hesitated. "Yeah?"

"Um... Can you tell me what number I got through to?" Colby rolled his eyes at himself.

Noah shrugged and rattled off the number.

"Thanks."

Noah went to hang up again.

"Are you okay?" Colby rushed out.

Noah frowned at the phone. "What?"

"I just... You sound... I just wondered if you're okay."

Noah's expression turned sceptical. "Why wouldn't I be?"

Colby kept his gaze on Noah through the telescope. "I don't know. You sound…" Wonderful was the obvious word. God, he really loved Noah's voice. But, at the same time: "You sound…sad."

"Yeah, well sometimes life sucks."

Colby nibbled on his bottom lip. "Bad day?"

"You could say that." Noah tentatively touched his injured cheek with his fingertips. He winced and studied his fingers, as if checking whether or not he was bleeding.

"What happened?" Colby asked.

"Why do you care?"

Colby smiled at Noah across the street—it was pretty much exactly the same tone of voice Noah had used when he'd walked Colby home from the club. "Why shouldn't I care?"

"Because no one gives a damn about a wrong number?" Noah suggested.

"I do."

Noah tapped the phone against his uninjured cheek. Colby could tell he was considering whether he should hang up. "I had an argument with…my date," he confessed.

"Sam—the person you thought was calling you?"

"Yeah. Sam h…she can be a bit out there sometimes—especially when she's had a few drinks." With a sigh, he leaned his back against the wall and slid down until he sat on the floor underneath the phone. He twirled the cable around his fingers, apparently deep in thought.

"What happened?" Colby barely risked making the words more than a whisper. One wrong move and he knew Noah would hang up on him.

Noah looked up at the ceiling. "Nothing important. Same shit, different day, you know?"

Colby closed his eyes, wondering just how many of Noah's days had gone like that. "Things will get better," he whispered.

"Ha! Yeah, right."

"They will," Colby said, putting every bit of certainty he had into the words. "You just have to wait a little bit longer, and you'll see."

Noah looked down. He didn't seem to be able to find the words to answer, and Colby couldn't let him struggle.

"It'll work out," he promised.

Noah made a sceptical sound in the back of his throat. "I wish I had your confidence."

"I can believe enough for both of us."

Noah smiled. "You sound like a message on a soppy greeting card."

Colby chuckled, so bloody relieved that Noah had smiled, even if it was because he thought he was talking to an idiot. "Maybe, but that doesn't mean I'm not right."

Noah pulled his knees up to his chest, curling into a ball where he sat on the floor. "God, I'm getting pathetic."

"Why?"

"When a wrong number turns into the highlight of your whole damn month, something is seriously wrong." Noah stood up, shaking his head at himself.

"Mine too," Colby said before Noah could hang up.

Noah hesitated again. "Thank you," he whispered, rushing the words out as if he was saying them against all his better instincts. He hung up and rested his forehead against the telephone for a full three minutes while the dial tone rang in Colby's ear. Noah rechecked that the door was locked before he switched off the lights and retreated into the rooms at the back of the studio.

Even after he disconnected his end of the call, Colby sat staring across the street, unable to convince himself to move away.

He didn't look up when Tony came in.

"Isn't he in bed yet?" Tony asked.

Colby had to clear his throat before he could answer. "Yeah, he has been for a while now."

"You know —"

"Don't," Colby cut in. "Yes, I know it's impossible for you to take me or any of this seriously, but no jokes, okay? Not tonight."

"What happened?" Tony pulled up another seat by the window.

Colby swallowed. It was crazy how difficult it was to get the words out. "Noah's date hit him."

"What? Is he okay?"

Colby kept staring straight ahead. "Physically, I guess he's fine. But no, not really, he's not okay at all. He didn't even seem that shocked—it was like it's happened to him before—as if it's happened so often he doesn't really expect anything better than that anymore."

"What about you, are you okay?" Tony asked, carefully.

"Besides wishing I was eighteen? And wishing that I'd been there for him—really there for him instead of over here, staring at him like an idiot, when he needed someone in his corner?" Colby sighed.

"You can't fix the world," Tony told him, with a pat on the shoulder.

Colby smiled slightly. "I know. I'm fine," he said, because there was no chance Tony would leave him alone until he said it. "But I'll be a damn sight better a year from now."

Chapter Four

Present day

Colby turned around, only to find Tony leaning against his wardrobe, completely blocking the doors.

"You're in my way," Colby said.

"If you change your clothes one more time I might have to kill you."

"You don't need to be here," Colby pointed out. "You could just leave me in peace."

"No. I'm coming with you."

"Like hell you are!" Colby stared at his brother as if he'd lost his mind, which he obviously had. "I'm going to a gay nightclub. I'm trying to get a date. This is not a scenario where an older brother, let alone one who can't decide which team he plays for, is going to be useful."

"I have picked a team — team bi," Tony pointed out, mildly. "And I'm not going to hold your hand — I'm just going to be there so I can keep an eye on you."

"No," Colby said.

Tony grinned.

"No," Colby repeated, more firmly. "It's not going to happen."

"If you wanted to go on your own, you should have snuck out again."

Colby looked heavenward. "I snuck out once, three years ago, and you've never forgiven me for it, have you?"

Tony's grin was still in place as he followed Colby out of the flat a few minutes later. It remained there as he kept pace with him down the street.

Detailed but discreet observations, always made from a polite distance, had proved that Noah always went to the same club. Purposefully ignoring Tony's existence, Colby walked a little faster. Noah had left for the club over half an hour ago. A man would have to be a fool to leave someone as hot as Noah alone in a nightclub for a second longer than he had to.

The queue to get into the club once more extended halfway down the side of the building. Colby joined the end of it, refusing to even glance toward his brother. With his luck, Noah would end up falling for Tony! Damn, he wished Tony had stuck to being straight, at least that way —

Tony chuckled, completely scattering Colby's thoughts. "Have a good time, kiddo. Try not to get into any more trouble than you can talk your way out of, but I'll keep my phone on just in case, okay?"

A surge of relief flooded through Colby. He'd never realised just how happy not having a babysitter on the most important night of his life could make him.

He smiled at the back of his brother's head as Tony wandered off, no doubt heading for another club — although it was anyone's guess if it would be a straight one or a gay one this time.

Colby was still smiling to himself about five minutes later, when a bouncer made his way down the row of guys waiting to get into the club.

"ID?"

Colby tried not to look as nervous as he felt when he handed it over. It was a genuine ID. He was old enough to get into any club he wanted. There was no reason why they shouldn't let him in now.

Despite all those very logical facts, it seemed a damn sight harder to get into the club this time. There was no offer to let him jump the queue.

* * * * *

Noah closed his eyes and let the beat push everything else out of his mind. Even as he stood in the middle of the dance floor, everyone around him faded away. It was just him and the music now. It pounded through every cell of his body, filling his whole world with a simple kind of perfection.

Guys came closer and went away again. One song blurred into another. Noah barely noticed any of that. He stayed on the dance floor not caring about anything other than the perfection of being lost in the music, of being able to really dance without having to worry if his students would be able to keep up, while his friends went back to the bar and got the drinks.

Finally, it became a choice between joining his friends or dying of thirst. Aware that he was probably already a few drinks behind everyone else, he grabbed one of the bottles of beer lined up on the bar in front of the group and tossed half of it back in one go. Smiling vaguely, he tried to focus on what his friends said to each other and to ignore the beat calling him back to the dance floor, but damn, it didn't come easy tonight.

As he drained the remainder of the beer, he glanced at his friends. Everyone was looking at him now, or more precisely, they were looking over his left shoulder.

Noah glanced around, wondering who'd caught their attention. He turned completely as he saw the man standing a few feet behind him.

Hot as hell, was the first thing he registered.

He looked up to the guy's hair or lack thereof. Trouble, his sensible side protested.

"Can I buy you a drink?"

"You're not his type," Kevin piped up from somewhere behind Noah.

"I can speak for myself," Noah corrected, looking the new guy up and down. Tight jeans, tight T-shirt—both emphasising a body that would probably look even better naked than it did clothed.

"God, Noah, only you would be stupid enough to hook up with a damn Nazi," Kevin muttered into his beer.

"A what?" The guy looked from Noah to Kevin and back again, big blue eyes open very wide, making him look genuinely confused.

"So the haircut's a fashion statement rather than a political one?" Noah asked glancing up at the guy's shaved head.

"Oh!" He ran his hand over the top of his head as if he'd forgotten all about his hair, or lack thereof. "No. Neither."

"Nothing personal," Noah said. "There's a local skinhead group that likes to send guys in here to cause trouble — some kind of warped initiation ritual."

"Oh, shit," Kevin muttered. He nudged Noah in the ribs. "Chemo."

The guy's eyes opened even wider. "No, it's nothing like that! Hydrodynamics — I do a lot of swimming."

Noah looked him up and down again. He had the height and build of a swimmer. It sounded plausible. There was only one thing that could stop him being damn near perfect. "What age group do you compete in?"

The guy grinned, looking far more pleased with the question than anyone in their right mind should. He took out his ID and passed it across without further comment.

Colby Landon.

Noah smiled when he saw the date on it. "Happy birthday. Eighteen today?"

Colby nodded. "You said to try again when I was eighteen."

Noah's eyebrows disappeared under his fringe. "You're that kid."

Colby seemed about to say something, but he stopped short. "Is there a way to say that I'm not a kid without sounding like a five year old?" he asked instead.

"Not a damn one." Noah chuckled.

"I'm surprised you remember me," Colby admitted.

"Cute teenage stalker — you do stand out a bit in my memory." Damn, but three years had turned cute into stunning. "You lived in the building opposite me, right?"

"I still live there, but I'm not stalking you."

"I'm not complaining. From what I recall, you seemed sweet…in an obsessive sort of way. And you're definitely hot enough to get away with a bit of eccentricity." Noah smiled. "If I remember rightly, I promised to show you a good time when you could get in here legally."

Colby blushed.

Noah grinned. Oh yeah, the boy *really* remembered that promise.

Colby cleared his throat. "About that drink?"

"Sure."

Colby caught the bartender's eye on the second attempt. "I'll have a Coke and…" He turned to Noah.

"Usual," Noah supplied.

The bartender turned away to fill their order.

"You know you're old enough to order a grown up drink, right?" Noah checked.

"Yeah, but I'm pretty sure I could be ninety and my coach would still kill me for it."

"For one drink?"

"We've got a big competition coming up. We're not supposed to drink until after it."

"And you always do what you're supposed to do?"

Colby shrugged. "Pretty much."

"Does your coach have any other rules about what you're not allowed to do before a big competition?" Noah was quite impressed with himself. He almost managed to pull off the innocent tone that seemed to come so naturally to Colby.

"Pages of them," Colby said with a wry smile.

"What does he have to say about sex?"

Noah grinned as Colby's blush came back full force.

"I know a lot of sports guys don't screw the night before a big game," Noah offered.

"He um… He's never mentioned anything about that." To Colby's obvious relief, the bartender brought their drinks across. Colby paid the man and turned back to Noah.

Noah tilted his head back to look up at Colby and waited with unaccustomed patience to see what would happen next.

Colby took a swig of his drink, but he seemed to have reached the end of what he'd planned out in advance.

Noah leaned against the bar. It was probably a good thing the boy was a good swimmer, because he was so far out of his depth his feet might never find the bottom of the pool again.

"Did you come here just to see me?" Noah asked, when he realised there was no way in hell Colby was going to come up with a topic of conversation any time soon.

As soon as Colby focused on him, Noah wrapped his lips around the rim of his beer bottle and swallowed down a few mouthfuls.

Colby watched the well-practiced move with embarrassed appreciation.

"Well?" Noah prompted.

Colby blinked. "Pardon?"

"I asked if you came here just to see me."

Colby nodded; he still hadn't looked away from Noah's mouth. Unless Noah was much mistaken, it wasn't a beer bottle he was imagining sliding against his lips.

"I'm still trying to work out what I did that made such a good impression on you that you'd want to come back and take me up on an offer I made, what, three years ago?"

"I watch you dancing."

"Just dancing?" Noah teased, trying to remember if he'd consistently made it all the way to his bedroom at the back of the studio before things got interesting.

The blush deepened. "Just dancing," Colby confirmed.

"I can't believe you haven't had plenty of other offers in the meantime." He said it mostly to enjoy the way the boy blushed, but Colby just shrugged.

Noah froze with his beer halfway to his lips. "Are you saying you've never taken anyone up on those offers?"

Colby shrugged again.

The words *you're a virgin* sprung to Noah's lips but, no. It was unlikely. It was also just possible enough that it might cross the line between making the boy blush and really humiliating him.

Noah looked across to the crowded dance floor. "Do you dance, or do you just watch?"

Colby shook his head. "Sorry. Two left feet."

Noah downed the rest of his drink and took Colby's barely touched Coke out of his hand. "Come on."

"I really mean it. I can't even clap to a beat."

"Then it's lucky clapping isn't involved, isn't it?"

Colby kept on protesting, but he didn't once try to shake off Noah's hand as Noah led him past the main dance floor and on to another one, which was less crowded. The music here was quieter; the other dancers were all paired up already. It was probably slightly closer to Colby's speed than the free-for-all Noah usually danced in.

Ignoring the men around them, Noah stopped in the middle of the dance floor and pulled Colby closer by his belt loops. "It's not complicated. You just move to the beat."

Colby remained entirely motionless, his expression highly sceptical.

Noah laughed. "Here, put your hands in my pockets."

He took Colby's hands and guided them around his body, into the back pockets of his tight leather trousers. The move immediately brought them up close and personal. Colby was quite a few inches taller than him, but not so much that their bodies didn't line up very nicely.

Noah put his hands on Colby's arse in return and pulled him nearer still, so their hips fitted neatly together.

Keeping it simple, Noah just rocked his hips in time to the beat, letting their bodies rub together.

"That's it," he coaxed, as Colby tentatively took up the movement.

In moments, Colby's erection was pressing against him through their clothes.

Noah smiled to himself. "That's right," he whispered.

The simple fact that the boy wanted him that much soon had Noah's cock hardening too. He adjusted their positions slightly, so Colby would know that he wasn't the only one getting off on humping another man on the dance floor.

Trusting Colby to keep their hips moving to the beat now, Noah slid his hands up Colby's shoulders. When he went to thread his hands into Colby's hair, he stopped short. He trailed his fingers over Colby's scalp, only the lightest stubble lingered where all the floppy blond hair had been three years before.

"That feels nice," Colby murmured. As he leaned into the touch, his eyes dropped closed.

"I've always liked it if a guy strokes my hair while I go down on him," Noah offered.

Colby bit his lip.

"Have you ever gone down on someone, Colby?" Noah whispered.

Colby shook his head very slightly, but he didn't open his eyes.

"Has anyone ever gone down on you?"

He shook his head again. In the dim lights it wasn't easy to tell if he was blushing, but it was impossible for Noah to believe he wasn't.

"Ever imagined me going down on you?"

Colby's steps faltered as the rhythm of the dance completely deserted him.

"I give great head."

Colby opened his eyes, but he didn't try to meet Noah's

gaze. "I believe you."

"You're that easy to convince? Pity. If you'd called me a liar, I'd have had to get down on my knees and prove it to you…"

Such a nice boy, such good manners; no accusation passed his lips. As Noah guided him to pick up the beat again, Colby even moved his hands from Noah's back pockets to rest on the small of his back.

Noah smiled and pulled him closer, keeping their bodies pressed tightly together. "I think I'll make a dancer out of you yet. You've got pretty good rhythm to start with. And, you know, rhythm's rhythm. If a man dances well, he'll screw well, too."

Colby didn't say anything to that, but Noah wasn't fooled. If Colby had been watching him in the studio after he'd got rid of all the students, then he had to know that Noah was a bloody brilliant dancer.

A movement caught Noah's eye. Somewhere among the crowd that filled the club, something sent up a red flag.

He looked over Colby's shoulder, turned them slightly, and glanced over Colby's other shoulder. There! Sam stood near the edge of the dance floor. A full year later, and Noah's first instinct was still to touch his cheek and test the bone to make sure it wasn't broken.

Sam was there, and he was watching them. For a moment, Sam met Noah's gaze, then his attention moved toward Colby.

No! Every muscle in Noah's body tensed. Maybe he'd just met the boy, but Noah was already sure that Colby and Sam shouldn't even be on the same planet, let alone in the same room.

"Come on, I've had enough dancing for one day." Noah took Colby by the wrist and led him toward the exit. He was reasonably sure Colby said something in response, but he couldn't make out any individual words over the pumping music.

Conversation wasn't his biggest priority then. Noah didn't stop, or even slow down, until they were outside.

"Where are we going?" Colby asked, as they stepped onto the pavement. His tone of voice was still polite, but it was also obvious he'd asked the question more than once on the way out.

"Home."

Colby stopped. Noah tugged at his wrist, but it made no difference. Colby was completely immoveable.

It took Noah a few seconds to realise why. "Don't look at me like that, darling—I mean my place not your doorstep. If you're very good you'll get a lot more than a kiss on the cheek this time around."

Colby's feet started moving again. Even when Noah released his wrist, Colby walked alongside him within easy touching distance, his loping stride easily eating up the pavement no matter what pace Noah picked.

Noah couldn't help but admire him out of the corner of his eye each time they passed beneath a street lamp. He was definitely hot in an innocent, puppy like way. Even without the mop of blond hair, he'd turn heads in any crowd of gay men once they worked out he wasn't a real skinhead.

Letting them into his building, Noah made his way quickly up the stairs. Colby seemed to hesitate for a moment in the lobby. Noah pretended not to notice that, but he couldn't help but smile when he glanced over his shoulder a few seconds later and realised that Colby had started moving again and was taking the stairs two at a time until he caught up.

Closing the studio door behind them, Noah flipped the lock and checked it. As he turned to Colby, Noah realised that he'd spotted the move.

Noah shrugged. "Can't be too careful, right?"

Colby nodded. "Right." He looked away, apparently fascinated by the rather bland room.

"I wouldn't want anyone to interrupt us," Noah said.

Colby nodded, but if he caught the invitation in the cue, he completely failed to jump on it.

He walked slowly around the room, studying every detail from the mirrors lining one wall, to the row of doors leading to Noah's flat, the studio's office and everything else.

It took Noah a few seconds to realise what Colby was doing. "Does it look different from this side of the street?"

"Yeah," Colby said softly. "Bigger."

"Bigger is always a good thing," Noah observed, leaning against the wall by the door.

Colby migrated slowly toward the large windows that almost filled the front wall of the studio and looked across the street.

"Which one is yours?" Noah asked, moving to stand next to him.

Colby pointed out a window on the fourth floor. The lights were off. It was impossible to make out anything from where they stood. Colby was a far more interesting sight, and Noah soon turned his attention back to him.

As if he could sense he was being watched, Colby also looked away from the view. He stared at Noah, but made no effort to close the gap between them.

Noah smiled. "Why do I get the feeling you've never thought past this point?" And, God, had Noah ever been as innocent as this boy was at eighteen?

"I don't want to do the same as all the other guys you bring back here," Colby blurted out.

Noah saw Colby regret the words a second after they hit the air. "If you're intending something really kinky you should probably tell me in advance."

"Would you have dinner with me?"

"Dinner?" Noah repeated, blankly.

Colby nodded.

"Cards on the table, darling. I've brought you back to my place. Dinner really isn't necessary at this point. Honestly, I have no problem screwing *before* the first date."

Colby didn't drop his gaze. "Is that a yes or a no to dinner?"

Noah tilted his head to one side. "You came all the way up here and the only thing you can suggest we do is make a date for dinner? Isn't there anything else on your mind?"

Colby blushed. "I think we should have dinner first."

Noah stared at him for a long time, thrown completely off his stride. "Dinner," he mused. "Um… Yeah, sure. If you'd like."

Colby grinned. Then, he didn't seem to know what to do with himself. Noah, now fully realising that he was the only person in the room who screwed before the first date, smiled at Colby's predicament.

Pretty sure he didn't have the heart to venture back out to the club, and having effectively lost any chance of getting laid that night, Noah wasn't above watching Colby blush for a while instead.

Colby turned his attention back to the room. "You really are a great dancer."

"Thanks."

"I watch your classes sometimes. You're a fantastic teacher, too."

"I've taught for four years without killing any of my pupils — that's a damn sight better than I ever thought I'd do."

"The guys you dance with on Wednesday nights — they're not a class, are they?"

Noah shook his head. "A dance company."

Colby nodded. "You run it?"

"No, but I do most of the choreography, so I do get to tell people what to do most of the time." Noah frowned as he considered the evidence. "Just how much time do you spend watching me?"

"Too much, according to Tony."

"He's your brother right — the one whose ID you stole last time we met."

Colby nodded. Pale blond eyebrows went up. "You

remember?"

Noah ran a hand through his hair, pretty sure he hadn't intended to acknowledge any such fact. "You're not like most of the guys I meet. I guess you made an impression."

Colby smiled and ducked his head, obviously pleased with the mild compliment. He looked back across the street. "I should probably get going."

He took a few paces toward the door. He hesitated. Turning back, he returned to Noah's side and brushed his lips across Noah's cheek.

Noah chuckled. "You're eighteen, darling. No one is going to think you're a slut for trying out the grown up version."

Noah leaned up and brought their lips together for the first time. Sliding his tongue against Colby's mouth, he gently requested admittance. Colby's lips parted. He gasped against Noah's mouth as their tongues touched.

Keeping it purposely simple, Noah cupped Colby's jaw in one hand, tilting Colby's head slightly to one side, so he had the perfect angle to work with.

Colby's lips were soft against Noah's mouth, so cautious, so gentle. Noah stretched out the kiss, letting their lips linger together long after he'd have usually pulled away. Colby reached out and put his hands very carefully on Noah's waist.

Noah tugged Colby closer to him in return. Stepping back, he took Colby with him and kept them moving until he found the wall. Resting his back against the old plasterwork, Noah closed his eyes and let himself relax into the kiss.

He had no idea how much time passed before one of Colby's hands left his waist. A second later, Colby slid that hand behind Noah's head, coaxing him forward an inch or two in the process.

Noah leaned up into the kiss, automatically trying to work out what Colby was trying to achieve and whether it was something he needed to be worried about. But, that seemed to be it. Colby just left his hand there, pinned between Noah's head and the wall.

Noah gave a mental shrug. It was a damn sight more comfortable to lean against a hand than the wall. Noah blinked. That was it, wasn't it? The sweet guy was trying to make sure he was comfortable.

Noah deepened the kiss and let Colby have a little bit of control over it, confident that he didn't have to worry where that would lead. He was right. Colby seemed content to just kiss and be kissed for the rest of his life. He didn't try to dirty it up at all. His free hand remained politely on Noah's waist, resisting any temptation to wander elsewhere.

Slowly, and with obvious reluctance, Colby broke the kiss. He rested his forehead against Noah's temple and took a deep breath.

"I should go." He seemed to be trying to convince himself of that, as much as anyone else.

"You could stay," Noah offered.

Colby closed his eyes for a moment and let out a frustrated little moan. "You have no idea how much I want to stay here with you."

"So stay."

Colby shook his head. "Dinner." He took another deep breath. "Dinner." He repeated the word like a mantra as he pulled back.

With a soft moan he brought their lips together one last time in a sweet, closed-mouth kiss. "Dinner," he whispered against Noah's lips before he pulled away again. "Tomorrow, after your last class, I'll come and get you?"

Noah nodded. "Okay."

Colby nodded as well. He stepped back and finally headed for the door. Noah watched him go. When he was out of sight, Noah let his head drop back to rest on the plasterwork.

"Ouch." The wall was a damn sight less comfortable now that Colby's hand wasn't there to soften it up for him.

* * * * *

The light hadn't been on in the flat when Colby had looked across the road from the studio, but it was on now. Tony was home and no doubt waiting up for him.

Colby closed the flat's front door behind him. In the little passageway that led toward the living room, he paused and pressed the heel of his hand against his erection, wishing it away — at least until he could get some privacy to take care of it.

"How did it go?" Tony asked, the moment Colby stepped into the living room.

Colby considered the question. "Okay."

"So, was he there?" Tony prompted, from where he lounged on the sofa.

"Yeah, he was."

Tony sighed and cast a glance up to the heavens. "You haven't stopped talking about him for three years. Now, when you might actually have something interesting to say, you're taken mute?"

"We're having dinner tomorrow night," Colby offered.

"That's good?" Tony hazarded.

Colby smiled. "It is good."

Tony just stared at him. "And?"

Colby wandered across to the window. The studio was in darkness now. "I bought him a drink. We danced."

"Wait." Tony held up a hand. "You mean he danced and you watched, right?"

"No, we danced together."

Colby looked over his shoulder just in time to see Tony cover his eyes with both hands. "And he still wants to have dinner with you?"

Colby laughed. "It went kind of well. He was nice."

"Nice is…nice," Tony said.

"I wasn't looking to get laid," Colby protested. "He can

get that any night of the week. He needs some nice in his life."

Tony's expression softened. "You're a good kid. You're as soppy as hell, and I have no idea how our parents ever managed to raise two sons who were so different, but you're a good kid. Now, go get some sleep, because if you're out on your feet tomorrow, your coach will keep you behind. It won't do to be late to your first date."

Colby didn't need to be told twice. The sooner he could retreat to his bedroom, the better. Closing the door behind him, he quickly shrugged out of his clothes and dropped them in the hamper. Settling himself between the sheets, he stared at the ceiling and tried to take in everything that had happened that night.

It was a damn sight harder to be nice than he'd ever imagined it could be. Noah, up close and personal, was so much more tempting than Noah on the other side of the street.

Colby ran his fingers over his lips. Closing his eyes he imagined the touch was Noah's mouth. He trailed his other hand down his body and wrapped his fingers around his erection. Noah's hands were smaller than his, his grip would probably be tighter, but his touch would be softer too.

Colby rocked his hips, just as he had when they'd danced together, and pushed his cock up into his grip.

Noah would know what he was doing. Colby's fingers teased at his foreskin, gentler than he'd ever touched himself before, wondering how Noah might touch himself when he was alone in his own bed on the other side of the street.

Images flickered across the insides of Colby's eyelids as he imagined what might happen after their date tomorrow. The brush of Noah's lips against his. Noah's skin under his fingertips as he carefully explored Noah's body.

Noah's hair sliding through his fingers as Colby tilted his head back to be kissed. Maybe even Noah's cock in his mouth as he wrapped his lips around the hard shaft and—

No, that shouldn't be tomorrow—that would come later, much later. But, damn, it would feel so good to learn how to please Noah that way, to work out exactly what Noah liked a man to do to bring him off.

Colby imagined curling up behind Noah in Noah's bed, feeling Noah's bare skin brushing against his softened cock as he snuggled closer after they were both finished. He imagined hardening against Noah's body during the night and the smile in Noah's eyes as he looked over his shoulder at him in the morning.

Pushing his hips forward into his hand again, Colby's gasped. His cum spilled across his stomach. Tomorrow couldn't arrive soon enough.

* * * * *

Having locked the door in Colby's wake, double checked it, and switched off the lights, Noah retreated into the small flat attached to the studio. Tossing his clothes on the chair in the corner, he crawled onto the bed and lay on top of the blankets. The whirl of the generator in the neighbouring room hummed in the background. One of the central heating pipes running along the ceiling clunked. He wriggled until he found a comfortable position on the lumpy mattress.

Whichever way Noah turned things in his head, he came to the same conclusion — nice boys were a lot more fun when they were willing to be at least a little bit naughty.

God, the last time he'd brought a man home and hadn't had sex with him was that night with Sam. Noah turned his face to the side and rubbed his cheek against the pillowcase.

Stupid to think about that tonight, stupid to think about Sam at all. It had hardly been a slap, more a shock than anything else. Noah closed his eyes. Damn it — he'd been so bloody sure he was past that stage in his life.

He could demand better from a man these days. He could throw out any guy who got too rough with him — even if that guy was Sam. Noah swallowed rapidly. No one had a hold over him anymore. Everything was fine. And Colby was…

Noah chuckled as he tried to imagine Colby in that scenario and failed. The idea of Colby getting violent with anyone was crazy. He was probably one of those guys who fished spiders out of the bathtub and sidestepped rather than tread on ants. Too good for his own good, too innocent for the real world. But, damn, wouldn't it be fun to work some of that innocence out of him, piece by adorably shocked piece?

Dinner…

Noah shook his head. He couldn't remember the last time he'd gone on an actual date.

If Colby wasn't a screamer then Noah was quite willing to take his dessert under the table. Colby would be quick at that age. As inexperienced as he was, it wouldn't take more than a few minutes for any guy to have him spilling into his mouth, rich and salty. No need to be overly safe when Colby hadn't had the chance to catch anything. Noah licked his lips.

If he tasted half as sweet as he acted, it would be better than any dessert they served with dinner. Colby hadn't mentioned a place. Food out with a teenager? Cheap and cheerful. McDonalds or Pizza Hut. No table cloths. Kids around. Under the table fellatio probably wasn't going to be an option.

Noah shrugged. So, they'd have to wait until he got the boy home. He could live with that. But if there was one thing he was sure about it was that tomorrow night they'd have to get past first bloody base. Nice could only keep a guy happy for so long.

Chapter Five

"Hello? Noah?"

Damn! Noah hurried out of his bedroom and to the door leading into the studio. "Colby?"

"Yeah, I..." Colby trailed off as he turned and faced Noah. His eyes opened very wide. His gaze slowly descended. When he saw the towel wrapped around Noah's waist he seemed to relax slightly.

Noah smiled, wishing he hadn't bothered with the towel, just to see the look on Colby's face if he had found him stark bollock naked when he arrived.

Colby cleared his throat. "Hi."

"Class ran late. I won't be a minute."

Colby nodded, although Noah doubted he had any idea what he was agreeing with. "It's no problem — the reservation's not until eight."

Now it was Noah's turn to look Colby over. The jeans and trainers he'd anticipated were gone, replaced by black trousers and dress shoes. A carefully ironed white shirt replaced the expected T-shirt. Add in the mention of a reservation and it seemed safe to guess that dinner wouldn't be at McDonalds after all.

"You want to come in?" Noah asked, when Colby didn't seem about to move on his own.

Colby quickly shook his head. "I'll wait out here."

Noah smiled as he retreated to his bedroom. It was always a good sign when a guy didn't trust himself to be alone with him while he was naked. The clothes he'd picked out before he went into the shower were irrelevant now. He dug his interview suit out from the very back of his wardrobe and grabbed the trousers.

A little bit of brain wracking and he remembered where he'd stashed his only suitable shirt. That would have to do — if for no other reason than because they were pretty much the only clothes he owned that weren't designed for dancing or clubbing.

Five minutes later, Noah strode back into the studio fully dressed. Colby stood looking out of his window, but he turned as Noah shut the door to his flat and automatically locked it behind him.

Colby only ran his gaze over him once, quickly. Then he looked him in the eye. "You look great."

Noah smiled, far more inclined to let his gaze linger when he returned the inspection. "You clean up pretty well yourself, darling." The blush arrived right on cue. "So, where are we going?"

"Harrison's, on Franklin Street." Colby held the door open for him as they left the studio.

Noah hesitated. "Are there two restaurants with that name? Because there is no way you got a reservation at Harrison's."

Colby waved the issue away. "I called in a favour."

Noah nodded vaguely to let Colby know he'd heard, but most of his mind was focused on trying to remember exactly how much he had in his wallet. He gave a mental sigh. It solved the problem of what he'd order anyway — the cheapest thing on the menu was the only option in a place like that.

Ten minutes later, as they stepped into the restaurant, a waiter hurried across to them. Noah eyed him warily, hoping that Colby really did have a reservation.

"Mr. Landon." The waiter gave a half bow. Noah raised an eyebrow. "Always an honour to see you visiting our humble establishment."

Colby laughed and shook his head. "Noah, this is Jordan Harrison — butterfly and the medley relay."

Noah cautiously nodded a greeting, wondering if this was the point where everything was going to get complicated, but Jordan just smiled as if he wasn't the least bit surprised Colby was bringing a man to dinner.

"I shuffled people around and got you a good table in my section." As Jordan led them through the restaurant, Colby stepped back to let Noah go ahead. When Jordan took a reserved notice off a table next to a big picture window overlooking Franklin Street, Noah sat down before Colby had a chance to hold his chair for him.

"I'm supposed to recommend the confit of wild salmon, served with spring vegetables. But if I were you, I'd go for the eight ounce fillet steak with the peppercorn sauce and get the triple cooked chips on the side." Jordan handed them the menus. "I'll be back for your order in a few minutes."

Aware that Colby was watching him across the table, Noah kept his attention on the menu as he played out the odds in his head.

"The steak sounds good," Colby observed. If he was trying not to sound as nervous as hell, he was failing.

Noah looked up from the menu. "Who did you tell them you were having dinner with?"

Colby blinked, as if confused. "You. Who else would I say I was having dinner with?"

"So, he knew you weren't bringing a girl?" Noah hinted.

Colby seemed to catch up then. "You mean, do my friends know I'm gay? Yeah, they all know."

"Must make things difficult?" Noah hazarded.

Colby looked blankly at him across the table. "Why?"

Noah put the probabilities together. "You're not the only gay guy in the swim programme?" He'd have put money on Jordan being straight...

"No. It's just me." Colby thought about it for a few moments. "Maybe it was strange for some of them at first—

but I think anyone who had a problem with me got over it once I made it clear no one else on the team was my type."

"Just like that?" Noah said sceptically.

"Pretty much," Colby nodded. "I might be the only gay man in the swim programme, but there are quite a few guys who do other sports. Tony's got a few gay friends in the athletics department—and he's kind of bi-ish in his own right."

"Bi-ish?" Noah asked.

Colby smiled slightly. "He mostly dates girls, but every now and again he comes home with a guy instead. I'm pretty sure there's a gay guy in the archery programme who Tony would love to get to know better, except the guy won't give Tony the time of day—that doesn't happen to Tony often. It's kind of fun to watch him chase his tail for once."

Noah studied Colby for a few moments. When Colby talked about being gay it all sounded so...easy. "You're seriously telling me that no one has ever had a problem with you being gay?" It was better than blurting out the question he really wanted someone to answer. How the hell did Colby always manage to meet the gay-friendly part of the population, when Noah found himself continually bounced from one bigot to the next?

Colby shook his head. "Not a *problem*, not really. A few sarcastic comments here and there. The most annoying thing I find is people assuming that I want them to set me up with every single gay man they know—as if the fact we're both attracted to men means we'll automatically be perfect for each other."

Noah couldn't help but smile at his exasperated tone. "It sounds like a promising start to me."

Colby shrugged. "I just think that if you're going to have sex with someone, it should be someone who you want to do more than have sex with."

Noah stared at Colby, trying to work out if he was serious or not. "You do realise that we have absolutely nothing in common apart from the fact that we both like to have sex with men?" Noah asked. Well, he already enjoyed having sex with men, he was confident that Colby would enjoy joining in once they got started.

"Why do you say that?" Colby asked.

"You're…" Noah waved a hand at him and shook his head.

Colby blinked. "I'm what?"

"You're," Noah sighed. "You're a…nice boy."

"And you're not?"

"No, I'm not. And I'm not the sort of guy someone like you has anything more than casual sex with," Noah said with complete certainty. "So, I don't know what you've got going on with this whole dating thing, but if it's all the same to you, we can just skip it and go back to my place."

"Someone like you?" Colby echoed.

Noah put his menu down. "Look, darling, I don't know what you want me to say. You like watching me dance, that's great—I'm very flattered. And if you've developed some sort of crush on me, that's really sweet. But, if you've built some sort of fantasy version of me in your head you are going to be very disappointed."

"I'm not disappointed."

Noah rolled his eyes. "Of course you're not—you don't know me."

"You could tell me a bit about yourself?" Colby suggested.

Noah closed his eyes for a moment, wondering what he had done wrong in a previous life to deserve this. "Fine, you can have the speed dating version—my whole life story in less than three minutes. Hi. My name's Noah. I'm twenty-three years old. I'm a dancer—well, I say that, but I really just scrape by teaching classes to people who treat dance like it's something to fill up a few spare hours—as if it's a sodding hobby. And, every day I have to bite my tongue to stop myself shouting at the top of my lungs that dancing isn't a *leisure activity*—it's my whole life. I have no family that will speak to me, or even admit that I'm alive. And I like casual sex, usually with vastly unsuitable men—although I think I've hit a whole new level of unsuitability with you."

Noah looked over his shoulder, hoping like hell he'd kept his voice low enough that no one else had heard him.

Colby just stared at him, obviously having no idea what to say.

Noah sighed. "Look, you're a nice guy. I'd quite like to have sex with you. The only things you actually need to know before we do that are that I'm healthy, and I intend to stay that way—I don't do bareback. I'm versatile as well as very flexible—I don't really care who tops. Oh, and I'm as willing to get kinky as the next guy, but I don't let anyone tie me up unless they've already proved they're not a serial killer."

Colby blushed, but he didn't look away. He didn't flinch. "I do want more than just sex with you. And yes, it does make a difference to me if we just go back to your place, because I don't want you to think I'm just using you the way other guys have.

"I used them, too," Noah cut in.

Colby completely ignored him. "I can think of a few things we have in common already."

"Name one," Noah demanded, leaning forward in his seat.

"We're both athletes."

Noah let out a bitter laugh. "Trust me, darling, there are quite a few things I wouldn't mind doing with a football team, but none of them involve anything you were taught in gym class."

Colby leaned forward in his seat. "You're forgetting—I've watched you dance—a lot. You could run rings around half the guys at the institute. You've got more stamina and better cardio than anyone I've ever trained with. If I tried to swim for as many hours a day as you dance, I'd drown from sheer exhaustion. You didn't get a body like yours sitting around in front of the TV all day, did you?"

Noah opened his mouth.

"Ready to order?"

Noah looked up at Colby's friend. Considering he'd had no concrete idea what to say to Colby, he couldn't bring himself to be too pissed off with the interruption.

"I'll have the steak you suggested," Colby said easily, and he looked across at Noah.

Noah tried to remember what else was on the menu — and, more importantly, what had been the cheapest thing there. He came up blank. Mentally flinching at the blow his wallet was about to take, Noah smiled at the waiter. "I'll have the same, thank you." He'd just skip a few meals until his bank balance was back in the black. It wouldn't be the first time.

"Will you tell me about the dance company you work with?" Colby asked, as soon as they were alone again. "The one from Wednesday nights."

Noah gave up and went with it. He'd let Colby have his nice date. At least, Noah could look forward to getting laid at the end of it.

* * * * *

"Anything else I can get for you?"

Colby shook his head as Jordan cleared the dessert plates. He looked across at Noah, who did the same.

"Cool. I'll get your check." Jordan disappeared.

As Colby reached in his pocket for his wallet, he saw Noah do the same. Colby shook his head again. "I've got it."

Noah raised an eyebrow. "I'll pay my way, thanks. I may be a slut, but I've never been a whore." The edge that had faded from his voice as they chatted through the meal was back.

"I asked you out," Colby said, carefully. "So I'll get this one. You can get the next one, if you want to."

Noah reached across the table and covered Colby's hand with his own. "Colby, there is no next one on the cards. You understand that, right? This is just a date and some fun afterwards. We're not…going steady or whatever the hell you'd call it."

Colby met his gaze across the table and refused to look down. "It'll be whatever it's going to be. You shouldn't rush to write it off any more than I should rush to make it something you're not ready for it to be."

Noah didn't look happy about it, but he subsided in his chair. "Have you got enough to cover the check?"

Colby nodded. There was a reason why he'd asked for money rather than gifts for his birthday.

Noah let it go at that, but the friendly atmosphere Colby had built up as they ate was now completely gone. Noah remained silent as they left the restaurant and walked back to his place.

Colby scrambled through the corners of his mind and tried to think of something to say as they strolled home. By the time they reached Noah's doorstep, Colby hadn't thought of a single word that fitted the situation, but he was very sure he should progress no further than the front door.

Daydreams and fantasies be damned. He needed to walk away before he was tempted to do more than he should with Noah on what was only their first real date. Colby only glanced away from Noah for a moment, trying to work out what to say, but Noah was through the door and up the stairs before Colby realised what was going on.

Not seeing any other option now, Colby followed Noah up the stairs. He didn't rush, but took the time to repeat to himself the most important thing of all—he couldn't let Noah think that he was just using him for sex. If that meant being patient just a little bit longer, he could do that.

Three years down, he could last a few more days, really, he could. Somehow, he could.

The trail of discarded clothes began in the dance studio.

Colby closed his eyes and tilted his head back in silent prayer. His complete faith in his ability to wait faltered slightly as he picked up Noah's coat. His shirt lay on the floor a few feet further into the room. Colby picked that up too. A belt lay near the door leading into Noah's private space at the back of the studio.

Colby hesitated on the threshold. He tapped tentatively at the door. "Noah?"

Receiving no response, he pushed the door open a little. A pair of shoes lay on the floor in a tiny hallway. Another door was indicated by a trailing trouser leg. Colby tapped on that door, too. "Noah?"

He heard a soft swish of material inside the room. He nudged the door open. Socks led the way across to a pair of boxer shorts lying on the floor at one corner of a bed. Colby stood in the doorway, unable to stop his eyes following the breadcrumb trail to its ultimate destination.

Noah lay naked in the middle of a small double bed, his hand wrapped around his erection, gently stroking himself.

Colby somehow managed to look up further and meet Noah's eyes.

"Feel free to join in whenever you want." Noah smiled.

Colby tried to swallow and almost choked. "I..."

His brain gave up and his feet carried him across to the bed. He sat on the edge of the mattress, now completely mesmerised by the movements of Noah's hand.

Noah shifted on the bed, working his shoulder blades into the pillows propped against the headboard. He lifted his hips off the bed as he wriggled into a comfortable position. Closing his eyes, he turned his head slightly to one side and gave a contented little sigh.

Colby couldn't do more than stare at Noah's body. True, some of his dance clothes hid very little, but it still hadn't prepared him for seeing Noah completely naked.

"You know you're allowed to touch, too," Noah

offered.

Colby snapped his attention up to Noah's face, just in time to see him smile an invitation. He automatically smiled back because, well, he was there with Noah, and that alone made the inclination to grin like an idiot damn near overpowering.

Then, before his brain had a chance to properly process his options, Colby's body had taken over again and he was reaching out to take advantage of Noah's offer. The moment he realised what he was doing, Colby froze, his hand hovering in the air several inches above Noah's body.

Slow. He'd promised himself that so often. If he ever got another chance with Noah, they'd go slow. He'd give Noah time to understand that things were going to be different between them. He'd make it perfect for Noah.

Curling his fingers into a fist, Colby stared at his hand for several long seconds as he battled against a depth of temptation he hadn't even realised existed until that moment.

Slow. He could do this.

Colby tore his gaze away from his hand. Refusing to get distracted by any amount of gorgeous, naked skin, Colby looked Noah straight in the eye.

Noah's expression changed, just slightly. Tension flooded into the room.

Noah would never forgive him. In that moment Colby had never been more certain of anything in his life. Noah would forgive him for failing to make things slow and perfect, but, if Colby turned away from him now, when Noah had offered himself up on a damn platter, Noah would never forgive him for that.

Maybe Colby would have been able to resist naked skin and his own desperation to come, but that tiny note of uncertainty in Noah's gaze, the vulnerability Noah had almost succeeded in hiding…

Colby lowered his hand until his fingers brushed very gently against Noah's skin. Noah had an amazing build—all lean muscle and graceful lines. Trailing his fingers up the far side of Noah's torso, Colby explored him inch by inch, determined to savour each part of Noah that passed under his fingertips.

The tension faded from the room as quickly as it had arrived, and Colby knew he'd made the right decision. There wasn't a hint of uncertainty in Noah now—he kept slowly jacking himself off with smooth easy movements, as if it was perfectly natural to do that while someone else watched. Noah was once more in charge of the whole world and his rhythm never faltered.

A bead of pre-cum formed on the tip of Noah's cock. Colby leaned down and caught it with his tongue.

Noah gasped. His hips bucked as Colby's mouth left him, as if trying to push his cock properly between his lips. That was fine as far as Colby was concerned, he—

"No."

Colby pulled back, his eyes shooting up to Noah's face. Colby blinked, rapidly recalling that this wasn't his own private fantasy. He had to think about more than doing whatever the hell he wanted to do now. All his big talk about treating Noah better than anyone else had lasted all of thirty seconds once he was in Noah's bedroom. Heat raced to his cheeks. "I'm sorry."

Noah chuckled and shook his head. "Seriously, darling, you don't have to apologise for giving head, but condoms were invented for a reason."

Colby blinked. "You said you were healthy."

"I also said I don't do bareback," Noah said, firmly.

Colby frowned and looked down at Noah's cock. The stolen taste had been so perfect. "What if—?"

Noah's fingertip covered his lips. "Condoms are not an optional extra. No arguing."

Colby nodded. He still couldn't stop staring at Noah's cock.

Noah moved his fingertip under Colby's chin and tilted

his face up until Colby met his eyes again. "You're old enough to know better than to screw around without something covering your cock."

"I just wanted to taste you," Colby whispered.

Noah ran his hand over Colby's head, caressing the shaved skin. His fingers trailed down the back of his scalp to his shirt collar. They slipped under the starchy white fabric and teased the sensitive patch of skin on the back of his neck.

"Taste me up here instead," Noah suggested, pulling him forward until their mouths met.

Colby groaned his approval into the kiss. Tentatively, he returned his hands to Noah's skin, desperate to explore his body as their tongues explored each other's mouths.

"Are you so shy I don't get to see any more of you than this?" Noah teased, pulling back from the kiss.

Out of breath, his mind spinning, Colby peered down at Noah's naked form. Gradually, he realised what Noah was saying. He straightened up and shrugged off his shirt. As Colby dropped the shirt on the floor beside the bed, Noah ran his fingertips over Colby's chest.

"You've shaved?"

Colby tried to make his brain form words as Noah's fingers found a nipple and rolled it between his thumb and forefinger. "Swim team. Charity thing. Wax," he managed to stutter out.

Noah leaned up and licked Colby's other nipple. "When?"

Colby stared down in fascination as Noah's tongue swirled around the small dark peak, making lightning shoot through his body. "When what?"

Noah grinned. "When was the charity waxing?" he asked before sucking against his nipple.

"Ages ago," Colby managed to whisper. "Last year sometime."

"Nothing grew back?"

"Um... Hydrodyn-"

Noah bit his nipple, a sharp flash of pain. Colby yelped and tried like hell not to come in his pants.

Noah pulled back a few inches. "Liar."

Colby shook his head. "It's all to do with friction in the water and…" he trailed off when Noah's grin didn't fade.

Noah kissed his way back to his lips. "You liked it. Maybe you tried it once for charity, but I think you liked it so much you kept doing it, didn't you?"

Colby had to consider it was unfair that he was half naked in a man's bed and someone could still make him blush that easily.

"You like feeling all smooth and hydrodynamic, don't you?"

Colby nodded.

"I like it, too," Noah said, running his hand over Colby's chest. "All clean, and fresh, and kissable."

Colby nodded on the general principle that he had no intention of disagreeing with Noah about anything, ever.

"The really important question," Noah whispered into his ear, as he trailed the line of kisses up along where his hair line would have been if it had still existed. "Is: did you wax everywhere for me?"

Colby shook his head. "We were all wearing Speedos when we did the charity thing," he managed to whisper.

"I think you'll have to prove that to me," Noah said, nipping at his earlobe. "But first, I'm going to get something for you to slip back into later."

Noah leaned over Colby, damn near upending himself over Colby's lap as he grabbed his wallet from the floor alongside the bed.

Colby placed his hand on the small of Noah's back to steady him, and then trailed his palm down over Noah's buttocks, just because it was impossible to resist that kind of temptation. Noah smiled over his shoulder at him and raised no objection to the touch. He took a strip of condoms out of his wallet and tossed them on the bed.

Colby spread his fingers across Noah's skin, using the full span of his hand to touch as much of him as possible.

"Damn—your hands are huge!" Noah rolled over, still half lying on Colby's lap and grabbed his wrist. Turning it this way and that, Noah examined Colby's hand very carefully.

Before Colby had a chance to work out what was going on, Noah had leaned over again. He grabbed Colby's ankle, lifting his foot up to be inspected. Suddenly, Noah turned his attention to Colby's crotch. "Are you in proportion all over?" He scrambled off Colby's lap and back onto the bed. "Strip," he demanded.

The order gave up on Colby's brain and went straight to his muscles. He stood up, undid his fly, and pushed both his trousers and his boxers down his legs but the fabric refused to be kicked away.

He stared blankly at his shoes for a few seconds before he finally realised he'd have to take them off first. As he sat down on the edge of the bed and struggled to do that, Noah helpfully traced random patterns on his back, destroying anything that might have been left of Colby's thought process. Eventually, the shoes were gone, quickly followed by everything else Colby had been wearing.

"Big all over," Noah murmured, apparently to himself—which was good because it meant Colby didn't have to think about coming up with an answer.

Noah casually slid his fingers through the short blond hairs surrounding the base of Colby's cock and tugged firmly at them. Colby gasped, helplessly tipping back his head as pleasure shot through him.

"Tell me what you've thought about doing with me," Noah suddenly ordered.

"Everything," Colby whispered.

Noah stroked his hand up Colby's abs, his nails scratching against Colby's skin and sending a shiver through him.

"Did any of your fantasies have anything to do with

pain?"

Colby shook his head. He covered Noah's hand, stopping him stroking, so he could concentrate. "I would never hurt you." That was important.

Noah laughed. "Oh, I know there's no sadism in you, darling. But I do wonder if there's not a bit of masochism hiding behind all your boy-next-door niceness."

"You said you're not into all that," Colby reminded him. "Not unless you know someone and can trust him."

"I said I'm not into letting strangers tie me up. I never said I had any objection to tying you up." Noah took his hand out from where Colby had held it still against his abs and wrapped his fingers around Colby's wrist.

Good, his grip felt good. But Colby forced himself to shake his head. "I want everything to be nice for you."

"You let me worry about me," Noah said, brushing himself aside as if he didn't matter.

"No." Colby shook his head again, trying to clear his thoughts. "I do worry about you." He lifted his free hand and stroked Noah's cheek, across where the bruise had lingered after the guy hit him the previous year.

Noah turned his head away from the touch, as if his cheek was still sore. "Tell me you've never imagined me tying you up and we can change the subject."

Colby shrugged. "Sometimes, yeah. But not all the time. I—"

"Will you let me tie you up?" Noah cut in.

Colby studied Noah's expression carefully. "Do you want to?"

"Yes." As simple as that.

That one word changed everything. Colby nodded.

Noah seemed to think for a few moments. "I want your belt."

Colby clumsily retrieved the length of leather from the belt loops in his trousers and handed it over.

Noah immediately pushed him down to lie in the

centre of the bed. The next moment, Noah was straddling his waist. Sliding his hands up Colby's arms, Noah grabbed his wrists and pinned his arms to the bed above him.

In theory, Colby knew he was the stronger man; he could have rolled them over and reversed their positions. Except, Noah was there, naked and straddling him, bare skin pressed against bare skin, and there was no way in hell Colby could move a single muscle without a clear order to do so. Hell, he wasn't even sure he could take a breath unless some sort of command was issued to that effect.

Tugging Colby's hands toward the headboard, and then further up so they passed between the thin metal rails, Noah wrapped the belt tight around Colby's wrists again and again, trapping them in place on the other side of the headboard.

Colby tipped his head back, twisting his neck to study the arrangement. All the air rushed out of the room as he saw the leather wrapped around his skin for the first time. His hands weren't returning from the other side of the bed frame until the belt was undone — until Noah chose to undo it.

"You're all mine now, aren't you?" Noah asked.

Colby nodded.

"You make a gorgeous submissive."

"What?" Colby pulled his attention away from the belt.

Noah was still straddling his hips. He looked very pleased with the world. "I said you make a very pretty sub." He ran his hands idly over Colby's chest, letting his nails scrape against Colby's skin. "I think you like the idea of belonging to me, of me being in complete control of you, don't you?"

Colby just stared up at him, unable to deny a word of it. Did that make him a sub? He knew the word. He'd stumbled on the Internet porn more than once or twice. But this was different. Being tied to Noah's bed wasn't a word or an idea. This was real and it grabbed hold of a part of him that he hadn't really been aware of before.

"Survival instincts really are a mystery to you, aren't they?" Noah ran his fingers over Colby's cheek, with surprising gentleness. "It doesn't even occur to you that I might hurt you more than you'd enjoy. So sweet..." His fingers brushed across Colby's mouth. Without warning he pinched Colby's bottom lip hard, his fingernail nipping at the sensitive skin.

Colby jerked underneath him, only partly in shock. He had no idea how or why, but the spike of pain went straight to his cock—morphing into pleasure along the way.

Noah's eyes widened in obvious approval. Colby gasped and met his gaze, trying to work out what the hell was going on. Suddenly, it didn't seem like Noah was just humouring him with this—it looked more like Noah was loving every minute of it.

"I bet your coach adores you, doesn't he, darling? You're the one guy in the programme who'll be in agony during training and still love every moment of it. You like it, don't you—the burn in your muscles and the ache in your lungs when you push yourself so hard you can't breathe." Noah's eyes glinted as he looked him over. "I could do so much with you..."

"Do it," Colby whispered. "Whatever you want, do it."

Noah raised an eyebrow. "Be careful what you wish for, darling. There's no way in hell you're ready for the kind of games I'd like to play with you."

Sudden panic made Colby scramble for anything that might convince Noah to change his mind. "If you don't have the balls for it, just say so."

Noah immediately moved to the edge of the bed.

Colby was wrong, what he'd felt before, that wasn't real panic—this, *this*, was real panic. "Wait!"

"Oh, I'm not going far," Noah said, quite casually. "But you'd do well to remember who has the other guy by the balls in this particular situation." He crossed his legs so he could sit comfortably on the narrow edge of the bed, reached out and palmed Colby's sac.

Colby looked from Noah to his crotch and back again. "Can I retract my earlier statement?"

Noah chuckled and gently squeezed Colby's balls. Colby helplessly pushed himself into Noah's hand, his body eager for more of the same, even when his mind trembled in protest.

Noah leaned forward and dipped his head over Colby's lap. As Colby stared down his body, Noah turned his head to the side, providing him with a perfect view as he trailed his lips up the line of Colby's erection.

Colby whimpered as Noah's lips reached the tip of his cock, knowing that this was all going to be over embarrassingly quickly.

Noah wrapped his mouth around the head. Pleasure raced through Colby, more intense than anything he'd ever known, but hot on its heels was a far less enjoyable emotion.

"Stop," Colby ground out.

Noah pulled back, his eyes full of confusion.

Colby dropped his head back onto the pillow. God, that had to be the hardest word he had ever said in his life. He took a deep breath. "Bareback," he whispered at the ceiling. Noah had been very clear that Colby was supposed to remember that it wasn't an option—Noah wouldn't be pleased with him if he forgot.

"You haven't had a chance to catch anything," Noah said, amusement replacing the confusion of a moment before.

Colby frowned. "But you said..."

"Yes. And now I'm about to give you a very good blow job, so the appropriate response is to shut up and enjoy."

Colby turned his attention to the ceiling, not at all sure how to say what he was pretty sure he needed to make clear in advance. "Um..."

"There's a special offer on today, darling—two orgasms for the price of one. This is only the first round, just let yourself go, and enjoy it."

Colby blinked up at Noah, trying to work out if Noah was actually giving him a get out of embarrassment free card.

"I'll be very insulted if you don't come in the first few seconds," Noah clarified with a grin.

Colby nodded, relief rushing through him fast enough to make him dizzy. Noah's lips wrapped around his cock once more, all wet heat and pure perfection. Colby stared down at him, completely enthralled by the hollowing of Noah's cheeks as he sucked around him.

It took every ounce of self control Colby possessed not to thrust up into Noah's mouth. Unable to watch and not come that instant, Colby dropped his head back onto the pillow.

He closed his eyes tight, until little flashes of light burst behind the lids. A few minutes—if he could just enjoy this for a few minutes, he knew he'd be able to die happy when the sheer pressure of not coming sooner killed him off.

Noah dipped his head, taking more and more of Colby's shaft into his mouth each time. Then, he…stopped?

Gasping for breath, Colby lifted his head and frowned down at Noah. He hadn't said stop, had he? He couldn't have. Maybe he was a bit kinkier than he'd expected to be, but no one was that much of a masochist…

The moment he met Noah's eyes, Noah bobbed his head back down. Colby didn't dare look away now. Noah's eyes sparkled. As he pulled back, he moved his lips and gave Colby a great view of his teeth sliding against his shaft all the way up to the head.

Reaching the tip, Noah scraped his front teeth very gently across the glans. Colby bucked, unable to remain still a moment longer. Noah wrapped his lips around him again. That was all it took. Thrusting up off the bed, Colby came into Noah's mouth—unable to catch his breath well enough to scream.

The world went away for a little while. All that existed was bliss until Colby finally managed to open his eyes. Noah had pulled back. He now sat up straight, looking extraordinarily pleased with himself and the world. He trailed his fingers over Colby's flaccid cock as he smiled down at him.

Colby wondered if there was an appropriate turn of phrase for this sort of moment but, if it existed, he had no idea what it was.

"You really should be barred from ever getting together with someone who isn't a complete size queen," Noah observed. "You'd be wasted on anyone who's not one."

Colby wasn't sure the right way to form that question either.

"Oh, yes," Noah said. "I very definitely am."

He sat by Colby's side, caressing his body, occasionally scratching his skin or nipping at it as the mood took him. He didn't seem to be in any particular rush.

Gradually, Colby caught his breath. It seemed like he'd barely done that when his body began to respond to Noah's teasing. He started to harden. If Noah noticed, he gave no sign of it. He seemed more interested in the way Colby helplessly arched into his touch each time he scraped a thumbnail across his right nipple.

Colby clenched his fists above the belt. "I want to touch you, too." The words were little more than a rough whisper.

Noah looked up at Colby's hands, smiled, and completely ignored the hint to untie him.

Colby squirmed, not sure if he was disappointed or pleased that his wishes were being ignored that way. Noah chuckled, as if he could read his mind and loved how confused Colby was.

"Top or bottom?" Noah asked.

The belt was suddenly the last thing on Colby's mind. "Both."

"At the same time?" Noah asked, raising an eyebrow at him.

"Whatever you want," Colby rephrased.

Noah seemed to give the question careful thought, but

he shook his head. "Pick."

Colby shook his head, determined that Noah was going to have whatever he wanted.

Noah caught Colby's chin between his fingers, his grip firm. "That was an order, not a suggestion. Pick."

Colby swallowed. It was bloody hard to think clearly when Noah's tone of voice sent shivers through his brain. "Will you top?" he asked, softly.

Noah nodded. A smile played around his lips as he picked up the lube, as if he was surprised by Colby's decision, but quite pleased with it, too.

Colby quickly moved his legs apart and pulled his knees back toward his chest.

"Eager, sweetheart?" Noah teased as he moved across the bed to kneel between his legs.

Colby wanted it too much to lie. "Yes." Three years! "I don't want to wait any more."

Noah grabbed a pillow from the top of his bed and slid it under Colby's hips as he obediently lifted them off the bed. "Sorry, darling, but you'll have to be patient a little bit longer."

Colby shook his head. "Now." It was the only word left in his head.

"You've never heard of prep?"

"Now," Colby repeated.

"It'll hurt."

Colby found another word. "Good."

Noah looked down at him, amusement dancing in his eyes. "There's erotic pain, and then there's 'Ouch, I never want anyone's cock in my arse ever again' pain."

Colby grumbled irritably as Noah slicked his fingers with lube and rubbed them against his hole. "I know what I—"

Noah slid one finger into him, quick and rough. Colby groaned his pleasure, unable to stop himself arching on the bed.

"You like that?"

Colby nodded. "More. Please?"

Noah only made him wait a little while before he obliged him. Two fingers stretched him open and Colby pushed against them from the first moment, desperate to feel them deeper inside him. Looking up at Noah, he saw him smile. "You really are a genuine pain slut, aren't you?"

Colby nodded. Anyone who could make him feel that good just by crooking his fingers could call him whatever he wanted.

A few more frustrating minutes with his fingers and Noah finally relented. He rolled on a condom and slicked the latex with extra lube.

Colby pulled his knees further back toward his chest. Noah didn't waste any more time. He thrust forward, sheathing himself completely within Colby's body in one harsh movement.

Colby gasped as his whole body tensed up. Noah had been right. It did hurt. But as Noah remained perfectly still inside him, discomfort soon turned to pleasure. Colby stared up at him in complete awe.

Noah peered back down at him, his complete focus enough to make Colby breathless, regardless of everything else. Desperate to reach out to Noah and make sure he never pulled away, Colby tugged at the belt around his wrists. It made no difference.

A moment later, Noah began to rock his hips. Colby fell completely still. He felt every inch of Noah's shaft deep inside him as Noah began to move his hips in earnest.

Hard and fast, each thrust made Colby's mind disintegrate a little further. Noah set a punishing rhythm, and each time he thrust he sent waves of pleasure through Colby.

It was too much, impossible to process, impossible for Colby to keep up with. He tossed his head against the pillow, unable to control anything, unable to do anything but accept whatever Noah gave him and love every second of it.

Slipping a hand between them, Noah started to roughly jack Colby's cock. It took all of thirty seconds before he came, clenching around Noah's shaft as his second orgasm of the night tore him in half and made him scream up to the ceiling.

Noah moved his hand up and grabbed onto Colby's shoulder for leverage. A moment later, his other hand moved from the mattress to grip Colby's other shoulder.

If anything, Noah's thrusts became harsher, faster than ever. His fingers dug into Colby's shoulder muscles as he came, but the look of pure bliss on Noah's face made everything but his expression irrelevant.

A second later, Noah collapsed on top of Colby, panting for breath. Colby stared up at the ceiling, trying to remember exactly why breathing was supposed to be important as he struggled to get the right amount of oxygen into his own lungs. Noah rose and fell slightly with each breath Colby took, almost all his weight resting on Colby's chest.

Long before Colby was ready for either of them to move, Noah pulled away and dispensed with the used condom. Colby watched him, admiring every line of his body. Even when he wasn't dancing, he moved like a dancer, all grace and precision, as if he was always moving to music no one else could hear.

Noah undid the belt and let Colby move his hands, but he didn't say anything. Opening a drawer in his bedside cabinet, he tossed Colby a packet of wipes.

As Colby cleaned himself up, Noah lounged on the other side of the bed watching him with an unreadable expression.

Colby tried to think of something to say. He'd always been aware that Noah was intimidating to talk to, but it hadn't occurred to him that having a conversation with Noah would actually be even more complicated after they'd had sex.

"You'd better be getting home."

Colby hesitated. "I thought..."

Noah looked him over. For a moment, Colby thought Noah was pleased with the half uttered request to stay the night. Then, Noah's smile turned wry. "Yeah, I'm sure you did. You're a sweet guy. And you have some serious natural talent. If you want to get together again..." He looked down, but his hesitation only lasted for a second. "I usually go to the same club—you'll probably see me around some time."

"But—"

"You have more important things to worry about than not spending the night here," Noah cut in.

Colby stared at him in confusion.

"Your shoulders for a start."

Colby twisted his neck to look at his shoulders. Long scratches from Noah's nails decorated his skin. Colby ran his fingers over the damaged skin. "Cool."

Noah blinked. "Cool?"

Colby couldn't hold back a smile. "You thought I'd have a problem with you leaving a few marks on me?"

Noah made a less than impressed noise in the back of his throat. "Your shoulders show you had sex—fine. Do you really want the whole swim team to know you were tied up, too? Your Speedos won't cover the marks on your wrists. What are you going to tell your friends when they ask about them?"

Colby waited until Noah looked him in the eye. "I'll tell them I enjoyed every minute of it."

"Good luck with that." Noah's smile seemed more than a little strained now. "Go home, Colby."

* * * * *

"Have a good time?"

Colby jumped and spun around. Damn it, he'd barely had a chance to close the front door behind him. "Are you trying to scare the life out of me?"

Tony grinned from the shadowy doorway leading to

the living room. "I guessed when you didn't come home a few hours ago that you went to his place for extra dessert."

Colby couldn't help but echo the grin. "Yeah, something like that."

"You had sex," Tony observed.

Colby didn't say anything as he wandered into the kitchen and grabbed a drink from the fridge.

"That's a yes then," Tony observed. "I trust you had the sense to be careful?"

Colby nodded, never taking his eyes off his bottle of Coke. He had the terrible suspicion that Tony would see the change in him just by looking at him—as if a preference for being tied up was suddenly written across his forehead. It was all he could do not to tug his sleeves down to make sure his wrists were covered.

"It's natural to be a bit disappointed if someone you've fantasised about for a long time doesn't live up to your expectations," Tony offered.

Colby shook his head. "Better." He cleared his throat and managed to pitch his voice at something above a whisper. "He was better than I ever thought anyone could be."

"Yet you're not rushing in here five minutes before you need to leave tomorrow morning?" Tony leaned against the kitchen counter opposite him.

Colby shrugged. "He's not used to people staying the night. He'll get used to it in time."

"So you didn't screw your obsession out of your system?" Tony sounded resigned now.

Colby smiled. "I'm just as obsessed as I ever was. Only now I don't think he's perfect, I *know* he is."

Tony rolled his eyes and patted him on the head as he went yawning past Colby. "I've got a late training session tomorrow. Leave a note on the fridge if you go out before I get in."

Colby nodded at his brother's retreating back. He had definite plans to be on the other side of the street long before

Tony got home.

Chapter Six

"Bloody hell!"

Colby looked up. Trent—breast stroke and medley relay—was standing at the next locker, staring at him as if he'd grown another head. Colby followed the direction of Trent's gaze more carefully. The extra head was apparently located in exactly the same place as the scratches Noah had left on his shoulders.

Colby couldn't help but smile. There were faint bruises there too—Noah had gripped him that hard. Colby turned his attention back to his locker and hung up his T-shirt.

Noah had been right about the marks that lingered on his wrists, too. They weren't bruises, but there were definitely red marks where the leather belt had rubbed against his skin. Colby was pretty sure he'd never be able to wear that belt again without getting a hard-on.

"What's going on?" Jordan asked as he opened another locker a little way down the line.

"Colby finally got laid," Trent said, before Colby had a chance to say anything.

Colby wasn't going to blush—really, he wasn't. He sat on the bench running down the centre of the changing room and began to undo the laces on his trainers.

"Laid by someone kinky," Trent specified, as he apparently noticed Colby's wrists.

No, he wasn't going to blush at all. Colby looked up and met Trent's eyes. "And?"

Trent blinked at him. His lips twitched with amusement. "Well, they always say it's the quiet ones you have to watch out for…"

Jordan chuckled. "You're just jealous because he's actually getting some, and you're not."

Trent let out a long suffering sigh. "True. On the plus side, neither are most of the other guys on the team—that does make me feel slightly less pathetic."

Colby smiled and shook his head at them both.

"Was it the guy you took to dinner?" Jordan asked.

Colby hesitated. It was one thing to show some respect for Noah's privacy and not brag about how bloody wonderful their sex life was going to be. Refusing to talk about his boyfriend at all seemed different, like he thought they had something to be ashamed of.

"Yeah. Noah—he's a dancer, he lives in the building opposite me," Colby said, carefully. He glanced at Jordan, then at Trent.

Trent shrugged. "Hey, I don't care who you screw. I just hope that your luck rubs off on the rest of us. No group of guys who spend half their life in the water should go through a dry spell this long. It's just not right!"

* * * * *

Noah was almost halfway to the club when he sensed that something wasn't quite right about the world around him. Subtle glances along the street didn't throw up any obvious warning flags. It was late, but not that late. There were plenty of people around, but no one that appeared threatening.

All those nice, logical considerations changed nothing. There was something wrong and Noah knew better than to doubt his instincts.

Someone was watching him. Someone was following him.

Noah sped up a little.

Sam?

One of that group of skinheads who thought a gay-bashing was a rite of passage?

Stupid random drunk who wanted a fight, and who'd decided Noah would be a suitable opponent because wasn't it just so bloody typical that he would?

Noah ran through his options. It didn't take long. He didn't have many. He was still a couple of streets away from the club. Head home and make it obvious where he lived? No. Flight wasn't an option. Fight? He was feeling pissed off enough with the world to have a chance of coming out on top, and anyway, what choice did he have?

When he turned the next corner, rather than speeding up again, Noah stopped just a few yards down the street.

Footsteps came closer to the corner.

Noah tensed.

Colby took two paces down the street and came to an abrupt halt.

Noah pushed his hand through his hair and let out a little sigh of relief. "Are you trying to make me paranoid?"

"No?" Colby hazarded. He had his hands pushed into his pockets. He stood with his head slightly ducked down, as if trying not to stand out or draw attention to himself — as if he really didn't have a bloody clue how hot he'd be if he stood up straighter and got a bit of confidence.

"You were following me," Noah snapped.

"Would you believe that, since we live in the same street, it's just a coincidence that we're both taking the same route, to the same club, at the same time?" Colby asked.

"No."

Colby smiled good-naturedly. "Yeah, I didn't think you would."

Noah sighed and shook his head. Colby really wasn't an easy man to remain pissed off with.

"Sorry if I creeped you out."

Noah looked Colby up and down without any idea what he should do with him. Well, okay — he had lots of ideas for what he could do with a guy like Colby, but since he'd already made a very firm decision that the previous night was a one-time deal, he wasn't going to bloody well do any of them.

"No one freaked."

Noah blinked at Colby.

"My wrists. You seemed worried that the other guys on the swim team would have a problem with them."

Noah looked down at Colby's wrists, just visible beyond the ends of his sleeves. He knew he should have been more careful with the boy; he should have thought about the consequences before he tied him up. Slowly, Colby's actual words registered.

"What did you tell them?" Noah asked, his curiosity getting the better of him.

Colby shrugged. "I didn't need to say much, they can put one and one together on their own."

Noah stared at him with no idea what to say.

"You look great," Colby blurted out.

Noah blinked and looked down at his clothes—clubbing clothes. The club. Yes. That was where he was supposed to be going.

He turned on his heel and walked away before he ended up standing in the middle of the pavement and staring at Colby all night.

Meet a random guy. Push Colby out of his head. Get back to normal. That was the plan, and he was going to stick to it. Noah nodded to himself. It was a good plan.

He'd gone all of a few paces before Colby fell in step beside him. Noah bit back a curse, but it wasn't as if he could demand Colby take a different route to the club.

"Did you have a good day?" Colby asked.

"No."

"How come?"

Because I kept getting distracted by this sweet little swimmer and forgetting what the hell I was supposed to be doing. "Just one of those days," Noah muttered.

"Maybe it will get better as the day goes on."

Noah wasn't going to think of the many and varied things Colby could do to make his day better. He wasn't.

Finally, the club came into sight. Noah walked a little faster. Running his eyes over the queue at the door, he wondered if there was anyone he knew there tonight. Familiar would be good. Someone who was familiar, but who wasn't Colby, and...

Noah came to a complete stop.

Sam.

"Noah?"

Sam stood, not in the queue, but alongside it, as if he'd spotted someone as he was heading for the front of the line and stopped to talk.

A touch to Noah's arm jerked him out of his stupor.

Colby stared down at him, his expression filled with concern. "Are you okay?"

Sam was there. And Sam had seen Colby dancing with Noah the previous night. And Sam was sure to remember someone as hot and as obviously out of his depth as Colby was. And Sam might decide to investigate further.

"Noah?" Colby put his hand on Noah's shoulder as if he thought Noah needed to be steadied.

Noah peered up at him. It only took him a second to make his decision, once his brain came properly back online. "I've changed my mind. I don't want to go to the club tonight."

"Oh."

Noah turned away from the club and took several paces back the way they'd come. He stopped when he realised the only footsteps he heard were his own. He looked over his shoulder and caught Colby's eye. "Well, don't just stand there—come on."

Colby obediently caught up and once more fell into step beside him. "Do I get to know what's going on?"

"No." Noah couldn't explain what he didn't

understand himself.

"Okay...?"

Noah glanced at Colby out of the corner of his eye. The boy looked wary, but Noah was pretty sure that was only because he was trying to work out if the sudden change of plans made it more or less likely that he was going to get laid.

Noah smiled slightly. So much for all his plans to limit it to a one night deal. There was no way in hell his will power extended to leaving an eighteen year old version of Colby on anyone's doorstep.

At the door to the studio, Noah sensed Colby hesitate.

"My brother's out. We'd have my place to ourselves."

Noah paused, his keys almost in the lock. On one hand, a home court advantage was always a good thing. He was always safer on his own turf. On the other hand, Colby hadn't been enthusiastic about being kicked out last time. It would probably be easier to leave Colby's flat, than to nudge Colby into leaving the studio. And, hell, it was Colby—for once, safety wasn't a concern.

Noah looked up at Colby.

The boy just stood there, waiting for Noah to make his decision. No demands, not even a request for what he wanted—just the relevant information hanging in the air between them.

Noah nodded. "Okay." It wouldn't kill him to let the boy pick the venue.

Colby seemed to be trying not to grin, but doing a very poor job of it. Noah couldn't help but smile in return. Within a few minutes, they were in Colby's flat with the door shut firmly between them and the outside world.

A short hallway led past a kitchen door and into the living room. There was a chair in the window. In front of the chair stood a telescope. Noah stopped halfway across the room when he spotted it.

"Do you want a drink or anything?" Colby said from somewhere behind him.

The words snapped Noah back into action. "I'll have whatever you're having," he said, vaguely. By the time the last word left his lips, he'd reached the telescope. He placed his eye against the view finder and found himself staring straight into the studio. It was dark and impossible to spot anything but vague outlines, but in the daylight, or when the light was on in the studio, Noah was willing to bet he'd be able to make out every detail.

The coating on the building's windows and the differing angles meant that Noah hadn't even been able to make out the telescope from his side of the road, but Colby had obviously been able to see everything.

"If it helps at all—the only room you can see into from here is the main studio space."

Noah pulled back from the telescope, turned and looked over his shoulder. Colby stood a few paces away, two bottles of Coke in his hands and a nervous expression on his face.

Noah shrugged. "Dance is meant to be performed for an audience. It's meant to be seen."

"You're not mad?"

Noah closed the gap between them. Taking the drinks off Colby, he set them on the table near the telescope. Then, sliding one hand behind Colby's head, Noah pulled him down for a kiss specifically designed to know just how un-mad he was.

The idea of Colby watching him, of Colby wanting to watch him that much, didn't make him mad, it turned him on. He settled his other hand on Colby's arse, pulling him forward, pressing their bodies together and letting Colby know that.

Colby gasped into the kiss. When Noah nipped at his bottom lip, he whimpered.

"One day, I'm going to screw you in that studio, and you're going to know exactly how many people from this block of flats will be able to watch us," Noah whispered to him. "I wonder if any of the other flat owners have invested in telescopes."

Colby seemed to stop breathing at that point. That was probably the reason he didn't voice any kind of protest, because Noah was pretty sure that exhibitionism was one kink that Colby really didn't have.

Noah moved his hand from behind Colby's head to his shoulder. He was just about to nudge him down onto his knees when he hesitated. If Colby's brother came home unexpectedly and saw them, Colby would be mortified. Hell, come to that, Noah wasn't at all in favour of being throttled by an over-protective sibling.

He stepped back from Colby. "Your bedroom."

Colby blinked at him as if he'd never heard of such a place. A moment later, he nodded and led the way.

There wasn't a lock on the door, but Noah still felt better once it was closed between them and any unexpected visitors.

"Naked, now," Noah ordered.

Colby quickly obeyed. He hesitated when he noticed that he was the only one getting undressed, but only for a second. He pushed on without making any complaint and soon stood nude in the middle of the room.

Noah ran his gaze over Colby's body from the top of his head all the way to his toes. So perfect—right down to the slight marks on his wrists and the scratches on his shoulders. He remained perfectly still, as if he knew that Noah had the right to stare at him for as long as he wanted, or perhaps as if he'd decided he didn't have much cause for complaint since he'd spent so much time watching Noah from the other side of the street.

If being studied made Colby nervous, it didn't dent his erection in the slightest—not even when Noah began to circle him. There were so many things he wanted to do with Colby, it was almost impossible for Noah to decide what to do first.

He reached out and ran his fingers across Colby's arse

as he walked behind him. Colby tensed as if he'd been struck rather than caressed. God, it was suddenly so easy to know what he wanted to do with him first.

"How much does your swimming costume cover?"

Colby looked over his shoulder. "I've got a few different ones."

Noah stopped staring at Colby's arse for a moment and looked him straight in the eye. "Do you have one big enough to cover a spanking?"

"Yes."

As Noah considered the possibilities he ran his fingers back and forth over the skin he was so desperate to mark. Colby would thrive under a spanking—everything about him screamed it. And, Colby hadn't even blinked when Noah suggested it.

Noah paused for a moment. If Colby was thinking with any part of his body above his waist, he'd have blushed at the idea, even if he might not have protested against it. One of them had to keep higher brain function going...

"If I spank you, you'll have to wear a costume that covers you from here to here." He ran his hand over Colby's arse and down the backs of his legs. "Do you have one like that—one that won't raise any eyebrows if you wear it to training for the next few days?"

Colby nodded.

"Here?" Noah asked. "In this room?"

"Yeah."

"Show me."

Colby looked over his shoulder at him. It seemed to take him a long time to work out what following that order involved. Finally, he stepped away from Noah's stroking hand, dug around in a drawer and found the required item. He offered it to Noah.

"No, put it on."

Colby did as he was told. His erection was clearly visible through the stretchy fabric, but otherwise the swimming shorts fitted the way Noah assumed a costume the right size would fit, and it covered Colby from navel to knee.

"The shorts pass without comment at training?"

Colby nodded, but Noah would bet money on the boy not having any idea why his lover wanted to be damn sure he wasn't bluffing about his ability to hide his embarrassment just because he really wanted to be spanked.

Noah nodded to himself. That was as close as he could get to being a nice guy today. He stepped forward, slid his hand behind Colby's head and tugged him down for a kiss.

Colby's hands settled on Noah's back, pulling him closer as he steadied them both. He whimpered when Noah broke the kiss, tried to dip his head to bring their lips back together and failed.

"I'm going to spank you until you come," Noah whispered in Colby's ear.

"Yes." It was barely a murmur, but the word held so much longing, it went straight to Noah's cock.

"But first, I want your mouth."

"Yes."

Noah didn't release Colby's neck; he just changed his grip and pushed him down onto his knees.

Colby gasped, immediately tilting his head back to peer up at Noah.

Noah stared down at Colby for several long seconds. He didn't look the least bit bothered about being put on his knees. Hell, it didn't even seem to occur to him that anyone would have an issue with it.

"Have you thought about going down on me before, darling?" Noah asked. "Have you imagined me standing in your bedroom, ordering you to suck me off?"

Colby swallowed. He nodded. He never looked away from Noah's face.

Noah reached into his back pocket and pulled out his wallet. He had to release his grip on Colby's neck to get out a condom, but he had no doubt that Colby was more than willing to stay where he'd been put.

"I don't want to use —"

"Then it's lucky for you that I'm the one who's making the decisions here, isn't it?" Noah said, without missing a beat.

"But —"

"Your options are safe or not at all." Noah paused and met Colby's gaze. Maybe the risk was small, but he was still damned if he'd let Colby take it.

Colby stared up at him for what felt like hours. "Safe," he finally whispered.

"Good boy." Noah had his fly undone and the condom on in record time.

Colby's hands remained idle at his sides as he waited. Noah smiled. It really didn't seem to occur to him to reach out to another man without that guy's permission. Such a pretty sub...

Noah slid his hand behind Colby's head and guided him forward. Steadying his cock with his other hand, he placed the tip to Colby's lips.

Without any order needing to be issued, Colby opened his mouth in offering.

"Try to keep your lips over your teeth," Noah said. Considering the situation, he was impressed by how level his voice was.

Colby murmured his understanding as he followed the order. His tongue rubbed against the tip of Noah's cock in a move that Noah couldn't help but think of as the very best kind of beginner's luck. He gasped at the unexpected burst of bliss. It took all his self-control not to push deeper into Colby's mouth.

* * * * *

Colby blinked up at Noah. He'd never heard a more erotic sound in his life. He hesitated for a moment, then did his best to repeat what he'd just done with his tongue.

Noah tightened his grip on the back of Colby's neck. "That's right," he whispered. He rocked his hips, just slightly, pushing his cock a fraction deeper into Colby's mouth.

This time it was Colby's turn to moan his approval. He couldn't taste Noah the way he'd wanted to, but the simple fact that he could feel Noah moving inside him was pure ecstasy.

Lifting his hands, he cautiously placed them on Noah's sides, encouraging him to thrust properly between his lips.

For a second, Noah stilled. He stared down at Colby very intently for what felt like a long time before he seemed to come to a decision. He rocked his hips again. The thrust was shallow, but there was clear and conscious intent behind it. He wasn't just moving on instinct now; he was as in control of his own actions as he was of Colby.

"Do you like that, sweetheart?" Noah asked.

Colby made an approving noise in the back of his throat.

Noah's head tipped back as he moaned in response. He thrust just a little deeper.

"God, you're a bloody natural."

Colby was pretty sure Noah wasn't even aware that he'd said that out loud. He stared up at Noah, completely enthralled with the pleasure on his face. His own cock pressed against the inside of his swimming costume, hard, aching and completely untouched.

Noah kept rocking his hips. None of the thrusts were deep, but they were made according to a faultless rhythm, as if a beat played inside Noah's head and he couldn't help but dance to it.

Colby whimpered at the idea and pulled another gasp from Noah.

Vibrations. The moment he realised what was working, Colby threw both embarrassment and caution to the wind. If Noah liked to hear how much Colby enjoyed getting on his knees for him, Colby was more than willing to oblige.

He let Noah feel every bit of vibration his appreciation could produce as he worked his tongue against the tip of his shaft.

It was hard to know if he was doing the right thing or not. He only had that one time Noah had gone down on him to copy, and at that point, his brain really hadn't been capable of storing away specific details for future reference.

Noah's grip on Colby's neck tightened. His thrusts sped up, just a fraction. He opened his eyes and stared down at Colby. Unable to break his gaze, Colby peered up at him in return.

One harder, deeper thrust that almost reached the back of Colby's mouth, and Noah came. His other hand moved to the back of Colby's head, keeping him close and still as Noah spilled into the condom.

Robbed of the chance to even try to swallow, Colby stared up at Noah and concentrated on his expression. He wasn't going to sulk at not being able to taste Noah's orgasm. Hell, he was still willing to be bloody grateful he was in the room for it.

Noah's grip on Colby's head remained tight as Noah gradually caught his breath. He blinked open his eyes and looked down at Colby. Perfectly still now, Noah just stared at Colby, as if memorising the sight of him on his knees with his lips wrapped around his lover's softening cock.

"Are you sure you haven't done that before?" Noah asked.

Of all the stupid things to do, Colby felt himself blush at the idle compliment.

Noah chuckled as he pulled away. He left Colby kneeling in the middle of the room as he dispensed with the condom and did up his fly.

Leaning back against the chest of drawers against the opposite wall, Noah stared across at Colby for a long time, making no move to close the distance between them. "I promised you a spanking, didn't I?"

"Yes." He'd actually promised to spank him until he came, but Colby was willing to take whatever he could get. Anything that involved physical contact was better than being tortured by the sudden distance between them.

Noah turned away.

Colby tensed, until he realised Noah was moving toward the bed rather than the door. Still kneeling in the middle of the room, he watched Noah settle himself comfortably on his bed, resting against the headboard with a pillow behind his back. Noah made him wait several extra seconds before he called him closer.

"Across my lap—your head this side," Noah ordered.

Colby suddenly wished he was a hell of a sight shorter than he was. All his limbs seemed to have a mind of their own. Like a fish out of water, he was clumsy and awkward as he tried to arrange himself as Noah wished. Noah didn't help at all. He just sat there, waiting until Colby fell still.

Noah placed his hand on Colby's arse. It was only then that Colby remembered that he was still wearing his shorts. Before he had a chance to take them off, Noah was tugging them down himself. He stopped with the material bunched tight around Colby's knees.

Colby looked over his shoulder, about to suggest he kick them off altogether, but the look in Noah's eyes stopped him short. Obviously, Colby's opinion wasn't necessary at that point. He shifted across Noah's lap as he moved back to face forward.

His cock rubbed against Noah's leather trousers, pulling a moan from him. He bit down hard on his bottom lip.

"No holding back." Noah roughly tugged Colby's bottom lip from between his teeth. "I'm the only one in this bed who's allowed to bite anything."

"Okay." Everything was okay with Colby, because Noah's other hand was now resting on his bare arse, and Noah was stroking the skin there—back and forth—in a way that made Colby's brain melt.

"I'm not going to be pissed off with you if you ask me to stop," Noah said.

"Okay."

"But if you don't come from the spanking, you're not going to be allowed to come at all." He said it so conversationally, as if he really didn't mind either way.

Colby minded so much he didn't know any words strong enough to explain the situation. "Okay," was the best he could manage.

Noah took his hand away from Colby's arse. A second later, the sharp sound of skin against skin filled the air. Colby jerked at the unexpected jolt the spank sent through his body.

He barely had time to process it before Noah's hand fell against his other buttock. Colby's eyes dropped closed as if to cut off any distractions and let him concentrate on what was happening within his body.

Noah's hand briefly caressed the struck skin. Two more spanks. Colby murmured his pleasure. Those two were harder than the first pair, as if Noah was beginning to trust that he wouldn't freak out at a tap on the backside.

It took Noah no time at all to find a rhythm he liked. Colby helplessly rocked his hips, trying to push back into each set of spanks that fell against his skin. His cock rubbed against Noah's leg each time he moved, and that only made it more difficult to still himself.

The friction against his shaft was pure pleasure, but the heat building in his buttocks as Noah continued to bring his hand down against them was far more complicated to process.

It danced along the knife-edge between pain and pleasure, pirouetting and leaping high into the air with sheer joy at finally being experienced.

Colby moaned, unable to keep anything back from Noah as he squirmed over his lap. Colby had no idea if he was trying to move closer to or further away from the spanks any more. He had no idea about anything beyond the fact that

Noah was in complete control, and that was just as it should be.

The rhythm Noah set was strong, determined and unyielding. Nothing Colby did made any difference as Noah's spanks coated every inch of his buttocks and the backs of his thighs.

Colby bowed his head, resting his temple against the bed sheets as he whimpered. He wanted to beg, but he had no idea what to beg for. The possibility that Noah would think he was asking him to stop kept him from uttering a single word for a long time.

Then, eventually, it became impossible to stay silent. "Please?"

The next spank was harder, and all the more perfect for it.

Colby groaned with need. "Noah, please?"

The rhythm changed, becoming faster.

Colby rocked against Noah's thigh, his cock rubbing against the leather over and over again.

Another spank—harsher than any of the others and landing right on the line between buttock and thigh. Colby cried out as bliss burst through him. He jerked against Noah's leg as he came. Noah's spanking never faltered. He kept his rhythm going until Colby eventually fell still, completely spent and no longer able to move a single muscle.

The room was unnaturally quiet. All Colby could hear was his own ragged breathing. For a long time, he simply lay there, incapable of doing anything else. Noah's hand was on his arse, but it just rested there now, barely putting any pressure on the spanked skin.

Colby had no idea how long he remained there before his mind started to come back on line.

Noah had just spanked him.

He'd just come while Noah spanked him.

He'd just come all over Noah's leather trousers, and he wasn't sure if that was something he should be working out how to apologise for. Hell, he wasn't sure about anything.

Finally, Noah tugged at his shoulder, not so much encouraging him to move as making it clear that Colby was going to move whether he was ready to or not, so he'd better get used to the idea.

Slowly, and more clumsily than ever, Colby obeyed. He managed to get off Noah's lap and collapse on the bed next to him. In the process, he rolled over onto his back. His spanked arse came into direct contact with the sheets, making him gasp and arch against the bed.

"You might want to sleep on your stomach tonight," Noah said, with obvious amusement.

Colby smiled at him as he gradually relaxed and let his weight rest properly on his spanked backside. He made no move to roll over. "It kind of feels good."

Noah chuckled, delight dancing in his eyes.

Not sure what to do with himself, Colby dropped his gaze. He'd come over Noah's trousers.

"There's um…in the bedside drawer," Colby said.

As Noah cleaned himself up, Colby kicked off the swim trunks that had been around his knees.

When Noah turned his attention back to him, Colby knew he'd been caught staring at Noah, but he was pretty sure Noah was way past the point of being surprised by how much Colby loved looking at him.

"Will you stay?" Colby blurted out.

Noah shook his head. "I should get back to my place."

"Why?"

Noah was halfway to the edge of the bed when he hesitated. "It's just easier that way."

Colby knew in that moment that he should have made certain that Noah undressed at some point. He was sure it had to be easier to convince a naked man to stay in his bed than a fully clothed one.

Sitting up, he reached out and put his hand on Noah's shoulder. When Noah half-turned, Colby put his other hand on Noah's cheek. He leaned forward and brought their lips together. He had no idea how to make a kiss either as perfect or as erotic as the ones Noah so easily offered him. He didn't try.

Pressing his lips against Noah's mouth, he merely did his best to make it clear that he wanted to kiss him more than he'd ever wanted anything in his life. Noah made no objection. He even turned further on the bed to make the angle easier. For all of three seconds, Colby was aware of being in complete control of the kiss.

Then, without any warning, Noah pushed him down on the bed. His spanked skin was once more pressed against the mattress, this time beneath both their weights. Flames burned across his arse. Noah grabbed Colby's nearest wrist and pinned it to the blankets. There was no way for Colby to control the kiss then or to control the whole series of whimpers and moans that filled the air.

A lifetime might have passed before Noah lifted his head. He stared down at Colby, his expression completely unreadable.

"Stay?" Colby asked again. "Even if it's just for a little while."

Noah seemed to think about it for a long time.

"Please?"

"Plans for another round?" Noah teased.

"Just rest with me for a little while?" Colby asked.

Noah hesitated.

"And, maybe after we've rested…" Colby suggested.

Noah chuckled. He also relaxed — as if the idea that he was being kept around for sex made everything far easier for him to deal with.

Colby carefully felt his way forward in the conversation. "Maybe you want to rest naked?"

Noah raised an eyebrow. "Any particular reason?"

Colby swallowed. So you're less likely to leave, probably wouldn't win him any points. "I like you naked," he said. It was the truth, too.

Noah lifted himself up off Colby and looked down at his already naked body. "You're not so bad yourself, darling."

Colby's blush made Noah chuckle, but somehow it also seemed to convince him to shrug off his clothes and lay down on the bed next to him. There was at least six inches of empty blanket between them.

He'll be fine with it if he thinks it's all about sex...

Colby moved across the bed with all the confidence he could muster. He kissed Noah, just briefly. Noah didn't back away when Colby broke the kiss. Colby settled his hand on Noah's side and closed his eyes as if he just intended to doze until they were ready for another round. When he risked opening his eyes a few minutes later, Noah's eyes were closed.

Colby cautiously, and with what he hoped was appropriate sleepiness, tried to gather Noah into his arms.

Noah blinked open his eyes. He nudged Colby's shoulder, with what seemed to be genuine sleepiness.

"Roll over," Noah mumbled. He prodded Colby until he did as he was told. Noah spooned behind him then, his crotch pressed firmly against Colby's spanked arse. Colby bit back a gasp, desperate not to wake Noah any more than necessary.

Noah's breaths quickly settled into a slower, and Colby assumed sleepier, rhythm. The arm he'd thrown over Colby tightened around him; he pressed his crotch more firmly against his spanked buttocks and murmured his approval.

Colby smiled to himself as he let his eyes drift closed.

* * * * *

"What the—?" Noah threw himself into a seated position as he jerked awake. He turned in every direction, studying the space around him.

He wasn't in his own room. His heart rate doubled.

There was no one else there at that moment. He calmed

slightly.

A loud ringing noise still filled the air. He traced it to an alarm clock on the bedside table and switched it off.

Silence descended. Noah pushed his hand through his hair and tried to make his brain work.

Colby.

Yes. That was right. He must have fallen asleep. Damn it. He'd only meant to doze for a while.

He looked around the room again. There was no sign of Colby, but there was a note on his pillow.

Noah picked it up.

Noah,
I had to leave stupid-early for training. I didn't want to wake you, but I've set the alarm so you have plenty of time to get back to the studio in time for your first class.
Love,
Colby.

Noah raised an eyebrow, not sure what to make of that.

Sweet that Colby didn't want to wake him up early?

Stalker-ish that he apparently knew the times of all his classes?

Overly-trusting to leave a virtual stranger in his home on his own?

Annoying because they could have had morning sex if Colby had woke him up before he left?

Noah shook his head and pulled himself out of the bed. He should probably just be glad that he hadn't had to face Colby over the breakfast table.

Pulling on his clothes, he found his wallet, pushed it into his back pocket and headed for the door.

Halfway across the living room, he heard a noise. There was someone else there, someone that wasn't Colby. Shit!

"Good morning."

Noah's head jerked up. A man stood in the kitchen

doorway—a position that also put him between Noah and the flat's only exit. He looked a lot like Colby, but older, and without the shaved head. Brother. Tony. Damn!

Suddenly facing *Colby* the morning after didn't seem like such a bad prospect.

"Good morning," Noah echoed. It didn't really seem like enough, given the situation. "I'm a…friend of Colby's."

Tony's lips twitched into a smile. "I know. Noah—he's mentioned you once or twice. Do you want a coffee?"

No, Noah wanted to get out of there as quickly as possible. Killing Colby for putting him in this position was pretty high on his to do list, too. "Thanks," was what actually left his mouth.

Tony retreated into the kitchen. Noah followed, not sure what else to do. He poured himself a coffee, but couldn't think of a single thing to say.

"He's completely besotted with you," Tony offered, as an opening.

Noah sipped his coffee, focusing all his attention on his mug.

"He's a good kid," Tony added.

The coffee was so hot it burned Noah's lips, he still took another sip.

"Any time you want to speak up…" Tony offered.

Noah shrugged. "I figured you were working your way up to some sort of stay the hell away from my little brother speech. I wouldn't want to spoil your flow."

For the first time, Noah looked up. Their eyes met across the kitchen.

Noah sighed. "How about we do the speed version? Yes, he's a nice boy. Clean cut, white picket fences, helps old ladies across the street, whatever. If he's spent half as much time staring across the street as I think he has, we both know that I'm not the same kind of guy."

"I know that the first time you met him he was fifteen."

Noah straightened up. "Nothing happened then."

"I know," Tony sipped his coffee. "I also know that you could have had him with a click of your fingers, but you chose to tell him to come back when he was eighteen, instead."

Noah held Tony's gaze for several seconds. Apparently, this wasn't a speech he could anticipate and provide a speed version of after all.

"If you're waiting for me to throw a strop, you're going to have a long wait. I don't have any problem with you and Colby. Anyway, I'm under orders." He nodded to a pad of note paper hanging on the front of the fridge.

Tony,
Noah stayed over. He's sleeping in. If you see him before you go to practice be nice. Seriously – your sense of humour sucks – just be nice.
Colby.

Noah stared at the note a little while, not sure what to make of that either. "Oh," was all he could finally think of to say.

* * * * *

Noah looked up as the door to the studio swung open. A quick glance at his watch told him it was too early for anyone to arrive for the next class.

He smiled a moment later, unable to feel too surprised when he saw Colby step around the edge of the door.

"I'm over here," Noah said, from the far corner of the room.

Colby smiled, slightly nervously, as he came across the room. "I'm sorry about Tony this morning."

Noah raised an eyebrow. "Did he do anything that warrants an apology?"

"I don't know, but it seemed safer to apologise just in case. He has a really sarcastic sense of humour—especially before he's had his first cup of coffee. It takes some getting used to."

"He was fine," Noah said, purposely keeping most of his attention on the music he was sorting through. "Did you apologise to him for anything I might have said too?"

"No." Just that one word.

Noah glanced up. Colby didn't expand on his answer. Apparently, if Tony didn't like him, Colby had decided his brother would just have to deal with it. Noah's lips twitched.

"So," Colby said. "I know you don't have long between classes, but I've been thinking—"

"I've been thinking, too," Noah cut in.

He could almost see warning flags go up in Colby's mind. "That's...good?" he hazarded.

"I'm not looking for a boyfriend. I'm not looking to date anyone. That's not going to change."

Colby didn't rush to reply.

Noah took a deep breath. "However, I can't deny, we're bloody good together. If you want us to keep meeting up, just for sex... That could work."

Colby opened his mouth, closed his mouth, thought about it, and tried again. "And this is different from a boyfriend in that...?"

Noah kept his gaze on the music. "We won't be dating. No restaurants, no clubs, no romance, no fuss. It'll just be me and you—either here, or at your place if Tony isn't there. And we'll both know exactly where we stand. This isn't going anywhere. It's just sex." He glanced up.

Colby nodded slowly, his expression wary. "Will you still be seeing other guys?"

Yes. It was a good answer—the answer Noah had already decided he was going to give. But Colby was right there, and it would be like kicking a damn puppy. "No. Not while we have this...arrangement."

"Can we stay the night?"

Noah had pre-planned an answer to that one, too. Now

that Colby was there, it was a damn sight harder to ignore the fact that last night he'd had the best night's sleep he'd had in years. "Yeah, we can do that."

"Can we stop using condoms?"

Noah took a deep breath, determined not to falter on *every* answer he gave. Compromise. "I'll get tested. But we keep using them until it's definitely safe."

"But once you think it's safe?" Colby pushed.

Noah nodded, although he was pretty sure the chances of them still having their little arrangement in place by then was a million to one.

Apparently, that was it for the question and answer session, because Colby now grinned as if he'd won the lottery.

Noah shook his head at him, but he couldn't help but smile a little bit too. It wouldn't last, but while it did, he was pretty sure he was going to enjoy the hell out of it.

Chapter Seven

Three months later

"You know you're a much better dancer than any of those guys, right?"

Noah shook his head, but Colby was paying close attention—he didn't miss the way Noah's lips twitched into a smile at the compliment.

Colby grinned. He itched to reach out and take Noah's hand as they walked home from the railway station but he forced himself not to.

He'd actually managed to take Noah on something that was sort of, close to, an almost date. It had taken him three months to wear Noah down, and he hadn't managed to add in dinner alongside the modern dance performance they'd been to see, but Colby was still pretty sure the world was a bloody brilliant place. He wasn't going to risk it all by pushing his luck and asking for soppiness on top of everything else.

"Yours or mine?" Colby asked, as they turned into their street.

"Mine," Noah said. His smile twisted a little. Colby knew what that meant.

Part hard just because he was with Noah, Colby's cock suddenly jerked to attention. Hell, yeah, he knew that smile. Noah led the way up to the studio with Colby hot on his heels, but rather than head straight for his little set of rooms at the back of the building, Noah went to another door at the far end of the space.

The second studio space beyond the door was a lot smaller than the main one. The windows were partially obscured so dancers could use it as an overflow changing room and warm up space. Colby stood just inside the door and looked around as Noah switched on the lights.

The mirrors lining two of the walls reflected Noah's image perfectly, as he strode to the far side of the room and unearthed a wooden chair from beneath a jumble of props and old costumes. He set the chair in the middle of the room facing one of the walls of mirrors.

"I want you naked by the time I come back. You can leave your clothes over there." Noah waved his hand toward a rail where, under different circumstances, dance costumes might be hung. A second later, the door to the small studio swung shut behind him.

Colby didn't hesitate. He'd worked out a long time ago that when Noah was in this kind of mood it was best to just do as he was told and try to keep up as best he could. Colby grinned. He'd never regretted obeying Noah.

Naked, he looked around the room again. He'd seen Noah show dancers into that studio on occasions—and he'd seen dancers come back out, in costume and warmed up ready to perform. But, in all the times he'd watched from across the road, he'd never seen Noah take a date in there—not once.

He spun around as he heard the door creak. Noah had taken off his clothes too, only he'd put other clothes on in their place.

Colby stopped breathing.

Noah in anything, or nothing, was, by definition, as hot as hell. Noah dressed to go clubbing was a walking wet dream. This outfit was in a whole different league again. The shorts were tiny, made out of a fabric that just begged to be caressed. The outline of Noah's cock was clearly visible against it. The top was mesh and not much bigger than the shorts. Somehow, they made him look far more exposed than mere nudity ever could.

"Pick up your jaw and come here."

Colby blinked and quickly closed the gap between them. Noah stood by the chair he'd placed in the middle of the room.

"Sit."

Colby sat.

Noah stepped back several paces. He slowly ran his gaze over Colby's body, taking in every detail. It was one of those looks that made Colby forget that Noah had ever seen him naked before. Nervousness rose up inside him, and he felt an almost irresistible urge to cover his cock.

"I know you've watched me dance, a lot," Noah said with that same slightly twisted smile. "But tonight it occurred to me that you've never seen me dance *for you*." There was an edge to his voice.

An uneasy feeling trembled inside Colby at the altered tone. "Noah?"

Without another word, Noah walked away. Tracking him in the mirror, Colby saw him approach the sound system in the far corner. Music filled the room. Loud, with a thumping beat, something like the music they'd danced to in the club, but somehow harsher.

Noah turned. He caught Colby's gaze in the mirror, then Noah closed his eyes. Colby could almost see him putting himself in a different head space, the same way he did when he was moving from teaching one kind of dance to another.

When he opened his eyes, his expression had changed. Colby forgot how to breathe all over again. He shifted in his chair.

Noah smiled. His hips began to rock in time to the music.

Colby had thought that the way Noah danced in the club was pure sex. He'd been wrong. That had been the PG rated version. This was the X-rated, might–actually-be-illegal-in-most-countries version.

Colby swallowed. As Noah began to move and the

dance really started, every inch of Noah's body seemed to be about sex and raw need. It wasn't just the way he moved his hips. It was everything.

Colby stared, completely fascinated. He couldn't take his eyes off Noah. Slowly, he lifted his gaze until he looked straight into Noah's eyes. He was aware of Noah moving closer to him, but he couldn't break their locked gazes — not even for the privilege of seeing the way Noah's body moved.

Noah stopped just a foot away from him. Colby reached out without thinking.

Noah swayed neatly out of range of his touch. "No, you don't. The management reserves the right to throw out any customers who touch the dancers."

Colby blinked at him.

"Put your hands on the sides of the chair and keep them there." At least that was easy to interpret. Colby put his hands where Noah wanted them.

"Good boy." Just for a moment, Noah's smile seemed friendlier, gentler, and he was far more like the Noah that Colby was used to. Then, the predatory glint came back into Noah's eyes. Still well within touching distance, he began to dance for Colby in earnest.

A lap dance. And, in that moment, it was obvious that Noah had been that kind of dancer in the past. This wasn't a guy dancing for his boyfriend; this was a professional who knew he was bloody good at his job.

Noah twisted his body, moving closer, until there was just a breath of air between them, then pulling back — making it impossible for Colby not to want to lean forward and bridge the gap between them.

No touching.

Colby tensed every muscle in his body. He wasn't going to break that rule. Even when most of his brain was starved of a blood supply that had been diverted straight to his cock, he knew that particular order was more important than any other command Noah had ever given him.

It was a simple rule, but even while he was unable to maintain anything like a clear thought process, Colby knew the situation was anything but simple. Tearing his gaze away from Noah's body, Colby made a point of looking him straight in the eye and holding his gaze.

Noah smiled as their eyes met. Amusement lightened his expression. On the next beat, he turned away from Colby. There was no chance of eye contact then and Colby's attention slid helplessly down to settle on Noah's arse. He had to clench his hands into fists to stop himself from reaching out.

Another turn, and suddenly Colby was staring at Noah's crotch. The shorts he was wearing were so tiny, the outline of his cock so obvious, the zip running down the centre line so tempting. Colby's mouth watered with the desperate need to slide off the chair, drop to his knees and take Noah's shaft into his mouth.

He whimpered as Noah thrust to the beat, moving nearer, until he was standing so close their knees almost touched.

Colby jerked as Noah's hand came to rest on his shoulder. "You said no touching," he reminded Noah.

Noah raised an eyebrow. "I said *you* can't touch. But I can do whatever I want. Right?"

Colby nodded rapidly. "Right."

Noah dipped his head and brought their lips together, the kiss made it impossible to think about anything—not the music, not the dance, not Noah's strange mood, not even his fear of screwing everything up if he made a wrong move. The kiss was the only thing that existed.

By the time Noah pulled back an inch and allowed Colby to pick up a few of his scattered brain cells, Noah was practically straddling him. Trying to catch his breath, Colby stared down between their bodies. In spite of everything else, Noah was still moving to the beat. One of his hands cradled the back of Colby's head, the other ran down Colby's naked torso until it reached his cock.

Colby gasped.

A few strokes; complete bliss. Then, without any warning, Noah was pulling away.

"Wait!"

Noah chuckled. He didn't say anything, but he didn't need to. He didn't put any extra distance between them. He started to dance again. His every movement was a tease, a temptation. One moment, he'd lean in as if offering a kiss. The next second, he was pulling back making it impossible for Colby to bring their lips together without leaving the chair.

"Noah…"

As he danced, Noah ran his hands over his own body, leading Colby's gaze over him, making it all the more essential that Colby be allowed to touch him too. It was torture—but the kind any man in his right mind would volunteer to receive every day for the rest of his life.

Pulling back again, Noah reached for the zip on his tiny shorts. Colby followed the tab of the zip from the top of the shorts all the way down and back between Noah's legs. Even as he unfastened the zip and rendered himself completely accessible, Noah kept dancing, turning so Colby could see him from every angle.

With his back to him, Noah rolled his hips and arched his spine, and Colby realised something else. Noah was wearing a butt plug.

Colby's heart stopped beating.

Noah's next movement took him behind Colby's chair. He leaned over Colby and ran one hand down his chest. A tearing noise made Colby turn his head to the side. He was just in time to see Noah rip open a sachet of lube with his teeth. Reaching down Colby's body, Noah slicked his cock with the lube.

"Noah?" Colby could barely breathe well enough to get the word out.

"Yeah?" Noah asked, pressing a kiss just below his ear.

Colby forgot what he'd intended to say.

Noah circled around the chair once more. It took him all of a few seconds to discard the plug. Then, he was straddling Colby again, sitting on his lap.

Colby looked from his slicked cock, to Noah's own erection and finally up to Noah's face. He still didn't have any words.

His brain had died. He was pretty sure he was going to come before anything else could happen, and Noah was still moving to the damn beat as if this was all part of the dance.

As Noah rocked his hips, their cocks rubbed together.

"Please?" Colby had no idea what he was begging for—mostly because, at that point, *anything* would have been fine with him.

Noah reached between them. He squeezed the base of Colby's cock, pulling him back from the edge of his orgasm. Then, he lifted himself off Colby's lap.

Never losing track of the beat, Noah guided the tip of Colby's cock to his hole.

Colby held his breath as, very slowly, Noah lowered himself down his shaft until he once more sat firmly on Colby's lap, straddling his thighs, but now with Colby's cock buried to the hilt inside him. It was unlike anything Colby had ever felt—better than anything he'd ever been able to imagine.

Slowly, Colby dragged his gaze up to look at Noah's face.

Noah's smile seemed different now, less ruthless than it had been at the start of the dance. For the first time since the music started, every part of Noah remained still for several seconds.

"You're okay with this?" Colby managed to rasp out. Until a few seconds ago, he'd been pretty sure that Noah's original claim of being versatile about who topped didn't apply to their particular relationship.

Noah chuckled and looked down between them at his flourishing erection. "Very okay with this," he promised, dipping his head and leading Colby from one kiss into another, then another.

Colby was barely aware of it when Noah started to move. The way his hips rocked was so subtle, it was easy to miss, until it had taken over Colby's whole world and had suddenly become impossible to ignore.

"Noah." It was pretty much the only word in Colby's head.

Noah kept his hands on Colby's shoulders, but the rest of his body moved, slowly undulating as he rode Colby. For several seconds, his head dropped back and he seemed to lose himself in his own pleasure.

Colby ached to be able to reach out and wrap his hand around Noah's cock, to offer back some tiny part of the pleasure he was receiving. He gripped the edges of the chair instead, unable to move without permission, unable to pull together the words to ask for it.

Noah started to move more quickly. He brought their lips together in a scorching kiss. Thrusting his tongue into Colby's mouth he matched his rhythm to the way he rode Colby's cock.

It was almost too much. Colby whimpered into the kiss, struggling to hold himself back, but sure that he was going to fail at any moment. "Please?" he mumbled into the kiss. "Noah, please…"

One of Noah's hands left Colby's shoulders and dropped down between them. Colby had barely even worked out that Noah was jacking himself off before he felt Noah's hole clench around him. There was no way in hell he could hold back for another second then.

He cried out into the kiss as he came. The world faded away until there was only that perfect moment of ecstasy. When he finally succeeded in blinking open his eyes, Noah was staring down at him.

Colby managed a shaky breath as he took careful stock of the situation.

Noah was still astride his legs. Colby's cock was

softening inside him. Noah's cum was decorating Colby's chest. Colby's hands were still on the edges of the chair's seat.

If Noah felt half as shaky as Colby did, it was a wonder he could balance where he was.

"Hands," Colby whispered.

Noah blinked at him.

"Can I move my hands now?" Colby asked, forcing himself to speak loudly enough to be heard over the music.

* * * * *

Noah looked down to where Colby's hands remained clenched around the edge of the chair. He'd actually kept his hands there the whole time...

Noah nodded. "Yeah. That's fine. You can move your hands."

Colby lifted them, flexing the fingers as if his grip on the chair had been so tight he'd cramped up. But, when he placed his hands on Noah's waist, his touch was as careful and gentle as ever.

Noah leaned forward and rested his temple against Colby's forehead.

The music he'd set to play ended abruptly. The silence was sudden and intense.

"If the guys I used to dance for had all been like you, I might never have quit it." It was a whispered little confession, but the sheer absence of music made it seem loud and stark against the surrounding silence.

Colby slid his hands around to the small of Noah's back, encouraging him to lean forward and rest against his body. For a few minutes, Noah let himself stay there, unable to pull away and just as incapable of pulling together his thoughts.

"Come on," he finally said. He untangled them and stepped away, but against all sense or reason, he found himself reaching back and offering Colby his hand to lead him toward the bedroom.

At the door into the main studio, Noah paused and grabbed a towel someone had left behind, offering it to Colby to wrap around his waist. It was only a few yards to the other door, Noah didn't bother covering himself up to move through the studio.

Safely inside his bedroom, Noah busied himself dispensing with his clothes and cleaning them both up. Finally stilling in the middle of the bedroom, lacking anything else to fidget with, Noah pushed his hand through his hair.

He needed space to think. One glance at Colby sitting on the edge of the bed, and Noah knew that the only way the boy would leave was if he was physically pushed through the door.

Noah took a deep breath. Okay, so thinking could wait until tomorrow, or at least until Colby was asleep. He nodded to himself, slipped into the bed, tugged Colby to lie down next to him and switched off the light.

The silence stretched out for so long, Noah was half sure that Colby had fallen asleep the moment his head hit the pillow.

"Wow."

Noah smiled in the darkness. Perhaps he hadn't been the only one who'd needed a few minutes to pull his reactions together. "I'll second that," he said with a chuckle. He shifted slightly uncomfortably on the hard mattress. Damn, but Colby was hung...

More silence, but Noah no longer harboured any doubts—this was the kind of silence that meant Colby was working up to talking about something.

"You said you might have liked it if all the guys you danced for were like me," Colby said.

Noah mentally cursed. Just because it was true, that didn't mean he should have said it out loud. "Yeah."

"The way it really was..." Colby hesitated.

Noah said nothing, hoping against all probability that

Colby would drop it.

"You hated it," Colby said. It wasn't really a question.

Noah still nodded in the darkness. "Yeah. I did. Every single time." He sighed, shrugged. "It could have been worse."

"Tell me about it?"

As his eyes adjusted to the gloom, Noah frowned up at the outline of the ceiling. "Why?"

"Because I want to know everything about you," Colby said.

Noah tensed. "No, darling, you really don't." Unable to just lay there any longer, Noah shuffled toward the edge of the mattress and sat up, lowering his feet onto the floor alongside the bed.

Colby reached out and wrapped his hand around his wrist. "Noah—"

"Let me go."

Colby immediately released his grip on him.

Noah hesitated. Damn. He hadn't really expected Colby to do as he'd asked. Just like it hadn't occurred to him that Colby, that any man, would actually keep his hands to himself while getting a lap dance. God, sometimes it was impossible to wrap his head around just how different Colby was compared to the kind of guys he was used to.

Noah took a deep breath. If Colby had refused to release him, it would have been so bloody easy to keep trying to pull away. As it was... He closed his eyes. "What do you want to know?"

"How long ago did you start doing that kind of dancing?" Colby asked, choosing each word with obvious care.

"A few weeks after I came out—as soon as I got a fake ID." There wasn't a hint of emotion in Noah's voice—he made sure of that.

"Was it a good fake?" Colby asked.

Noah raised an eyebrow in the darkness. Not quite the

question he'd expected...

"You said before that you can spot even the best fake from across the room," Colby reminded him.

In spite of everything else, Noah found himself chuckling at the memory of their first meeting. "No. Mine was a bloody awful fake. But it wasn't the kind of club where they worried too much about that."

"So the manager, or whatever, he knew you were underage when he hired you?"

"Yeah, he knew."

Colby was quiet for a few moments. "In the club, was it just dancing?"

It took Noah a few seconds to realise what Colby was, very delicately, trying to ask. "A lot of the guys who danced there made money on the side. I stuck to dancing." He stared down at his hands in the half-light.

"I'm glad."

"It was a practical decision, not a moral one," Noah forced himself to say.

"I'm still glad."

For some reason, the fact that Colby wanted to think well of him was far harder to deal with than all the less than pleasant memories which wanted to force their way to the front of his mind. "I'd have probably picked up some extra cash the same way as the other guys, except..." He took a deep breath and forced himself to keep going. "There was an understanding that the dancers would all be very grateful for their jobs—and that meant being available to management whenever they wanted one of us. The owner of the club, he...took an interest in me. We had an on-off thing going on, almost right from the start."

Colby shifted on the bed behind Noah, as if he was sitting up properly, but he didn't reach out to Noah. "What was he like?"

"Sam? He was a complete bastard—he still is." Noah swallowed down the bitter taste in the back of his throat. "The arrangement we had, it didn't end when I got the job here and quit dancing in his club. He owns most of the gay nightclubs in the city. I still see him around sometimes." He couldn't keep back the bitter little laugh. "Even now, even though I know how it goes with him, I still come to heel whenever he clicks his damn fingers."

Noah waited for another movement on the mattress — one that would herald Colby getting up and walking away. God knew that if the boy had any sense, he'd have been out of there a long time ago.

Damn it — not a movement, not a word. Not even a question about when was the last time Noah had let Sam screw him. The silence stretched out, and, for once, Noah was the one who had to break it. "I haven't even spoken to him since we got together. I've never cheated on you."

"I believe you."

Noah was shocked enough to turn to face him. There was just enough light for him to make out Colby's features. He looked so bloody trusting, so damn sure that his trust would never be betrayed.

"Is there anything else you want to know or are you done with twenty questions for the night?" Noah demanded, but he couldn't bring the usual snap to his voice.

"Only one more thing," Colby said. "Will you come back to bed?"

Noah looked at the mattress between them. "Yeah."

And Colby smiled. He'd just found out that his lover used to be a lap dancer, only avoided being a whore by luck, and was likely to cheat on him whenever his ex demanded it. And Colby just smiled and welcomed him back into the bed alongside him.

Wrapping his arms around Noah, Colby held him close and pressed a kiss to his temple. Noah closed his eyes. Sometimes it seemed less like Colby was a different type of guy and more like he was a completely different bloody species.

Chapter Eight

Another three months later

"You were amazing."

Noah paused halfway out of the stage door at the back of the theatre. Colby stood a few yards along the alley, smiling broadly. Even though Colby wasn't supposed to be there, Noah couldn't bring himself to feel overly surprised by his presence.

He stepped out of the doorway to stand directly in front of Colby. "I thought we were going to meet up around the front of the building?" Noah had actually been quite specific about that. True, he'd managed to avoid admitting it had anything to do with him not wanting Colby walking down dark alleys on his own, but Noah was still sure he'd made the point very clearly.

"Everyone's trying to get taxis out there. I figured it would be easier for me to find you here," Colby said, easily. He touched Noah's cheek and encouraged him to look up. "You were fantastic."

Noah smiled. Colby said it as if he meant it, rather than because it was polite—as if he was a connoisseur expressing a carefully deliberated conclusion.

"It looked completely different than it did in rehearsals. Sharper, much more energy."

Of course, if a man spied on a dance studio for long enough, he probably did pick up a bit of knowledge...

Noah couldn't help but chuckle, but he didn't give Colby time to wonder what the joke might be. He put his hand on Colby's shoulder to steady them both as he leaned up for a kiss. Their lips met, and for a few moments the whole world faded away.

A wolf whistle from the stage door rudely jerked Noah back into reality.

"I guess this explains why you haven't been to the club for months."

Noah tensed, looking from Geraint, to James, to Thomas, and then back around the loop again.

"He's gorgeous," James drawled. His attention shifted to Colby. "I can see why Noah wants to keep you all to himself."

Noah glanced in Colby's direction just in time to see the blush touch his cheeks, but Colby's expression remained relaxed. He kept his hand on the small of Noah's back and didn't try to pull away from him.

As Noah forced himself to make civil introductions, he gripped the strap on his back pack very tightly. James had been right on both counts. Colby was gorgeous, and Noah didn't want to share. If he had his way, Colby wouldn't get within twenty miles of another gay man for the rest of his life.

All at once, the other guys in the dance company weren't just dancers or even possible sexual partners for himself, they were the competition—they were men that Colby might decide he'd be better off with.

Noah forced a smile onto his face and kept it there through sheer force of will as he watched his friends flirt with Colby.

James—his family had money, and they hadn't disowned him the moment he came out. Colby would have to be an idiot not to realise he'd be better off with him.

Geraint—he was closer to Colby's age. They probably had more in common. He wasn't as much of a slut as the rest of them. If Colby's dancer fetish was incurable, Geraint was probably the kind of guy he should end up with.

Thomas—he had all the right contacts in the business. He was going places, and he'd do it without ever giving a single lap dance.

Noah's hand was starting to cramp around the strap on his back pack. Colby wasn't actually flirting in return, but that didn't mean anything. He'd never really flirted with Noah. He'd gone straight to throwing himself at another man without any warning or preamble.

Noah shifted his weight from one foot to the other, knowing he couldn't demand that they leave without making a fool of himself, but sure that every moment they spent there made it more likely that Colby would realise that he had much better options than him, even among the local dancers.

"Here—let me take that."

Noah blinked as Colby took his bag off him and slung it over his own shoulder as if it was the most natural thing in the world.

"Hot and a gentleman," James said, leaning against the wall next to the stage door. "Do you have any brothers, angel?"

Colby glanced toward James for a second, but by the time he spoke, Noah knew most of his attention was already back on him. "Only one who lives down here—Tony, he's in the athletics programme at Falconer."

Noah's lips twitched as he realised that Colby had completely missed the reason for James' question.

"I don't suppose he's gay?" James finally hinted.

"He's bi," Colby said. His attention didn't waver from Noah at all. "I borrowed his car. It's in the car park in the next street." He hesitated for a moment. "Does everyone have a lift, or—?"

"They can make their own way home." Noah turned his back on the other dancers, damned if he'd stick around to hear anyone say that they'd love Colby to drive them home.

Colby fell easily into step alongside him. "How do you think it went?"

Noah glanced at him out of the corner of his eye.

"The performance," Colby hinted.

"Good," Noah said. "A lot better than I expected."

"You must be exhausted."

Noah glanced at him again, his lips quirking with amusement. "Is that why you're carrying my stuff for me?"

Colby looked down at the bag as if he hadn't really registered its existence until that moment. He shrugged, but didn't make any attempt to hand it back. When they got to the car, he put it on the backseat before sliding behind the wheel.

Already settled in the passenger seat by that time, Noah didn't give Colby time to put the key in the ignition. A hand on the back of Colby's neck was all it took to make Colby turn toward him.

Noah had no interest in making the kiss sweet or innocent. The kiss had one purpose, and that was to wipe away any possible interest Colby had in anyone else—to remind Colby that, even if he was far from perfect, Noah could still take a man somewhere very close to perfection whenever he chose—even in a public car park.

When Noah pulled back, Colby remained exactly where he was for several long seconds. His tongue snuck out to caress his lips. He blinked open his eyes and looked at Noah.

"Just making the situation perfectly clear," Noah said.

"Clear?" Colby whispered.

"After a performance, I'm not exhausted, I'm high on adrenaline. I don't want to sleep, I want to screw. Is that a problem?"

Colby took a deep breath and turned back to the steering wheel. For a few seconds, he didn't seem to know what to do with the wheel or how to answer the question. Finally, he cleared his throat. "No problem at all."

"Good."

It took Colby three attempts to get the key in the ignition. He drove very carefully, as if making a point of keeping all his attention on the road. Noah smiled as he relaxed back in the passenger seat. There was no way in hell

Colby was thinking about anyone but him now.

* * * * *

"Your place or mine?" Colby asked, as he switched off the engine.

"Is your brother home?"

Colby tried to remember Tony's schedule, but quickly gave the job up as impossible. Hell, it was only luck he could remember his brother's name. "I have no idea."

"I fully intend to make you scream loud enough to wake up anyone in the building," Noah said, far more calmly than anyone should be able to.

"Yours then?" Colby asked.

Noah chuckled. "Yeah, probably a good idea."

Colby nodded. After driving halfway across the city with an erection that wouldn't fade in the slightest, he'd have nodded to anything. He followed Noah up to the studio on autopilot, not sure what Noah was planning, but confident that he was going to enjoy every second of it.

The moment they stepped out of the studio space and into the corridor leading to Noah's bedroom, Colby's back hit the wall. Noah's lips covered his, and any brain cells Colby had managed to gather together since the last kiss scattered.

Noah pulled back as suddenly as he'd pounced; leaving Colby breathless and glad the wall was there to support him.

"Naked—now."

Colby's body took over. His hands were clumsy, but he managed to get his clothes off without popping any buttons or ripping any seams. That was probably the best he could hope for while Noah stood barely a step away from him, fully dressed and watching every move he made.

When there was nothing left for him to take off, Colby fell still.

Noah caught hold of his wrist and pulled him into the

110

bedroom.

"Kneel."

Colby obeyed. Sure now that he understood where this was going, he reached out to free Noah's cock.

Noah slapped his fingers away. "No. Put your hands behind your back."

Tilting back his head, Colby stared up at Noah, trying to work out what was going on and what mood Noah was in. But, he also put his hands behind his back.

Turning away from him, Noah opened the drawer in the bottom of his wardrobe.

If Colby could have got any harder he would have. He'd grown to love that drawer since they first started dating.

"For the rest of the night, you're going to do exactly as I say—*exactly* as I say. Understand?"

"Yes." Colby wasn't sure there had ever been a time when he'd done anything else in Noah's presence, but Noah's tone of voice easily bypassed any part of his brain that worried about anything so logical. There could be no answer but yes.

Noah caught hold of Colby's chin and held his head still so he could study him for a long time. "You are mine. I'm not going to let you forget that."

Colby swallowed. "Yes."

Noah remained very serious, but he nodded his apparent acceptance of Colby's answer. "Wrists."

Colby brought his hands from behind his back and offered his wrists to Noah.

The cuffs were leather and well padded. Colby felt something settle inside himself when they were fastened around his wrists. An order to remain still was wonderful, but the cuffs were something else again.

Colby took a deep breath as Noah went back to the drawer and took out several other items.

"On the bed, on your knees, facing the headboard."

Colby hurried into position. Noah immediately tugged

on the cuffs, pulling them up toward the headboard, forcing Colby to lean over so far that he had to lower himself to his elbows to stop himself from falling flat on his face. Cuffs fastened in place, Noah disappeared behind Colby. He pushed Colby's knees further apart on the bed. Within what seemed like a few seconds, he'd placed a spreader bar between cuffs wrapped around Colby's thighs.

Looking down beneath his body, Colby saw Noah attach a chain to a centre point on the bar. Floating on current happiness and the promise of future bliss, he watched with almost detached interest as Noah ran the chain up the bed and connected it to the headboard alongside the cuffs.

Turning his head, Colby managed to catch a glimpse of Noah's expression. He didn't look so much high on adrenaline as he appeared very focused and incredibly intense. Disappearing again, Noah moved down to the base of the bed. Colby felt cuffs being wrapped around his ankles, then chains pulling at the restraints as Noah, presumably, fastened them to the bottom legs of the bed.

"Test them," Noah ordered.

Colby obediently tried out the arrangement of cuffs and chains, trying to work out how much slack he had. The obvious answer was—not a lot. He could rock back and forth a little, but it was clear he wouldn't be getting off his elbows and knees until Noah decided he should be permitted to do so.

"It feels good," Colby whispered.

"Good…" Noah mused, running his fingertips from the top of Colby's spine down toward his arse.

The mattress shifted as Noah climbed onto the bed and knelt between Colby's widely spread knees.

"Good," Noah repeated, apparently not entirely impressed with the word. "We should be able to do a lot better than *good*, don't you think?"

His fingers abandoned Colby's spine in favour of running up and down the inside of his thigh.

A shiver raced down Colby's back. Even without looking over his shoulder, he was pretty sure Noah smiled when he noticed that.

Noah's other hand began to stroke Colby's cock very gently. It was barely more than a brush of his fingertips.

Colby bit his lip and rocked his hips, automatically trying to push his shaft against Noah's hand. Noah chuckled, but damn if he didn't make the touch even lighter in response.

Yes, Noah liked to tease. Colby had worked that out a long time ago. Hell, he loved that about Noah. But, he also had the strange suspicion that Noah's mood tonight was going to take his frustration to a whole new level.

"Noah." It was half a whisper, half a moan.

"Yes?" Polite curiosity, nothing more.

Colby whimpered. Closing his eyes, he bowed his head toward his forearms and tried to be patient. Gradually, Noah wrapped his fingers more firmly around Colby's shaft and began to stroke him very slowly.

Colby tried to rock his hips again, but Noah had a knack for riding out that kind of movement, never granting more than he wished.

"Please." Colby helplessly thrust into Noah's grip.

A second later, Noah's hand disappeared altogether.

Colby moaned, but he knew better than to voice a protest. He bit his lip and remained as still and silent as he could, hoping that might put Noah into a more lenient, less teasing, mood.

Noah chuckled, as if he could read every thought straight out of Colby's head, and he thought it sweet that Colby still harboured such hopes.

Noah's hand returned, but it ignored Colby's cock in favour of cradling his balls. Colby froze — not even breathing for several seconds.

Noah gradually tightened his grip. Colby wasn't entirely sure if that was a good thing.

Even when he had no choice but to start breathing

again, he tried to keep his breaths shallow and make sure he didn't move his rib cage any more than was absolutely necessary.

Tighter still, Noah's grip bordered on painful and blissful at the same time.

Colby swallowed rapidly. Bound, head down, arse up, there was nothing he could do but accept whatever Noah offered him and be grateful for each touch.

Noah rested his other hand on one of Colby's buttocks. Colby tensed with expectation, waiting for the palm to leave him, and then quickly return to slap down hard on his skin. Both Noah's hands remained completely motionless.

Colby let out a yelp as what he first thought to be slicked fingers, moved against the cleft between his buttocks.

Right hand on balls. Left hand on arse.

An image appeared perfectly formed in Colby's mind. In it, Noah dipped his head, and his tongue swiped across Colby's exposed hole. Just a second later, the real life Noah repeated the action.

Colby whimpered as pleasure rushed through him. Bondage be damned, he couldn't help but squirm—arching his back to make himself even more accessible to whatever Noah wanted to do with him.

Colby froze as Noah tightened his grip around his balls. His touch was still just short of hurting him—just. The message couldn't have been clearer. Colby would stay in position, one way or another.

Noah's tongue moved against him again, circling his hole. Colby bit down hard on his bottom lip and somehow managed to remain motionless. Perhaps his stillness was the cue Noah had been waiting for, because he began to work his mouth against him more firmly, teasing and testing the ring of muscle at the same time.

Colby closed his eyes so tightly he saw stars. It was impossible to remain still as Noah's tongue caressed him that way. The bondage only helped to a certain extent. Even

Noah's grip around his balls could only inspire so much control.

It was completely different to those times when Noah's fingers played against him. Colby gasped for breath as more pleasure than he ever believed possible rushed through him, making him shudder and whimper.

"Please," Colby whispered.

Noah murmured. Perhaps it was only an enquiry as to what Colby was attempting to beg for, but it felt like approval as his lips moved against Colby's hole.

It was unlike anything he'd ever felt, so perfect, and at the same, it was so obviously going to be impossible for him to come from just that.

Sex. Fingers sliding inside him and rubbing against his prostate. Noah's mouth on his cock. Noah's hand on his cock, for that matter. There were lots of things that Colby could get off on. But this, just this? Colby was sure it could melt his mind and make him lose control of every part of his body, but it wouldn't make him come. It would just hold him on the edge of his orgasm forever.

Noah's tongue moved nimbly against him, never repeating the same action for long enough for Colby to have any way of predicting what Noah would do next. His mouth was gentle one moment, the next his tongue pressed against the ring of muscle more firmly.

As more and more bliss burned its way through Colby's psyche, the tight grip Noah had on his balls ceased to be any sort of incentive toward obedience. It was no longer possible to tell if his touch promised pain or perfection. There was no longer any line between the two sensations.

The bondage became the only thing that kept Colby in place. He was aware of his lips moving, but he had no idea what he said, what he begged for, what he offered Noah if his pleas were granted. He didn't care what words left his mouth; he just prayed they were the right ones.

Suddenly, Noah was gone. His hand and his mouth

vanished from existence.

Colby twisted on the bed, knowing that Noah couldn't have actually disappeared, but unable to believe mere common sense on such a vital topic.

"Stay where you are." The words snapped like a whip.

Colby froze. Not having caught a glimpse of Noah, he held onto the words like a talisman and dropped his head back down to rest on his forearms.

Noah's hands settled on Colby's hips. The tip of his cock pressed against Colby's hole, slicked with lube. One harsh movement had Noah buried inside him.

Colby cried out, pure relief making him scream as Noah's hips connected firmly with his buttocks. There was no time for Colby to catch his breath. Noah's rhythm was both frantic and unfaltering, his grip on Colby's hips sure to leave impressive bruises the next day.

Rocking back into each thrust, tugging against his bondage in an instinctive effort to obtain every bit of free movement that was within his power, Colby gasped for breath.

Noah moved one hand up to his shoulder. "You're mine. Do you understand that, Colby?"

Colby tried to nod.

"You belong to me, body and soul. You're mine."

Colby whimpered.

"Say it."

"Yours," Colby gasped out. "I'm yours. Body and soul."

"Come."

It was easily the most beautiful word in the English language. A second before, Colby had been sure he lacked the ability to come on command, without even a hand on his cock to help him along. Apparently, Noah knew him far better than he knew himself.

Colby's orgasm tore through him just a second after the word hit the air. Noah kept thrusting through Colby's orgasm, seeming to draw out the moment of ecstasy until Colby's entire world collapsed in upon itself.

The world went black around the edges, and the darkened edges grew wider and deeper, until they met in the middle.

When Colby finally blinked open his eyes, he was on his back. Noah knelt on the bed alongside him, undoing the cuffs that had held the spreader bar between his thighs.

"Noah?"

Noah glanced up from his task. "You passed out. Just for a few seconds."

Colby nodded. Lifting his head, he stared up at Noah, aware that his brain was very fuzzy, but not sure whether or not that represented a problem.

"Okay, darling?" Noah asked.

Colby managed another nod and dropped his head back to rest on the mattress as Noah undid the remaining chains, and finally the cuffs.

Lifting his wrists, Colby studied them. Not a single mark—which was good of course. Noah had made it clear that he didn't want him turning up at training looking as though he got arrested every other weekend. But, damn, those marks after the first night had been pretty. He'd have loved to have seen them back there every chance he got.

Colby dropped his hands onto the mattress and turned his attention to where Noah sat alongside him, studying him carefully.

"Noah?"

Noah smiled, but a second later he got off the bed. Colby tightened his hand into a fist at his side, determined not to reach out or ask him to stay. He was in Noah's bed. The guy wasn't going to go anywhere. Colby just needed to learn to trust him; that was all.

Almost as soon as he stood up, Noah began to undress. Colby turned sleepily onto his side and watched, enjoying seeing bare skin revealed just as much as he always did.

117

Naked, Noah lay down on the bed alongside him.

Colby shuffled closer, and Noah lifted his arm to welcome him nearer for a while.

"I told you I was going to make you scream, didn't I?" Noah said.

Colby chuckled. From how sore his throat was, he guessed it was only luck that stopped him waking everyone in the street. "You always keep your promises."

Noah trailed his fingers up and down Colby's spine, so relaxed now compared to when Colby had met him around the back of the theatre.

"You also said you own me, body and soul," Colby mentioned.

Noah's fingers only paused for a second before resuming their caresses. "Is that a problem?"

"Hell, no!" Colby grinned as he snuggled in closer to Noah's side, already more than half asleep. "I don't think I've ever loved you as much as I did when you said that."

* * * * *

Noah allowed his hand to drop onto the mattress behind Colby as he felt Colby fall fast asleep.

It was said so bloody casually. Out of all the things he could have been panicking over, that was the thing that stood out first and foremost in Noah's mind. No big declaration, no fuss, just a few little words said in a tone of voice that made it completely clear that Colby meant every one of them.

Not *I love you* — because I'm sweet and naive and I think I'm supposed to say that after sex.

Not *I'm in love with you* — an announcement full of uncertainty and nerves, because what if the other guy doesn't feel the same way?

I don't think I've ever loved you as much as I did when you said that. As if Colby was so used to being in love with someone, with being in love with Noah of all people, it no longer occurred to him to consider the matter worthy of comment. It was just mildly interesting to compare how intensely he felt that love at different times.

Noah took a slow, deep breath.

It didn't seem to occur to Colby to worry that he wasn't loved back. It was as if he knew, without any shadow of a doubt, that Noah was head over heels, completely besotted with him.

No need for anyone to say anything. Colby just knew. And Noah was really glad he'd taken that deep breath, because he'd suddenly lost the ability to breathe at all.

He was in love with Colby. Noah closed his eyes, but it wasn't so easy to hide from reality. He was in love with Colby. He wasn't sure when it had happened, but it had crept up on him when he wasn't paying attention and now... And now, he was in love with Colby.

Noah's heart raced. He finally managed to take a breath, but it didn't help. He was in love with Colby. He was reasonably sure he was also on the verge of a panic attack.

He shook his head in the darkness of the bedroom. This wasn't happening. It couldn't be happening. It was just supposed to be sex. Damn it, they'd agreed right at the start — it was only supposed to be sex.

But he'd never cared who else the guys he had sex with screwed. He'd never been jealous when his friends flirted with someone who he just did scenes with.

Noah bit down on his bottom lip. He'd never stuck with the same guy for this long, either. And he never went back to their place. And he never stayed the night. And he never went on soppy dates. And he never, *never*, danced for the men he screwed — not the way he'd danced for Colby a few months back.

And now, Noah's lungs seemed to want to catch up on all that time they'd spent frozen in place because his breathing turned fast and shallow. Was that another symptom of a panic attack? He didn't know. Another new experience Colby was going to introduce him to. Great.

Forcing himself to exert every scrap of his self control, Noah gradually pulled his body back into line. His heartbeat and his breathing slowed. Everything was okay. He just had to look at the problem calmly.

Colby was in love with him. He was in love with Colby. Noah wasn't sure which statement constituted the biggest disaster.

Being in love with Colby was stupid. It was an invitation to get his heart broken the moment Colby got into a room with a couple of other gay men and realised that he had options that couldn't be spotted from his living room window.

He'd said there were other gay athletes at the institute. How long before Colby met one of them and realised he could be doing a lot better than a penniless dance instructor?

On the other hand, Colby being in love with him was...

Noah swallowed.

All at once, it was obvious that that was an even bigger problem. Because, when Colby worked out he could do better it would only hurt Noah, but Colby never realising how much better he could do — that would end up hurting Colby.

Sex. Casual. Just for a while. Keeping Colby on those terms was one thing. But anything more than that? Noah closed his eyes. It would be cruel to lock Colby into anything that wasn't entirely casual and inherently temporary.

Colby could do so much bloody better. He needed to realise that, and...and Noah needed to make sure Colby went and did that, before either of them fell even further.

Colby deserved something much better than Noah could ever offer him. And Noah needed Colby out of his life — right   now.

Chapter Nine

Noah tensed as he heard the door into the studio swing open behind him. For once, it had nothing to do with the possibility of it being Sam. Right then, Sam would have been a blessing — he knew how to deal with Sam.

Noah took a deep breath and forced his words to come out calm and steady. "Sorry, all the classes are over for the day."

"It's me."

Like he hadn't been able to distinguish Colby's presence from anyone else's for months. "Oh," Noah forced himself to keep his tone disinterested through sheer force of will. "Hi, Colby."

"Hi." Colby's footsteps stopped halfway across the studio, as he seemed to realise that he wasn't receiving the welcome he expected.

"Did we have plans for this evening?" Noah asked.

"Not that I know of..."

Noah pushed another breath into his lungs. It would be kinder on Colby in the long run if Noah simply killed Colby's crush on him right now. Noah may have come to that conclusion in the early hours of the morning, but in the cold light of day, he still knew it was the right decision. "So, why are you here?"

"To see you..." The honest confusion in Colby's voice tore at him.

Noah plastered a mockery of a smile onto his lips and turned to face Colby. "You mean you want to get laid."

Colby frowned. "I mean I want to see you."

Noah raised an eyebrow. "So you don't want to fuck

me?"

Colby's expression became wary. He made no attempt to close the gap between them. "Bad day?" he guessed.

Yes. Bad days happen when you can't remember the steps because you're too busy thinking about a boy you had no business taking to your bed in the first place. "Not particularly."

Colby stood in the middle of the room, hands pushed deep into the pockets of his jeans. He rocked back on his heels, obviously at a loss. Rescuing him would be counterproductive; Noah let him struggle to find something to say on his own.

"Some of the guys I train with are coming around for pizza tonight," Colby finally said. "I thought you might want to—"

"Thanks, but I'll pass," Noah cut in.

Colby seemed to be deep in thought for quite some time. Finally, he spoke. "I've been thinking—"

"So have I."

It didn't even seem to occur to Colby to insist on being allowed to finish his own sentence first. Somehow, that made it so much harder for Noah to push on and say what needed to be said. "The arrangement we had. It was fun—I'll give you that. But it's run its course. It's time to go our separate ways."

Colby blinked at him. "You're breaking up with me, just like that?"

Noah held back a sigh. "No, darling. We're not breaking up—we were never together. We just had an arrangement, which is now over." His tone was just as patronising as he'd intended it to be. Noah was in complete control over every word that left his mouth. That knowledge failed to make him feel any better.

Colby clenched his jaw, obviously gritting his teeth, but his tone was mild when he spoke. "I don't know what's going on with you today."

"Why would you? You don't know me. We were fuck buddies, not soul mates. A deep understanding was never required." Noah leaned back against the wall on the far side of the studio, partly to look as if he didn't care, but mostly to make sure he didn't accidentally close the gap between them.

Damn it, Colby should have gone by now. He should have stormed off the moment Noah cracked reality open for him. What the hell was he still doing there?

Noah gave a theatrical sigh. "Sadists outnumber masochists." He had no idea if it was true, but it sounded good.

"What?"

"It'll be easier than you think it will be for you to find a guy who wants to tie you up and order you around," Noah said.

"You know that's not all we're about—" Colby began.

"Yes, I know. You've been day dreaming about me for years. You're actually madly in love with me and want to help me straighten my life out," Noah drawled. "Darling, it's all just masochism by another name."

Colby shook his head.

"Oh, for fuck's sake, grow up!" Noah snapped. "The masochist in you likes me because I'm the only guy you've met who's screwed up enough that being with him will hurt any chance you have of happiness." He forced himself to hold Colby's gaze. "The only reason you waited around to screw me was because three years of frustration appealed to the side of you that loves how it feels when someone twists the knife in you. You didn't stay celibate for three years because you cared about what I said to you, Colby. You're just submissive enough to like doing what you're told—to like doing what *anyone* tells you to do."

Colby took a step back. "Why are you—?"

"You're wired to look for trouble, darling. Look somewhere else."

Colby swayed away, then suddenly stepped forward, closing the gap between them with several quick strides. "Noah, I don't know what's going on, or what I've done to make you think I'm not serious about us." And, in spite of everything, his voice stayed gentle.

Noah turned away from him, no longer able to maintain any sort of eye contact. "You don't want me—you'd stick around for anyone who hurt you, because you like it."

"Noah, you're not listening to what I'm trying to tell you," Colby said, from a few feet behind him.

"Maybe I don't want to hear it," Noah snapped.

"If you'll just—"

Noah mentally cursed. Just how hard did he have to push to get rid of the boy? "I've always liked my lovers dominant," he blurted out. "I have no interest in wasting any more of my time with a submissive little boy."

"You'd prefer to be with a guy who'd hurt you?" Colby said. For some reason, that seemed to annoy him more than any of the insults Noah had pitched at him.

"No. I said dominant, not sadistic. I wouldn't stick around with anyone who hurt me." And wasn't that the biggest load of bollocks of it all? "I'm not like you, Colby. I don't get off on pain." He forced himself to turn to face Colby.

Colby's eyes narrowed. "I think you can take or leave that sort of pain, no problem at all," he snapped. "You're not scared of being hurt that way, not anymore. It's the idea that I care enough about you to try *not* to hurt you that's always scared the hell out of you."

"You don't know me!" Noah yelled. He swung away from him and suddenly he was past Colby and standing all alone in the middle of the studio.

"Really?" Colby made no move to close the gap between them. He stood perfectly still. "I know you've convinced yourself you'd prefer a guy to fuck you than make love to you—you'd prefer him to lash out at you than hold you close. I know you'd prefer a guy to act like a bastard and treat you like a cheap slut because that means you don't ever have to risk hoping he'll give a damn about you—because you don't have to take the chance that he'll fall out of love with you if you know he never loved you in the first place."

The breath caught in Noah's throat. "Get out!"

Colby shook his head, his eyes filled with sadness rather than anger.

Noah stormed forward and pushed at his chest. "Don't you dare come in here and tell me how to live my life. I got on just fine before you tried to turn my world upside down, and I'll get on just fine once you leave. You're not the solution, Colby, you're the problem! Get out."

Colby took a step back. "Fine! If you want to go back to that—fine! I can only love you, Noah. I can't force you to face the fact you deserve to be loved—not if you hate yourself this much!" He strode toward the studio door and jerked it open. "Let me know when you're ready to grow up and take a risk."

Noah turned to the window and stared down into the street. He watched Colby leave the building, cross the road and disappear into the block of flats opposite. The moment he knew he wouldn't run into Colby outside, Noah stormed out of the studio and down the stairs.

He'd show Colby that he didn't need any of that soft sentimental bullshit to have a good time. He'd show everyone that he was just fine without Colby in his life. He'd—

It was only when he stood outside the closed club that he realised it was far too early for anyone to be there. The damn place wouldn't be open for hours yet.

Muttering curses under his breath, Noah rubbed his hand against his face. Slowly pulling himself together, he began to retrace his steps home. It was okay. It was just a couple of hours, he could wait that long. Then, he'd go to the club, pick up his old life and everything would be fine.

It only hurt right now because he was trapped in no man's land, without Colby, and without everything that had filled up his life before Colby descended upon his world.

A glance down the alleyway at one end of the club and Noah stopped short. Sam's car was parked near one of the club's side doors. The door was ajar.

Sam was in there. And Sam was as unlike Colby as any man could ever be. And Sam was familiar and understandable in ways that Colby would never be.

Noah stared down the alley, but the only thing he really saw was the look in Colby's eyes just before he left the studio.

If Noah had said even a fraction of the things he'd thrown at Colby to Sam, the guy would have had him pinned against the wall with his hands wrapped around his throat choking the air out of him, and that would have only been the start of the fun for the night. Noah swallowed. He was pretty sure Sam's reaction was exactly what he'd deserved.

Without making any sort of conscious decision, Noah found himself halfway down the alley and stepping through the side door of the club. Sam stood next to the bar discussing some sort of liquor order with the bartender.

Noah froze. If he turned and walked away now, Sam would never know he'd been there and —

It was as if some sort of sixth sense kicked in. Sam looked up, straight at Noah. Their eyes met.

A few brisk words to the man behind the bar and Sam strode toward the doorway Noah lingered in. Brushing past Noah, Sam led the way further down the alley, away from where anyone looking down between the buildings would be able to see them.

Noah wrapped his arms around his waist. He hadn't even thought to grab his coat before he left, or change out of the clothes he'd been dancing in. It hadn't seemed that cold when his anger had been burning inside him. Now, it seemed as if he was freezing to death from the inside out.

Sam pushed his hands into the deep pockets of his coat and studied Noah for what felt like a long time.

Noah swallowed, but he made damn sure he kept the rest of his body completely still. Pissing off Colby was one thing. Making Sam angry was nothing short of suicidal.

"I knew you'd come crawling back soon enough," Sam

drawled.

Noah kept his mouth shut. Sam was right. He always went back to him, sooner or later. Sam was where he belonged. Fighting it for more than a few months had always been pointless. Eighteen months was a new personal record. He doubted he'd ever manage to avoid Sam for that long again, not without Colby there to make the effort worthwhile.

Sam stepped forward. He was shorter than Colby, and he carried less muscle. But, his posture, his attitude and his expression all made him a threat in ways Colby would never be.

Sam took a tight grip on Noah's hair, tugging painfully at the strands as he forced his head back.

"You owe me an apology for the way you acted last time we met up."

Noah met Sam's eyes. That night seemed like a lifetime ago now.

Sam laughed. There was no humour in the sound. "Did you think you wouldn't pay for ordering me out of your precious little studio like that?"

Noah swallowed down the bile in the back of his throat but he managed not to lift his hand and touch his cheek.

"All that pride," Sam sneered. "Do you really think what you do now is any different to shaking your arse for a drunk's loose change?" His grip on Noah's hair tugged him off balance.

"On your knees."

For a second, Noah just stared at him.

Sam didn't wait around for obedience. He grabbed Noah's wrist with his free hand and twisted his arm, forcing him down on his knees in the dirt of the alley.

"If you want this, you're going to have to prove it," Sam bit out. "You're going to have to show me that you remember your real place in this world. Afterwards, maybe, I'll let you beg me to take you back. But first—"

He released Noah's hair. A second later, the back of his

127

hand connected with Noah's cheek, in exactly the same place as it had last time. Noah's head snapped to the side, his whole body jerked with the force of it.

It was what he expected. It was what he deserved. It was even what he needed. But in that moment, the words in Noah's head weren't his own, and they weren't Sam's either.

If you want to go back to that...

If... As if there was a choice. As if, somehow, it was okay not to want to go back to the way his life had been before he met Colby.

Noah stared down at the ground at Sam's feet, not really seeing it. "I don't want this," he whispered. He looked up at Sam. "I don't want this." Even to his own ears, the words sounded off, as if they came from a long way away, as if he was only then realising that it was possible to want something else, okay to want something else for more than a few months.

Sam loomed above him. "What?"

Noah blinked at him, as if he'd never seen him before. He was half sure that was the truth. As Noah looked up at him, Sam seemed to be a very different man than he'd been when Noah had worked at the club, when he'd been unable to get in or out of the building without passing Sam's office, without being called into Sam's office.

"No."

Back when he hadn't really had a choice, the answer had always been yes. But now? No. Noah pulled himself to his feet. Apparently caught off guard by any hint of resistance from him, Sam's grip failed. Noah turned on his heel and took several paces toward the mouth of the alley, barely even registering the other man's existence now.

"You don't walk away from me!"

"I don't want this," Noah repeated to himself, realising even as he said the words that Colby was right. Familiar be damned. He wasn't going to do this, not again, not if there was a chance of having something different.

Sam grabbed his arm, tearing his shirt at the shoulder as he dragged Noah around to face him. "Don't play games with me, Noah. You know what will happen if you do."

Noah looked him up and down, strangely calm now that he'd moved through his panic and into a crystal clear world on the other side of it. "Colby was right."

"Who the hell is Colby?"

"You don't scare me," Noah said, still more to himself than the man facing him. "Not any more. I don't care enough about you to actually give a damn what you could do to me."

Sam frowned.

"I stopped being afraid of you the day I walked out of that damn club—it just took me a long time to realise it." He pushed Sam's hand off his shoulder.

Sam stared at Noah in obvious confusion.

Noah turned away from him again. Thoughts twirled through his mind so fast he couldn't focus on any of them or take in any details about the world around him.

Sam grabbed his wrist and pulled Noah back around. A blow to Noah's face pushed him toward the wall. His temple slammed into the rough surface. He automatically rolled against the wall, putting his back against the brick work. He looked up at Sam and saw the anger in his eyes. "No."

"Since when do you give enough of a damn about who screws you to say no to anyone?"

"Now," Noah said. "Since now." *Since Colby.*

Sam laughed. "Don't bother playing hard to get— you're not worth it." He stepped between Noah and the end of the alley way. "You really think anyone would bother if you didn't offer it up from the first second. This is all you are, and this is all you will ever be, Noah, a cheap back-alley fuck."

Colby waited three years for me. Noah couldn't help but smile at the knowledge.

"I don't know who this Colby is, or what stupid ideas he's been putting in your head, but you're too smart to believe he actually gives a damn about you, aren't you?" Sam laughed again. "Maybe I'll ask around and find him. We can have a threesome. You can take two easily enough, can't you, Noah? Or maybe I'll just fuck you each in turn." He stepped forward, until he was right in front of Noah.

Noah shook his head, trying to push the idea of Sam and Colby out of his mind. "That's not going to happen." He wasn't sure which of them he was trying to convince.

Sam laughed, stepping closer again, obviously thinking he'd found the perfect way to bring Noah back into line. But the image of him laying a hand on Colby was right there in Noah's head and, suddenly, doing something that would make Sam angry wasn't the worse possibility the future could hold.

Noah brought his knee up, hard.

Sam doubled over with a soft groan, his eyes full of shock before they closed in pain.

Noah stepped over him, heading quickly for the end of the alley. Instinct kicked in, pushing him to rush home, lock the door and lick his wounds. But as he stepped into the dance studio, his eyes went straight to the view through the window, to the building across the street.

Colby was over there.

Let me know when you're ready to grow up and take a risk.

Not: I hate you. Not: I never want to see you again. Not even: you'll pay for that next time I see you.

Just: *Let me know.*

Noah didn't stop to think it through. He raced back down the stairs and across the street to Colby's building. A car honked at him when he was halfway across the street, but Noah wasn't in any mood to notice things like that. He only paused when he saw the rows upon rows of buzzers and realised he had no idea which button would take him through to Colby's flat.

He closed his eyes, trying to picture the door leading into Colby's flat. He hadn't looked. He hadn't cared, hadn't been there unless he was with Colby and thinking more about sex than door numbers.

Noah's fingers shook as he pressed the first button. Colby didn't live there. Noah pressed the next button, then the next.

"Hello, I'm looking for Colby Landon's apartment," he said again.

"You want number forty-nine."

"Thank you."

Noah pressed the button for number forty-nine.

"Hello?" With the distortion from the intercom, it didn't sound like Colby. Maybe it was Tony, maybe one of Tony's boyfriends?

Noah hesitated. "Hello, I'm looking for Colby Landon."

"Come on up. Forth floor, just opposite the elevator."

A buzzer sounded, and the electric lock on the door released to let him in.

On the way up in the lift, Noah tried to get his thoughts in some sort of order and work out what he was going to say.

Sorry.

I'm an idiot.

I didn't mean any of it.

I love you.

Noah pushed his hand through his hair. He was reasonably certain, considering the way he'd acted in the studio, that there would be a fair amount of begging for forgiveness in his future. That was okay. And, since he'd probably be down on his knees anyway, a blow job was always an acceptable form of apology, wasn't it?

Noah shook his head as he reached the fourth floor. No, Colby wasn't Sam. Colby didn't even like him saying he was a slut, acting like one for Colby's amusement probably wouldn't do him any favours.

He'd… He'd ask Colby what he wanted him to do to make it up to him. Nice and simple. Yes. Colby would know the answer.

Stepping out of the lift he saw number forty-nine, exactly where he remembered the door to Colby's flat being. He didn't give himself any time to change his mind before he knocked at the door.

The guy who opened the door wasn't Colby. Noah hesitated.

"You're not the pizza man," the guy observed when he seemed to realise that Noah wasn't going to utter a word on his own.

"I'm looking for Colby Landon," Noah managed to say.

The guy smiled, shrugged slightly. "Come on in then."

Noah stepped into the little hallway and shut the door behind him.

"Colby! There's a guy at the door for you!" the other man yelled, as he strolled back toward the living room.

Through the open door, Noah saw a group of guys sitting around and chatting to each other. A memory picked that moment to float up to the front of his mind.

Swim team. Pizza. Tonight.

Damn!

Noah took a step back, then another. He turned toward the front door and reached for the handle.

Chapter Ten

"Noah!" Colby broke into a grin the moment he spotted him. As he rushed forward, he took the first full breath he'd managed since he'd stormed out of Noah's studio over an hour earlier.

Noah hesitated, his hand still on the door handle. For a moment, Colby thought Noah wasn't going to turn to face him at all. When he did, all the oxygen disappeared from the world.

It was like being thrown back in time, only this time Noah had a split lip to go with the bruise on his cheek. There was another mark on his opposite temple. Colby stepped forward, hurrying to close the gap between them. "What happened?"

"I'm sorry," Noah said, stepping back toward the door. He glanced over Colby's shoulder. "I forgot you had company. I'll go."

"No!" Colby caught hold of Noah's arm before he could retreat any further.

Noah tensed, but he didn't try to pull away, he didn't order Colby to let him go.

"Stay, please?" Colby glanced toward the living room. He couldn't just drop Noah in the middle of them all, not like this. He slid his hand down Noah's arm until he held his hand instead, and led him into the kitchen. "Just give me a few minutes to get rid of them?"

Noah shook his head, looking everywhere but directly at Colby. "You don't need to do that. I shouldn't have just turned up on your doorstep. I can go."

Colby nudged Noah's jaw as gently as he could, until

Noah finally looked up and met his gaze. "You turn up whenever you want to—no exceptions." He studied the bruises on Noah's face, doing his best to keep his expression blank. "Can you tell me what happened?"

Noah blinked at him. "I'm sorry about earlier. I just, um, kind of freaked out. You're not like normal guys, and—" He shook his head. "No. That sounds like an insult. I don't mean—"

"Hush," Colby whispered, stroking Noah's uninjured cheek with his thumb. "We'll work all that out. Can you tell me about this instead?" He released Noah's hand and gently touched the other side of Noah's face, just below the bruise.

Noah lifted his hand and pushed Colby's touch aside in a polite sort of way. "It's nothing."

"It doesn't look like nothing."

Noah glanced down for a moment. "I ran into a guy I knew before I met you."

Sam. Colby forced himself to do nothing more than nod his acceptance. This wasn't the time to get jealous. It wasn't the time to track Sam down and kill him, or even to mention the fact he wanted to kill the guy.

Noah still must have caught something off in his expression. "I didn't have sex with him."

Relief rushed though Colby, but he did his best to hide that, too. Not sure what was best to say, he just nodded again.

Noah's eyes narrowed slightly.

It only then occurred to Colby that Noah really hadn't expected to be believed. Leaning forward, Colby brushed his lips against Noah's uninjured temple.

Colby took a deep breath. On the one hand, he had no doubt that Noah had been telling the truth about what he'd *willingly* done with Sam, but... "Is this the only way he hurt you?" he asked, as carefully as possible.

Noah seemed to take a few moments to translate the question into something without euphemisms. "Nothing happened."

Colby nodded his acceptance once more.

"It was just a slap." Noah waved a hand, as if it was something that could be brushed away as nothing. His sleeve slid back slightly.

Colby carefully took hold of his fingers and held his hand still so he could examine the mark that lay around Noah's wrist. His stomach turned over.

Noah seemed confused for a moment, then he realised what Colby had spotted. He looked down, then he glanced at his sleeve, where it had ripped at the shoulder. He took his wrist carefully out of Colby's grip and wrapped both his arms around his waist, hiding the injured wrist in the process. "I should go."

"No. There's no need for you to leave," Colby protested. It was all he could do to stop himself trying to wrap his arms around Noah and keep him safe there with him forever.

Noah shook his head. "I'm a mess. And I'm embarrassing you in front of all your friends and—"

Colby put one fingertip against Noah's mouth, carefully avoiding the small split toward one side of his bottom lip. "Don't talk about yourself like that."

"I'm sorry," Noah whispered behind his finger.

Colby gave in to temptation and very gently wrapped his arms around Noah. For a moment, he thought he'd made a terrible mistake. Noah stood as stiff as a rod in his embrace. Then, very slowly, he leaned forward and tucked his face into the crook of Colby's neck.

Colby took a deep breath and cautiously strengthened his hold on Noah, welcoming him properly into his arms.

"If you two are finished making out, the pizza's here!" someone shouted from the living room.

Colby pulled back just far enough to look down at Noah. "Will you stay? The pizza won't last long. Once they're gone, we can talk things through properly."

"I'm a mess," Noah whispered, glancing at his ripped

sleeve.

"You can borrow one of my shirts if you like."

Noah lifted one hand to his face. Colby didn't bother to pretend a fresh shirt would conceal everything. All he could do now was wait patiently until Noah told him his decision.

"If you're sure you don't mind me staying," Noah finally whispered.

Colby left Noah in the kitchen while he grabbed a clean shirt from his room. Relief rushed through him as he watched Noah exchange one top for another. There weren't any more bruises.

Not giving Noah any extra time to get nervous about meeting his friends, he took Noah's hand and led him into the living room.

Jordan looked up from the pizza boxes he was sorting through. He smiled as he recognised Noah from their date at the restaurant. "Hi." His expression changed as he studied Noah's injuries. "Are you okay?"

Colby opened his mouth to speak, but he didn't get the chance to say a word.

"Face verses pavement," Noah said, his tone full of self-mocking humour. "Not my best moment ever."

Jordan raised his left hand to show the bandage on it. "Fingers verses kitchen knife," he said in much the same tone. "I'm banished back to being a damn waiter again."

Colby glanced at the other guys sitting around his living room. Everyone seemed to have caught the exchange. No one seemed to question Noah's story. Colby felt his stomach knot as he wondered how many times Noah had made up a similar lie. He squeezed Noah's fingers, in what he hoped was a reassuring way and led him across to the smaller of the rooms two sofas.

Trent was sitting on one end of it, but the other seat was empty.

"There's Coke in the fridge, if you want some," Colby mentioned.

Trent went off to get it, leaving his seat vacant. Colby calmly stole his friend's place so he and Noah could sit next to each other.

Walking back into the room with several bottles of Coke, Trent raised an eyebrow at Colby, but he took the theft in good part, sitting on the floor alongside the coffee table to find the pizza box he wanted.

"You should try some," Jordan said, pushing one of the boxes toward Noah. "It's good."

Trent huffed. "It had better be, after you made us wait for it to be delivered from halfway across the damn city, rather than just letting us order it from two streets away like any sane person." He opened his box and took out a slice. He took a bite.

Jordan waited for his verdict.

Trent shrugged. "What do I know? I liked the one you said shouldn't even be fed to livestock."

Colby kept most of his attention on Noah as the other guys good naturedly argued around them. Gradually, he felt Noah relax—even going so far as to back Jordan in the great pizza debate.

"So, dance, right?"

Noah nodded, his expression entirely neutral. "That's right." His tone was polite and unconcerned but, even if no one else could see it, Colby knew that Trent's question had Noah back on the knife-edge he'd been balancing on when he'd first arrived at the flat.

Colby tilted his head, trying to catch Trent's eye, but the other guy's attention never wavered from Noah.

"Coach suggested I take a few classes last year because my flexibility really sucked. So, Sarah, she's my little sister, dragged me along to this ballet class she goes to. It took me about ten minutes to work out that dancers are freaks of nature."

Noah didn't say anything sarcastic. If Colby had any doubts about how off balance he was, that fact sealed it. He slid his arm around Noah's waist but, before Colby could think of something appropriate to say, something that would make it damn clear that he was on Noah's side without embarrassing him, someone else threw a napkin from the pizza place at Trent. They had good aim—it bounced off his temple.

Trent picked it up and tossed it back in the general direction it had come from. "Hey, I'm being serious, here. That class nearly killed me. And my little sister, never been inside a real gym in her life, ran rings around me. It was a one hour class and I could hardly walk the next day."

Colby smiled as he felt Noah relax again.

"It's just different to what you're used to," Noah offered.

Trent considered him for a moment, as if deep in thought. "You're a real dancer—I mean, you do the whole dance thing full time?"

Noah shrugged. "Teach it mostly, at the moment."

Trent nodded, as if that decided everything. "It's really lucky you're gay."

A little bit of tension made it back into Noah's shoulders.

"Why?" Colby asked, carefully, more than happy to throttle Trent if necessary.

"Because if there was a straight dancer going to all the swim meets, I'd have to find some way of convincing my sister not to turn up. At least this way, if she gets a crush on you, which she probably will, I don't have to do the whole big brother thing." His smiled turned into a grin. "Hey, in fact, even if she's blatantly throwing herself at you, I can just leave it all to Colby to tell her to stop hitting on his boyfriend, right?"

A burst of surprised laughter left Noah. Suddenly, the whole room seemed to loosen up.

Relaxed was nice. Noah being willing to meet his friends was nice. Finally getting his friends out of his flat so he could be alone with Noah was in a different league of wonderfulness.

Pizza finished, and Jordan content that everyone, bar Trent, had admitted he should always be allowed to choose where they ordered their food, Colby nudged his friends toward the door as politely as possible. Halfway down the hall, Trent turned back to where Noah remained on the sofa in the living room. "You going to be at the next swim meet?" he called out.

Noah glanced to Colby. "I don't know if…"

"If you can make it, it would be great," Colby said, not for the first time since they started dating. Noah had always been particularly stubborn in his belief that his boyfriend watching him swim would somehow cause trouble for him, but maybe meeting the other swimmers had changed things. Colby couldn't help but hope it had.

"Just let me know closer to the time if you're going to be there," Trent suggested. "I'll tell Sarah to save you a seat."

"Thanks," Colby said, as they reached the front door and found themselves out of earshot of everyone else.

Trent shrugged. "If someone didn't speak up and mention the fact that there are two gay guys cuddling in the middle of the room, the guy was going to have a damn heart attack. I figured it was better to say about Sarah being into dance than it was to point out you're still pretty much the only guy on the team getting any…"

Colby smiled and shook his head as he shut the door in Trent's wake. His expression turned more serious as he went back down the hall toward the living room.

Noah had moved away from the sofa to stand by the window, looking across the street toward the studio. He didn't turn away from the view as Colby approached, but the tension in his shoulders made Colby feel sure that Noah knew he was there.

"Are you up to having that talk now?" Colby asked, carefully.

The darkened glass was almost as good as a mirror. Colby watched the reflection as Noah closed his eyes for several long seconds.

"There's not much to say," Noah finally whispered. "You were right—about everything. You do scare me more than any of the guys who've ever slapped me around, even more than Sam."

Colby waited out the long silence, sure there was more to come.

Noah took a deep breath. "I know I've given you no reason to want to give me a second chance—"

Colby quickly stepped forward. With his hands on Noah's shoulders, he turned him away from the window and encouraged him look up. "You've given me every reason," he said seriously.

Noah hesitated. "I know I'm not exactly an attractive prospect at the moment," he said softly, waving a hand at his bruised face. "But if you want to do something…"

Colby nibbled at his bottom lip. "A bit more talking first?"

Noah seemed to think about the request for a long time, but finally he nodded.

"Did I do something that pissed you off and started all this?" Colby asked.

Noah thought for even longer that time. "I realised I'm in love with you."

Colby stared down at him, trying to make the connection between that and deciding to break up with him. "You do realise that I'm in love with you, too?" he checked. "What I felt a few years ago might have just been a crush on someone I didn't even know, but this, now, you do know I love you, right?"

Noah nodded. "Yeah, I know." His lips twisted a little. "Knowing that was probably what took the freaking out to an extra special level."

Colby smiled slightly. He still didn't get it, but from

Noah's wry smile, Colby was pretty sure he wasn't supposed to be able to understand that particular thought process.

"It might take me a while to get used to the idea," Noah said.

Colby kissed him gently on the temple and, while he would have loved to have simply spent a few moments relishing the fact that Noah had just said some incredibly important words out loud for the first time, he forced himself to push forward.

"Tell me what happened after I left?" he asked, making the words as gentle and non-threatening as possible.

"I went out to prove you wrong," Noah admitted, his voice strangely devoid of all emotion. "I thought going with another guy would push you out of my system, and everything would go back to normal. Next thing I knew, I was with Sam in the alley behind the club. Suddenly, I realised you were right. I didn't want to go back to the way things were before we met. I didn't want to break up with you. I told Sam that, and..." He waved his hand to indicate his bruised face.

"I'm so sorry," Colby said, tilting Noah's head back so he could study the bruises in a better light. "I should never have..." He mentally cursed himself. If only he'd stayed in the studio rather than stormed out. If only he hadn't let Noah's words get to him. He touched the side of Noah's face very gently.

Noah shook his head. "No, it was all my fault. I shouldn't have pushed your buttons like that. I really had it coming after the way I acted, and—"

"Colby!"

Colby jumped at the unexpected voice. He looked across the room. Tony stood in the doorway leading out to the hall.

"I want to talk to you. In the kitchen—now."

"I'm—"

"Now," Tony repeated. He sounded more pissed off than Colby had ever heard him.

Colby looked from Tony's angry expression to Noah's wary one. There was no way in hell he could deal with both men at the same time, and Tony didn't sound like he was in any mood to wait his turn.

"I'll just go see what he wants. I won't be a minute," he promised Noah.

"It's okay. I should go anyway," Noah began.

"No! I'll be right back," Colby rushed out. "Can you wait here for me?"

Noah glanced past him to where Tony still lingered in the living room doorway and nodded.

Colby offered Noah a reassuring smile before heading into the kitchen.

Tony moved out of the doorway and leaned against the far cabinet.

Colby glared at him from the position he took up on the other side of the small kitchen. "I was in the middle of something."

"Define *something*," Tony demanded.

Colby frowned. "I was talking to Noah about something important."

"So I heard."

"Then why the hell did you interrupt us?" Colby hissed, not at all inclined for Noah to hear them arguing on top of everything else.

"Because I want to know why you're apologising to your boyfriend for a black eye."

Colby's jaw dropped as it all clicked into place inside his head. "You think I hit him?"

"You tell me," Tony bit out.

Colby shook his head, sure now that his brother had completely lost his mind. "I'm not listening to this." He turned to the door.

He hadn't gone more than two steps before Tony grabbed his arm and pulled him back around to face him. "You'll listen."

Colby pushed him away. "Would you listen to me accuse you of hitting one of your dates?" he demanded.

"If you walked into a room and heard anyone say to me what he just said to you, I wouldn't expect you to give a damn if I wanted to listen or not. I'd expect you to deal with it—just like this."

Colby stared at him, slack jawed.

"Damn it, Colby—he's half your size. What buttons could he possibly push to make him deserve a black eye?"

"*I* didn't say he deserved anything," Colby snapped. "I would never hurt Noah."

"Really? Because it sure as hell didn't sound like it out there. And, I'm telling you right now—"

"It wasn't Colby."

They both turned toward the kitchen doorway.

Noah stood there, his expression devoid of any emotion. "It wasn't Colby," he repeated, all his attention on Tony.

Just like that, Colby sensed his brother relax. Tony's anger faded away, and as it went, Colby saw the fear underlying it. He hadn't been furious that he'd hit Noah, he'd been terrified that he'd hit him.

Noah glanced toward Colby. "I'm going back to my place, I just wanted to clear that up before I go. It wasn't Colby," he told Tony again.

"Stay?" Colby stepped forward and put his hand on Noah's arm.

Noah hesitated, then he shook his head. "No. You're not going to screw things up with your family." He turned to go.

"Please, stay," Colby whispered, sure that if Noah walked out of the flat now, it would take months to convince him to set foot in the place again.

"I knew dating me would cause trouble for you, but it never occurred to me that…" Noah shook his head again. "I won't cause trouble between you and your family. I just… I won't."

A little thud echoed around the room as Tony dropped his head back to rest against the high cupboard behind him. "Dad warned me this would happen," he observed to the ceiling.

At least his words caught Noah's attention and made him stall on the threshold.

"What did he say?" Colby asked, warily.

"Don't be smug, sooner or later Colby will start dating, and then the 'responsible adult of record' stuff gets a whole lot more complicated." Tony looked across at them both and sighed. "Lacking a kitchen table to talk around, let's go back to the living room."

Colby smiled, remembering his parents dragging either him or Tony to the kitchen table for various 'talks' over the years. Out of the corner of his eye, he saw Noah looking back and forth between them and Colby knew he was trying to decide if he should leave or not.

Colby slipped his hand into Noah's and led the way back to the living room. If Noah didn't seem entirely enthusiastic, he didn't fight to regain control of his hand either.

When Tony put his hand on his shoulder, Colby looked away from Noah for a moment. He wasn't sure if the squeeze to his shoulder was supposed to be an apology for thinking he'd hit Noah, or a reassurance that everything would be okay. Either way, he was pretty sure the move said everything Tony intended to say on that particular topic.

"What happened?" Tony asked, as he folded himself into the arm chair that didn't face the window.

Colby guided Noah to sit on the sofa, just where they'd sat while the other swimmers were there. He didn't let go of Noah's hand.

"Colby didn't do anything wrong," Noah was very firm about that.

Tony looked from Colby, to Noah, and back again.

"You had an argument," he started for them.

"I started it," Noah said.

Colby slid his arm around Noah's shoulders. Noah's attention didn't stray from Tony.

"Okay," Tony said, rubbing at the bridge of his nose. "Let's assume that I'm not going to freak out at Colby again." It was the same tone of voice Colby remembered Tony using during kitchen table talks with his parents—the one that said he really didn't want to be there, but he was going to see it through regardless. Apparently, even being the supposed adult in the scenario hadn't convinced Tony to like the talks one little bit.

"We had an argument. I stormed off," Colby said.

"Bloody hard not to after the way I spoke to you," Noah muttered.

"Noah," Colby chided.

"Sorry." He didn't sound especially sorry.

"What happened after Colby left?" Tony butted in.

"I decided to get Colby out of my system," Noah said.

"Great, so my brother's not hitting you, you're just screwing around on him," Tony looked up to the ceiling and Colby just knew that he was wishing his little brother was still at the 'watching things happen from the other side of the road' stage.

"If I'd gone through with it and let him screw me, I wouldn't have a black eye."

Colby pulled him closer into his side.

"Nothing happened," Noah said. He turned to Colby, only to close his eyes for several seconds. "I know it doesn't change that I went to him, but honestly, nothing happened."

Colby stroked Noah's hair back from his face as he nodded his understanding.

Noah met his gaze for a second. "You believe me?" He still seemed confused by the idea.

"Of course."

Noah stared up at him, now back to being completely

off balance. He only looked away when Tony stood up.

Colby looked up at his brother.

"I'm going to bed," Tony announced.

"Talk over?" Colby checked.

"You're not hitting him. He's not screwing around on you. I'm supposed to be your responsible adult of record while you're down here at the institute—not a damn relationship councillor. You're on your own from here, kiddo."

* * * * *

Noah watched Tony walk out of the room, heading for his bedroom. When Tony was out of sight, Noah risked a glance at Colby. "So, that's it?"

"He was just looking out for you," Colby said. He still had his arm around Noah's shoulders. "I think the idea that I'd hurt you scared the hell out of him."

"If he thinks you're capable of hurting anyone, he doesn't know you at all," Noah said.

Colby stroked his fingers up and down Noah's arm. "I don't know how much you overheard when we were in the kitchen, but he made it pretty clear that if I ever suspected there was even a million to one chance that he'd hit someone he was with, he'd expect me to jump on him exactly the same way."

Noah frowned at the door Tony had left through. If Tony was that freaked out about someone hurting a complete stranger, Noah could only imagine what would happen if the guy found out someone was hurting his little brother. He doubted an explanation that Colby actually liked it would do him any good in that situation.

"Do me a favour," Noah said. "Never tell him you're kinky. Just…don't. Okay?"

Colby chuckled and pressed a kiss to his uninjured temple. "You know, while he'd happily lynch me if I ever did

146

anything to hurt you, he'd probably just roll his eyes if he ever found out that I like it when you tie me up and stuff."

Noah shook his head. "No. You're wrong. He cares about you." He cared more about Colby than Noah's whole family cared about him. Hell, Tony seemed to care more about a complete stranger than Noah's whole family had ever cared about him.

Noah looked down at his hands. It was only then that he realised that he was twining his fingers together. He quickly stopped doing that. He cleared his throat. "Have you decided if you want to do something tonight or if you'd rather leave it until…?" He waved a hand to his face.

Colby touched his jaw, very gently, and encouraged Noah to turn to face him. He brushed their lips together, very gently, almost chastely.

Noah parted his lips, but Colby didn't take up the invitation, and Noah still wasn't sure enough about how forgiven he was to take the initiative himself.

"I want you to stay here tonight," Colby whispered, breaking the kiss but tilting his head so their foreheads rested together.

"Okay," Noah said.

"Even if we don't have sex."

Noah closed his eyes. Staying when he had nothing to offer, nothing to hide behind? Against all his instincts, he forced himself to nod very slightly. "If that's what you want."

Colby smiled as he pulled back. He held out his hand and led Noah into his bedroom as if it was the most natural thing in the world. But, it wasn't natural. Getting into the same bed as someone who he wasn't about to have sex with wasn't natural. Someone forgiving his screw ups without making him get down on his knees to beg as well as suck wasn't natural.

Noah lay next to Colby in his bed. When Colby turned on his side and looped an arm around his waist, encouraging him to loosely spoon in front of him, Noah knew that he should feel accepted and forgiven, but he didn't. Unable to get into a comfortable position, Noah squirmed, instinctively moving closer to Colby in the process.

His buttocks brushed back against Colby's crotch—against Colby's half-hard cock. Noah froze, trying to work out his next move.

"You know we don't have to just sleep, right?" he asked in the darkness of the room.

Colby stroked his hand gently along Noah's side. "Hush. It's fine."

Noah frowned. "Just so I'm clear on this, are we not having sex because you're still pissed with me, or because you think I'm going to have a panic attack if we do anything?"

Colby leaned over and switched on one of the bedside lamps. A tug at Noah's shoulder encouraged him to roll over to face Colby.

"We're not having sex because you're not yourself right now," Colby said, choosing each word with obvious care. "And because there are some things we should probably clear up before we do—but I don't think now's a good time for us to have that discussion."

Noah studied his expression for several seconds. "What needs to be cleared up?"

Colby hesitated, but only for a moment. "When we talked at the studio earlier…" He paused, giving Noah a chance to stop the conversation before it started. "Did you mean what you said about preferring to submit?"

It was on the tip of Noah's tongue to say that Colby was right, he didn't want to have this conversation tonight after all. He took a deep breath and pushed the instinct aside. "If you want us to switch, we can do that. It's not a problem."

"That doesn't really answer my question," Colby said, his tone still mild. "Do you prefer that?"

Noah swallowed. "If you want to play the dom, then—"

Colby pressed a finger against Noah's lips. "What do

you prefer?"

Noah looked up. Their eyes met.

"You hate the idea of switching," Colby realised.

Noah closed his eyes, scared that Colby might see something else in his expression that he really didn't want him to know.

"You were lying at the studio—just saying whatever you thought would piss me off, right?"

"Yes." Noah forced himself to open his eyes, but he didn't meet Colby's gaze. "Submission's never been my thing. I can play the part if I don't have a choice. But actually enjoying it the way you do? That's not in me." He swallowed down the bitter taste in the back of his mouth. "I don't like doing what I'm told. I hate being tied up. Pain doesn't feel good to me, it just hurts." He made sure the truth came through in every word, holding nothing back, letting Colby know exactly what to do to punish him most effectively.

Colby was silent for a long time. "But you do like your side of things. You like tying me up and everything else? You're not doing it just because I like it?"

Noah bit back an automatic response. It was only fair that Colby should know what to take away as a punishment as well as what to initiate. "I'm not into the extreme end of it all, or hurting someone more than they get off on, but yeah—I love the dom side of things."

"I'm glad."

Unsure of what to say, Noah settled for nodding.

"If you love your side of things and would hate subbing, why offer to switch?" Colby eventually asked.

"Because you've got every right to be pissed with me, and…" Noah rolled onto his back and stared up at the ceiling. "Because, if I'd gone through with it, that's how it would have been with Sam. He'd have made me do everything I hate, and I'd have let him—hell, I'd probably even have thanked him for it, too. I can't offer you less than I'd have done for him."

Noah risked a glance at Colby. For the first time, he

saw real, deep seated anger in Colby's eyes. So this was it then, that was the admission that would change everything between them.

"I never realised just how easy it is to want to kill someone before," Colby said, reasonably calmly, all things considered.

Noah turned his head toward Colby, ready for the worst.

"When I think of the way he's hurt you..." Colby shook his head.

Noah knew his eyebrows went up at the idea that Colby was angry at Sam rather than him.

Colby looked up. "I want to kill him. If I was ever face to face with him, I think I'd try."

Noah held his gaze for several seconds. There was something about the way he said it that made Noah tense up in a way that a threat to his own life would never have achieved. "No."

Colby didn't even blink.

Noah shook his head. It would be too easy for Colby to run into Sam in a club and twig who he was. "You're going to stay away from him. Next time we go to a club, if he's there, I'll point him out to you. But, that's only so you can make sure you stay the hell away from him. Understand?"

Colby didn't rush to agree with him the way he normally did.

Noah felt his stomach turn over. He knew he had no right to demand Colby's submission right then, but he needed it. "Colby?"

Finally, Colby dropped his gaze. "You don't have to point him out to me."

Noah tried to work that out. "Are you saying you've met him?"

"No," Colby whispered. "I've only ever seen him from a distance. From the other side of the street..."

There was something so confessional about his words.

It took Noah a few seconds to put the pieces together. "You saw him with me in the studio." Noah closed his eyes. "You were the wrong number." Why the hell hadn't he realised that before?

"Yes."

Colby had seen it. Noah closed his eyes tighter, not caring that it made the bruise on his cheek ache.

"You threw him out before I had a chance to get across the street."

"Good," Noah bit out. He forced himself to open his eyes, knowing he didn't have the luxury of wallowing in embarrassment right then. He had far more important things to deal with. "I still mean what I said. You have to stay away from him. You don't speak to him, you don't go near him, understand? It's important, Colby. I want you to promise me you'll stay away from him, no matter what."

For a long time the room was completely silent.

"Okay," Colby finally said. "I promise."

Noah felt the tension drain out of him. He stared up at the ceiling as he fought to pull himself together, knowing that the conversation as a whole wasn't over, but needing a few moments to recover from the idea that Colby had come so close to going after Sam and getting himself completely screwed over in the process.

A few minutes passed before Colby touched Noah's cheek and encouraged him to turn his head on the pillow. "Will you promise me something?"

Noah nodded, knowing that after everything that had passed between them that day, he wouldn't be able to refuse Colby anything he asked for.

"If you ever feel like you want to go and see Sam, for any reason, at any point in the future, will you promise me that you'll come and talk to me first?"

Noah had no idea what he'd been expecting, but it wasn't that. "Why?"

"Because I think you know deep down that you

deserve better than the way he's treated you, but sometimes, maybe when things get hard, you forget all that. So, when you forget, I'd rather you come to see me." Colby took a deep breath. "If that means you venting at me or trying to push me away, I can deal with that. Honestly, there's *nothing* you'll ever say to me that will make me walk away from an argument with you again—but the idea of him hurting you..."

Noah stared at Colby for several seconds, completely speechless. Colby was trying to protect him. He was doing it with requests rather than demands, he was asking for Noah to check his instincts rather than completely deny them, but all that changed very little. Colby was effectively asking for the same promise that Noah had insisted on receiving from him. *Stay the hell away from someone who'll hurt you.*

"Do you think you can promise that?" Colby finally prompted.

Noah nodded. "Yes, I promise."

And, in spite of everything, Colby smiled as if Noah had given him the best present ever created.

Noah cleared his throat. "You know, you still haven't told me what you want me to do to make things up to you—what it will take for you to really forgive me for today."

Colby blinked. "The promise you just made—that's it."

Noah hesitated. "Let's be completely clear about this, we're talking about sex now. You do get that, right?"

Colby shook his head. "I don't want you doing anything to make it up to me. That's..." He shook his head again.

Noah raised an eyebrow.

"You know I love you to bits, right?" Colby said. "But, you have some seriously screwed up ideas about the right reasons to have sex with someone."

Noah stared at Colby for a long time. The boy really didn't get it. The idea of putting someone on their knees to beg for forgiveness didn't just fail to press his buttons, it actually turned him off.

Noah felt his lips quirk into a smile. He'd been right before. Colby really was a different species than men like Sam. Noah leaned forward and pressed a kiss against Colby's lips. It was almost chaste—almost.

When Noah pulled back, it was only to dip his head and press another kiss on Colby's neck, as he began to make his way down his body.

Colby's hand on his shoulder stopped him short. "What are you doing?"

"I'm going to suck you off," Noah said, very simply.

All credit to Colby, he seemed to make a hell of an effort to look like he thought that was a bad idea. "Maybe I wasn't clear a minute ago—"

"You were very clear," Noah cut in. "You don't want an apology blow job."

Colby nodded.

"Which is good, because that's not what you're going to get," Noah said. "This is a celebratory blow job, it's very different."

Colby blinked at him. "We're celebrating?"

"We are," Noah agreed, pressing a kiss halfway down Colby's chest.

"Anything in particular?"

"The fact that, in spite of having had extremely bad taste in men for as long as I can remember, I've actually managed to fall in love with someone who's not only not a complete bastard, but who might actually be the sweetest guy on the planet." He placed another kiss low down on Colby's abs. "And, even more unlikely than that—for reasons beyond my understanding—he loves me back."

Colby swallowed.

"Doesn't that sound worth celebrating?" Noah asked. He placed a kiss on the tip of Colby's quickly stiffening cock.

Colby seemed to realise that this wasn't an argument he was going to win—or one that any sensible man would want to win. He nodded his acceptance and smiled down the bed, as easy in his submission as Noah had ever seen him.

"Good boy," Noah whispered. "Now, where was I...?"

Author's Note.

There's a free short story that catches up with Noah and Colby as their relationship progresses. It's called Another Six Months Later... and you can find it on my website.

Worth a Shot

Chapter One

"Here's to more time spent sprinting and less time spent screwing."

The words pulled at Donovan's attention, dragging it back toward the same table of guys that he'd been discretely observing ever since he'd plucked up the courage to start drinking in that pub.

Luck hadn't been with Donovan that particular night. By the time he'd arrived, all the seats that would have allowed a clear view of Tony Landon had already been claimed. Still, the occasional glimpses he caught of Tony's profile from his current vantage point were something. Donovan wasn't above taking what he could get.

As Tony's companions laughed and drank to the toast, Tony shook his head and slumped back in his seat.

"To the longest three weeks of Tony's life," Cosmos, a long distance runner from the Falconer Institute of Training's athletics team, suggested. Once more, everyone in the group raised their drinks.

Tony drained the last of his beer and glared at each of the men around his table. "I'm so glad you all find our coach's decision to torture me amusing."

"Haslet does have a point. You are kind of slutty," Cosmos pointed out. "You'll have much more energy for training if you're not getting any."

"Pot, kettle, black?" Tony shot back, without missing a beat.

Cosmos smirked. "Call me what you like, sweetheart— I'm not the one who promised Haslet he'd stay celibate until after the Trentmoore meet."

Donovan looked from Tony to Tony's friends wishing, not for the first time, that he had the confidence to sit with them around that table and joke about things the way they did. But, no. It was useless, even the thought of joining them was making his grip on his glass turn white knuckled and his throat close up.

"It's only a couple of weeks," said another man at Tony's table, Mike—the team's shot putter, in a more sympathetic tone of voice.

Donovan lifted his gaze just in time to see Cosmos pat Tony on the shoulder. "Yeah, Tony. It's only the longest you'll have gone without sex since you turned legal…"

Tony glared down at him. "You're a real bastard at times. You know that, right?"

"Yep," Cosmos said, more cheerfully than ever, obviously not the least bit worried by the fact he was half Tony's size. Everyone at the table laughed.

Tony pushed his hand through his spiky, blond hair as if he was at his wits end. But, when he turned to get up from the table, Donovan saw that Tony was smiling too, as if he didn't really mind their teasing. "I'm going to get another drink."

"Careful, Tony," Cosmos called after him. "Too much of a good thing and Haslet will probably make you give up alcohol, too."

Tony didn't bother to turn around. He just held two fingers up to the whole group as he walked away. Donovan watched him go, automatically dropping his gaze to admire the way tight jeans stretched across Tony's arse.

As Tony moved out of Donovan's line of sight, the jokes Tony's friends had been making gradually presented themselves for Donovan's consideration. Tony had promised his coach he'd give up sex for the next three weeks.

Donovan frowned at his drink.

Tony and sex were so closely linked in his mind, it was almost impossible for him to think of one existing without the other. Tony not being intimately entwined with the very essence of sex was wrong. But at the same time…

It probably wouldn't make any difference, but it was worth a shot. Hell, anything that might tip the balance in his favour and make it possible for Donovan to speak to Tony without hyperventilating was worth investigating. Donovan abandoned his lemonade and headed after Tony.

As he rounded the corner, he saw Tony standing halfway along the bar, waiting to be served.

He hesitated. At the last moment, his courage deserted him. He changed course and ended up standing about two metres to Tony's right. Donovan stared down at the battered wooden surface, cursing his own cowardice. Maybe if he tried to —

"Hi."

Donovan jerked his head up. He didn't need to sidle down the bar. Tony now stood right alongside him. For a few seconds, Donovan's vocal cords refused to cooperate, just as they had so many times before. All he could do was stare at Tony like a prime candidate for the post of village idiot. Finally, he managed to clear his throat.

"Hi." It might not have been the height of wit, but it was pretty close to a normal pitch. It could have been worse — it had been worse on several other occasions when Tony had tried to start conversations with him.

"How did the nationals go?"

Donovan blinked at Tony. "The nationals?"

"The archery nationals, they were last week, right?" Tony asked.

Donovan nodded. "Yes, they were." Except nobody knew that, because while athletics might be popular enough that everyone at the institute would recognise half the team, archery wasn't the kind of sport that anyone who didn't own a bow ever noticed.

"So…?" Tony promoted.

Donovan managed to pull a few brain cells together.

"They went well. The institute's team came third."

"What about the individual event—how did that go?" Tony prompted.

As Donovan stared up at him, he had the strangest sensation that Tony already knew the answer to that question. "I won," he blurted out.

Tony failed to look the least bit surprised. "Congratulations."

"What can I get for you?"

Donovan jumped at the sudden interruption from the other side of the bar.

The bartender looked at the empty beer bottle Tony had placed on the bar. "Same again?"

Tony shook his head. "Coke this time, thanks."

That meant he was driving. Donovan had been paying attention over the months. If Tony was driving, he stopped after one. If he wasn't driving, he drank every one of his friends under the table and still never slurred a word.

As Donovan watched, Tony pulled his wallet out of his jeans pocket and turned to him. "What are you having?"

No – that was what he always said. Whatever Tony had suggested each time he'd approached him, Donovan always panicked and said no, regardless of the answer he actually wanted to give.

Not for the first time, he tried to pull sensible thoughts to the front of his mind and push his nerves aside. *Tony isn't a psychopath. Tony isn't a complete bastard. Tony isn't Ryan.* None of it helped. *Tony can't expect anyone to fall into bed with him tonight, he's not allowed to have sex.* Bingo!

"The same, thank you." To Donovan's amazement, the words sounded completely calm.

As the barman got their drinks and Tony handed over the money, Donovan stared straight ahead. *It might work. God help him, but this might actually work...* Apparently, the sure and certain knowledge that Tony wasn't going to assume they'd have sex that very moment really did make it possible for Donovan to have a drink with him without completely freaking out.

"Come on, there's a free table over there." Tony pointed to a completely different part of the pub to where his friends were sitting.

Relaxing slightly as he realised that he wasn't going to have to face an entire group of guys, Donovan made his way to the empty table. Jacket in one hand and his bottle of Coke in the other, he shuffled his way awkwardly onto the bench that half-encircled the corner table. Tony slid in after him, every movement fluid and confident.

Silence. Damn. Donovan's nerves made it impossible for him not to attempt to fill the hush with words, any words.

"How did you know the nationals were last week?"

"Well, I kind of know one of the guys on the institute's team," Tony said. "Although, if I'm honest, I don't really know him that well yet. We've just flirted now and again. At least, I've flirted with him. Until this evening, he's always just nodded politely and rushed away at the first opportunity."

Donovan met Tony's eyes for a horrified moment as he recognized his own behaviour being quoted at him. "I don't flirt." Not anymore.

"Never?" Tony asked. "With anyone?"

Donovan shook his head.

"Good," Tony said, with an easy smile. "In that case, I won't take it personally." He took a sip of his Coke.

Donovan gulped down some of his own drink. He tried not to stare at the way Tony's mouth caressed the rim of his Coke bottle. He tried not to imagine that it was his cock pressed against Tony's lips. He failed on both counts.

"So, flirting aside, do all bi men make you nervous, or am I special?" Tony asked.

The question hit the air just as Donovan was taking another swig of his drink. He promptly choked on it.

Tony reached out and patted him helpfully on the back. Donovan caught his breath, but somehow, Tony's hand stayed there, resting high up, near his shoulders. The heat from Tony's skin soaked through the thin fabric of his shirt. Donovan waited for air to stall in his lungs and his heart to race, but for some reason, it didn't happen. The only reaction his body offered up in response to Tony's touch was a rapid hardening of his cock. He discretely moved his jacket to rest over his lap.

"Well?" Tony asked, with an unrepentant little grin. "Should I feel special or not?"

Donovan took a careful sip of his Coke while he played for time. Glancing up, he met Tony's eyes. He had the distinct impression that lying to Tony wouldn't do him any good. "Maybe you do make me more nervous than most men in here," he confessed.

"Because I'm bi and most of them are gay?" Tony asked, conversationally, as if he really wouldn't take offense if Donovan said yes.

Damn, but it was tempting to say yes. The only other option was the truth and there was no way in hell he could actually say: *Because I really want to have sex with you, but I think I might have a panic attack if I try to do that.*

Heat rushed to Donovan's checks at the very idea of uttering those words. He looked up from his inspection of the table top and accidentally caught Tony's gaze again.

Tony's eyes sparkled, as if he'd guessed at least part of what the honest answer would be. "How long have you been out?"

Donovan remembered how to breathe. "About three years. I came out when I was nineteen. What about you?" That was three calm and reasonably complete sentences in a row. Donovan couldn't help but feel a little proud of himself.

Tony chuckled. "I wavered between thinking I was straight, then gay, then straight again for so long I'm pretty sure my family thought I was going to build a revolving door on the closet by the time I finally shrugged and settled on being bi. Since that happened, oh, all of eighteen months ago, I guess I was twenty-three."

Donovan smiled. It was easy to smile at Tony, even while Tony's hand lingered on his back. The last time he'd been that comfortable smiling at a guy had been back before —

Donovan shut that train of thought down very firmly. "I think it's different if you're gay," he babbled, eager for any distraction. "I always knew."

Tony still gave no sign of thinking he was sitting next to a mad man. "My little brother was the same. He's in the swimming programme here. He's been out since..." He frowned slightly. "Damned if I can actually remember him not being gay." He shook his head and pushed his hand through his hair, disordering the blond spikes as he apparently dismissed his brother from his mind.

Donovan watched with appreciation as Tony's lips caressed the rim of his Coke bottle once more.

"You haven't dated anyone since you joined the institute," Tony said.

Donovan just blinked at him. That had definitely been a statement rather than a question.

"I asked around," Tony admitted, without any trace of embarrassment. "I found lots of guys who'd struck out with you, and a few girls who've tried their luck with just as little success, but no one you've actually dated."

"Oh." Donovan couldn't think of anything else to say except possibly: *I could name at least twenty of your previous lovers off the top of my head. They all say you're kinky as hell.*

"So, I'm left wondering if you dated anyone before you came here," Tony added.

"Are you trying to ask me if I'm a virgin?" Donovan closed his eyes, but yes, he had apparently said that out loud.

When he forced his eyes open, Tony was making an obvious attempt not to laugh. "I thought I was being subtle, but yeah, pretty much."

Even though he was sure he was blushing bright red, Donovan couldn't help but chuckle at the easy way Tony had of taking anything anyone said in his stride.

Tony took another sip of his drink. "Well?"

Donovan's laughter faded away. "No, I'm not a virgin. There was a guy at university."

"Didn't end well?" Tony asked, his voice gentler than it had been before.

"We weren't dating. He wasn't my boyfriend or anything like that."

Tony didn't say anything. The silence demanded words. Unfortunately, the only words Donovan had to hand were the truth.

"It...it all kind of... Suddenly, he assumed we were going to... I mean, it wasn't that I didn't want to... But, I..." He shook his head as he felt memories and panic start to bubble up inside him. "I'm sorry—I'd rather not talk about it."

Tony's hand started moving against his back for the first time since Donovan had choked. It travelled in slow circles, rubbing his back through his shirt. It felt nice and, maybe because of Tony's temporary vow of celibacy was tipping the balance and reminding Donovan that this situation was very different to the one he'd been in with Ryan, it didn't feel at all threatening.

"Suddenly things were going faster than you wanted them to go, but you couldn't pull the brake?" Tony suggested, still in that softer tone of voice.

Donovan nodded—that sounded so much more sensible than his fractured explanations had.

"So maybe that's made you nervous about getting to know any guys here—you're worried that if you tell someone you're interested, things will start to go too fast and you won't be able to slow them down again?"

Donovan stared at his Coke bottle. "I know it's stupid. Logically, I know that—"

"It's not stupid," Tony cut in. His tone changed and suddenly allowed no argument. He seemed to think for a few seconds. "I have an idea."

166

Donovan glanced up at him. "An idea?"

"Yeah." Tony turned a little more in his seat, pulling his knee up onto the bench between them. "An idea. Will you do me a favour?"

Not sure what else to do, Donovan nodded.

Tony set his drink down on the table. "I'm going to do something. I'd rather you didn't slap me without at least hearing me out first. Okay?"

Still no closer to understanding what the hell was going on, Donovan nodded again. "Okay."

Tony smiled. A second later, he leaned forward and dipped his head.

His lips brushed against Donovan's mouth, both firm and gentle at the same time. Then, before Donovan had a chance to register anything else, Tony pulled away.

Donovan gasped. He looked down. That was the only reaction he managed to scrape together. The rest of his body remained completely frozen in place.

Panic. There should be panic. There was always panic. Even those times he'd managed to get drunk enough to talk to another man, any movement toward doing anything other than talking always brought a wave of memories that swept away any possibility of wanting to be within a hundred miles of another living person.

"Donovan, look at me."

There was nothing harsh about the words, but they were undeniably an order. They demanded to be obeyed.

Donovan slowly looked up at him.

"You were only going to get more and more nervous, sitting there wondering what would happen if I made a move on you. So—I've made my move."

Donovan swallowed. He could still feel Tony's mouth against his lips.

"That means the next move is yours," Tony added. "Nothing past a kiss will happen until you decide you want it to."

Donovan merely stared at Tony's mouth in complete fascination.

"You've heard me out. This is the point where you're free to slap me if you want to."

Donovan was shocked into lifting his gaze far enough to meet Tony's eyes. "I don't want to slap you."

Tony smiled down at him. "I won't pretend I'm not glad about that."

Donovan smiled back. It was only then that he registered what Tony had actually said, rather than how much he wanted to kiss Tony when his lips moved to form words. "Did you mean it—about the next move being mine?"

"Yes." Just that one word, but said in a way that made Tony sound completely confident in his decision.

Donovan took a deep breath and pushed his hand through his hair as if that would help him sort through his thoughts. A second later, he nodded his understanding, and he did understand. Even if Tony was used to dating people who jumped into bed at a moment's notice, the fact that he couldn't do that without pissing off his coach made things different.

Donovan nodded again.

Even if Tony wanted them to have sex, which he'd always been quite clear about, he wasn't going to want them to have sex tonight. Everything was fine. Donovan had three weeks to psyche himself up for it, before sex would be required. He could do this. Donovan was repeating that reassurance to himself in a very firm tone of voice when Tony dipped his head and brushed their lips together again. Donovan jerked in surprise.

Tony pulled back just far enough to meet his eyes.

"I thought you said the next move was mine," Donovan whispered. Their lips were just a few inches apart. The temptation to lean up and try for another kiss was almost over powering.

"I said that nothing past a kiss will happen until you

make it clear you're up for it," Tony corrected, still not retreating at all. "I never said that I wouldn't kiss you every chance I got."

"Oh."

"That okay with you?" Tony asked.

Donovan nibbled at his bottom lip. "I... You don't mind just kissing someone and not..."

Tony smiled and stroked his fingers along Donovan's jawline. "Sometimes a kiss is just a kiss. It doesn't have to be foreplay, you know?"

Donovan merely stared at him.

"Just kissing someone can be fun on its own. Right?"

I don't know. I've never done that. There was never much kissing with —

Donovan swallowed several times in quick succession. This was different. Tony wasn't Ryan. Different rules applied. He settled for nodding.

Tony immediately brought their mouths back together. It was just a kiss, not the start of anything else. With that thought fresh in his mind, Donovan found himself cautiously parting his lips, but Tony didn't rush to accept the invitation. He just brushed their mouths together over and over again until Donovan thought it might drive him crazy.

It wasn't until Donovan whimpered that Tony finally traced his tongue against his bottom lip and began to explore his mouth in earnest. It was a slow and almost sleepy kiss. Tony slid his free hand behind Donovan's head and encouraged him to tilt his head to a certain angle, but the other hand stayed on Donovan's jawline.

There was no attempt on Tony's part to close the gap between their bodies. There was no hint that things would suddenly spiral out of control. Gradually, Donovan felt himself relax.

Tony kissed like a man who knew exactly what he was doing. All Donovan had to do was follow his lead, which was probably a good thing because Donovan was vaguely aware that any ability he'd ever had for complex thought was gently slipping away.

His hands itched with the desire to reach out to Tony in return, to find out if those blond spikes would be as rough against his palms as he'd always imagined they would be, or if Tony's jawline carried a hint of stubble.

No, that would be too big a risk. Donovan kept his hands where they were, one resting on the table, the other on the seat alongside him. His heart beat faster, but it was nothing like the start of his usual panic. It all felt quietly sublime.

Eye closed, completely absorbed in the kiss, Donovan lost all sense of where he was or even who he was. The kiss—that was the only thing that was important. A kiss that wasn't the start of something else, but just perfect in its own right. Part of Donovan wanted to sob with relief at the pure magic of it.

When Tony began to pull away, Donovan moaned his disapproval. He clenched his hand into a fist, but he couldn't quite bring himself to reach out and stop Tony. He remained very still. He had no idea how much time passed before he was able to open his eyes.

Tony just smiled as he slid his fingers through Donovan's hair. "Okay?"

Donovan nodded. He really wanted another kiss, and he was pretty sure he was making a fool of himself in front of the hottest man he'd ever met. But, as Tony stroked his hair back from his forehead, Donovan was surprised to find that he really was okay.

"Do you drive?"

It took Donovan a hell of a long time to wrap his mind around the change in topic.

Tony waited patiently, as if he was quite used to melting men's brains and no longer found their drop in IQ worthy of comment.

"Yes, but I don't have a car," Donovan finally offered.

"Good."

Donovan frowned, sure it wasn't just his addled brain that made that seem like a strange response.

"That means you don't have any excuse not to accept a lift home," Tony explained.

"Oh."

"They rang the bell for last orders a few minutes ago. It's chuck out time."

Donovan looked past Tony's shoulder. He hadn't heard a bell, but there did seem to be a lot of men moving towards the doors. "Oh," he repeated.

Tony pulled himself gracefully to his feet. He held a hand out to help Donovan do the same. Trying to navigate his way around the edge of the table one handed probably didn't help him move less clumsily, especially when he really needed his only free hand to hold his jacket in front of his tenting fly, but Donovan couldn't quite bring himself to pull his hand out of Tony's grip.

Their hands were still joined together a few minutes later when Tony brought them both to a stop alongside a car in the street outside the pub. A fresh breeze whipped down the road. It cleared Donovan's mind a little and offered up certain facts for his consideration—such as, all of Tony's friend's teasing aside, there was no guarantee that Tony had any intention of keeping that promise to his coach, and that it was quite likely that Tony would expect to be invited in when they reached Donovan's place.

"You don't have to drive me home," Donovan rushed out. Even to his own ear his voice sounded off. "It's not far. I can—"

Tony good-naturedly nodded his agreement with everything Donovan said, but he still nudged him firmly into the car.

Sitting in the passenger seat, Donovan watched Tony slide behind the wheel, not sure what to say or how to explain himself. When Tony caught his eye and smiled, Donovan quickly turned his attention to where he'd placed his jacket across his lap.

"You'll either need to give me directions or an address," Tony said, starting the car.

"I'm sorry. I thought... I mean..." Words faded away. He didn't look up until Tony reached out and touched his jawline, encouraging him to turn his head so he could look him in the eye.

"I keep my promises, sweetheart. The next move is yours. I'm just going to drive you home. I'm not going to invite myself in when we get there."

As easily as he said that, as if no words Tony uttered could possibly be a lie, Donovan felt some of his tension drain away. He nodded. A few seconds passed before he realised that he still needed to follow that up with some sort of concrete information on where he lived.

He'd been telling the truth about not living far away from the pub. It seemed to him as if mere seconds passed before Tony had pulled up at the kerb outside the appropriate block of flats. Tony killed the engine. The car filled with silence.

"Are you completely out?" Tony suddenly asked.

Donovan was pretty sure he should have been used to the sudden changes in topic by that point but, once more unsure what to say, he just nodded.

"So, if one of your neighbours walks past the car and sees me kissing you goodnight, that's okay?"

Donovan nodded.

He immediately parted his lips under Tony's kiss. Perhaps Tony was starting to trust him not to freak out, because this time he didn't make Donovan wait before he deepened the kiss and sent little electric shocks of pleasure tingling through Donovan's body.

Seconds, minutes, maybe even hours might have passed, but when Tony pulled away it was still far too soon.

"Will you be at the pub tomorrow night?" Tony asked.

Donovan quickly nodded, only to falter. "No." Damn. "I'm on the late shift at work." He looked down. "Maybe I can—"

"It's okay," Tony cut in, before Donovan had a chance to offer to try to swap his shift with someone else. "How about...?" Tony trailed off. "No. I've got a training session booked late on Wednesday."

All Donovan could do was listen helplessly as the days between then and Trentmoore slipped away. Damn it, three weeks to work himself up to having sex wasn't going to help if he didn't get to see Tony in those weeks!

"Friday?" Tony finally said. "I'm meeting up with Cosmos for a training run, but I'm free after that."

Donovan quickly nodded.

"How do you feel about meeting up at my place instead of the pub?" Tony said.

Donovan was about to nod. Then reality reasserted itself. Tony and him—alone. It was a panic attack waiting to happen.

Tony stroked Donovan's hair back from his face. "The same rules would apply—the next move will still be yours."

Between that promise and the one to Tony's coach, maybe he could be alone with him without freaking out. Or, to look at it another way, if he was destined to freak out, maybe it was better to do that in private rather than in the pub.

Donovan nodded with all the confidence he could muster. "That sounds great."

* * * * *

"Good day?"

Tony paused halfway along the corridor leading from his flat's front door and glanced into the kitchen. How had his day been? "It had its moments," Tony said.

His younger brother, Colby, looked up from a half-made sandwich. "What kind of moments?"

Tony let a self-mocking smile rise to his lips. "The kind where Haslet catches me checking my texts in the middle of a very long, very boring department meeting."

Colby's mouth formed a neat little O.

"In my defence, he wasn't talking about anything that was even vaguely to do with me or any other sprinter in the programme," Tony said, leaning against the kitchen door frame.

"Has he rescheduled all your training for five AM again?" Colby asked. "Because if he has, I'm relocating to Noah's for the duration. You and mornings that early are not a good combination."

Tony shook his head. "It's even worse this time."

Colby blinked at him. "Seriously?"

"Yeah," Tony said. "He apparently made a suggestion, which I, of course, wasn't taking the blindest bit of notice of. The first thing I registered was... 'That's okay with you isn't it, Landon?' I look up and everyone in the room is staring at me."

All interest in his half-constructed sandwich abandoned, Colby leaned back against the counter, his eyes already sparkling with amusement. "And you, of course, said 'Yes, Mr. Haslet'."

Tony nodded. "Cue much laughter from everyone I train with. Cosmos damned near fell off his chair."

Colby's smile got wider by the moment. "Well, don't keep me in suspense. What was the suggestion?"

"That I give up sex until after the Trentmoore meet."

Colby's jaw actually dropped a bit. "That's three weeks, right?"

Tony sighed. "Yeah."

Colby's eyes narrowed. "You're taking it scarily well..."

Tony shrugged.

An image of Donovan appeared in the front of his

mind. Hazel eyes, light brown hair, a nervous smile and a body that never failed to have Tony hard in an instant.

"The day got better as it went on," he acknowledged.

"Better how?"

Tony took a deep breath. *You know that archery guy I was telling you about. After over a year of me chasing after him, he finally let me buy him a drink. He's hot, and sweet, and awkward, and nervous as hell. And —*

Tony chuckled to himself as he pushed his hand through his hair. And, there was no way in hell he was going to say any of that to his little brother. "I'll tell you when you're older."

Colby rolled his eyes, but he smiled at the familiar brush off, taking it in good part. "Want a sandwich?"

Tony shook his head. What he wanted was Donovan Matthews. Happily, for the first time, it seemed like he might actually get him.

Chapter Two

Donovan took a deep breath and pressed the buzzer labelled for flat forty-nine. Everything was going to be fine. They were just going to...

Okay, so Donovan wasn't sure what they were going to do, but he was very sure of three things. The next move was his. Tony wasn't allowed to have sex. And Tony was nothing like Ryan.

Everything was going to be fine.

Donovan stared at the rows of buttons. Tony had definitely said flat forty-nine. Donovan shuffled his feet, wondering if he should press again, just in case Tony hadn't heard him the first time. But, if he had heard him, that would be rude and —

Donovan took a step back from the door, trying to work out what the best course of action would be. Maybe if he —

"Are you really early or am I even later than I thought?"

Donovan looked over his shoulder. Tony! Tony in a running vest and a pair of very short shorts. Donovan couldn't have quoted the time accurately for a fortune.

Tony jogged along the last few metres of pavement that separated them, pulling out a set of ear buds and switching off an i-Pod worn strapped to one arm.

"If a long distance runner ever invites you on a *nice short little run* — kill him," Tony recommended, with a chuckle as he pulled out a key that had been tucked into the i-Pod's holder.

Donovan managed to drag his gaze away from Tony's body for long enough to look down the street. "Is Cosmos coming here?"

"No. He's still running. He wants to get another couple of miles in today."

Tony pushed the door open and stepped back to let Donovan in. "Were you waiting long?"

Donovan shook his head.

"Nervous?" Tony asked, as they stepped into the lift.

Donovan managed a small smile. "That obvious?"

Tony's smile looked far more genuine. "Yeah."

The fact that Tony saw no reason to lie about it surprised a burst of laughter out of Donovan.

"I'm not a serial killer," Tony offered, as they stepped out of the lift on the fourth floor. "Promise."

"Good to know," Donovan murmured.

"Or a sex maniac who's going to jump you the moment I get you alone."

Donovan nodded his agreement. "I know."

They made their way into Tony's flat. A short hallway led to a large, bright living room. The width of the farthest wall was almost entirely taken up by three big windows. Donovan automatically made his way across to them, trying to appear completely relaxed.

A telescope was set up in front of the central window. It was too early and too light to have much chance of seeing anything, but it was just the kind of distraction he needed. Careful not to adjust the settings, Donovan bent over and peered through the view finder.

His eyebrows rose as he found himself looking straight into the building opposite. There seemed to be some sort of dance class going on.

"The guy teaching the class is Noah."

Donovan jerked upright and stepped quickly away from the telescope, a hurried apology for prying rushing to his lips. The words died as he turned to Tony.

Tony didn't look angry, he seemed amused. "Noah's my brother's boyfriend. Colby's the one who plays voyeur

177

with him, not me."

"I'm sor—"

Tony shook his head and waved the apology away. "Colby's actually much less creepy in person than that telescope makes him look."

Donovan couldn't help but smile at the blend of affection and resignation in Tony's voice.

"Make yourself at home. TV remote's on the coffee table. There's beer in the kitchen. Help yourself to whatever you can find food-wise," Tony said over his shoulder, as he walked down a corridor leading off the living room. "I'm going to hit the shower."

Too nervous to eat and having long since realised that alcohol was no help dealing with sex related nerves, Donovan stood idly alongside the telescope for a few minutes. There wasn't really much to do except look through the view finder again.

The class seemed to be breaking up. A guy, who Donovan assumed had to be Noah, was ushering people out of the studio. Another man, a tall guy with a shaved head, seemed to be staying behind.

Donovan stepped away from the telescope and paced around the living room a little. Everything was fine, he knew that. But, for better or worse, it was a lot easier to really believe that Tony was nothing like Ryan when Tony was actually in the room—possibly because it was harder to think clearly about anything when all his blood was diverted away from his brain and straight toward his cock.

Donovan crossed his arms before lifting one hand up and nibbling at the corner of his nail. There was no reason to believe everything was going to go to hell at any point in the near future. Really, there wasn't.

When he heard a door click open, Donovan turned toward the corridor leading, he supposed, to Tony's bedroom.

Tony didn't appear, but two men's voices floated through from the direction of the front door. They'd barely uttered a few words before it was clear that it had to be Colby and Noah. Donovan's nerves doubled.

Words disappeared and were replaced by what sounded very much like one man pinning another man to the wall and kissing him senseless. A quick analysis of the flat's lay out made it all too clear that anyone heading toward the bedrooms would have to walk through the living room first. Suddenly, the living room was the last place Donovan wanted to be.

Without even bothering to stop and wonder if he was about to make the biggest mistake of his life, Donovan ducked past the door leading to the front hall and hurried along the corridor Tony had disappeared down. There were only two doors. One opened onto an unlit room. One was shut, but a strip of light showed along the bottom edge. Donovan quickly opened the closed door and stepped into the room beyond it.

Tony wasn't there.

Donovan let out a relieved breath and shut the door behind him. All he had to do now was work out what to say when Tony found him lurking in his bedroom.

Without warning, the door on the adjacent wall swung open a few inches. Steam escaped through the gap as Tony peeked past the door. "Don?"

"I'm sorry, your brother and his boyfriend came home. They were, um... Do you mind if I wait for you in here?"

Tony chuckled. "No problem. I won't be a minute." He closed the bathroom door again.

Donovan pushed his hands into his pockets. Did barging into Tony's bedroom count as having made his move? Ryan would definitely have said it constituted a move, and an invitation, and a whole host of other things.

Was it Tony's turn again? What were the exact terms of Tony's promise to his coach? Were there things they could do without breaking the promise—bloody hell, was it a good thing if there were or not?

Donovan pulled one hand out of his pocket and nibbled

at a finger nail as his thoughts spiralled faster and faster.

Going into another man's bedroom did imply an inclination to go to bed with him, didn't it? Come to that, the erection that had been straining against Donovan's fly ever since Tony said hello certainly hinted he was very much up for it. And, if everything a man did indicated his willingness to have sex, he couldn't complain if a guy took him up on that offer. If a man acted like a slut around his university roommate, he had to be willing to deal with the consequences, right?

Donovan paced up and down the strip of carpet to the side of Tony's bed that was furthest from the bathroom door. He could leave. He could go back into the living room and brave coming face to face with Colby and Noah the way he should have in the beginning. He could leave completely, give up on the idea of ever having a sex life that didn't involve his own hand and—

Donovan stopped halfway along his pacing-route. On top of a chest of drawers set alongside the wardrobe rested the kind of clutter that almost anyone would accumulate if they weren't a complete neat-freak. Except, Donovan was reasonably sure that most people's bedroom clutter didn't include a pair of shiny silver handcuffs.

He stared at them, completely transfixed. Without thinking about it, he wrapped one hand around his opposite wrist. It was so easy to imagine the cuffs encircling his skin, trapping his hands, rendering him completely helpless. His breath caught in his throat as blood rushed to his cock faster than ever.

Rumours really didn't lie. Not about Donovan Matthews never having dated anyone at the institute and not about Tony Landon being kinky as hell, either.

Donovan's mind raced back—but not to the time it visited so often when he tried to take a step closer to another man. Suddenly, Donovan's psyche reeled under the recurrence of every Tony related fantasy he'd let creep into his mind when he worked his cock.

The Tony he'd imagined in a hundred different scenarios stared down at him. Donovan's hands were bound, pleasure danced through his veins and there was the kind of peace that most people only found in worshiping a one true god.

A click snapped Donovan back to the present. He spun around just in time to see Tony step into the bedroom, a large blue towel slung casually around his waist. Donovan took a step back as he found himself forced to confront not only the fact that Tony might not be exactly like the guy who starred in all his fantasies, but the possibility that, even if Tony really was that guy, Donovan still didn't have the balls to play his part in his own wet dream come true. Another step back and he only just avoided stepping into that chest of drawers.

"Your brother and his boyfriend," Donovan tried to explain. "They were…"

Tony nodded without forcing Donovan to try and find suitable words to describe what the other two men were doing in the hall, or why he would probably freak out if they tried to do that together.

"I told Colby that I had a date after my run. They probably assume we've gone out and they have the flat to themselves."

Donovan had been staring fixedly at the carpet since almost the first moment Tony stepped into the room. Now, as Tony's bare feet moved into his line of sight, Donovan was helpless to resist the temptation to drag his gaze slowly up Tony's practically nude body.

A touch to his jawline coaxed Donovan to look up further and meet Tony's gaze. "Remember what we said about the next move being yours?" Tony said.

Donovan nodded.

"That means you don't have to worry I'm going to pounce on you, whatever room we're in." Tony whispered the words in his ear as if they were a delicious little secret.

Donovan felt the heat go to his cheeks, but the teasing was so gentle it made him smile as well as blush.

Tony pressed a kiss next to his ear and another against his cheek as he traced his way to his lips.

They were in Tony's bedroom. Tony only wore a towel. The kiss wasn't entirely chaste. The uncertainty Donovan expected to bubble up inside him remained conspicuously absent. He leaned up into the kiss, doing his part in bridging the difference between their heights. Lifting himself onto his toes took away most of his ability to balance. He reached out and put his hand on Tony's shoulder to steady himself.

Bare skin. Donovan snatched his hand away the moment he remembered that Tony was damn near naked. Did that count as making a move?

Tony paused for a second, but it didn't seem so much like a hesitation as a moment's reflection. Donovan felt something brush against his forearm. He didn't have time to pull away. Suddenly Tony's fingers were wrapped around his wrist.

Never breaking the kiss, Tony guided Donovan's hand back up to his shoulder.

"That's fine," Tony whispered into the kiss. When he released Donovan's wrist, he moved his hand to rest on the small of Donovan's back.

Tony's skin was warm under Donovan's palm, but it was the skin around Donovan's wrist that tingled with pleasure. He wanted Tony's hand around his wrist again. He wanted to regain that brief moment of certainty he'd felt when Tony was in complete control of his wrist.

It had all been so simple. His hand would be where Tony wanted it. The possibility of his hand being in the wrong place, of him doing the wrong thing had vanished. Perfection had taken its place, just like in the fantasy. And he hadn't freaked out when Tony held his wrist that way. Maybe he could do this after all. Maybe he could have just a taste of the things he'd seen in all his favourite bits of internet porn.

Maybe if he just made sure it happened while Tony was keeping his promise to his coach...

It was a cheap shot, one Donovan knew he shouldn't take, but he could pay Tony back for that in the future. And, God, Donovan needed to feel that moment of perfection again.

When Tony broke the kiss, he didn't rush to step back. His hand stayed on the small of Donovan's back, inviting him to linger close while he pulled himself together. Donovan blinked open his eyes. His gaze fell on Tony's shoulder, where his hand still rested. He stared at his wrist, imagining that Tony's hand encircled his skin.

"Okay, sweetheart?"

Donovan nodded, not trusting himself to say anything sane if he spoke.

Tony stepped back. "I'm going to get dressed. It's up to you if you want to turn around or close your eyes."

Donovan did turn away from him, although he wasn't sure if he intended to give Tony privacy to dress or himself space to think.

He found himself facing the chest of drawers, and the clutter on top of it.

The handcuffs stared up at him, very shiny and oh-so tempting.

The idea of feeling completely certain that he was where he should be and that he was doing exactly what he should be doing; the impossibility of doing the wrong thing – all his fantasies coming true with the hottest man he'd ever known. It was impossible not to be drawn to so many wonderful prospects.

With their conflicting schedules, it was impossible to tell how often they'd be able to see each other before the Trentmoore meet. If Donovan didn't do this now, he might never have another chance this good.

He reached out and picked up the handcuffs. The metal links rattled.

"Don?" Tony said, from somewhere behind him.

Donovan stared down at the cuffs, but he didn't give himself time to think or to panic. He tightened his grip around the cold metal. He had to try.

Tony's hand came to rest on Donovan's shoulder. Tony turned him around so they stood face to face. He was still wearing his towel.

"You said the next move is mine. This is my move." Donovan watched, as if from somewhere outside his own body, as he reached out and offered the cuffs to Tony.

* * * * *

Tony couldn't remember any point in his life when he'd been innocent enough to find a pair of handcuffs shocking. Right then, with Donovan, they managed to render him completely speechless.

He stared down at the cuffs as if he'd never seen them before, as if he hadn't used them to tie up a whole string of men and women. Just as Tony tore his gaze away from them, Donovan glanced up. Their eyes met. The mixture of emotions in Donovan's gaze hit him like a punch to the stomach — the uncertainty, the fear, the desperation and, running through it all, a streak of pure, bloody-minded determination.

Tony wasn't sure what he'd expected Donovan's move to be. It had been a hell of a long time since he'd dated anyone who wasn't more than happy to jump into bed from the word go. Come to that, it had been over a year since he'd been with anyone who wanted to wait for a bed rather than make do with a wall in a club. Tony had vaguely supposed there would be a certain amount of making out, or maybe — damn it, he didn't know what the steps were, exactly. But he did know that there should be some stepping stones between innocent little kisses and even the mildest form of kink.

As Tony watched, the emotions that had filled Donovan's eyes gave way to straight forward embarrassment. He began to drop his hand and turn away. Tony couldn't let that happen. He caught hold of Donovan's hand and took the cuffs from him.

I've wanted to tie you up since the first moment I saw you, but since you're barely keeping it together for a conversation, we should probably wait before we bring out the toys, or have sex, or pretty much do anything past a kiss.

"Okay."

Donovan glanced up at him, relief wiping away any trace of another emotion. "It's okay?" Donovan checked.

"Of course." Tony smiled, and was rewarded with a return smile from Donovan.

Obviously it was okay with Tony. Handcuffs were always okay with him. But at the same time, he knew there was no way in hell he could tie Donovan up. Bloody hell — Tony didn't know exactly what had gone on with Donovan and the guy he was in uni with, but there were times when a single touch seemed to be enough to cause Donovan to hyperventilate. Bondage wasn't going to help with that.

Tony glanced down at the cuffs in his hand. There was only one choice he could make. The fact it was one he'd never made before wasn't important. Because, Donovan was Donovan, and after waiting all this time to get a chance with the guy, Tony wasn't going to let anything happen that would scare Donovan off — not even if it was Donovan's idea.

Tony walked across to the bed and sat down on the edge of the mattress. It only took him a second to have one half of the cuffs cinched around his left wrist. Lying down on the bed, he reached up to the headboard, guided the other cuff behind one of the metal rails and fastened it around his right wrist.

He didn't pause, didn't hesitate and he didn't look toward Donovan until it was done. When he finally turned his attention to Donovan, it was hard to imagine anyone looking more shocked. It had obviously never occurred to him that Tony would be the one who wore the cuffs.

"Donovan?" Tony prompted.

His only response was to move his gaze from the cuffs to Tony's face.

Tony smiled at his confusion. "Come here."

Donovan obeyed.

Tony waited until Donovan reached the side of the bed before he said anything else.

"Sit down." He nodded to the bed alongside him.

It didn't seem to occur to Donovan that it was traditionally the man wearing the bondage who obeyed the orders. He lowered himself carefully onto the edge of the bed.

"Everything's fine," Tony said, firmly, and told himself that it was only Donovan he was trying to reassure. The cuffs were the kind that could be undone without access to the key if necessary; knowing that wasn't making Tony feel any better about being bound.

Donovan nodded. His gaze slipped back to the handcuffs. Whatever his reason for suggesting bondage, he'd apparently had very specific expectations of who would be doing what. He still seemed to be having trouble making the leap from what he'd thought would happen, to what was actually happening.

"It's your move again," Tony prompted.

"I thought..." Donovan looked Tony straight in the eye. "You're okay with this?"

"Yeah." Tony's heart was racing so fast it might burst through his rib cage. He was tied up, and every instinct he had told him that was all kinds of wrong. But he couldn't worry about any of that right then. "Are you?"

Donovan blinked at him.

"Are you okay with this?" Tony prompted.

Donovan seemed to think about the question for a long time before he finally nodded.

Silence.

Tony took a deep breath and forced himself to at least try to relinquish a little bit of control over what might happen next. If he put his mind to it, he could keep his mouth shut and wait for Donovan to speak first—if not out of submission then at least out of curiosity about what Donovan might choose to say.

"I don't know what you want me to do," Donovan whispered. A blush touched his cheeks at having to make such a confession.

Any uncertainty Tony felt about being tied up dissolved. The pure submission in Donovan's words made the cuffs irrelevant. He wasn't submitting to Donovan, he was just...just stressing that Donovan was completely safe and free to set whatever pace he wanted. He was just making himself less intimidating while his new boyfriend found his feet. The difference was subtle, but it was important. When Tony smiled up at Donovan this time, it was a genuine expression, unhampered by any hint of nerves.

"Don't try to work out what I want," he offered. "Just do what you want."

Donovan met his gaze for a moment before quickly looking down. He didn't reach out to Tony; he didn't seem to know where to look, let alone where to touch. It wasn't in Tony to let him flounder, not when there was one thing that he knew was in Donovan's comfort zone.

"Kiss me." Tony had intended it to sound like a suggestion, but it hit the air like a clear order.

Before Tony had time to regret that, Donovan lowered his head and brushed their mouths together. He'd already started to pull back when Tony slid his tongue out to caress Donovan's bottom lip in an invitation to linger.

Donovan hesitated, but he didn't retreat. Tony only had to lift his head a fraction off the pillow in order to deepen the kiss. Donovan willingly parted his lips, welcoming Tony into his world and giving up control to him as if it was the most natural thing in the world.

Above the cuffs, Tony tightened his hands into fists. His inability to reach out to Donovan tore at his instincts. It wasn't even about wanting to cop a feel. He just wanted his hands on Donovan, sliding through light brown strands of hair as he pulled him closer; welcoming him into his arms, letting him know everything was fine.

A frustrated noise escaped from the back of Tony's throat. Donovan instantly tensed. He lifted his head. Staring down at Tony from just a few inches away, he licked his lips, as if savouring the sensations of the kiss. He looked so damn shell-shocked.

"Good boy," Tony murmured.

Donovan's eyes opened wider. They were hazel, with little flecks of amber in them, and beautiful. His blush came back, but it seemed to be more about enjoying being praised that way than embarrassment.

"Good boy," Tony repeated. Yes, he'd been right. The only thing that deepened in Donovan's expression when he heard those words repeated was pleasure. He might not have played before, but Tony had no doubt that his first read on Donovan was right. He was sub to the bone.

Donovan hesitated, but only for a moment. He dipped his head and brought their lips back together.

Tony smiled into the kiss. Even when Donovan was leaning over a bound man, his first instinct was still to follow his lover's lead. Whether he understood Tony's cues on a conscious level or not, Donovan responded to them all. As Tony brought the kiss to an end, Donovan obediently lifted his head. His eyes remained closed for what felt like a very long time.

Tony stared up at him, simply waiting him out.

Donovan nibbled on his bottom lip. "I think it's your move now," he whispered, as he opened his eyes.

Tony shook his head. "Your move lasts until you take off the cuffs."

Donovan glanced up at them. "Is there a key?"

Tony nodded toward the bedside table. It was hard to miss it. There was a bright red key ring attached to them to make them easy to find in a pinch.

Donovan picked up the keys and reached up toward the cuffs.

"Put the keys in my hand."

Donovan instantly stopped searching for the lock and did as he was told.

Tony wrapped his fingers tightly around the key ring. "You can have them back when you've finished your move properly."

Donovan tensed. "I...I don't know what you want me to do."

"Look at me—look me in the eye."

It took a long time, but eventually Donovan obeyed.

"If this is as far as you want to go, that's fine. But I get the feeling that maybe there are other things you'd like to do."

Donovan dropped his gaze. Tony followed his line of sight. Donovan's hands were at his side, his fingers furled into fists as if he was keeping his hands to himself through sheer force of will.

"You're allowed to touch me if you want to," Tony offered.

Donovan looked at the cuffs. "Even though you can't?"

"I don't mind." Okay, so that wasn't entirely the truth, but Tony was going to call the lie very small, and definitely white. "And I'm not going to think I can do whatever I want once the cuffs come off, either," he hazarded, wondering if there was a specific piece of reassurance Donovan needed.

"If I start something—" Donovan whispered.

"There's no starting anything," Tony cut in, very firmly, wondering just how pushy Donovan's ex had been to make Donovan so nervous about that. "Things are what they are. A touch doesn't have to be anything more than it is—just like a kiss."

The comparison seemed to snap everything together in Donovan's mind. He reached out and settled his fingers on Tony's cheek. It took Tony a second to realise that he was copying his way of coaxing Donovan to look up at him.

Tony smiled at the realisation. It was hard to believe an ex even existed in that moment. It really seemed like the only person Donovan had to copy was Tony himself. Turning his head, Tony pressed a kiss against Donovan's fingers.

Donovan responded by tracing his fingers across Tony's lips. About to open his mouth and wrap his lips around Donovan's fingertip, Tony hesitated. He had a horrible feeling that Donovan would take that as an order to suck him off. Forcing himself to remain perfectly still, Tony just let Donovan brush his fingers back and forth across his lips until he was ready to move on.

Very slowly, Donovan trailed his fingers down over his chin and to his throat.

Donovan seemed far more fascinated by his explorations than anyone Tony had ever met. It was as if he'd never had a chance to simply get to know another man's body before.

But, what had he said? Tony tried to remember Donovan's actual words rather than the anger he'd felt toward his ex when Donovan offered his stumbling account. The guy hadn't been Donovan's boyfriend. They hadn't dated. So, what did that mean? A one-night stand? A friend who'd been more interested in getting benefits than Donovan had been in offering them? Donovan didn't seem like the type to go for either kind of hook up—or at least, not the type to enjoy it if he did.

As Donovan ran his hands over Tony's shoulders and down his chest, it was impossible to imagine him enjoying a drink in a nightclub, let alone getting laid in the back room of one.

As minutes ticked slowly past, Tony stared up at Donovan, completely engrossed by tracking the different emotions that passed through his eyes. It seemed as if he didn't know how to hold anything back—or maybe as if, despite all the reasons to assume otherwise, Donovan didn't even know why someone would want to hide anything from his lover.

Donovan's fingers traced down Tony's abs, making his muscles twitch and his cock stiffen far more quickly than such a chaste touch warranted. Donovan only faltered when he reached the edge of the towel wrapped around Tony's waist. He looked up at Tony, as if seeking his advice.

Advice, Tony repeated to himself—that's what Donovan was looking for, not an order.

"Your choice," Tony said, far more casually than he felt. "I'm not going anywhere either way."

* * * * *

Maybe it was the handcuffs. Maybe it was Tony's promise to his coach, or the promises he'd made to Donovan. Maybe it was the fact that, even while he was in handcuffs, Tony still seemed to be perfectly calm and in complete control of the entire world.

Whatever the reason, as Donovan stared down at Tony, no man had ever seemed less like Ryan. Donovan failed to feel any cause for concern. So, stop now and savour the fact he'd managed to do so much without freaking out, or keep going and see if he could gain some even better memories while he had the chance.

For a few more seconds, Donovan's fingers remained on the edge of the towel. The corner was tucked into the top, precariously holding it wrapped around Tony's body.

Tony had given him the out. But, God help him, Donovan didn't want to take it. He was sick of running scared, of turning his back on what he really wanted. He was sick of letting a guy he hadn't even set eyes on in years rule his sex life.

Moving slowly, feeling like he was looking down upon himself and watching everything happen from outside his body, Donovan unwrapped the towel from around Tony's waist, rendering Tony completely naked.

Tony's cock was already half hard. Tony wanted to have sex with him. But that was okay because he couldn't actually do that. And, while he didn't have to worry about them actually having sex, Donovan found himself relieved to know that he wasn't the only one who was turned on. Maybe he wasn't screwing this up as much as he'd thought he was.

Donovan glanced up to Tony's face. Naked and bound in front of a fully dressed man, he still managed to look completely in charge. He smiled at Donovan when their eyes met.

Donovan couldn't hold his gaze for more than a few moments. His attention was drawn inexorably back to Tony's cock. He was uncut, the hairs around the base were trimmed short, and he was perfect. Donovan reached out and, before he lost his courage, trailed his fingers lightly along the stiffening length.

A glance up to Tony's eyes proved that Tony didn't look pissed off with him. Everything was still fine. Donovan carefully wrapped his fingers around Tony's cock. It was so different to touching himself. As Donovan stroked Tony's shaft, it rapidly hardened against his hand. Donovan watched it happen, as fascinated as someone who had never seen an erection before.

He was sure his own cock would have hardened at the sight, except he was already as hard as he could get, his erection pressing uncomfortably against the inside of his jeans.

Donovan swallowed, wishing he had the courage to unzip and take himself in hand too. Almost as soon as the idea occurred to him, Donovan pushed the possibility aside, sure that it would prove too much for his nerves to take. Ryan had hated it when he wanted to—

No. He wasn't going to think about that. He was only going to think about Tony. Yes—just Tony. He could wait until he was back in his own flat to take care of himself. For now, it was far more important to concentrate on Tony.

Donovan stroked from the base of Tony's cock all the way up to where his glans peeked past his foreskin and back, again and again. His hand fell into an easy rhythm, as if this were no big deal, as if he actually had plenty of experience with jacking a cock that wasn't his own.

"That's right," Tony murmured.

Donovan glanced up. He gasped when he saw the pleasure in Tony's eyes. His hand faltered for a moment before picking up the movement again. He had no idea how long he'd been playing with Tony's cock, but it had obviously been long enough for Tony to really start to enjoy the attention.

"Tighten your grip a fraction," Tony ordered.

Donovan hurriedly did as he was told, eager for any guidance on how to please Tony—especially when that didn't come in the form of a demand that they have sex that second.

"Perfect."

Tony thought he was perfect? The possibility made Donovan's cheeks heat up.

Tony shifted on the bed. His eyes dropped closed. He seemed completely lost in his rising pleasure and showed no hint of embarrassment as he rocked his hips and pushed his cock up into Donovan's fist, encouraging him to pick up the pace.

Pre-cum leaked from the tip of Tony's cock and slicked the strokes. Donovan stared down at him, enthralled by everything from the way his hand looked around Tony's erection, to the way Tony's abs flexed when he pushed himself up into his grip, and the ecstasy that flashed across Tony's face.

"Close."

Donovan automatically tightened his grip just a little more, the same way he did when he was alone in his own bedroom with his own cock in his hand.

Tony gasped. He arched on the bed, thrusting hard into Donovan's grip as he came.

Donovan stared down at him, wide eyed and awestruck as Tony spilled long ropes of cum across his stomach.

For several minutes after Tony fell still, they both remained locked in place, Donovan's hand still wrapped around Tony's slowly softening shaft. The important thing was to make sure he memorised every detail so that he could replay it all with perfect accuracy when he got home.

Tony opened his eyes. Suddenly, Donovan found himself thrown back into the real world — into a world where he couldn't just sit there staring at Tony for however long he wanted without worrying about what the repercussions of his recent actions might be.

As moves went, he was pretty sure his was now officially over.

As if reading his mind, Tony smiled and looked up at the cuffs. Donovan followed his gaze and saw Tony open his fist, offering him the keys.

Donovan's hands were none too steady, his fingers more than a little cum stained, but he managed to get one of the cuffs undone. Tony lowered his arms.

Donovan pulled away. He was about to stand up and put some extra distance between them when a gesture from Tony stopped him short.

"Wait there a second."

Donovan froze. He couldn't bring himself to look Tony in the eye but he couldn't make himself disobey either. He remained perched on the edge of the bed, just waiting for whatever was about to happen next to happen.

A touch to his cheek was Donovan's only warning before Tony's lips met his. The kiss was strong. Tony's mouth was firm against his, but it was the same as his earlier kisses. Every movement of Tony's lips against his seemed to be designed to make it completely clear that nothing had changed. A kiss could still be just a kiss. Nothing had to be the start of anything else.

When Tony ended the kiss, he took hold of Donovan's wrist. Donovan tensed, sure that he'd somehow misread the situation, but all Tony did was hold his hand still so he could use the discarded bath towel to clean up his fingers.

When he released Donovan's hand, Tony turned his attention to swiping at the lines of semen trailing across his stomach. Donovan didn't try to retreat again. He was still sitting on the edge of the bed when Tony tossed the towel aside.

"What about you?" Tony asked.

It was pointless to deny that he was turned on. Donovan knew his erection was clearly visible through his jeans. He'd given Tony every reason in the world to believe that he'd do whatever he wanted, and now —

"I should go," Donovan said, pulling himself jerkily to his feet.

Tony caught hold of his hand and tugged gently at his fingers. "Sit."

The breath stuck in Donovan's throat as he retook his seat.

"It's not a trick question, sweetheart," Tony promised. "All you have to do is tell me what you want? Do you want me to get you off or not? There's no wrong answer."

Donovan glanced at Tony. The voice in the back of his mind told him that wasn't the way things worked in the real world, but at the same time, it was hard to look Tony in the eye and believe that he was lying.

"Yes or no," Tony prompted.

Donovan shook his head.

"That's fine," Tony said.

Donovan had to ask. "You're sure?"

"Of course." As if the idea of him not being sure of everything was a strange, alien concept.

Donovan managed a smile.

"But you don't have to rush away just because we've gone as far as you want to go," Tony said, stroking Donovan's jaw with the fingers of his free hand.

"I should probably go anyway," Donovan whispered. "I've got a session booked at the archery range before work tomorrow."

"That's okay, too."

Donovan felt his heart gradually return to something closer to its usual pace. For now at least, Ryan's voice faded a little from the back of his mind.

"How about you just rest here with me for a few minutes while I get my breath back, and I'll drive you home?"

Donovan was reasonably sure that Tony was trying to make it sound like a question on purpose, but it somehow still sounded more like a statement of fact to Donovan's ear. He nodded his acceptance.

Tony tugged at his hand until Donovan lay down next to him, curled into his side with one of Tony's arms around his shoulders. As the seconds gradually ticked by, Donovan slowly relaxed against him. Tony still didn't seem to be the least bit bothered by the fact he was still the only naked man in the room.

* * * * *

"I thought you promised your coach you were going to live like a choir boy until Trentmoore," Colby said, the moment Tony stepped into the kitchen the following morning.

"So?" Tony asked, reaching instinctively for the coffee.

"You brought a date back here last night. I heard you leaving to drive someone home. You didn't even last three days, let alone three weeks!" Colby said.

Tony glared at his little brother as he poured his coffee. "I didn't say I wouldn't date. I promised I wasn't going to have sex." And a hand job was not sex. Tony was very sure about that and more than willing to argue the point with his coach if necessary.

Colby looked at him as if he'd lost his mind. "Haven't

you always said that dating someone you weren't having sex with was like getting a new bike for Christmas but not riding it until Easter?"

Tony glowered at him over the top of his coffee mug as he took his first sip.

"What did she—?"

"He," Tony cut in. "He's a he, not a she, and his name's Donovan Matthews."

Colby blinked at him. "The archery one? The guy finally gave in?"

"Something like that." Tony was still damned if he knew what had changed to make Donovan give him a chance, but even though it was stupidly early in the morning, he couldn't help but grin at the fact he'd actually managed to get something past a 'hello' out of him.

"What did Donovan say when you told him about your promise to Haslet?" Colby asked, his voice dripping with curiosity.

Tony stared down into his coffee.

"You haven't told him yet, have you?" Colby pushed, amusement forcing everything else out of his tone.

Tony pointedly ignored him.

"Who hasn't told who what?" Noah enquired, from the kitchen doorway. His hair was sleep mussed. He headed for the coffee just as quickly as Tony had.

"Tony hasn't told Donovan that he can't have sex with him until after the Trentmoore meet," Colby said. If he noticed the way Tony shot daggers at him, it didn't make any noticeable difference.

"Obviously, darling."

Tony was aware that he and Colby both turned their full attention to Noah at that point, but Noah had his back to them and seemed not to realise everyone else in the room was focused of him.

"Obviously?" Colby prompted.

"No guy wants to tell a potential lover he's pretty much

signed control of his cock over to another man. You can play that kind of bull off as a joke with friends and little brothers, but..." He shook his head. "No, it would be like telling his date he was wearing a chastity belt and his coach is his key holder. Not a good first impression." Noah took a deep pull from his coffee cup and finally turned to face them.

Tony didn't look toward Colby, mostly because he was pretty sure that his little brother would be grinning like an idiot at Noah's description of his supposed predicament.

"I'm not going to tell Donovan about it because it's irrelevant. He's not the kind of guy who falls straight into bed with someone," Tony said. "We wouldn't be having sex in the next few weeks even if Haslet didn't want to teach me a lesson about checking texts in meetings."

Noah raised an eyebrow at him. "That's the only reason?"

Donovan's important. I'd cut off my right arm rather than risk doing anything that might screw things up with him, and if that means breaking my promise to my coach the moment Donovan wants me to, I won't hesitate for a second. Tony huffed. He'd cut off a few things before saying any of that out loud in front of Colby or Noah, too.

He glared at Noah. "You know, I liked you much better when you were too worried about pissing off any member of Colby's family to get sarcastic with me."

Chapter Three

Tony smiled when he drove around the corner and spotted the signpost for the archery centre, then he promptly rolled his eyes at himself. Bloody hell, he was getting as soppy as Colby. The realisation did nothing to help him feel in control of his emotions. He'd always known his interest in Donovan was more intense than what he'd felt for the other men and women he'd dated, but this was getting crazy.

A group of people were standing outside the main door leading into the centre. Donovan was easy to spot. He had his back toward the road, but Tony had spent months staring at his arse, he'd know it anywhere.

As he drove closer, Donovan must have heard the engine. He looked over his shoulder. Saying a few quick words to the people he'd been chatting to, he turned and left the group without a backward glance.

Leaning across the car, Tony pushed the passenger door open for him. "Hi."

Donovan slid into the car. "Hi."

At some point over the last week, Donovan's nerves had come back. Tony glanced across at him as he pulled away from the kerb. Donovan had been carrying his jacket. It now lay across his lap and he appeared to be completely fascinated by the folds in the dark blue fabric.

"Good day?" Tony asked.

Donovan nodded. He nibbled on his bottom lip.

Tony turned the corner, making his way around the edge of the car park, toward the exit.

"Bad training session?" Tony hazarded.

Donovan shook his head and fiddled with the sleeve of

his jacket.

It was like being thrown back to those months when Donovan refused to even give him the time of day—which was both terrifying and making it damn near impossible to have a conversation while driving.

Tony pulled into an empty parking space.

Donovan tensed, but he didn't even glance in Tony's direction.

"Tell me what's wrong," Tony ordered.

Donovan studied the dashboard.

"Donovan?" Tony nudged.

"Whose move is it?" Donovan blurted out.

"Yours," Tony said, without making any effort to work out if that was in any way accurate.

Donovan nodded slowly, as if taking time to settle that fact in his mind. A little of his tension faded.

Tony found his free hand curling into a fist on his lap. Damn, but it was a good thing he didn't know who Donovan's ex was. Intentionally or not, the guy had done one hell of a number on Donovan.

"Believe it or not, sweetheart, I'm not a complete bastard."

Donovan did look up then, his eyes full of confusion.

"I'm not going to rush you into anything you're not ready for," Tony expanded.

Donovan nibbled on his bottom lip. "I…"

Unable to let him struggle, Tony dipped his head and brushed their lips together in a gentle kiss. That seemed to calm Donovan's nerves far more quickly than any of his clumsy attempts at verbal reassurance.

"I don't think you're a complete bastard," Donovan whispered, as Tony broke the kiss. His tone of voice was completely different now. Almost every trace of tension was gone.

"So what then?" Tony asked, gentling his voice in an effort to match Donovan's more hushed tone.

"I think you're perfect," Donovan said, very simply.

Tony smiled down at him as he filed that statement away to be enjoyed later. "I'm not that, either. But what I meant is — am I doing something in particular to make you nervous?"

Donovan lowered his head. His temple came to rest on Tony's cheekbone. "You're not doing anything. I'm just being an idiot."

Tony quickly pulled back and slid his knuckles under Donovan's chin to make him look up. "No, you're not." His tone allowed for no disagreement on the matter.

Donovan glanced up at him through his lashes. He didn't argue the point. He tilted his face up for another kiss.

It was such a sweet little request for reassurance; Tony couldn't have refused it for the world. He brushed their lips together, slow and tender. He did his best to make it chaste, but God it was hard to make even a single second about something other than sex when Donovan called to him in ways no other man or woman ever had. Tony finally convinced himself to pull away.

He had no interest in sharing Donovan with a pub full of men. "My place or yours?"

"Yours," Donovan said, with apparent calm, as he straightened in his seat and turned to face the windscreen. He seemed to be at ease now, as if he had somehow made room for their date inside his head. Or maybe as if he'd thought himself into a worry when they were apart, only to realise there was nothing to worry about once they were back together.

He still seemed to be relaxed, or at least as relaxed as Tony had ever seen him get, when they stepped into the flat.

All Tony's past experiences told him the appropriate thing to do was to grab Donovan and take him straight back to his bedroom.

Tony glanced at Donovan. All his previous experience with other people didn't count for a damn thing. Tony had never felt more clueless in his life, or more certain that one wrong move on his part would have his date walking out of his life, never to be seen again. The sight of the kitchen gave him inspiration.

"Coffee?"

Donovan nodded. "Thank you."

As he made it, Tony kept a careful eye on Donovan, trying to work out what the hell was going on in his head and where he should be trying to lead the date.

Conversation. Non-threatening, non-flirtatious, conversation. He could do that—probably. He wiped his hands on his jeans as his palms turned damp.

"Does your family live around here, or did you move here for the institute?" As a first attempt, Tony didn't think that was too bad.

Donovan glanced at him before turning his attention to an apparently detailed study of the kitchen worktop. "My parents are divorced. My dad lives up in Yorkshire now, but my mum and my stepdad are only about fifty miles away."

"Are you close?" Tony asked, cautiously, as he handed over one of the cups.

"Not so much with my dad," Donovan said. He leaned back against the counter and studied his coffee for a few seconds. When he looked up, he met Tony's gaze and smiled slightly. "Not because he has a problem with me being gay. We just..."

A tiny frown appeared between his eyebrows. It took all of Tony's self-control to remain leaning against the cabinet on his side of the kitchen and give Donovan time to speak, rather than step forward and kiss the frown away.

"I don't think he's ever forgiven me for quitting football. Archery isn't really his kind of sport." His tone of voice was light, but the look in his eyes made his flippancy sound painfully false. He'd been more comfortable talking about being gay.

"How did you come out?" Tony asked.

"Unexpectedly," Donovan said with a slight smile. "I'd...um...I'd been trying to work out how to break the news to my mum and my stepdad for months. Then one Sunday, the three of us are sitting around the dinner table and my mum just asks me outright—are you gay? I was so shocked I blurted out—yes. And that was pretty much it."

Tony's couldn't help but smile at the rueful note in Donovan's voice. "No one knew before then?"

It was like someone pulled the plug. The light drained out of Donovan's smile. "Only one guy—I didn't actually come out to him either. He guessed, too."

There was no doubt in Tony's mind; they were talking about the guy Donovan had sex with. His grip on his coffee mug turned white-knuckled.

Tony hesitated, knowing he needed to ask, but damned if he could think of the right words to frame the question. He took a deep breath. "When we spoke about him before, I'm not sure you told me the whole story."

Donovan tensed as if Tony had slapped him.

"Did he...hurt you?" Tony asked, as gently as he knew how.

Donovan shook his head. "No." It didn't sound like the truth.

Tony stared down into his coffee. It was pretty much their second date. Calling him on that lie when he hadn't a chance to prove that Donovan could trust him with the truth, whatever that was, was unthinkable. Letting the lie pass was—

"It wasn't... I agreed to everything that happened between us. He never forced me to do anything. But..."

But, Tony thought—that was the important word.

"He...wasn't the most pleasant of people," Donovan said softly. "My memories of my time with him...aren't good."

"Was he kinky?" Tony asked.

Donovan shook his head so firmly, his entire body

seemed to move with the gesture. "He was nothing like you. You're nothing like him." He sounded very certain about that, but also as if he was working very hard at maintaining that certainty. "I'd prefer not to talk about it." Donovan's Adam's apple bobbed as he swallowed several times in quick succession. "Please?"

It was the plea that did it; Tony had never heard a man sound so close to bolting. Needing to find a different topic, fast, Tony grabbed the first one that came to mind. "How did you get into it—the archery, I mean?"

Donovan smiled, so relieved—perhaps not just by the change of topic, but because Tony had changed it the moment Donovan had asked him to.

Tony watched while Donovan took a moment to pull himself together. When he spoke, he sounded as if he'd successfully dragged himself out of the headspace that had scared him so much and was mentally back with Tony.

"The year he married my mum, my stepdad bought me an archery taster course for my birthday." A touch of colour rose to his cheeks making him look far healthier than he had a few minutes before. "I...um...I was really into the whole Lord of the Rings thing at the time. I used to spend hours watching the DVDs over and over again..."

Tony grinned as he filled in the blanks the way a parent with a supposedly straight son couldn't have. "You mean, you liked watching the movies and crushing on the pretty elves, but your stepdad thought you were admiring their skills with a bow and arrow."

The blush deepened, but amusement danced in Donovan's eyes as well. "Something like that. I was fifteen. I wasn't even out, let alone..."

"Let alone willing to admit to an interest in elf porn to a grown up?" Tony asked.

Donovan let out a burst of laughter. "Yeah. I mean, we get along great, and he didn't even blink when I came out as gay, but there are some conversations that just shouldn't happen."

"You'd make a cute elf," Tony said, tilting his head to one side and making a point of assessing him very carefully.

Donovan dropped his gaze, but he smiled at the teasing, too. Tony had won national sprinting competitions and felt less like a champion. He was the one who'd made Donovan smile, and laugh, and relax.

"Tie me up."

Tony sipped his coffee as he tried to work out what the hell to say to that. Fantasies. Porn. Bondage. Perhaps it wasn't that big a leap, really.

Donovan cleared his throat. "What we did last time, but this time, put the cuffs on me instead?" His glance up at Tony was so quick, so fleeting. His sudden lack of confidence tore at something in Tony.

"You know there's no rush, right?" Tony said.

Even though he was already leaning against the kitchen counter and couldn't possibly back away, Donovan gave the impression of retreating several paces, just as he had when Tony asked him about his ex.

Tony instinctively stepped forward to stand directly in front of him. "Donovan?"

"I'm sorry. I got the impression you might want to—"

Tony put a fingertip over Donovan's lips. "Yes."

The simplicity of the answer seemed to prompt Donovan to lift his gaze, if only to work out what was going on.

"Yes, I do want to tie you up. I've wanted to do that from the very first moment I saw you." He held Donovan's gaze, refusing to act like he thought that desire was anything to be ashamed of. "But I'll still want that next week, or next month." He kept *next year* back through sheer force of will, not about to scare Donovan with predictions about the future and predilections toward bondage at the same time. "And what I want doesn't mean a damn thing, unless you want it too."

Donovan stared up at him, unblinking.

"There's no rush," Tony promised him, as he took his finger away from Donovan's mouth. "And there's no need for us to get kinky at all, unless you want us to."

Donovan stared at Tony's shoulder for what seemed like a very long time, and all Tony could do was wait for his verdict.

"I do want to. And, if you don't mind, I'd prefer not to wait. I'd like to do this now," Donovan whispered.

"Any particular reason?" Tony asked, carefully.

* * * * *

Because I don't think I'll be brave enough to let you tie me up after Trentmoore.

Donovan couldn't say that. He took a deep breath and tried to think of something else to say, something that would make sense.

If Tony hadn't been standing directly in front of him, he was pretty sure he'd have given way to an inclination to pace. As it was, there was little he could do to expel his nervous energy.

He wanted this. If there was one thing he was sure of; it was that he wanted this. He wanted to feel the cuffs around his wrists and know that he'd made the only decision he needed to make. He wanted the fantasy he'd seen in so many internet videos. But, God help him, he really wanted all that to happen while Tony's promise to his coach meant that there were certain things that Tony couldn't decide to do to him while he was tied up.

"Donovan?" Tony prompted.

Donovan took another deep breath. "I want this." That was as true as anything could be. "Ever since we... Ever since you wore the cuffs that night, I can't stop thinking about what it would have been like if I'd been the one wearing them." He cleared his throat. "I can't sleep for thinking about it. Every time I close my eyes, I see how it might be. And, I think I'll

206

love the way it feels, but I can't know for sure until I try it. And I need to know."

He looked up and met Tony's gaze. Instinct kicked in almost immediately, pushing him to drop his gaze, but Donovan fought against it. He needed Tony to understand, even if he didn't really understand it all himself.

"Please?" Donovan whispered.

Tony dipped his head. It was nothing like the kiss in the car. That had been gentle and sweet—this was everything that kiss hadn't been but which Donovan had wished it was. One of Tony's hands slid into Donovan's hair and took a steady grip on the strands, holding his head at just the right angle for Tony to be able to explore his mouth just as he wanted.

As Donovan leaned into the kiss, their bodies rubbed together. With their bodies lined up as they were, it was impossible to believe that what he'd said to Tony hadn't appealed to at least part of him. Tony's cock was just as hard as Donovan's was.

When Tony broke the kiss, it was only to move his lips alongside Donovan's ear and whisper to him. "There's very little I won't do if you ask me to in that tone of voice." The whisper was so rough, it sounded more like a growl than anything else.

Donovan gasped for breath. At some point, he'd moved his hands to rest on Tony's shoulders. Each of his fists was wrapped around a handful of Tony's shirt. Slowly, having to concentrate in order to find any kind of coordination, Donovan released his hold on Tony and flattened down the material.

Tony smiled as he slid his fingers through Donovan's hair. When he spoke again, his tone was different, as if he was making an effort to be practical and sensible no matter how turned on he might be. "Sometimes, a guy might like the idea of being tied up, but when he actually tries it, it can freak him out."

Donovan stared up at Tony, wanting to promise he wouldn't be one of those guys, but not sure he'd actually be able to follow through on any such claim.

"And that's fine," Tony went on. "If you ask me to take the cuffs off, I will—that's not a problem. But, if we're going to do this, I need to know that you will tell me the moment you want the cuffs taken off. Can you do that?"

Donovan nodded.

"I'm serious about this, sweetheart," Tony said, stroking his fingers through Donovan's hair again. "It's important."

Donovan stared at Tony's shirt for a few moments. "I can promise to do that, but…" He took a deep breath. "If I do freak out, I'm pretty sure it will be as obvious as hell without me needing to say a word."

Tony continued to card his fingers through his hair. "What do you think the chances of you panicking are?"

Donovan swallowed. "High."

"But you're still sure you want to do this?" Tony checked.

Donovan nodded. "I'm sure." He'd never been more certain of what he wanted in his life. He just wasn't so sure he could cope with getting what he wanted.

Tony took one of Donovan's wrists in his grip. His fingers wrapped all the way around until the tip of his index finger touched his thumb, creating a complete loop. Donovan stared, completely captivated. Without thinking about it, he offered his other wrist up to Tony's other hand.

"Perfect," Tony murmured, mirroring his grip on Donovan's left wrist. "Ready to play, sweetheart?"

Donovan nodded again, still completely focused on the sight of his skin in Tony's grip.

Tony stepped back without releasing either of Donovan's wrists. Another step back, a tug, and Donovan went with him. In order to maintain his grip on Donovan, Tony had to walk backwards, but that didn't seem to dent his confidence. He moved with complete certainty, as if nothing could ever faze him, could ever scare him. Donovan had never seen anything so beautiful in his life.

Tony opened his bedroom door with an elbow against the handle. A moment later, the door was closed behind them, and they were all alone in the world.

Tony still had a small smile playing around his lips.

"I'm going to have to let go of you for a second or two, but you're not to take that as permission to wander off, understand?"

The teasing made Donovan smile. If Tony was relaxed enough about it all to joke, it seemed silly for him to cling so tightly to his own nervousness. Ryan had never teased about things like that.

Tony released Donovan's wrists and scooped up the cuffs from the bedside table. In just a few seconds, it was all done. Donovan went seamlessly from standing in front of Tony to lying on the bed with his hands cuffed to the headboard.

Donovan looked up at his wrists, quietly fascinated by the sight of them restrained that way for the first time. Tony didn't pull his hand away as soon as the lock snapped into place. He stroked his thumb across the inside of Donovan's wrist, just below the line of the cuff, where his pulse raced beneath his skin.

Donovan swallowed, wondering if Tony could feel how fast his heart was pounding, wondering what Tony would think of it if he could.

Very slowly, Tony trailed his fingers down Donovan's arms, over the fabric of his long sleeved Falconer T-shirt, until he reached the neck line. From there, he ran his fingers up underneath Donovan's jaw.

"Now that I've got you all tied up, what should I do with you?"

Donovan met his gaze for a moment, then looked away.

"Any ideas?" Tony asked. His fingers stroked back and

forth up the line of Donovan's neck, making it impossible for Donovan to think, let alone speak. He shook his head.

"No ideas at all?" Tony asked.

Donovan licked his lips. "It's your move." The words came out softer than he intended, little more than a whisper.

Tony sat on the bed just where Donovan had sat when Tony was bound the same way. Except, when Tony had been cuffed there, he'd worn nothing more than a towel. Donovan nibbled at his bottom lip, wondering if he should have offered to undress before they got out the handcuffs, but the very idea of it sent a blush to his cheeks.

Any hope that his heightened colour was subtle enough to escape Tony's notice died when Tony brushed his knuckle across the heated skin.

"Tell me," Tony ordered.

Donovan glanced up at him. Refusing to answer was out of the question. If Tony wanted to know, it wasn't in Donovan not to try and give him what he wanted.

"I realised I'm not dressed quite the same way you were when we did this before," he whispered.

Tony smiled. "True."

Ryan would have been pissed with him for not thinking of that before they got started. Tony seemed to find the difference interesting. He slid his hand away from Donovan's face and down to rest on the neckline of his shirt. From there, he kept trailing his hand lower, brushing over the fabric. It was all Donovan could do not to squirm in an effort to push himself up and gain a firmer touch.

"Fewer clothes could be arranged," Tony offered.

Donovan glanced up. His gaze locked with Tony's and he suddenly found it impossible to look away.

Tony hadn't actually asked a question, but it was obvious that he wanted an answer. His fingers stilled on the hem of Donovan's shirt. Several seconds passed and Donovan realised that this was as far as anything was going to go until he said something.

Another realisation came quickly on its heels. If he said no, Tony wouldn't go any further. As he looked up at Tony, it couldn't have been clearer that Tony was completely in control of every action he made. There was no getting carried away for Tony; there was no runaway chain reaction that might send everything to hell.

Maybe it was because his promise to his coach was right in the front of his mind and that changed everything, but Donovan couldn't imagine Tony being anything other than completely in control of every action he ever made. He'd been right when he said that Tony was nothing like Ryan.

Donovan nodded. "Yes." He could do this.

Tony didn't say anything. There was no praise for being good, no suggestion that any answer he could have given would have been any less acceptable.

Donovan squirmed on the bed as best he could, trying to make it easier for Tony to pull his shirt up his body and over his head.

The cuffs made it impossible for Tony to push the shirt completely off. It bunched around his forearms, but Tony wasn't looking at the fabric, his attention was all on the bare skin he'd just revealed.

Donovan watched carefully for his reaction. Even if he stacked up okay against most guys, Donovan was well aware that Tony was in another league again. Archery didn't require the deep, perfect lines of muscle that Tony carried. Donovan was paler than Tony, and more lightly built, and none of that mattered because Tony had dipped his head and brought their lips together.

Tony balanced himself with apparent ease, his hands on the mattress either side of Donovan, but he didn't linger over the kiss. When Tony pulled away, Donovan tried to lift his head off the pillow and bring their mouths back together. Tony either didn't notice or wasn't inclined to grant that particular request. He placed a kiss against Donovan's jawline instead, then another on his neck.

Donovan helpfully tilted his head back, baring his neck for Tony. Another kiss, lower down his neck, just above his collarbone, and this time Tony sucked against the skin very gently. It felt like a test, to gauge Donovan's response more than anything else. Donovan turned his head to the side, making it clear he welcomed whatever Tony wanted to do with his neck.

Apparently, Tony believed him. Donovan closed his eyes as Tony placed a love bite on his skin, low enough for it to be hidden by most necklines. He gasped as Tony nipped at the skin he'd just kissed, before pulling away, moving further down Donovan's body.

There was stubble lingering on Tony's jawline. It scraped against the smooth skin across Donovan's chest as he kissed him. His movements were all very slow, very controlled, as if he purposely wanted to give Donovan time to object at every turn.

Lifting his head, Donovan peered down at him. At almost the same moment, Tony looked up.

Smiling, Tony pressed another kiss against the centre of his chest. His hands came to rest on Donovan's waist and ran up his sides, making Donovan wriggle, trying to push himself into both hands at the same time.

Tony chuckled against Donovan's sternum and dropped another kiss onto the skin there.

"Do you like being tied up as much as you thought you would, sweetheart?"

Donovan nodded.

"Out loud," Tony corrected.

"Yes," Donovan managed to whisper. "I like it." *And I'm not freaking out. I can do this without panicking. I can do this…*

There was a part of Donovan which wanted to yell out with the sheer joy of finally knowing that. He could do this.

Tony trailed his way across Donovan's chest until his lips brushed across one of Donovan's nipples.

The breath stalled in Donovan's lungs as Tony circled

his nipple with his tongue before closing his lips around it and sucking firmly. Electricity crackled through Donovan's body. He'd never felt anything like it, never guessed that something like that could feel so good.

Donovan let out a whimper. He couldn't hold Tony's gaze, but every time he looked back to him, Tony was still watching his face.

"What do you like about it?"

Donovan blinked at Tony.

Tony blew across the nipple he'd been toying with, making him shiver. "What do you like about being tied up?"

Donovan just stared at him. Tony wanted him to talk and make sense now?

Tony smiled, as if he knew he was asking for something damn near impossible, but still as if he expected to get what he wanted all the same.

"I can't do anything wrong," Donovan blurted out.

Tony trailed kisses across to Donovan's other nipple and took it into his mouth. "You didn't do anything wrong when I was the one who was tied up," he pointed out, as he eventually pulled back, blew across the kissed skin and made Donovan shudder with pleasure. "I've never known you to do anything wrong, full stop." He traced his way back to the centre of Donovan's chest.

"I..." was all Donovan managed.

Tony made a vague noise in the back of his throat, as if encouraging Donovan to keep trying to speak.

"I...I like being able to let go. I like knowing you're in control." He said the words so softly, he wasn't even sure Tony would be able to hear them. Even as close as they were to each other, the words seemed so insubstantial as to be irrelevant.

"Completely in control," Tony said. Looking up, he caught Donovan's eye and held it. "You never need to doubt that, sweetheart."

Donovan took a deep breath as he felt himself relax.

Tony understood, and Tony was nothing like Ryan.

Straightening up, Tony ran his hands over Donovan's torso, setting millions of nerve endings alight with every movement of his hands, and there was nothing Donovan could do but lie there and accept it. That fact combined with every touch, making each one all the more perfect.

"Has anyone ever gone down on you?" Tony asked.

Donovan opened his mouth, then he closed his mouth. He completely failed to utter a word between times. Images of his cock and Tony's mouth getting intimately acquainted filled his mind and made complicated things like syllables impossible. He took refuge in shaking his head.

"Have you ever gone down on another guy?" Tony asked.

* * * * *

The second the words left his mouth, Tony knew he'd made a mistake. All at once, every muscle in Donovan's body knotted up. He stilled beneath Tony's hands, no longer trying to move and compliment every offered caress.

For a long time, Donovan remained frozen in place. He broke that spell with a nod, but he didn't relax in the slightest.

Donovan's words from earlier floated up to the front of Tony's mind. *My memories of my time with him…aren't good.*

Tony carefully kept his own reaction in check. He didn't let any of his anger at the man who gave Donovan those kinds of memories show in his expression. No hint of his own tension made it through into his body language. He didn't even allow himself to show the slightest concern for Donovan. He was sure that concern wasn't what Donovan was looking to him for.

Moving up the bed, Tony brushed his lips against Donovan's. He did his best to make the kiss reassuring, but not too obviously sweet. Donovan helped by parting his lips almost immediately, welcoming him in, making it obvious that he relished the actual kiss as well as the comfort Tony wanted to provide.

Very slowly, Donovan started to relax again.

"Have you ever imagined me going down on you?" Tony whispered, when it finally seemed safe to trail kisses back towards Donovan's ear.

"I..." Donovan gave up on words and nodded. A little bit of his tension came back, but that seemed more of a natural response, as if Donovan was just a little wary, unsure if Tony would be pleased with him for fantasising about that or not.

"I've imagined it," Tony said. "I've pictured you exactly as you are so many times. And I've imagined taking your cock in my mouth, sucking around you until you're squirming and desperate to come."

Donovan whimpered. He rocked his hips as if trying to find Tony's mouth in the most basic of ways.

"Shall I do that, sweetheart?" Tony whispered to him, pulling back so he could look him in the eye.

Donovan bit his bottom lip. "Whatever you want."

Tony shook his head. "Yes or no. If you don't say yes, it doesn't happen."

Donovan's eyes opened wide. A touch of uncertainty came back, but it seemed to revolve around the fear that his lover might retract the offer of a blow job at the last minute.

"Yes or no," Tony repeated.

"Yes." The word sounded stronger than damn near any other he'd uttered since the handcuffs had been brought out.

Tony ran his knuckles over the line of Donovan's erection through his track suit bottoms. Perhaps it wasn't a huge success to get a man who was that turned on to admit that he wanted a blow job, but it felt like a huge victory to Tony in that moment.

Donovan wanted this. Donovan wanted him. And Donovan trusted him enough to state both things out loud.

Pushing down his inner tease, Tony didn't waste any time before he undid the draw string at the top of Donovan's track suit bottoms, and pulled the fabric down.

Catching Donovan's boxers along the way, Tony quickly had Donovan completely bare all the way down to his knees.

Donovan cooperated and lifted his hips off the bed to make it easier for Tony to half-undress him, but at the same time, Tony couldn't help but be aware that Donovan wasn't the kind of guy who'd find it easy to be exposed in front of anyone for the first time.

Happily, there was one very easy way to distract him from any fleeting embarrassment. Tony immediately dipped his head and wrapped his lips around the tip of Donovan's cock.

A gasp made him look up. The surprise on Donovan's face quickly gave way to pleasure as Tony swirled his tongue around the head and teased his foreskin.

It had been so long since he'd dated anyone who was inexperienced enough to find a blow job shocking, Tony couldn't help but slow everything down to give himself time to admire each reaction. There was a simple honesty in Donovan that none of Tony's previous lovers could claim. Everything he felt passed across his face, and it was gorgeous.

Tony dipped his head, taking Donovan deeper, letting the glans rub against the back of his mouth. Both his hands rested on Donovan's hipbones, steadying him and supporting him. His own cock throbbed inside his jeans as every reaction Donovan offered dropped straight to his crotch. The taste of Donovan's pre-cum leaking onto his tongue made Tony moan his approval around his shaft.

Donovan arched, tugging at the cuffs. Tony would have grinned, if he hadn't been keeping his teeth carefully covered by his lips. He wondered if Donovan would have reached out to him if he hadn't been bound. It was easy to imagine Donovan's fingers in his hair, all his manners forgotten in favour of trying to hold his lover in place and make sure that he didn't vanish like a mirage before he came.

Damn, but it was just as easy to imagine Donovan fumbling at the blankets on either side of his body, grabbing fistfuls of fabric as he fought against that instinct to reach out, not wanting to take that kind of control over what was happening between them, because... Well, what other reason could there really be apart from the obvious one? Inexperienced and shy as hell, perhaps. Hurt in the past, definitely. But Donovan was also beautifully eager to follow rather than lead.

Tony moaned his approval around Donovan's cock once more, making Donovan whimper and thrust up into his mouth. Tony easily stilled Donovan's movements, pressing him down against the bed and holding him motionless so he could go down on him exactly as he pleased.

A good memory—that was important. It was obvious that the last guy Donovan had been with hadn't bothered to try to make anything good for Donovan. Hell, Donovan had said the guy hadn't even gone down on him.

This time Tony was going to make sure he had a good memory.

Slow enough to make sure Donovan had plenty of time to enjoy the ride; quick enough that he didn't drive Donovan too mad with frustration. Tony kept his gaze on Donovan's face, doing his damnedest to read every thought out of Donovan's head and adjust his actions accordingly. He never remembered being so intently focused on a lover, so determined to make everything absolutely perfect for another person.

Donovan twisted, pushing against Tony hands, trying to rock his hips and get more friction, more depth. Tony held him in place as he dipped his head more rapidly; letting Donovan have exactly what he wanted, while making damn sure Donovan remained certain who was in control of those kinds of decisions.

"Please..." The word was just on the edge of hearing. Donovan lifted his head and peered down at Tony. "Please?"

It wasn't so much the word, it was the way it was said. It sounded less like he was begging for an orgasm, and more like he was praying that Tony would prove that Donovan had been right to trust him when he put himself in his hands and gave up control to him.

Not—*please let me come*. It felt more like—*please make the right decision for me when you decide if I should be allowed to come*.

Nothing the most experienced lover could have done would have been better calculated to grab Tony's inner dom by the throat. Almost without thinking about it, he bobbed his head lower still, taking the tip of Donovan's cock into his throat as he brought him off in a few easy movements.

Donovan tossed his head back, but he didn't scream. Tony was reasonably sure that was because Donovan had completely forgotten how to breathe.

Swallowing rapidly around Donovan's cock, Tony took every drop that was offered with practiced ease. Even as he watched Donovan come slowly back to earth, Tony kept his lips around Donovan's softening cock, simply holding him in his mouth.

He didn't lift his head until Donovan looked down and made eye contact. He looked so bloody awestruck, and that didn't change at all as Tony let Donovan's shaft slip from between his lips. Donovan stared at him as if he was a not so minor miracle.

Tony tried to remember how he'd felt after his first blow job. It was a long time ago, with a girl in the back seat of his parents' car—of all the bloody awful clichés! One thing Tony was sure of—he hadn't looked anything like as angelic as Donovan afterwards.

Tony straightened up. Donovan lifted his gaze and tracked his movements. For the first time since they met, eye contact seemed to be easy for him. There were no nerves, no signs of hesitation in him now. Wonderful stuff, afterglow.

Donovan's tongue snuck out to moisten his lips.

Tony couldn't resist, he leaned down and brushed their

mouths together, soft and sweet. He didn't make any attempt to deepen the kiss until Donovan traced his tongue across his bottom lip and shyly asked for more.

Parting his lips, Tony let Donovan steal a taste. And there it was; a stunned little gasp—the first time Donovan ever tasted himself in another man's mouth.

Tony didn't pull away. He kept the kiss going, until Donovan once more gained the courage to try to deepen it. A pleased little whimper filled the air, letting him know just how much Donovan loved the simple intimacy of a shared taste.

Finally, Tony forced himself to sit up straight.

Donovan blinked at him, staring at his mouth as if it was the eighth wonder. It wasn't until Tony saw the blush touch Donovan's cheeks that he knew Donovan was back with him.

A glance down—but there was nothing submissive about it. Donovan's attention went straight to Tony's crotch and the way his erection tented his jeans.

Donovan nibbled at his bottom lip. "If you'll uncuff me, I can sit up and…"

Tony stared down at him. Maybe it was possible to get away with the theory that oral wasn't really sex, no matter who was getting sucked off, or—

Oh, to hell with it, Tony knew damn well that if Donovan had been ready, as well as willing, to have any kind of sex with him, he'd have gone for it and to hell with Haslet.

The uncertainty in Donovan's voice was the only thing that stopped him short.

"I'll uncuff you, but we've both made all the moves we're going to make tonight."

Donovan glanced down at Tony's crotch once more.

Tony pretended not to notice. He turned his own attention to Donovan's body. He ran his eyes over him, taking in every inch of bare skin from his knees all the way up to where his shirt was still wrapped around his forearms. Bloody gorgeous.

A tiny shift as Donovan fought against the instinct to squirm under his gaze, and Tony reluctantly abandoned his inspection but, rather than reach for the handcuffs, he reached for Donovan's clothes.

It only took him a few moments to have Donovan's track suit trousers pulled up. It turned out to be far less easy to get his shirt back down over his head, but a little bit of fumbling and a lot of helpful wriggling on Donovan's part finally got everything where it should be.

Unlocking the cuffs, Tony helped Donovan to sit up. No time for nerves, no opportunity for Donovan to wonder exactly how to leave a guy's flat with style when they were done. Tony kissed Donovan before he had a chance to say anything. This time he didn't try to make the kiss sweet or innocent. Then, while Donovan was still blinking in the aftermath of that kiss, it was easy for Tony to take complete control of the drive back to Donovan's flat.

Chapter Four

"I'm so sorry!"

Tony raised an eyebrow. It wasn't quite the greeting he'd expected when he arrived at Donovan's flat to collect him for their third date.

"I wanted to text you, but I haven't been able to grab a minute, and—"

"Calm down," Tony cut in. They'd been effectively dating for three weeks, and even if they hadn't managed to meet up too often during that time, Tony was starting to get quite used to Donovan's nerves peaking at the start of each date. Stepping into the flat, he politely nudged Donovan back until he had room to close the door behind him. "Tell me what's wrong."

Donovan shook his head. "Nothing's wrong. I just..." He glanced over his shoulder. "Something's come up. I can't make it tonight after all, and I—"

Tony put one hand on Donovan's cheek and another on his shoulder. "Calm," he repeated. "You need to take a rain check on tonight?"

Donovan nodded.

"That's fine, sweetheart. It's not the end of the world."

"Yes, it is," Donovan hissed, with another look over his shoulder. "I... You... We were going to—"

Tony smiled. Donovan had obviously had very definite plans for that night. "We can do whatever you want, tomorrow, or another night. It's fine."

Donovan shook his head. He looked so bloody heartbroken.

"Hey! It's fine. I promise." Tony dipped his head and

brought their lips together in as sweet a kiss as he knew how to give. "Everything's fine."

"At least this explains why you've sounded so distracted the last couple of weeks."

Tony froze. He felt Donovan tense. A glance over Donovan's shoulder and he saw a woman standing in the doorway leading back to Donovan's living room. For a moment, he harboured the hope that she was just one of Donovan's friends from the archery department, but she looked to be in her late forties, and she had the same light brown hair and hazel eyes as Donovan. Her lips were pressed tight together, as if she was trying to hold back her amusement and only just succeeding. She looked suspiciously like the kind of woman who would take outing her son over Sunday dinner in her stride.

"Everything's fine," Tony whispered to Donovan, and hoped like hell he was telling the truth. He squeezed Donovan's shoulder as he took half a step back and put a little distance between them.

Parents. Okay. He could do this. Tony stepped forward with his hand held out. "Hello, you must be Mrs. —" Tony stopped himself short. Damn. Remarried. "I'm sorry, I'm not sure if the surname is the same?"

"Anna Marshal." She shook hands with him as another person joined her in the doorway. He looked about the same age as Anna, and seemed to share her amusement with the situation.

"Fred Marshal," the man said, also holding out his hand to be shaken.

"Tony Landon. I'm in the athletics programme here." In that moment, it was the only perfectly unobjectionable fact about himself that he could think to offer up.

Parents. Suddenly, he understood why Noah had been so petrified at meeting the rest of his and Colby's family.

Tony kept a friendly, relaxed smile pinned to his lips as he frantically tried to work out what the hell he was supposed to do now.

"You didn't mention you were dating anyone." That was Anna—and it was said to Donovan, rather than Tony.

One glance at Donovan, and Tony was reasonably sure that there was no way in hell Donovan was up to answering for himself. Tony held out a hand to him and, just as he suspected, instinct, or perhaps good manners, kicked in. Donovan stepped forward to take his hand.

"We haven't been dating that long," Tony said, with a reassuring smile down at Donovan. He squeezed Donovan's fingers, promising him that everything would be fine.

Donovan offered him a far more nervous smile in return.

"So, the athletics programme?"

Tony tore his gaze away from Donovan. "Yes. I'm on the athletics team—the two hundred and four hundred metre sprints, and the four hundred metre relay."

When Donovan's parents retraced their steps to a small living room, there didn't seem to be much to do except follow along and make the best of it. If he was aware that he'd have felt a somewhat ignoble inclination to get the hell out of there if he was with anyone else, then the fact he was with Donovan made him feel more protective than he'd ever thought possible.

Tony took a seat on the sofa as if it was the most natural thing in the world, keeping hold of Donovan's hand. It was something like sitting opposite his parents at the kitchen table back home. Tony had the horrible suspicion he'd be lucky to get out of there without being grounded.

"So, where did you two meet?" Donovan's mother asked.

Institute dining hall. I spotted Donovan the first moment he walked in and kept hitting on him every time I saw him, until he finally gave in and let me buy him a drink. No—that wasn't the right answer, even if it was an honest one. Damn.

Another truth then. No lies, just skirt around the bits

parents probably didn't need to know about. "The institute's not that big a place. We saw each other around a few times before, but I don't think we really got a chance to speak properly until we were at one of the institute's fundraising events. Right?"

Donovan nodded.

Tony was reasonably sure he would have agreed with a statement that they'd first met when little green men abducted them both and flew them off to Mars for the weekend.

"They had everything arranged alphabetically by department. Athletics was next door to archery," Tony said. Flirtation had been made slightly more difficult by the fact Donovan had quickly retreated to the far side of the archery section and hadn't come back within earshot the whole evening.

Tony tightened his grip around Donovan's fingers. When he looked down, Donovan was looking up at him. His nerves seemed to have eased slightly. Now he only looked as if the world was going to end at some point that day, rather than at that very moment.

Parents. Conversation. Tony turned his attention back to Anna and Fred. This time, his attention settled on Fred. "Donovan mentioned that you were the one who got him into archery."

Providing he remembered to avoid the whole elf-porn thing, that was another safe topic, right? It even had the additional benefit of making it sound like he and Donovan spent a large portion of their time talking about perfectly innocent things.

Maybe this talking to Donovan's parents thing wasn't going to be so bad after all…

* * * * *

Donovan knew that his mum and stepdad couldn't have actually been there for several consecutive hours, but by the time he walked them to the door, it seemed like they had. Alone with them for the first time since Tony arrived, Donovan stood in the flat's tiny hallway without any idea what to say.

They'd never had a problem with him being gay. Tony was right. Everything was fine and—

"He seems lovely."

Donovan looked up and met his mother's eyes. "He is."

"Were you going to tell us about him at any point?" she asked.

"I guess I thought I should see how things went first," he said. "We've only been seeing each other a few weeks." *And I didn't want to have to explain why we broke up if it all goes to hell after Trentmoore.* Donovan nibbled on his bottom lip.

His mother smiled, hugged him and pressed a kiss against his cheek. "Well, I'm glad we called in and had a chance to meet him. Remember to ring your gran next Tuesday, okay? It's her birthday."

Donovan nodded. It was a damn sight easier to talk about grandmothers than boyfriends.

His step-father hugged him before he left, too. "I'll make sure we phone before we turn up on your doorstep in future," he promised, too low for his mother to hear.

Donovan smiled his thanks as they stepped back from each other. A minute later, he was standing on his own in the hall, trying to work out what the hell he was supposed to do now.

How long have you been training at the institute?

Do your family live around here?

Oh, your brother's here too! What sport does he do?

The sheer number of questions that had been put to Tony made Donovan's mind swirl. He pushed his hand through his hair as he tried to change mental gears for the fifth time in way too short a period.

Going from planning out their last evening together before Trentmoore, to answering the door and finding his mother there rather than Tony; then actually answering the door to Tony; then going from trying to make some sort of sense with both Tony and his parents in the same room, to now being alone with Tony—it was all too much. And, through it all wound the fact that Ryan would have been pissed as hell if he turned up expecting to get off, and ended up having tea with his parents instead.

Donovan closed his eyes and tried to work out what the hell he could reasonably say when he went back in the living room. No suitable turns of phrase presented themselves to his rather addled mind.

When he opened his eyes, Donovan glanced at his watch. Tony was leaving for Trentmoore at the crack of dawn the next day. He should probably have already been asleep.

"We've got a little while before I need to head home."

Donovan jerked his head up. Tony stood in the living room doorway, leaning against the doorframe, looking just as relaxed as he had when he sat on the sofa opposite his parents.

"I'm so sorry," Donovan said.

"What for?"

Everything? "This wasn't what we were supposed to be doing tonight."

Tony smiled good-naturedly. "There'll be plenty of other nights."

Donovan nodded, relieved at yet more evidence that Tony was nothing like Ryan. But, at the same time, the knowledge that there wouldn't be any more nights before Trentmoore made it impossible for him to return Tony's smile.

Tony stepped back into the living room. Donovan trailed after him. When Tony sat on the sofa, Donovan lowered himself down onto the seat next to him.

"Why do I get the feeling there's something you're not telling me?" Tony asked, as he stroked Donovan's hair back from his face.

Donovan blinked at him.

"What's going on in that head?"

Donovan leaned helplessly into Tony's touch. "Nothing at all."

Tony raised an eyebrow.

"There's nothing going on in my head. That's part of the problem. I think my brain kind of shut down."

Tony chuckled. Sliding his hand around to the nape of Donovan's neck, he tugged him forward, encouraging him to snuggle into his side.

Donovan went with the movement, resting his head on Tony's shoulder.

"It didn't seem to go too badly to me," Tony said after a while.

"They really like you," Donovan whispered.

"I like them too," Tony said easily, as he shifted in his seat and relaxed more comfortably back against the sofa cushions. He stretched out his legs and gave a contented little sigh.

As being alone with Tony allowed a little of his tension to slip away, Donovan carefully rearranged himself to fit neatly against Tony's side.

"What did you have planned for tonight?" Tony asked after a while.

Donovan had one hand resting on Tony's chest. He traced his finger around the logo on Tony's T-shirt as he tried to work out what would be the best thing to say.

"You seemed to have your heart set on something particular," Tony prompted.

Donovan shook his head. "Nothing particular, I just thought we'd have time to…"

"Don?" Tony twitched his shoulder.

"I bought a pair of handcuffs online," Donovan blurted out. Heat raced to his cheeks. "When I heard a knock on the door, I thought you were early. It was only luck I didn't have the cuffs in my hand when I answered the door to them."

Tony chuckled and pressed a kiss to the top of his head.

"Now, that would have been an interesting conversation for me to have with them the first time we met…"

Donovan smiled. He had no doubt that Tony would have been able to take that as calmly in his stride as he took everything else. It also didn't escape his notice that Tony both assumed that he would be the one giving the explanations on their behalf, and that Tony was okay with that.

A moment later, Tony tucked a knuckle under Donovan's chin and encouraged him to tilt his head back and look up at him.

"Who was going to be in the cuffs?" Tony asked, although Donovan was pretty sure he already knew the answer.

"Me."

Tony moved his hand to Donovan's wrist and wrapped his fingers around the joint. It was all Donovan could do not to whimper. Even that casual grip called to something inside him, promising him it would all be okay because Tony was in complete control of everything.

"Tomorrow night, we'll do whatever you want, handcuffs and all. Promise."

"I'm sorry I won't be there to see you compete," Donovan said. "I tried to swap my shifts around, but—"

"It's not a problem," Tony cut in, before Donovan's rushed explanation could descend into complete incomprehensibility.

Donovan glanced at him.

"Are you still up for tomorrow evening?" Tony asked.

For the first time since they started dating, Donovan had the strongest desire to lie—to make up a shift, or a training session, anything at all.

He glanced up at Tony once more. Maybe it would be okay. Maybe it wasn't Tony's promise to his coach that was letting him hold it all together by a thread. Maybe the magic ingredient was actually Tony. Maybe they could have sex without it freaking Donovan out at all.

Donovan took a deep breath and let it out very slowly. Maybe none of that mattered. He'd come this far. He had to at least try.

"Tomorrow evening will be fine," Donovan said.

"Here or at mine?" Tony asked.

"Yours," Donovan said. He wasn't sure about anything else that might happen the following night, but he knew that if Tony suddenly turned out to have more in common with Ryan than Donovan had thought he did, then he'd be better off if he could leave — or if he at least had a space of his own to retreat to when it was all over.

"Do you want me to pick you up?" Tony asked.

Donovan shook his head. "I'll make my own way to you." If everything was going to change after Trentmoore, Donovan wasn't going to risk things getting started in a car.

Chapter Five

"I can't have sex with you."

Even though unexpected announcements weren't exactly an unknown quantity in their relationship, those still weren't quite the first words that Tony had expected to hear when he opened his front door to Donovan. His first instinct was to laugh at the sheer randomness of the statement, sure that there must be a punch line coming. But Donovan didn't just look dead-pan serious, he looked completely freaked out.

"Okay."

Donovan blinked at him. "Okay?"

Tony nodded and stepped back to let Donovan into the flat, as if they always greeted each other that way, as if his thoughts weren't racing in a million different directions as he tried to work out what had changed since the previous evening.

Donovan took half a step forward, then hesitated.

"Tea?" Tony asked, with a glance toward the kitchen. You couldn't get less threatening than tea. A hot drink had helped Donovan find a calm headspace before—Tony saw no reason to mess with a system that worked.

Donovan looked from Tony, to the kitchen door, and back again. He met Tony's eyes for a moment. "Tea?" he repeated blankly.

"There's coffee if you'd prefer," Tony offered, still carefully keeping his tone casual.

Donovan opened his mouth. He closed his mouth. "Tea's fine, thank you."

"In here, or out there?" Tony asked.

Donovan still stood in the hallway outside Tony's flat.

He looked down at the dark green carpet beneath his feet. It was now more than a little damp from the rain water dripping off his clothes.

Tony studied Donovan carefully, ignoring the very interesting way his long sleeved T-shirt clung to his skin, the thin white fabric so wet it was almost translucent, in favour of trying to work out if there was anything other than nervousness to be discerned from his expression.

His hair was dripping wet. His face streaked with water. The lines down his cheeks were almost certainly caused by the rain rather than by tears; Tony still wanted to gather him into his arms and promise him that everything was going to be okay.

"Inside is fine," Donovan finally decided. He stepped into the flat.

Tony retreated into the kitchen, leaving Donovan to close the front door behind him, in a vague hope that it would stop him feeling trapped. He heard the door click shut, but he didn't turn away from the sink. He kept all his attention on filling the kettle, as if his heart wasn't pounding—as if he had no doubt that Donovan had closed the door from the inside rather than shut it behind him when he left.

A noise behind Tony placed Donovan in the kitchen doorway. He was still there. Tony breathed a little easier. "How was your day?" he asked.

"What would you have done if I'd said I wanted my tea out there, rather than in here?" Donovan asked, at the same time.

"Taken it out there to you," Tony said. He put the kettle on to boil and leaned against the edge of the counter. "What else would I have done?"

"Decided I was completely insane and shut the door in my face?"

"Just because you wanted your tea in the corridor?" Tony asked.

Donovan smiled slightly. Stepping into the kitchen, he

took up a position leaning against the counter top opposite Tony. "I..." He took a deep breath. "I know that things are...that you might have different plans for us tonight."

Tony raised an eyebrow. "Then you know more than me, sweetheart."

Donovan stared at the worktop for a few seconds, no longer smiling at all. "I know about Trentmoore, about your promise to your coach," he whispered.

Every muscle in Tony's body knotted with tension. For the first time in over a decade, he realised he didn't know enough swearwords for his present situation. He'd been so focused on what Donovan thought about their sex life. All that bull with his coach had become nothing more than something stupid he'd said, something that his friends liked to tease him about, but which was otherwise irrelevant. It hadn't actually affected anything, hadn't been worth thinking about for weeks. But, now...

"I know that your promise to him ended today," Donovan added.

"And what about the promises I've given you since we started dating," Tony asked. "Was there an expiry date on them, too?"

Donovan nibbled on his bottom lip and subjected the kitchen floor to a detailed study. He'd wrapped his arms around himself, as if trying to hold himself together.

It was impossible for Tony to stay on his side of the kitchen a moment longer. He moved to stand directly in front of Donovan. Tucking a knuckle under his chin, Tony coaxed him to look up and meet his eyes. "Did you know about that bull with my coach when you let me buy you that first drink?"

Donovan nodded. "I'm sorry."

Tony kept his knuckle under his chin, keeping Donovan looking up while he hushed the apology away.

His thoughts were hurtling through his brain so fast, Tony found it nigh on impossible to catch hold of any one of them. Donovan had believed that... All this time, Donovan had thought that… Donovan had only ever trusted him not to be like his ex because…

Tony took a deep breath. It was time Donovan realised the truth. "If you'd been able to look me in the eye and tell me that you genuinely wanted to have sex with me that first night in the pub, I'd have broken my promise to my coach without the slightest hesitation and taken it with good grace when he decided to move all my training sessions to stupid o'clock in the morning in retaliation."

Donovan stared up at him, but he didn't venture any sort of opinion.

"We haven't had sex because you don't want to—simple as that."

"I do want to," Donovan corrected.

It was such a blatant lie, Tony found himself smiling. The fact Donovan thought he'd believe such a bad bluff was actually quite sweet.

A touch of colour rose to Donovan's cheeks as he seemed to realise his poker face sucked. "I've never said I don't want to," he said, softly. "I just said I can't." He looked Tony straight in the eye. "That's nothing like the same thing."

Tony nodded very slowly, sensing how important the difference was to Donovan. "Just like me not rushing you because I have no interest in doing that, is different to me simply pretending to be a nice guy while I was waiting out all that stupidity with my coach?" he suggested. "That's nothing like the same thing, either."

Donovan bit his bottom lip again. Tony wanted to kiss it better, but forced himself to resist.

"I'm not going to try to jump you, no matter what my coach's opinion on my sex life might be."

The wording made Donovan smile slightly, but it didn't last. "I just… Logically, I know you're not…" He closed his eyes.

"Not like your last boyfriend?" Tony suggested, gently.

"He wasn't my boyfriend."

Yes. Tony remembered him saying that before. "That difference is important, too," he agreed. Stepping forward, he wrapped his arms around Donovan.

He wasn't sure how Donovan would react to that right then. He got the impression that Donovan wasn't entirely sure either. For several seconds, Donovan stood very still, as if waiting for the different parts of his brain to come to a consensus. Then, very slowly, he put his arms around Tony in return. He dipped his head and rested his temple against Tony's shoulder.

Tony closed his eyes, tightening his grip on Donovan as he rested his face against Donovan's wet hair and took a deep breath. Donovan's caution, the fact that someone had obviously taught him he needed to be that cautious with another man, killed something in Tony.

He rubbed Donovan's back through his wet T-shirt in a clumsy attempt to soothe him.

Donovan had managed to soak up a hell of a lot of rain water on his way to Tony's place — possibly because he hadn't been in that much of a rush to get there. Shit!

As Tony held Donovan, he was aware of the dampness leaching through his own clothes. He wrapped his arms a little tighter around him, trying to warm him against his body until such time as he worked out a way to suggest that Donovan get out of his wet clothes, without making it sound like he just wanted to get him naked.

"When you let me buy you that first drink, did you have a clear idea in your head about what you wanted to happen from there?" Tony asked.

Donovan nodded.

"A kind of fantasy version of the future — in a perfect world, this is what would happen?" Tony suggested.

Donovan offered a rather more wary nod.

"Will you tell me what it was?"

Donovan shifted slightly within Tony's embrace, but he didn't go so far as to pull away from him. "Why?"

So I can make sure you get exactly what you want. "I'd like to know," Tony said, simply.

Donovan was silent for what felt like a very long time.

"There's no wrong answer, sweetheart. I'm not going to be angry whatever you say."

Donovan took a deep breath. "I'm not completely delusional," he finally said. "I didn't have some huge fairy tale romance planned for us or anything stupid like that. I just thought we'd have sex, it would be fun, then we'd go our separate ways."

Tony hesitated.

"Things didn't go well with the last guy I..." Donovan shook his head, as if to clear the memory of it from his mind. "But I thought that three weeks would have been long enough to get me into the right head space with you. Even when we didn't manage to meet up that often, I thought... Right up until I got out of the taxi outside, I really thought I could come up here, we'd have sex, and it would all be fine."

It would be fun, then we'd go our separate ways... Tony thought, glad that Donovan couldn't see his expression. "And the only reason why you picked me to do this with was because you heard them all winding me up about that promise to my coach?" Tony asked, maintaining his calm tone through sheer force of will.

Donovan shook his head. "Not the only reason."

Tony waited.

"You're you."

That sounded more promising.

"You have a reputation for..."

Tony thought back to that first move Donovan had made — the handcuffs. "You wanted someone who was kinky?"

"That and..." Donovan cleared his throat. "You have a reputation for...knowing what you're doing."

"So, all those things together made me a good choice for someone who was looking for a guy to..." It took Tony a few seconds to think of a term that fitted the kind of arrangement Donovan seemed to be seeking. "Tutor him in sex?" Tony longed to shy away from the idea, but that was exactly what they were talking about. Donovan wasn't looking for a boyfriend, he was looking for someone who could sort out his nerves about sex, get him back into the saddle and bugger off when he was no longer needed.

He felt Donovan tense. "When you put it like that, it sounds—"

"Fine," Tony cut in. "It sounds fine."

Donovan looked up at him. "It does?"

Tony avoided his gaze for a moment, in favour of staring over Donovan's shoulder at the kitchen cabinet behind him. If it was anyone else, the arrangement really would have suited him fine. Pity he couldn't have claimed to have been as lacking in delusions as Donovan, really. For the first time in his life, that fairy tale ending had sounded so good.

Run! The word screamed through Tony's mind. He needed to get as far away from Donovan as he could, before he fell even further in love with him, before anyone other than himself realised how far he'd fallen already.

He met Donovan's eyes and—

Everything Tony knew he needed to say in order to give himself any hope of getting out of the situation with any kind of pride intact died on his lips. He couldn't do it. He couldn't walk away from him. "Yes," he said, more softly than he intended. "There's no reason why we can't do that."

"There isn't?" Donovan said.

Tony nodded to himself. If Donovan wanted someone who could get him through his nerves and make it possible for him to have sex, then that's what Donovan would get.

"So, we...keep hooking up?" Donovan asked.

Tony swallowed down a bitter taste as it flooded the back of his mouth. "No. You said he wasn't your boyfriend. Well, if this is going to have any chance of working, we're not going to be hooking up—I'm going to be your boyfriend. That

236

means neither of us sleeping with other people, or dating other people, or anything else like that, either." There was no way in hell he'd keep his sanity if they couldn't at least agree on that.

When Donovan hesitated, the air stalled in Tony's lungs.

Donovan cleared his throat. "I don't know how quickly I'll be able to... I wouldn't mind if you want to keep —"

Tony started breathing again. "No. If I'm single, I screw around. If I'm dating someone, I don't. That doesn't change just because we're going to take things slowly. You're still going to be my boyfriend." He allowed no room for argument in his tone. He might not be able to get his happy ever after with the guy he was falling in love with, but he'd be damned if he'd just pretend it was a business arrangement while whatever it was that they were going to have together lasted.

"So, until we can have sex?" Donovan said.

"We'll keep going as we have so far. Whatever you're up for, we'll do. Whatever you're not, we won't."

Donovan smiled. "You make it all sound so simple."

"It is," Tony said, and it was. Donovan not having whatever he needed wasn't an option. If that meant Tony keeping how he really felt to himself and acting like it was only ever about sex, he'd just have to find a way to deal with that. Simple.

* * * * *

Donovan nodded, not immediately able to wrap his mind around the fact that the sky hadn't fallen in when he made his big confession. He took a deep breath. He was fine. Tony wasn't pissed with him. Tony was willing to keep dating him — even if that was only until they had sex. That wasn't just okay, that was so bloody marvellous Donovan could barely breathe through his relief.

Finally, because it was obvious that he needed to say

something, and the words were right there in the front of his mind. "It's your move."

Tony kept on stroking Donovan's back while he apparently gave the situation deep and considerable thought. "I think our next move should involve getting you warm and dry," he eventually announced, his tone of voice was ever so slightly off.

Donovan looked up. Tony didn't look angry. If anything, he looked a little amused.

"Wet is a very good look on you," Tony said. "But I'm pretty sure hypothermia isn't fun."

Donovan looked down at his clothes. He hadn't really thought about how long he'd stood on the other side of the road while the rain pelted down around him, trying to work out what the hell to say to Tony when he got up to the flat.

Another fact registered. "I'm getting you wet too," he realised. Was that why Tony sounded less than happy? He tried to take a step back, but Tony's arms were still around him and they made that impossible.

"No, I'm getting me wet," Tony corrected, firmly. "I'm the one who came to join you on this side of the kitchen, remember?"

Donovan blinked at him. Ryan would never have taken the blame for anything, even if it really had been his fault.

Unsure how to actually ask, Donovan tilted his head back a little further, offered his lips up to be kissed, and hoped.

Tony dipped his head and brushed their mouths together as if it was the most natural thing in the world. Donovan immediately leaned into the kiss. For some reason, Tony refused to make the kiss anything other than entirely sweet. He didn't relent in the slightest, until Donovan whimpered a plea against his lips.

Finally, Tony began to explore his mouth, leading him to kiss him back and let their tongues dance and slide against each other. Donovan had no idea how long they spent there.

He was as unaware of time as he was of everything else. He only remembered a world outside that kiss existed when Tony pulled away.

"Warm and dry," he reminded Donovan.

Donovan nodded.

Tony took hold of his hand and led him through to his bedroom.

"Hot shower, then dry clothes," Tony ordered, nudging Donovan toward the en-suite. "You get in. I'll find something for you to wear while your clothes dry out."

Donovan automatically complied. He already had his hand on the bathroom door handle before an alternative presented itself to him.

"Don?" Tony prompted, when he noticed that his order hadn't received instant obedience.

"You're almost as wet as I am." He couldn't quite meet Tony's gaze. "You're probably cold too. You should have a hot shower as well."

"I can go in after you."

Donovan forced himself to lift his gaze. The moment he saw the complete understanding in Tony's eyes, he realised that, even if he didn't have to explain what he was asking for, he would have to state it out loud.

"Whose move is it now?" Donovan asked.

Tony still stood on the other side of the room, next to the wardrobe he'd been looking through. "Yours."

Donovan swallowed. "We could share the shower."

"Is that what you want?" Tony asked, crossing the room.

Donovan nodded.

"Even though the idea makes you nervous as hell?" he whispered in his ear.

Donovan nodded again.

"Don't you think maybe your nerves are telling you to slow down, sweetheart?"

Instinct almost had Donovan nodding his head again,

on the basis of whatever Tony said was fine with him. He stopped himself just in time and shook his head.

"I meant what I said," Tony promised. "I'm fine with...helping you work through everything you want to do. But, I don't think rushing is going to make anything easier."

"I think my nerves are saying that I wouldn't have liked the way it would have been with him."

Tony stroked Donovan's cheek and kissed him gently on the lips.

"I think I'm going to be nervous the first time we do anything. But after we've done something once, maybe my brain will realise how things are with you instead of focusing on how they were with him," Donovan said, softly.

Tony nodded, as if that made perfect sense, but Donovan wasn't entirely sure if that meant anything. Tony tended to do the same no matter how bizarre a statement he came out with.

Silence descended. Donovan's nerves suddenly turned on their heel and strode off in a different direction. "Are you trying to be polite while you tell me you don't like the idea?" he blurted out.

Tony chuckled. "Any guy who doesn't want to join you in the shower is either stupid, or straight, or both. I'm neither."

Donovan swallowed.

Tony nodded toward the door. "I'm flexible about where we drink tea, but it's probably going to be easier to shower in there than in here."

Donovan looked at where his hand rested on the door handle. Slowly, he managed to prompt the right pairs of muscles into action. He stepped into the bathroom, aware that Tony was right behind him.

Turning to face him, Donovan stood in the middle of the room and waited to be told what to do. It was Tony's move now, and everything was always much better when Tony was calling the shots.

"If you want to leave your clothes in the sink, I can throw them in the dryer afterwards," Tony offered.

As Donovan took off his wet clothes, he was aware of Tony doing the same on the other side of the small room, but he didn't look in Tony's direction. There was a subtle tension in the atmosphere that hadn't been there the other times they'd met up, and Donovan didn't know what to do about it.

He heard Tony turn on the shower. A moment later, the sound of the water changed, as someone stepped under the spray.

"Coming in?" Tony invited.

Not looking in Tony's direction ceased to be an option. Donovan turned toward him. Entirely naked, standing under the spray, Tony was more gorgeous than ever. The sight of him went straight to Donovan's cock. His nerves trembled as he stepped into the small shower enclosure.

Trying not to rub up against Tony without a very definite invitation to do so, Donovan tipped his head back and let the water run through his hair, slicking it back from his face.

When he opened his eyes, he found Tony studying him with a surprisingly serious expression on his face. He parted his lips to ask what was wrong.

"Want me to wash your back?" Tony asked, before Donovan had a chance to get a single word out.

Donovan nodded.

Tony took his shower gel off the shelf at the back of the shower and poured some onto his hands. His touch was slick with bubbles as he ran his palms over Donovan's shoulders and down the outsides of his arms. It felt strangely chaste and intensely erotic at the same time.

"Have you ever shared a shower with another guy?" Tony suddenly asked.

Donovan shook his head. "Only at the gym, not like this." He waited a few moments, to see if Tony was going to say anything else, but that seemed to be it. "Am I doing something wrong?" he asked, glancing over his shoulder.

Tony smiled slightly, as if he thought the question a silly one, but was too polite to say so. "There's nothing you can do wrong, sweetheart."

Tony's hands seemed to move more confidently over Donovan's body now. He didn't pause once, until Donovan cast a quick glance up at him and caught his eye.

"Can I?" Donovan looked at the shelf where the shower gel stood.

Tony handed it to him with an easy smile. "Of course."

It was an intimate thing to do, sliding his hands over another man's wet skin. Donovan instantly fell in love with the sensation. He wondered if Tony would let him come over and share his shower every day.

"I was right," Tony whispered in his ear after a few minutes. "You do look great wet."

Donovan knew he blushed at the compliment. He parted his lips, but closed them without saying anything. A few seconds later, he tried again.

"Thank you." The words came out at such a rush, they blurred together.

"For what?"

"Everything?" Donovan suggested.

Tony pressed a kiss against his temple. "You're welcome."

Donovan smiled up at him, before turning his attention back to where his hands were gradually working their way down Tony's body.

Sharing a shower had them both hard, but Tony didn't seem to have a problem with that. He didn't appear to be in a rush to get them out of the shower and move them on to something else. He wasn't trying to start anything in the shower either. The atmosphere was almost companionable.

That didn't change when they got out of the shower and dried themselves. Donovan could never remember feeling so calm, so relaxed in another man's company.

In the bedroom, Tony went across to the wardrobe. "I don't have anything that will fit. But I reckon, if we roll the legs up a bit, then these should be okay." He held up a pair of track bottoms with a drawstring waist. "What do you think?" He glanced over his shoulder.

Donovan stood next to the en-suite's door. He had a towel slung around his waist, the same as Tony. The lines of both their towels were disturbed by their erections. Donovan looked up and met Tony's gaze.

"Do you want a blow job?"

Chapter Six

Donovan forced himself to hold Tony's gaze as he spoke, sure that would be the quickest way to convince Tony that he was serious about the offer.

"What happened to our plan to go slow?" Tony asked.

Donovan took a step back, physically as well as mentally. "I—"

"I'm not saying I don't want to, or that it's a bad idea," Tony cut in. "I'm just wondering what changed between the kitchen and here."

Donovan took a step forward. "I think I can." God help him, but he really did. His mouth watered at the prospect of finally being able to drop to his knees in front of Tony and, as relaxed and as turned on as he was after the shower, he knew this was the perfect opportunity.

"Do you think we should try it tonight because you want to or because you think I want you to?" Tony said, moving closer, doing his part in closing the gap between them.

"I want to," Donovan whispered. He could hear the truth in the words. Tony seemed to sense his honesty too.

"Then, we try it. We go as far as you want, and then we stop," Tony decided.

Donovan nodded.

"Will you tell me when we've gone as far as you want to?" Tony asked, seriously. "Can you do that?"

Donovan nodded again.

"Okay, then—it's your move," Tony said.

Donovan swallowed. He'd kind of expected Tony to take over at that point and tell him what was going to happen next. Having to actually make a move rather than just tell Tony what he would like their next move to be was slightly terrifying, but he could see from Tony's expression that it was his only option.

Tony would help him, but he wasn't going to pressure him. If he really wanted this, he had to prove it.

Donovan stepped forward until he stood directly in front of Tony. There was no reason why he couldn't get on his knees right where they were, but before he had a chance to do that, Tony touched his jaw and guided him to tilt his face up.

A kiss. A kiss that didn't have to be the start of anything. Donovan smiled. Tony must have felt the movement against his lips, because he smiled too, and lifted his head.

"Maybe you could sit on the edge of the bed?" Donovan suggested.

Tony walked backward until the backs of his legs touched the mattress. His fingers still rested against Donovan's jawline and his touch invited Donovan to come along with him.

When Tony sat down, Donovan once more went to lower himself to his knees. Tony stopped him short again, grabbed one of the pillows and dropped it on the floor. Then, he finally let him kneel.

Ryan wouldn't have given a damn how hard the floor was. Another little bit of concrete proof who he was with. Donovan looked up at Tony.

"Condom or no condom?" Tony asked.

Another difference between the two men, but this time Donovan didn't want to take advantage of it—tasting Tony was too important. He shook his head.

His gaze went to the towel covering Tony's crotch. The fabric did little to hide how hard Tony was. He was about to reach out and move Tony's towel aside when it occurred to him that it might be worth making a request before he got started. Even if Tony said no, he probably wouldn't be pissed off with the question.

"Do you mind not…" Donovan faltered.

Tony stroked his fingers through his hair, pushing the damp strands back off his face. "Not what?"

"Not putting your hand on the back of my head, just this time. I—"

"That's fine," Tony cut in. He stroked his fingers through Donovan's hair once more, before dropping his hand down to rest on his shoulder.

No more hesitations now, Donovan was determined about that. Everything was going to be fine. Tony was Tony and Donovan could do this.

He moved the towel aside, just as he had that time he gave Tony a hand job. The comparison helped settle his nerves further. He reached out and wrapped his fingers around Tony's cock. The angles were different, but as he stroked him, Donovan felt a calm settle over him. Jacking Tony off was definitely a good memory.

He leant forward and kissed the tip, just letting his lips move against the glans. No wave of panic threatened to overtake him. His mind remained serene, his cock remained hard. Donovan stilled his hand and steadied the length as he took the head into his mouth and swirled his tongue around it.

The flavour of Tony's pre-cum danced on Donovan's tongue, making him moan his approval. His own pleasure danced faster through his veins. No memories threatened the edges of his mind.

Tony stroked Donovan's shoulder.

Donovan risked a glance up. Tony was watching him as if enchanted. He couldn't have been, of course. The guy probably had half a dozen blow jobs a week. If he felt anything, it was almost certainly boredom. Donovan knew he wasn't doing anything that would impress anyone. Ryan hated being kept waiting.

If Donovan was going to suck him off, he should do it

properly.

He dipped his head, taking a few more inches past his lips. Keeping his teeth carefully covered, he worked his tongue against the underside each time he leaned in to let more and more of the length fill his mouth.

Gradually, Donovan managed to take another inch. That was important. If he was going to suck cock, he should do it properly, and that meant taking the whole thing, not just however much was convenient. His heart sped up as he realised just how badly he was screwing this up.

Sucking to hollow his cheeks and create a firm seal, just as he was supposed to, Donovan closed his eyes and pushed himself to bob his head lower still.

The tip hit the back of his throat. He pulled back quickly, spluttering.

There was nothing in his throat, nothing in his mouth. He could breathe fine; except he couldn't, because his lungs were refusing to cooperate.

Donovan bowed his head and closed his eyes even tighter, knowing that he was going to catch hell for screwing up, and that he was only going to make things worse by kneeling in front of Ryan like an idiot, not even trying to make up for his lapse. But all he could do was kneel on the thin carpet in his room at the university and —

"Okay. It's okay." The words seemed to come from a very long way away, but they were persistent, repeating themselves over and over again. "It's okay."

Slowly, a few of Donovan's other senses nudged his brain, creeping through the storm of panic to point out that they had interesting things to report, too.

There were arms around him. His temple rested against someone's shoulder. Someone's hand was on his back, stroking large, soothing circles against his bare skin. Ryan had never done anything like that, no matter how freaked out Donovan had been. Ryan would have been furious with him for screwing up a simple blow job.

This person was different. He smelled like Tony's shower gel. Donovan took a deep breath, filling his lungs with the scent.

"That's right. I've got you. You're going to be just fine." The tone as much as the words confirmed exactly where Donovan was and who he was with. Slowly, what he'd thought was reality faded away in favour of a solid, substantial version of the present.

He lifted his head and blinked open his eyes. "I'm—"

A hand covered Donovan's mouth.

"I know damn near gagging you is an incredibly stupid thing to do right now," Tony said. "But I've got a horrible feeling you were just about to try to apologise to me, and I can't let that happen."

Donovan blinked at Tony.

"If you were going to say anything else, I'm sorry for cutting you off. But not so sorry that I'm not going to take complete advantage of the situation and have my say first anyway. Okay?"

Donovan smiled slightly behind Tony's hand. There was a strangely comforting sense of complete honesty surrounding Tony's words. Donovan nodded his willingness to wait his turn.

"You only need to apologise to someone if you do something wrong. You haven't done anything wrong. There is nothing you need to apologise for. *We* tried something. *We* found out it's a good idea to wait a while before *we* try again. That's all."

Donovan felt the heat rush to his cheeks as he heard the stress Tony put on every word that shared the blame out equally between them.

Tony seemed to wait for a few moments, as if giving Donovan time to process everything he'd said. Then he moved his hand away from Donovan's mouth and slid his fingers through his hair. "Okay?"

Donovan nodded. If he wasn't allowed to apologise, he

wasn't sure what he was supposed to say. He looked down. For the first time, he registered that Tony wasn't where he'd expected him to be. Instead of sitting up on the edge of the bed, he was sitting naked on the floor alongside Donovan, his back resting against the side of the bed. Donovan hadn't even been aware of him moving.

"Can you tell me what happened?" Tony asked.

Donovan took a deep breath, still shaking slightly with lingering panic. Even knowing how bad the truth sounded, he found himself unable to lie. "I forgot who I was going down on," he whispered.

Tony kept stroking his hair, as if there was nothing wrong with that admission, as if people mistook his cock for someone else's on a regular basis. "Have you had a flashback before?"

Donovan glanced up at him.

"Isn't that what happened?" Tony asked. "Suddenly you were back there with him?"

Donovan nodded and tried to ignore the shiver that rushed through him as the past tried to creep up on him again.

Tony leaned forward and brushed their lips together. It was the last thing Donovan expected him to do and the kiss was over before he had a chance to return it.

"It helps, doesn't it?" Tony asked. "Being kissed is something that reminds you who you're with."

Donovan swallowed. "We... Kissing wasn't really his thing."

Tony nodded as if Donovan had just confirmed something important. He offered him another of those brief kisses before he spoke again. "I know you said before that you prefer not to talk about him. But I think we'll have a better chance of making this work if you decide you are willing to talk to me about what happened, at least a little bit." His voice was hushed, as if he was trying to break the news to him gently.

Donovan stared at a point on Tony's shoulder as his heart raced faster and faster. No tone of voice could make it easy to face that particular reality. He closed his eyes and pulled together what bits of courage he could muster. "What do you want to know?"

* * * * *

Tony cursed himself for an idiot all over again. "I don't mean right now, sweetheart. There's no rush. We'll talk about it when you're ready."

"I... If I know the conversation's coming, I'll just work myself up to the point where I can't say anything that makes sense," Donovan confessed, fidgeting with the end of the towel still wrapped around his waist.

As Tony studied Donovan, it was easy to believe a single question might break him.

Donovan glanced up. "Please?"

A question *might* break him, but a rejection certainly would.

"We should get dressed and take the conversation out into the living room," Tony decided, in the vague hope that doing that would keep Donovan's memories of that bastard as far away from their bed as possible.

It didn't take long to have them both dressed and making their way toward the sofa. Tony wouldn't have minded if it had taken an extra hour or two—the extra time to get his head in order would have been a godsend.

He closed his eyes, but quickly opened them again. The panic on Donovan's face as the flashback had hit him, hard and sudden, was apparently indelibly etched on the inside of Tony's eyelids. It was hard to believe he'd ever be able to shut his eyes and not see it.

Idiot!

He'd known they were going too fast. Whatever he'd said to Donovan, *they* hadn't tried something which didn't work out. Tony had let Donovan do something before he was ready for it, and now he had to find a way to fix that.

Donovan was trusting him to help him because he was supposed to know what he was doing, and this was how Tony proved he deserved that trust—by making stupid decisions right out of the gate?

Tony turned toward Donovan.

He was wearing Tony's clothes. They'd rolled up the sleeves and the bottoms of the track suit trouser legs to make them come closer to fitting him, but the effect made him look very young and more vulnerable than ever.

Tony took a deep breath and sat down on one end of the sofa. Leaning back, he rested one arm along the back of the cushions, making sure he appeared completely relaxed in the hope that would let Donovan feel a little less stressed out by the conversation.

Donovan perched on the edge of the cushion next to him. "What do you want to know?"

"Whatever you can tell me," Tony suggested, sure that Donovan had a better idea of what he needed to be aware of than he did himself.

Donovan closed his eyes for several seconds. "I can't just talk about it like that. If you ask me questions, I think I can answer them, but I can't just…"

"Okay," Tony said, there went that plan. Pot shots in the dark it would have to be… "What was his name?"

Donovan glanced very briefly in his direction before turning his attention back to the floor.

"I have no problem referring to him as *that bastard*, if that makes it easier," Tony offered. "That's what I've been calling him in my head for weeks."

Donovan let out a surprised little chuckle. Lifting a hand, he covered his mouth as if unsure it was an appropriate reaction considering the topic. Tony smiled slightly in spite of everything, thrilled to have eased Donovan's stress for a few moments, even if it was only with a bad joke.

"Ryan," Donovan finally said. "His name was Ryan." He swallowed, but he pushed forward without waiting for another question. "He was my roommate my first year at university." He tugged at the sleeves on his borrowed shirt, unrolling them and pulling them down over his hands. "And he was gorgeous."

"Okay," Tony said, when some sort of response seemed to be required.

"I'm not exaggerating," Donovan said, apparently to the carpet rather than Tony. "If a cat walk model and a porn star had a son—he'd look just like Ryan. The moment I saw him, I fell in instant lust."

Tony reached out and stroked his fingers through Donovan's hair, pushing the damp strands back from his face. "Sounds like a perfectly sensible reaction to me."

Donovan smiled, but he didn't manage to look in Tony's direction. Eye contact obviously wasn't going to happen at any point soon. That being the case...

Donovan looked confused when Tony slid an arm around his shoulders, but when Tony guided him to curl into his side and rest against him, he seemed to welcome both the contact and the excuse not to look him in the eye.

"Did you get on well?" Tony asked, pitching his tone to roughly where it would be if they were discussing the weather.

"We were on different courses. We had different friends. We didn't really see much of each other except when we were in our room." Donovan shifted positions slightly, leaning more firmly into Tony's embrace.

"But at some point that changed?" Tony prompted gently.

"I thought I was being discrete," Donovan whispered.

"Discrete?"

"I had a crush on him, but I didn't think I was obvious about it. I didn't think anyone at uni had even guessed I was gay, let alone that he'd realised I was interested in him."

Donovan turned his head, tucking his face into the crook of Tony's neck.

Tony stroked his hand up and down the outside of Donovan's arm, concentrating on keeping his breaths slow and steady while Donovan was pressed against his rib cage.

"It wasn't until he called me on flirting with him that I realised I wasn't being as subtle as I thought I was." Donovan took a deep breath. "At first I was sure he was going to be furious with me—I didn't know he was gay then. But he was really nice about it."

Tony had severe doubts about the bastard ever having been nice to anyone in his life, but he stroked Donovan's hair and kept that to himself.

"We had sex," Donovan said. "It...wasn't what I thought it would be like."

Tony pressed a kiss against the top of Donovan's head. "Once?" he asked.

Donovan shook his head. "Lots of times. Whenever he wanted us to."

Tony only hesitated for a second. "What about what you wanted?"

Donovan was silent for a few seconds. "I did want to. Even after I realised that it was never going to be the way I thought it would—I still couldn't look at him without getting instant wood." He ran his fingers over the logo on Tony's shirt, tracing out each letter of the institute's name. "There were times when I... At one point, I decided that I wasn't going to have sex with him anymore, but..."

Out of Donovan's line of sight Tony looked up to the ceiling and wondered if it was possible to track the other man down and kill him.

"It wasn't... He just... Saying no to him wasn't easy—sometimes, I'd manage to say it, but..."

"But he didn't listen?" Tony said.

Donovan took a shaky breath. "He never forced me to do anything. He never hit me or pushed me around. It wasn't like that... He... It sounds stupid, but at the time..."

Tony pressed another kiss against the top of his head, silently promising to accept whatever it was like and never consider Donovan in the least bit stupid.

"He knew exactly how hot he was, and how much I wanted him," Donovan whispered. "He knew that I thought about him when I jacked off, and he made it seem like I owed him—that saying no to him would be so stupid, so ungrateful. He used to say that since I got off thinking about him, it was only fair that I got him off in return and..."

Tony said nothing. He wasn't sure he could have got a single syllable out without making it obvious just how much he wanted to kill the bastard.

"And, once I said yes to one thing, once I let one thing happen, stopping wasn't really an option. And, he had this way of making everything he said stick in my mind and sound like the truth." Donovan swallowed. "Logically, when I was alone, I know it was all bullshit. But when he was there..."

Tony tightened his hold on him.

"I know everyone's not like him, and you are *nothing* like him, but..." Donovan lifted his head and looked Tony straight in the eye, damn near begging him to believe him. "I know it's stupid—"

"It's not stupid," Tony cut in. "It's not stupid at all." He brushed their lips together, hoping Donovan got some kind of comfort from it. "How long did it go on for?"

"Months," Donovan whispered. "Until I managed to move rooms."

Tony pressed a kiss against his cheek, then another one, sweet and gentle, against his mouth.

"I know it sounds like I'm making a fuss about nothing—"

Tony covered Donovan's mouth with a hand once more.

Donovan only looked shocked for a second, after that,

he seemed to be strangely reassured by it. Tony mentally filed the move under the same heading as handcuffs, kisses and shared showers. It was something else that Ryan had never done—something that it was safe for Tony to do without stirring up any memories.

"It sounds like he was a manipulative bastard who got inside your head and did his damndest to completely screw you over," he corrected.

Donovan held his gaze, apparently searching his expression, desperately hoping that Tony was telling the truth. Tony let him look until he finally seemed to realise there was no lie to spot, then he dropped his hand away.

"It's not you," Donovan suddenly blurted out. "It's any guy who likes men. Or straight women—if they don't back off when I tell them I'm gay, they freak me out too. All someone has to do is flirt with me and suddenly Ryan's voice is back in my head and..." He looked down. "I did try to date before. But saying yes to anything, even a drink was..."

"It made you remember how saying yes to one thing with him meant giving him something he could use against you. It made you feel like you'd end up not being allowed to say no to anything else," Tony filled in.

Donovan nodded.

Tony found himself nodding too, as several minor mysteries resolved themselves.

"What about with me?" Tony asked, carefully.

Donovan squirmed a little closer into his side as if he was scared that his support was going to be taken away. Tony automatically held him tighter. "Before, when I used to flirt with you, you found that intimidating, right?"

Donovan shook his head. "Right from the start, I wanted to flirt back. I just froze up and..."

Tony mentally translated that to—*yes, as intimidating as a black widow in the bathtub.*

"Okay, what about now. Do you feel safe with me?" Tony somehow resisted the attempt to hold his breath while he waited for an answer.

Donovan nodded.

"Does that go for the time since that stupid promise to my coach ended, too?" Tony asked.

Donovan hesitated.

"There's no right answer. But you need to tell me the truth, sweetheart. Did you feel safer when you knew I'd promised my coach I wouldn't have sex?"

Donovan still didn't answer. He traced the line of the logo on Tony's shirt again.

"Because if you did," Tony added. "You know we can fix that, right?"

"Fix it?"

"I'll phone my coach and promise not to have sex for another three weeks."

Donovan pulled back far enough to look up at him. He blinked. "You're serious."

"Of course."

Donovan opened his mouth, and closed his mouth. "What would your coach say?"

Tony was on the verge of saying that he didn't give a damn what his coach said—which was perfectly true. Then, the facts of the matter nudged at the back of his mind. "I'm pretty sure he'd either order a drug test or a psychiatric assessment," he admitted. The look on his face would be priceless.

Donovan chuckled.

Tony stroked the backs of his fingers down Donovan's cheek as he smiled in return. "Want to stay here while I make the call?"

Donovan shook his head. "You don't need to do that."

Tony raised an eyebrow. If that's what would take the pressure off Donovan, it was exactly what he needed to do.

"I'm not worried that you'll act like him," Donovan said. "I'm worried that I'll freak out even though you're not acting anything like him." He cleared his throat. "I think what you promised your coach helped me accept that first drink. But I know you better now. You were right earlier — it's the promises you've given me that made the real difference."

As far as Tony could see, Donovan believed all that was true. It was selfish to think of himself when all his focus should have been on Donovan, but he'd have been lying if he'd said he didn't take his own comfort from what Donovan had just told him.

"I won't call Haslet right now," he allowed. "But I'm keeping it as an option."

Donovan seemed to be deep in thought for a few seconds. When he looked up, he met Tony's gaze for a second. "Is there anything else you need to know?"

"Only one more thing for now," Tony said. "Have you seen him since uni? Has he tried to contact you or anything like that?"

Donovan shook his head.

Tony breathed slightly easier. "Will you tell me if he does?"

Donovan met his eyes for a moment. "Why?"

Because I'd quite like to string him up from a lamp post by his balls. "Because if I'm going to help you, I need to know about anything that happens that stirs up bad memories for you."

Donovan said nothing.

"I'm serious, sweetheart — will you let me know?"

Donovan nodded. He was silent for a few seconds.

Tony waited him out.

"What happens now?" Donovan finally asked.

Now, I try to work out how the hell to make everything right for you without screwing it all up and hurting you in the process. If I can do that without letting on how I really feel about you, that would be good too.

Tony smiled. If he could somehow convince Donovan to fall in love with him while he did all that, it would be even better. He cleared his throat. "Now, we order take out and watch bad TV."

Donovan couldn't have looked more shocked if Tony had suggested sky diving.

Tony glanced at his watch and considered the options. "You have a choice between bad pizza delivered very quickly and an apparently fantastic Chinese place that doesn't deliver, but which is pretty close by. I can be there and back in about fifteen minutes."

"Pizza sounds good," Donovan said.

Tony was pretty sure Donovan wasn't aware of the way he tightened his grip on the edge of Tony's sleeve when he made his decision. He was also sure he shouldn't like Donovan wanting him to stay close as much as he did.

"After that, I'd like you to stay here tonight. Not to screw, just to sleep," Tony specified. *I don't want you to be on your own tonight.*

Donovan hesitated.

"Have you ever just shared a bed with someone and slept next to him?" Tony asked, but he was pretty sure he already knew the answer. Ryan wouldn't have invited him to do that. That would make it a safe thing to do.

"That's okay? Just sleeping?" Donovan asked.

Tony smiled. "It's very okay indeed." Practical considerations aside, Tony would have been quite happy never to let him out of his sight ever again.

Chapter Seven

If sharing a bed with another man had turned out to be a lot easier than Donovan had ever thought it could be, working out what to say to that same man the following morning was a hell of a lot more complicated.

Donovan hesitated in the kitchen doorway, watching Tony savour his first cup of coffee of the day. "Thank you for letting me stay here last night."

Tony looked up as he realised he was no longer alone. His lips quirked into a smile. "I liked having you here. You're really snuggly in your sleep—it's nice."

Donovan fiddled with the sleeves on his borrowed shirt. They'd unrolled again during the night and were now so long they completely covered his hands. "I understand if you've changed your mind after sleeping on it." Donovan forced himself to get the words out at a volume where they could be heard and understood, but it wasn't easy. Even though he knew he had to give Tony the out, the idea that Tony might take it stabbed deep inside him.

"Changed my mind about what?" Tony said. He held out a hand to Donovan, and against all his intentions, Donovan found himself stepping forward and taking it. Suddenly, he was standing directly in front of Tony.

"About everything. About us. About getting me to the point where we can..."

"I haven't changed my mind about anything." Tony slid his arms around Donovan and settled his hands on the small of his back. "But I'm glad you asked."

Donovan glanced up at him. "You are?"

"Of course. If you don't tell me what you're worried

about, I can't fix it." *If you do tell me what you're worried about, then I will fix it.* Even if Tony didn't say the last bit out loud, Donovan still got the message. There was no doubting Tony's complete confidence in his ability to fix the whole world.

Donovan smiled as he dipped his head and pressed a kiss against Tony's shoulder, loving how safe that made him feel. "What happens now?"

"Now," Tony said. "I kiss you good morning, like this." The kiss was soft, and sweet, and tasted like coffee. "Then, I drive you home so you can get dressed for work. Then, I drive you to work so you won't be late. After we're done with work or training or whatever else we have to do, we meet up tonight." He seemed to pause to think for a moment. "In the pub. Is eight okay for you?"

Donovan nodded, sure that was safer than having to find words. If Tony wanted to go to the pub, that's where they'd go.

Tony stroked his cheek. "You have lots of great qualities, sweetheart. The ability to lie worth a damn isn't one of them."

"I'm…not always good at remembering that other men aren't Ryan," Donovan admitted. Even as he spoke, a hundred memories of minor and not so minor humiliations nudged at the corners of his mind. "There'd be less chance of me embarrassing you in front of your friends if you…kept me and them in separate parts of your life."

"No."

Donovan glanced up at Tony. "No?"

"If you tell me you don't want to go to the pub, that's one thing. But, I'll be damned before I act like I'm ashamed of you." Tony tightened his embrace, as if to reassure Donovan that he wasn't pissed off with him, but his tone of voice invited no debate on the matter.

Donovan looked down.

"Did you and he ever go out anywhere together?"

Donovan shook his head. "He wasn't my boyfriend."

Tony dipped his head and whispered in Donovan's ear. "But I *am* your boyfriend, remember?"

Donovan felt a touch of heat rush to his cheeks at the reassurance.

"I meant what I said last night, sweetheart. I'm happy to help you through your nerves, but the only way I'm going to be able to do that is as your boyfriend."

Donovan hesitated, sure there had to be a catch. Reality was never this kind.

"You need to see the complete flipside of the coin," Tony said. "That means someone who cares about you — not just someone who turns up, fools around with you, then buggers off."

Donovan risked a glance up. Tony looked more serious than normal. "You're okay with that, with us...with me being your boyfriend until we can...?"

Tony smiled. The expression was slightly off. He seemed more wry than anything, as if there was a joke that Donovan was unaware of. "I have no problem being your boyfriend, or with giving a damn about you, for however long we're together."

Donovan took a deep breath, savouring the honesty in Tony's voice.

"Any doubts about that?" Tony asked.

Donovan glanced up at him. "No doubts."

Tony studied him for several seconds before he seemed to be willing to take his word for that. Then, he nodded, as if the matter was now settled.

"One of the reasons why I suggested we go to the pub is because I don't think a good boyfriend would let you go on being nervous around other gay men forever. I'm sure that if you get to know some of the other guys in the pub as actual people, it will get a lot easier for you to see that they are nothing like Ryan."

Donovan had thought that too. He'd been wrong.

"Or you could get to know Colby and Noah first," Tony

mused. "That could work."

"No!" Donovan blurted the word out before he could think better of it.

Tony peered down at him, obviously surprised.

"I'd rather not meet them straight away. The pub is fine. Eight o'clock, I'll be there." The prospect of humiliating himself in front of Tony's friends had to be better than doing that in front of Tony's family…

* * * * *

"You're going to go cross eyed if you stare at the door any harder."

Tony ignored Cosmos in the vague hope that, just this once, the guy would take the hint and shut up.

Cosmos chuckled. "You really are besotted with him, aren't you?"

Yes, but Tony didn't see any reason why he should share that information with Cosmos. Hell, he was willing to cut out his own tongue before he told Donovan anything of the sort. Unless he somehow managed to convince Donovan to fall for him in return, of course. That would make things very different.

The door swung open. Two guys from the institute's weight lifting programme came in, along with Mike.

As soon as Mike spotted them, he broke away from the other two guys and came to join them at their table.

"Tony's waiting for Donovan and watching the door like a puppy desperate for his master to come home. It's very sweet," Cosmos explained, as Mike took a seat at his side. "He's also completely refusing to give up the details of his first night in the sack after Trentmoore."

Mike mumbled something that sounded vaguely sympathetic, although it wasn't clear to Tony exactly who Mike was sympathising with.

"We could always ask Donovan when he gets here,"

Cosmos mused.

"No." Tony wasn't sure what expression showed on his face when he turned toward Cosmos, but it made Cosmos smirk with obvious amusement.

"Scared he'll blush?"

No, I'm scared he'll have a panic attack. He glared at Cosmos.

"If I play nice with your new boyfriend, you know you'll owe me, right?" Cosmos said.

"Fine. That's a deal," Tony said, without hesitation. "You keep the conversation clean. You don't offer up any anecdotes about my sex life. And you don't flirt with him — at all."

He glanced back toward the door just in time. Donovan!

Tony was on his feet the moment he saw him. Donovan barely had time to glance around before Tony was right there in front of him.

"Hi." Tony touched Donovan's cheek and tilted his head back to kiss him. He didn't rush it. He let their lips linger together until he felt Donovan start to relax.

Aware that if Donovan's nerves were going to peak, it would probably be right at the start of their date, Tony took careful stock of Donovan's expression as he lifted his head. He looked calm, if far from comfortable with his surroundings. The pub was busier than Tony had expected it to be mid-week.

"We won't stay long, just for one drink," Tony promised. "Just long enough for you to meet a couple of people." Which should also be long enough for everyone to see that Donovan was now officially off the market — that held an undeniable appeal of its own.

"Everyone knows everyone, right?" Tony said, as he nudged Donovan into one of the seats on the opposite side of the table to Cosmos and Mike before sitting down himself.

Donovan offered up a nervous smile, but didn't

actually say anything.

"We're both in the athletics department with Tony," Cosmos said, as he shook hands with Donovan across the table.

When Tony nudged a bottle of Coke towards him, Donovan wrapped his hands around it like a lifeline. "Long distance, right?" Donovan asked Cosmos. His tone made his nerves obvious. Tony settled his arm across the back of Donovan's chair in an effort to reassure him everything was fine.

"Yep," Cosmos said. "Anything under five thousand meters isn't real running. Never let the sprint boys tell you differently." Tony held his breath, but Cosmos didn't go straight for his usual line about him being the only one in the group with any endurance in the sack. Either it was Donovan's blatant nervousness that tipped the balance in Tony's direction, or Cosmos really wanted whatever favour he intended to get out of Tony in return, but it seemed Cosmos really did intend to play nicely.

"Cosmos' just bitter because our coach made him do sprint training with me for a week last year," Tony explained to Donovan. "He's not used to losing."

Cosmos raised an eyebrow at him. "Careful, darling. I haven't given up trying to convince Haslet to turn the tables and make you join me for a few weeks worth of *real* training runs. Let's see how you find getting a solid hundred miles under your belt every week."

Tony smiled. "You'll excuse me for being bloody glad he hasn't taken you up on that offer." Especially since, if Haslet had gone for that rather than celibacy as a punishment, Tony was pretty sure that Donovan would never have let him buy that first drink.

"Real men run marathons," Cosmos announced, with complete confidence in his position and obviously relishing having a fresh audience who gave no sign of wanting to say anything himself. "Real men don't require starting blocks."

"Meaning he almost fell flat on his face the first time he tried to use blocks. He blamed them every time he lost to me," Tony translated.

"I did not lose—I merely let Tony win," Cosmos corrected. "It would have been rude to show him up in his own event."

"Yeah, like I *let* you cane me every time you drag me on a run with you," Tony said.

Cosmos shrugged, completely unrepentant. "Not my fault you don't have any stamina." He met Tony's eyes across the table, but he didn't add his usual line about how Tony's sexual partners would all be grateful if he learned how to compete in an event that wasn't over in less than a minute. Good behaviour indeed.

As Cosmos turned his attention toward Mike, Tony dipped his head slightly, and he managed to catch Donovan's lowered eyes.

Donovan didn't say anything, but he smiled as if he wanted to let Tony know he was okay. As much as Tony would have loved to have taken that on faith, he automatically took stock himself.

Donovan's nerves hadn't faded away completely, the way they sometimes did when they were entirely on their own, but they hadn't peaked dramatically either. Donovan hadn't managed to say much—but there again not many people did around Cosmos. He'd appeared nervous, but hadn't drawn anyone's attention in a way that might make him feel self conscious.

Tony leaned back in his chair as he sipped his Coke and listened to Cosmos nagging Mike about some plan or other that he was cooking up. He was tempted to consider their first venture out to the pub a success.

* * * * *

Donovan let out a relieved little sigh as he stepped into

Tony's flat later that evening.

"What do you think?" Tony asked, as he closed the door behind them. "Cosmos and Mike aren't too bad, are they?"

Walking ahead of Tony, Donovan wandered into the living room and over to the window. "Is Cosmos his real name?" he hedged.

"Yeah. His parents were really into the new age thing. I don't think they considered what kind of attitude a guy would end up with after having to go through school with a name like that." He paused for a second. "You didn't say what you thought of them."

Damn. "They seemed nice," Donovan hazarded. Well, Cosmos had seemed hyper, and Mike had barely got a word in edgewise, but they were Tony's friends—Donovan was willing to consider that qualified them both as nice.

"But?" Tony asked, from somewhere toward the middle of the room.

Donovan sighed. Rather than face Tony, he studied Tony's reflection in the window. "I just don't know what to say to guys without giving them the wrong impression."

As Donovan watched his reflection, Tony stepped up behind him and slid his arms around his waist. A tug encouraged Donovan to lean back against him. "Did he accuse you of that—of giving him the wrong impression?"

Donovan nodded.

"A lot?"

Donovan nodded again. Every other thing he'd said to Ryan had been twisted into an invitation, but...

He took a deep breath. It took all his courage to make the next admission. "Not just him."

Tony didn't pull away. It was only when he failed to do that, that Donovan realised he'd expected him to.

"Every time I go to a gay pub, guys always think I'm flirting with them, that I want them to flirt with me," Donovan blurted out.

"I've never seen you give any guy the slightest encouragement to think you're interested in him, and trust me, I've been paying really close attention every time you stepped into that pub."

Donovan breathed a little easier with the reassurance. Ryan would have said it was his fault for acting like a slut. Donovan leaned a little bit more firmly into Tony's embrace.

Tony pressed a kiss to his temple. "It will be easier now."

Donovan hesitated. Being able to occasionally talk to Tony in complete sentences wasn't the same as talking to a stranger whose reactions were, by definition, a hell of a lot less predictable. "It will?"

"Of course," Tony said. "If a man hits on you now, you just tell him you've got a boyfriend. And if someone doesn't get the hint when you give him the brush off, you can tell me and I'll be more than happy to get the guy to leave you alone."

When Tony encouraged him to turn around within his embrace, Donovan went with it. He looked up.

Tony looked very serious. "Do you think that might help?"

Donovan nodded. "Thank you." He was silent for a few seconds, but when Tony didn't speak up, Donovan pulled together his courage and took the initiative, sort of. "Whose move is it?"

Tony brushed their lips together, but he didn't accept Donovan's offer to deepen the kiss.

"You know that neither of us has to make a move every time we meet up?" he asked, as he lifted his head. "It's part of the being someone's boyfriend rather than a casual hook up."

Donovan didn't retreat. Tony wanted to have sex with him—he'd made that very clear. Donovan couldn't keep on doubting that every time Tony failed to act like Ryan. "But maybe we want to, even if we don't have to?" he suggested, quite proud of himself for sounding sane, even if he hadn't managed to sound flirtatious.

"Then, it's your move."

Donovan hesitated, sure it was nothing of the sort. But, if Tony was offering...

"Handcuffs." Donovan was pretty sure any other man on the planet would have thought he was insane for just blurting out that one word. Tony simply nodded as if it was the most logical and complete answer anyone could have given.

"On me or you?" he asked.

"Me!" Donovan bit his bottom lip. He really hadn't meant the word to come out as vehemently as it had. "I mean, unless you..." If the rumours he'd heard about Tony's sex life weren't as complete as he'd assumed they were, if Tony liked wearing them as much as Donovan did, it wasn't fair that he hogged them. "If you prefer to—"

Tony put a finger over his lips this time, rather than his whole hand. "We're not talking about what I prefer."

"We should be," Donovan said, behind his fingertip.

Tony shook his head.

"Please." The finger was still there, but it was easy to talk past it. And, really, if Tony seriously wanted him to shut up, he'd have used his whole hand, like before. "Tell me what you prefer?"

Tony paused for a second. "I prefer to be the one tying someone else up," he said eventually. "But that doesn't mean we can't switch things up whenever you want to." He finally moved his finger away from Donovan's lips.

Donovan looked up at him, studying him very carefully. "I don't think you liked being cuffed at all."

"I liked everything we did when I was tied up—if I didn't, I'd have said, straight away," Tony said, stressing that last bit as if it was important. "But, you're right; wearing the cuffs doesn't do anything for me."

Donovan bit his bottom lip. "They don't make you feel..."

Tony slid his fingers through Donovan's hair. "Feel

what, sweetheart?"

Donovan frowned. He wasn't sure there were any words that actually fitted how he felt. "Safe?" he hazarded. "Peaceful?"

"Is that how they make you feel?" Tony asked.

Donovan nodded, but he couldn't meet Tony's gaze. "It sounds stupid."

"It sounds beautiful."

Donovan glanced up at him. Tony didn't look like he was making fun of him. He seemed more intrigued by the idea than anything else. He took hold of Donovan's hand and led him back toward the bedroom without any further delay.

When Tony released his hand, Donovan went straight to where the cuffs rested on the bedside table, but Tony didn't. He went across to the chest of drawers instead. He took something out of the top drawer before he came to stand at Donovan's side.

Tony held a different pair of cuffs in his hand, leather ones.

"Do you think these would make you feel safe too?" he offered the cuffs to him to inspect.

Donovan ran his fingers over the well padded leather. He'd seen similar ones used in scenes on the internet, but he hadn't actually seen a pair in real life. The very sight of them went straight to his cock. The scent of the leather made him harden even more rapidly.

"Why these and not the others?" he asked, trusting that Tony wouldn't mind the question.

"They're more comfortable than the other ones," Tony said, very simply.

Donovan nodded. He handed them back to Tony. His sleeve slid back slightly with the action, showing his watch. That would be in the way. Donovan took it off and put it on the bedside table.

He hesitated then, remembering how Tony had lain naked on the bed, and how awkward it had been to move his own clothes out of the way when he'd worn the cuffs while dressed.

"Should I?" Donovan touched the neckline of his shirt.

Tony nodded. "Go for it."

As soon as he'd tossed his shirt aside, Tony fastened one of the cuffs around Donovan's wrist. Donovan looked down at it. He watched in fascination as Tony unclipped the cuffs from each other to make it easier for Tony to bind his other wrist the same way.

"Better or worse than the metal cuffs?" Tony asked.

Donovan didn't even need to think about it. "Better."

"Why?"

"It feels more like you're holding my wrists." Donovan glanced up, not sure if Tony would approve.

"Do you want them to be held in front of you, or behind you tonight?" As he spoke, Tony guided Donovan's hands behind his back, letting him know what his suggestion would be.

Donovan considered the question carefully. "Behind feels good," he offered.

Tony pressed a kiss against his temple as he moved to stand behind Donovan and fasten the cuffs together. It was different to being cuffed to the bed. More free in some ways, less free in others. Donovan took a deep breath and let it out slowly. Everything was fine, and his cock was now hard enough to make him wish he'd worn looser jeans.

Tony dropped a kiss on Donovan's shoulder as he moved back in front of him. A few quick movements and Tony had taken his shirt off over his head, so they were both stripped to the waist.

When he stepped forward to kiss Donovan again, their bodies brushed together, bare skin against bare skin in a way that Donovan had already fallen in love with when they were in the shower.

Donovan gasped. He sensed Tony move away slightly, as if he wasn't sure it was a good kind of a gasp or not.

Donovan closed the gap between them, pressing their bodies together. He couldn't help but moan his approval into the kiss. He was pretty sure no one could misinterpret that as being a panicked kind of sound.

Tony deepened the kiss. One of his hands was on the back of Donovan's head, holding him at just the right angle. Tony's other hand rested on his side, steadying him as he rose up onto his toes to bridge the height difference between them.

By the time Tony broke the kiss, Donovan knew he wasn't the only one whose cock was hard and pressing against the inside of his fly. He blinked up at Tony.

"Last time you wore cuffs I sucked you off," Tony said.

Donovan nodded his acceptance of the statement. He hadn't been able to return the favour last time he'd tried, but maybe this time, with the cuffs to remind him who he was with, he —

"I want to do that again."

It took Donovan a few seconds to realise that the conversation wasn't going the way he'd expected it to. "Why?" he blurted out.

"Because one of the good parts of not rushing is being able to take the time to revisit things we've enjoyed doing before, rather than trying to do something new every time we get together," Tony said. "So, unless you can look me in the eye and tell me you don't actually want a blow job…"

"I do want that!" Donovan was pretty sure no sane man would have said anything else at that point. Maybe he'd said it really enthusiastically, because he made Tony smile.

Tony turned them so Donovan's back was to the bed. He undid Donovan's fly without any hint of fumbling. In seconds, he was guiding Donovan to kick off his trainers and step out of the tangle of jeans, boxers and socks, all at the same time.

Donovan was completely naked as Tony guided him to sit on the edge of the bed. He watched Tony's movements with an almost detached kind of interest. He half expected a flurry of uncertainty to rise up inside him regardless of which of them knelt and which of them sat on the edge of the bed, but it didn't happen.

Maybe Tony was onto something with the whole re-visiting good things plan. For the first time, Donovan realised that he was actually able to think about something to do with sex and call to mind the memory of enjoying it in the past.

He'd liked feeling Tony's mouth around him when Tony went down on him before. Getting a blow job was a good thing. Tony wanting to do it again was a very fantastic thing.

Donovan watched Tony lower himself to his knees in front of him. He knew that Tony was studying his reactions, working out if the little changes between last time and this time were making him nervous.

He didn't want Tony worrying. While Tony rested his weight forward over his knees rather than sitting back on his heels, they were close to the same height. It was easy for Donovan to lean forward and press their mouths together. It was brief and chaste, and almost as soon as he did it, Donovan was sure he'd made a mistake by taking so much control of things. He pulled back quickly. But before he had a chance to apologise, he saw the look in Tony's eyes.

Tony didn't think he was trying to take over. Tony liked that he'd kissed him. He liked it a lot.

Donovan was sure that a naked man shouldn't blush at a kiss, but he felt the heat race to his cheeks and there was nothing he could do about it. And maybe there was nothing he should want to do about it because Tony grinned when he noticed.

Tony pressed a kiss to his cheek, just where the flush would be deepest. Donovan thought that he intended to trail kisses down his body the way he had last time, but Tony sat back on his heels.

All his movements just slightly slower than seemed natural, as if giving Donovan plenty of time to react, Tony wrapped his hand around Donovan's erection.

Donovan bit back a gasp.

Tony smiled as he began to move his hand around Donovan's cock in slow, easy movements.

Donovan couldn't help but rock his hips in time with the strokes. His eyes dropped closed. His brain went into neutral. His first hint that something might have changed was a breath of air moving against the tip of his cock.

He looked down just in time to see Tony run his tongue over the head. He might have cursed out loud at the sight. He couldn't be sure. From that point on, he had very little idea what words stayed inside his head and which ones he shared with Tony.

The sight of Tony on his knees, the image of Tony's lips wrapped around his cock, was almost enough to make Donovan's eyes roll back in his head — except that would have meant not being able to take in that same beautiful view for every single moment it remained available.

Even though he was sure Tony tried to make everything last for as long as possible, it quickly became obvious to Donovan that there was no way in hell he was going to be able to hold back.

Tony barely dipped his head. His tongue worked against the tip as his lips wrapped around the very topmost part of his shaft. Hardly any of his cock was even in Tony's mouth, and it still felt so close to ecstasy, it couldn't possibly be legal.

The relief he'd felt at Tony still being interested in him despite how screwed up he was. The cuffs around his wrists. The simple fact Tony was undeniably and perfectly who he was. It all collided with the bliss rushing through his veins, and restraint became impossible.

Donovan let out a yell as he came.

All the energy seemed to drain out of him as the intense waves of ecstasy gradually faded away. He slumped back and lay across the bed. His cuffed hands were trapped behind him.

That didn't matter. The cuffs still felt good, reassuring and strong around his skin.

The mattress dipped as Tony joined him on the bed. Half laying down alongside him, propped up by one elbow, Tony smiled as if it was Donovan who had just done something nigh on miraculous for him, rather than the other way around.

Donovan nibbled on his bottom lip. Completely relaxed and at ease with the whole world, he still wasn't sure how exactly to offer to do the same for Tony the very moment he got his breath back.

"What about you?" Donovan whispered. He didn't raise his head to look, but he was pretty sure if he did glance toward Tony's fly, he'd see that he was still hard and straining against the material.

"I'm fine as I am."

"I thought. I mean…" If his hands were in front of him, Donovan would have lifted his fingertips to his lips and made his offer clear that way. Unable to do that, he found himself floundering. "You don't want me to suck you off?" he finally rushed out.

"No," Tony said. "We're not going to try that tonight."

Donovan blinked. "We're not?"

* * * * *

"No, we're not." Tony said, very firmly. He'd made that decision long before they'd got up that morning, let alone returned to his flat. He wasn't going to let them make the same mistake they had the previous night. They were going to go slow, and they weren't going to do anything that Donovan was nervous about for the foreseeable future.

"Because?" Donovan asked, cautiously.

"It's not tit for tat, sweetheart. You don't owe me an orgasm because I got you off." He let his tone of voice make it clear how serious he was about that. That was one of the very first things he needed to push out of Donovan's head. "And we're not in a rush. I think that's why things didn't go to plan last night—all the ideas we're trying to put in your head were just too new. So, we're going to let everything settle into your mind properly before we try any new moves."

Donovan turned his attention to a detailed examination of the ceiling.

Tony watched, warily. Knowing that his decision was a good one wasn't quite the same as knowing that his decision would go down well with Donovan. There was definitely a line to be aware of—one that separated a guy who kept hold of the reins while he helped Donovan do whatever he wanted to do, from a guy who took so much control of the situation that what Donovan wanted became as irrelevant now as it had been when he was with that bastard.

Handcuffs upon request were one thing. Tony letting his dom side run free was out of the question. It had to be Donovan's show, and—

"I've been jacking off while thinking about going down on you for months."

Tony blinked at the unexpected statement. If it hadn't been for the way the blush across Donovan's cheeks deepened, he might have pulled off sounding far less innocent than he actually was.

"Just because you like thinking about something, that doesn't mean you have to actually do it," Tony said, stroking his fingers down Donovan's cheek. And, God, how much courage had it taken Donovan to admit to thinking about him that way after everything Ryan taught him that would lead to?

Damn, but it was hard not to fall a little further in love with him every time they met up.

"I just mean that I've had plenty of time to get used to the idea that I want to suck you off," Donovan added. "I know I screwed up last time, but—"

Tony put a fingertip briefly to Donovan's lips, silencing

him as politely as possible. Their eyes met for a moment. Donovan seemed to realise that he'd miscalculated. "I know last time didn't end the way we both hoped it would?" he offered, as an alternative.

Tony brushed a kiss against his lips in praise.

"I think, with the cuffs, it might end better this time," Donovan whispered.

Tony stroked his fingers through Donovan's hair and pushed it back off his face.

There was something about Donovan's eyes—a calmness in them that hadn't been there last time Donovan wanted to suck him off. Tony had spent the better part of the previous night working things out and making little lists inside his head. He'd suspected that afterglow belonged firmly in the list of things that helped Donovan feel calmer. Now, he was sure he was right.

"Please?" Donovan said.

With that one word, two things became clear. Donovan would take any attempt to talk him out of it as a rejection, and Donovan wanted to go down on him for his own reasons rather than because he thought that was what Tony wanted.

Donovan didn't need his boyfriend to be patient or to slow things down. He needed the guy who was supposed to know what he was doing to get him through this blow job without inspiring another flashback. And Donovan had to have whatever he needed—failure on that score wasn't an option.

"We'll try it again and see what happens," Tony decided, with complete, if entirely faked, casualness.

Donovan smiled at him, managing to look both shy and full of afterglow at the same time. Yes, afterglow, that was important, and it wouldn't last forever. If they were going to do this tonight, the sooner the better.

Tony pulled himself off the bed and kicked off the remainder of his clothes, but he stopped Donovan short when it became clear he intended to slip off the bed to kneel alongside it.

Donovan made no objection when Tony prompted him to kneel on the bed instead. It was only when Tony reached for the cuffs that Donovan spoke up.

"Tony?"

"I'm not taking them away, I'm just…" He unclipped them and brought them around in front of Donovan. "Rearranging things, to make it easier."

"Oh… Thank you." So polite…

"Condom or not?" Tony offered.

The shake of his head was just as firm as it had been last time. "Not."

"Okay." Tony tilted one of the pillows on end so he could lie down with his head tilted up just enough to be able to keep a good view of Donovan's face.

Even if Donovan didn't want control, if Tony had his way, everything about this was going to give Donovan a head start in feeling like he was the one with all the power. Arranging them so that Donovan would be the one who loomed above him was as good a place to start as any other.

Tony stroked his thumb across Donovan's lips as he guided him to kneel between his extended legs. "Just keep it simple," he said, doing everything in his power to make it clear that he was offering a suggestion, not issuing an order. "Just take the tip in your mouth and move your tongue against it. That's all you need to do."

Just like I did with you. There was a reason why he hadn't tried to show off when he went down on Donovan. Even if it hadn't registered with Donovan on a conscious level, perhaps subconsciously he'd have realised that a complicated technique and deep-throating wasn't in any way necessary.

A quick brush of the lips and Tony lay back.

With his hands in front of him now, Donovan was able to wrap his fingers around Tony's erection. He glanced up at Tony for a moment, but he didn't try to keep eye contact as he dipped his head and carefully encircled the topmost inch of

Tony's cock with his lips.

Wet heat enveloped the head. Donovan's tongue moved slightly clumsily against the glans.

Tony silently cursed. Damn it, he was supposed to be the guy who knew what he was doing when it came to sex. It was one of the main reasons Donovan had chosen to date him in the first place. Tony didn't need to come the first second he felt a guy's mouth on his cock. Really, he didn't. Not even if it was Donovan's mouth and Tony had spent over a year imagining it getting better acquainted with his erection.

Donovan soon took more of the length between his lips and began to bob his head a little more quickly. His lips slid further down the shaft. He was rushing again. Advice and examples hadn't worked.

As good as what Donovan was doing felt, Tony couldn't risk Donovan being upset by needing to stop again— not even for something that felt like a tidal wave of pleasure that was determined to show him just how much fun it could be to drown beneath the waves.

Tony reached down. He knew the moment Donovan spotted his hand in his field of vision that he thought Tony was going to put his hand on the back of his head. Tony expected him to pull back, but Donovan held his ground, his mouth remained around Tony's cock.

His movements more cautious now, Tony carefully guided the hand Donovan had wrapped around the base of his cock up so it encircled further along the length. Donovan wouldn't have to dip his head more than an inch in order to kiss his fist.

"Just the tip," Tony reminded him. His voice was raw and deep, it was impossible for him to make the words as gentle as he would have loved them to be.

Donovan made a sound that was probably meant to indicate agreement. Vibrations surrounded Tony's cock, sending shock waves through his body. "Perfect," he whispered.

Another set of vibrations. It only took Tony two more bits of praise before he became sure that Donovan was going to acknowledge everything he said with another of those spine tingling little sounds.

Because he liked being praised or because hearing Tony's voice reminded him he wasn't with Ryan? Did it really matter which?

Anything that Donovan liked was by definition a good thing, a thing that should be repeated at every possible opportunity. Tony stared down at Donovan as he whispered snippets of approval to him.

Donovan's lips were narrowed into a thin pink line. His cheeks hollowed as he sucked around the tip. He was gorgeous.

Closing his eyes, Donovan began to work his tongue more confidently against the tip of his cock, diligently repeating all those moves that Tony had praised over and over again.

Tony gave everything he had to keeping his hips still and not pushing up into Donovan's mouth, but he refused to close his eyes as he fought for control. He kept all his attention on Donovan, searching for clues.

He noticed the moment tension began to creep into Donovan's muscles.

"Donovan. Look up. Look at me." Just a touch of an order in his tone saw Donovan obeying him instantly.

Donovan's gaze met his. Tony smiled down at him. "That's right. Let me see your eyes."

Donovan hesitated for a moment. He looked down. Then he pulled his gaze back up. A touch of colour made it to his cheeks as if the idea that Tony liked looking at him while he sucked him off was a strange and fantastic concept.

"That's right," Tony murmured again, meeting Donovan's gaze every time Donovan managed to look up at him.

There would be no doubting who Donovan was going

down on this time. There would be no room for anyone other than Tony in Donovan's head. Success rushed through Tony's veins almost as fast as Donovan pushed more and more pleasure into his body. It made it even harder not to come long before he should have needed to.

Tony gasped as Donovan's tongue swirled against him again.

He tugged gently at Donovan's shoulder, encouraging him to pull away, sure that him coming in Donovan's mouth would be a step too far for that night.

Donovan looked up, but he made no attempt to obey the prompt.

"Gonna come," Tony explained, as best he could while Donovan's lips were still wrapped around the tip of his cock.

Donovan made a noise that sounded like it was full of approval. Its pitch was higher than the other sounds he'd offered Tony. The vibrations were faster and a whole new kind of wonderful.

Tony's control faltered. His climax caught him off guard. He managed to keep his hips still as he came, but there was no way he could actually stop his orgasm thundering wildly through him.

His breath caught in his throat, stopping him from crying out. It was impossible for him to keep his eyes open as he came. The first moment control of his body came back to him, he looked down at Donovan.

He expected him to have pulled back—to have been put off balance, if not thrown into a complete flashback. He had a whole string of reassurances ready on his lips and—

They weren't needed.

As their eyes met, Donovan pulled back and let Tony's softening shaft slip from his mouth. His lips were reddened by friction, but both pleasure and satisfaction danced in his eyes.

Tony caught hold of the links between his cuffs and tugged him up the bed to lie down next to him.

"I did it," Donovan whispered to him, as if Tony might not have noticed. "I actually managed to do that without completely freaking out."

"You were amazing." Tony smiled and brushed a chaste kiss against his lips.

Donovan snuggled into his side, just the way he had the previous night. He didn't seem the least bit bothered about the way the cuffs remained around his wrists. He let out a satisfied little sigh as Tony wrapped an arm around his shoulders and welcomed him close.

I love you.

Directly after a blow job wasn't the right time to say it.

While Donovan didn't feel the same way wasn't the right time to say it either.

Neither of those facts stopped Tony wanting to say it.

He settled for pressing a kiss against Donovan's temple and keeping the confession inside his head, but that didn't mean it wouldn't have been the truth if he had said it out loud.

Chapter Eight

I've been thinking about when we finally manage to have sex...

Donovan shook his head at himself as a wry little smile twisted his lips. He hadn't been thinking about anything other than having sex with Tony for so long, it was a small wonder he hadn't gone mad. But actually saying that to Tony, starting that conversation...

Taking a deep breath, Donovan let it out slowly.

Including the time before Trentmoore, they'd been dating for almost three months now. Which, as far as Donovan could work out, was the longest Tony had dated any one person since he'd joined the institute.

Donovan closed his eyes. Whichever way he cut things, his time had to be running out by now. He pushed his hands through his hair. Tony being patient and giving him time was all well and good — as long as Tony didn't give him so much time they completely failed to have sex before he decided he'd spent long enough pretending to be Donovan's boyfriend and pandering to his complete inability to pull himself together.

A sound from the corridor leading from Tony's front door to his living room made Donovan look up. He glanced at his watch. Tony had only left two minutes ago. He'd said the take away place was close, but even so...

Donovan automatically looked around, fully expecting to see whatever Tony had come back for lying on the sofa, or perhaps on the floor alongside it. Clothing had gone a bit askew before Tony left. His wallet could easily have fallen out of his pocket.

A movement on the other side of the room made him

stop searching and look up. "Did you forget...?" Donovan pulled himself jerkily to his feet. Tony hadn't forgotten anything. It wasn't Tony who'd come in, and all the hard work Donovan had put into avoiding meeting Tony's brother was ruined in an instant.

Donovan stared, unable to bring a single word to his lips.

When Tony's brother saw him, he halted on the threshold. In that moment, Donovan realised that he wasn't the only one who'd been working very hard to avoid running into anyone but Tony on the nights he stayed there.

Suddenly snapping back into action, the guy smiled. "Hi. I'm Colby."

Damn it, if he'd realised how mortifyingly awkward it would be to meet Colby on his own, he would have taken Tony up on one of his invitations to introduce them. For several seconds, there were no words in his head.

Still standing alongside the sofa, Donovan pushed his hands into his pockets to stop himself making his nerves even more obvious by fidgeting. "Yes. Tony mentioned you," he finally managed to stutter out.

"What did he say?" Colby asked, his curiosity clear.

"That you're not actually as creepy as the telescope makes you look." The moment the words left his lips, Donovan pulled one hand out of his pocket and pressed it against his mouth. He hadn't really just said that. He couldn't have.

Colby's easy laughter caught him off guard. "That sounds like Tony."

"I'm so sorry. He didn't mean it like that. He—"

Colby grinned and made his way further into the room. "Yeah, he did mean it like that. It's okay."

"He said you were dating the man who teaches the dance classes," Donovan tried to clarify.

"Yeah, I am. His name's Noah."

Donovan nodded, quietly determined to stick to

nodding or shaking his head for the rest of the conversation. It was probably the only way he could get through it without either making any more of a fool of himself, or dropping Tony any further into it with his brother. Damn it, this was exactly why he hadn't wanted to meet Colby, or Noah, ever.

"Is Tony around?"

Bugger, a nod wasn't going to cover that. "He went to get food," Donovan said, picking each word with care, just in case he should stumble across something else he really shouldn't say. Perhaps something along the lines of — *You're supposed to be at Noah's. You left a note on the fridge door saying that you weren't coming back tonight. I checked.*

"Food? Where from?"

"A Chinese place. I can't remember the name." Donovan nibbled on his bottom lip. "He said a friend of yours recommended it to him. It doesn't deliver."

Colby's eyes lit up at the mention of the recommendation. "How long ago did he leave?"

"Only a few minutes."

By the time Donovan had finished giving his answer, Colby was already on his mobile. "Are you at one of the places Jordan likes? Will you get some for me and Noah, too?"

Donovan shuffled his feet as Colby took a seat on the sofa and rattled off an order which seemed to be enough for six people. When he was done, Colby listened to whatever Tony was saying on the other end of the line, his expression becoming more serious. Then he handed his mobile across to Donovan.

"Hello?" Donovan hazarded, as he held it to his ear.

"Everything's fine," Tony said.

Donovan wasn't sure that was true, or what sort of response was required. Taking a step back, he took a seat on the room's other sofa. "Yes?"

"He's a bit weird, but it's a very harmless sort of weird," Tony went on. "Seriously, think of him as a slightly dopey Labrador — he's no more likely to think you're flirting with him than a puppy would be."

Donovan felt the heat go to his cheeks. Apparently, he hadn't been as subtle as he'd liked to think he'd been while putting off the introduction. But, as much as he loved the reassurance, how the hell was he supposed to reply to that when Colby was sitting right there? "Okay," he settled for.

"I'll be back in ten minutes at the most," Tony promised. "If you get stuck for conversation, ask him something about Noah—anything at all. He'll babble about him for hours, no problem."

"Okay," Donovan said again. "I..." He knew his blush deepened at the simple fact that Tony had cared enough to say all that. "Thank you."

When Tony disconnected the call, Donovan handed the mobile back to Colby. "Thank you."

Colby pocketed the phone. He was just about to speak when the front door opened again.

It was the guy Donovan had seen briefly through Colby's telescope. Noah. Donovan wasn't sure if that made the whole situation better or worse.

Colby got to his feet, his whole face lighting up with a smile that bordered on a grin. "Hi." He brushed his lips chastely against Noah's cheek before stepping back. Noah seemed slightly amused by something, as if that wasn't the way Colby usually greeted him.

"This is Donovan," Colby added. "Tony's boyfriend. Tony's getting Chinese for us all."

Noah extended a hand to Donovan as Donovan pulled himself to his feet. If Noah was shocked at running into him, he was a lot better at hiding it than Colby had been when he first walked into the room.

"Noah Stephens."

"You're the dancer." God, could Donovan be in any less control of his mouth if he tried?

Noah's apparent amusement with the situation deepened. "You're the archer."

"More someone who works in a call centre and occasionally gets to the archery range," Donovan said. He was quite pleased to think that comment sounded sane, even if nothing else he'd said that evening had.

"I know the feeling. I mostly teach dance classes — generally to people who should never be allowed within twenty miles of a dance floor."

"Bad day?" Colby asked. His hand came to rest on the small of Noah's back as he spoke.

"I didn't say anything to any of my students which will get me fired," Noah said. "So I'm going to count it as a success. Although, if I ever get one that can read minds, I'm going to be up the creek without a paddle." He took a seat on the sofa, and stretched out his legs, looking perfectly relaxed. "There are some days when mental sarcasm is really not an optional extra."

"It's not their fault they can't dance like you," Colby said, mildly, as he sat next to him. "No one can."

Donovan couldn't help but smile at the way Colby spoke to Noah. It was also suddenly much easier to picture him as the puppy that Tony had compared him to — a puppy who was overjoyed to have his master home again. He sat down on the opposite sofa.

"Most of them can't even find the beat," Noah said, although he sounded like he wasn't finding it easy to cling to his annoyance at his students now he was with Colby.

Colby smiled. "Neither can I." He glanced across at Donovan, neatly welcoming him into the conversation. "I have two left feet."

"Colby does fine," Noah corrected. He seemed to consider that statement carefully. "As long as you don't let him lead."

Colby shook his head. "Noah dances like it's what he was born to do. I dance like a swimmer."

"Where as I swim like a dancer…" Noah murmured.

Colby shook his head, obviously not happy with even

the mildest criticism of Noah, even from Noah himself.

Noah's expression as he looked up at Colby was a strange mixture of tolerance and resignation, as if he had tried to explain a version of reality in which he wasn't perfect to Colby, but had eventually given it up as impossible.

This time, when the door opened, Donovan really hoped it was Tony. He wasn't sure he could take another surprise addition to the group.

* * * * *

"Well?" Tony asked, an hour or so later, as he led Donovan into his bedroom and finally got him on his own for the first time since he'd brought the take away back. "Was I right about Colby — a slightly dopey Labrador?"

Donovan bit his lip in an apparent effort to hold back a chuckle.

Tony grinned, thrilled to see Donovan relaxed enough to enjoy the joke.

"He's nice," Donovan said, softly. "He's...very focused on Noah, isn't he?"

Tony laughed, that was one way to put it. He also had a horrible suspicion that Colby and Noah were having a similar conversation about exactly how besotted he was with Donovan. Even if Donovan hadn't seen the amusement in Noah's eyes as he looked from Tony to Colby and back again, Tony definitely had.

When Donovan's expression turned more serious, Tony tensed, not sure what to expect. He'd had the chance to prime Colby slightly on the phone, but that had only been a few rushed words warning him to keep everything between him and Noah to a kiss on the cheek at the very most.

"Do you remember saying that he's not as creepy as the telescope makes him look?" Donovan asked.

Tony nodded, taking a seat on the edge of the bed and tapping the mattress alongside him, inviting Donovan to join him.

"Before you got home," Donovan continued. "When Colby introduced himself, I said you'd mentioned him. He asked what you said and…"

Tony laughed. Was that all?

Donovan smiled cautiously as he sat down next to Tony. "He didn't seem to be offended," he offered.

"I've been saying it to his face for years," Tony said. "He doesn't take any notice any more." He considered that statement. "He didn't take any notice to begin with. Brothers are allowed to wind each other up." Which reminded him… "You're an only child, right?"

Donovan nodded.

"I thought so," Tony said. "My coach is going to be heartbroken."

Donovan tilted his head slightly to one side as he tried to follow. "He is?"

Tony nodded. "He thinks you're a good influence on me. He was hoping you had a brother he could set Cosmos up with."

Donovan ducked his head, but there was a pleased little blush across his cheekbones, showing he was quite flattered by the praise, even if it was strange and came from a coach he'd never met.

"Probably a good thing you don't have a brother after all," Tony said, idly. "I don't think he'd have ever forgiven me if I landed him with someone like Cosmos."

Donovan was slowly getting used to Cosmos and Mike. Tony was pretty sure he would find Colby and Noah even easier to get along with, now that he'd actually met them.

Tony ran his fingers up and down Donovan's back, wondering if he should apologise for not being there when Donovan first met Colby and Noah, or if it was better to pretend that he hadn't noticed how nervous the idea had always made Donovan.

"Do you know, once upon a time, I tried to set Colby

up on a date with Cosmos?" Tony said.

The look on Donovan's face was a perfect mixture of shock and scepticism. "You're joking."

Tony shook his head. "Although, in my defence, I had just met Cosmos. He seemed like a really sweet guy." Whereas Donovan really was a sweet guy.

"I'm sorry I made so much fuss about not meeting them before," Donovan suddenly rushed out. "I just…"

"You were just nervous," Tony said, complete acceptance hanging on every word.

Donovan offered up a jerky nod.

"Because Colby's my brother or because he and Noah are gay?" Tony asked, keeping the real question back for now. *Did Ryan have a brother – is that the problem?* Because, really, how did he fix that problem? Nudging Colby into staying over at Noah's on the nights Donovan came to the flat was one thing, but he couldn't actually magic his little brother completely out of existence.

Donovan seemed to think about the question Tony had actually asked very carefully. "Because I've been nervous around other gay men for so long, it's become a habit." He glanced up at Tony. "I know they're not going to think I'm flirting with them. I just… I also know that I could panic and make a huge fool out of myself in front of your family, and –"

Tony laughed, cutting Donovan off before his words could end up rushing out so fast they descended into complete confusion. "I'm pretty sure they wouldn't even notice if you did flirt with them, or panic. Half the guys in the institute could dance through the flat nude and up for it – if Noah was in the room, Colby wouldn't even realise there was anyone else there. Noah might notice, but he's almost as bad as Colby at this point. He'd probably complain that their dancing wasn't up to scratch and try to teach them some new steps."

And, God help me, but all I'd do in that situation was worry that they'd either make you nervous or that you'd want to wander off and have sex with them rather than me.

Tony smiled wryly at the reality of his situation. Despite all his best efforts, Donovan still didn't seem at all inclined to fall for him in return, or even to date him for any longer than it took him to get laid.

As Tony studied Donovan, he gradually became aware that they'd reached the part of the evening where Donovan was no longer thinking about any man who wasn't in the room.

Donovan remained deep in thought for a little while, but while he also stayed relaxed, Tony was quite content to wait him out and simply admire the view. He'd find out which direction things were going to go in soon enough. Once Donovan made his decision, it usually became very obvious whether the evening was going to involve kinkiness very quickly.

A few more seconds ticked passed. Donovan looked up and met Tony's gaze. Tony knew that look. It was what Tony had come to think of as Donovan's 'handcuffs expression'. There was a certain amount of nervousness in it, but there was a streak of rock solid determination there, too. It was an expression that said he was wary of trying something new, but he was bloody well going to do it anyway.

Tony loved that look, and not just because it tended to lead to very intense orgasms for them both. There was a strength and a confidence visible in Donovan in those moments. The only other time he seemed to be that sure of himself was when he held a bow in his hands.

If he held true to form, Donovan would blurt out what he wanted right about —

"What else do you have in the top drawer?" Donovan said, rushing through the words in his apparent haste to get them out.

Tony didn't pretend to misunderstand. He'd caught Donovan eyeing the chest of drawers more and more speculatively ever since Tony had taken the leather cuffs out of the top one. "There are a few other toys in there," Tony acknowledged.

It took a few moments, but Donovan eventually dragged his eyes up and met Tony's gaze. "Whose move is it?"

"Yours," Tony said. He was reasonably sure that Donovan knew there wasn't even the pretence of taking turns anymore. It was Donovan's show. For the first time in his life, Tony wasn't the one making any of the big decisions in a relationship.

As much as it scared the hell out of him, he was just along for the ride. All he could do was try to steer things slightly to give Donovan the best possible chance of being able to do exactly as he pleased, and try to keep his dom side to himself whenever possible.

"I'd like to see what else is in the drawer, please."

Tony's lips quirked. The please was a nice touch — even if it was all about vanilla flavoured politeness rather than the kind of formal submission Tony had received in some of the local clubs and had hoped to one day enjoy with Donovan.

Levering himself up off the bed, Tony walked across to the chest of drawers. Rather than try to carry bits and pieces across the room, he took the whole drawer out and placed it on the bed next to Donovan, ensuring that Donovan would know that he wasn't hiding a single thing from him.

Donovan turned sideways on the bed and pulled his legs up in front of him as he positioned himself to get the best possible view of the contents.

Tony wasn't entirely sure what sort of reaction he'd expected. There were a fair number of things in there and, if Tony was confident that the various restraints would find favour with Donovan, he was equally certain everything else would be well outside his comfort zone for a hell of a long time to come.

Calm. That was the first thing that Tony noticed. Donovan was completely calm. His breathing was slow and steady. His shoulders were relaxed. There was a slight blush on his cheeks, but Tony could only consider that a good thing—it meant that Donovan wasn't white as a sheet, and that meant there was nothing in there that reminded him of Ryan.

Donovan reached out, but paused, with his hand a few inches above the drawer. "Can I?"

"My toy drawer is your toy drawer," Tony said, stretching out on the bed on the other side of the drawer, leaning on his elbow and making sure he had a good view of Donovan's expression while he explored the contents.

Donovan ran his hands over the ankle cuffs that matched the wrist cuffs they'd already used. Tony could so easily picture Donovan tied spread eagle on the bed, squirming as he was teased right to the edge, before Tony finally let him come. He'd thrive on that kind of bondage.

"I thought those might catch your attention."

"You know it's not only about feeling safe, right?" Donovan blurted out. "I…"

"You find them hot, too?" Tony suggested, when he realised that Donovan wasn't sure how to finish the sentence on his own.

Donovan nodded. His blush was beautiful.

Tony's lips twitched. "Snap."

Donovan chuckled at his childishness, but his attention went quickly back to the toys.

A blindfold passed under Donovan's inspection. A gag was carefully inspected. He still didn't seem to be the least bit nervous.

Tony was more than a little fascinated by the idea that Donovan found his toy drawer less intimidating than he'd found meeting his little brother. He couldn't help but smile.

"Where did you get the idea to try kink?" Tony asked, after a few moments, making sure it sounded more like idle curiosity than something he'd been wondering about more and more as the weeks passed and Donovan's interest in handcuffs remained as strong as ever.

Donovan met his eyes for a moment before turning his attention to the blanket next to the toy drawer.

"Don?" Tony, prompted, wondering if he'd miscalculated somewhere along the line and brought back memories that had no place in that conversation.

"Internet porn," Donovan mumbled. "The...um..." He cleared his throat. "The kind without elves in it."

Tony grinned. "Snap," he repeated. Well, porn and an older woman he'd dated not long after he left school. It was close enough to count in Tony's book.

Whatever kind of kinky porn Donovan had been watching, it was obvious that he'd seen enough of it to get comfortable with the sight of paddles and floggers. Even if he wasn't interested in using them, he didn't seem worried by the fact that Tony owned a fair selection.

The tails on one of the floggers seemed to fascinate him. He ran his fingers over the lengths of suede again and again.

"If you want to try it you can," Tony said, still in that casual tone of voice, as if he hadn't been hard as a rock ever since Donovan first mentioned wanting to explore the drawer.

Donovan jerked his head up to look at Tony. He turned his attention back to the flogger, picked it up by the handle and offered it to Tony.

Tony smiled, but he merely turned the toy around in Donovan's grip, so that it was obvious he'd been offering to let Donovan wield it rather than feel its kiss.

Donovan stared at him as if he'd lost his mind.

Tony held out his arm offering his forearm as an easy target. "There's nothing to it. Just a flick of the wrist."

Donovan continued to stare at him.

When he finally turned his attention to the toy again, he seemed to fall into deep thought. Pushing his sleeve back, he brought the tails down against his own forearm instead, firmly, but not hard enough that Tony worried he might hurt himself.

"Well?" Tony asked.

"It feels good. I always wondered, when I was…"

"When you were exploring the internet?" Tony suggested.

Donovan blushed, but nodded. "It's the same as the handcuffs, isn't it?" he asked, carefully. "You own them to use on other people, not because you want anyone to use them on you."

Tony considered the drawer for a moment. If it had been anyone else sitting on his bed, that would have been a pretty thorough understanding of the situation. With Donovan, the usual rules weren't so much different as non-existent. "I tried out pretty much everything when I first bought it. I wouldn't use anything on someone else unless I had a good idea what I was doing. If you want to try something out on me, that's fine."

Donovan stared at him, unblinking. "Which is nothing like saying you'd actually like it, right?"

Tony smiled at the challenge. Donovan's confidence had come a long way—especially when they were alone together. "It's not my usual thing," he allowed.

Donovan went back to looking through the drawer. He ran his fingers along the length of a crop before coming to a halt at the end. In the corner of the drawer was a slim, black vibrator.

It seemed to shock Donovan more than any of the kinky bits and pieces. Tony analysed his expression carefully. Ryan didn't seem to have been the type to have played with a lot of toys, but at the same time, he'd obviously been a bastard as a top. Tony was pretty sure the idea of any kind of anal play still scared Donovan more than anything.

One blink of big hazel eyes and he looked to Tony, as if for an explanation.

"One of my ex girlfriends wanted to try a double penetration thing," Tony said, honestly.

Donovan nodded his understanding. He cleared his

throat. "Did you, try it I mean?"

Tony shook his head. "We never got around to that particular idea." *We went with the idea of a threesome and used two real cocks instead of a real one and a fake one...* No. There was such a thing as offering no more truth than was actually necessary—especially when Donovan was one lover that Tony would never be willing to share with another person that way. Even the thought of someone else touching Donovan made him want to string that person up. "It's pretty much the only toy in there that's never been used," he said, more for something to say than anything else.

Donovan stared down into the drawer for a little while, his expression unreadable. "Will you use it on me?" He hesitated then. "I mean... Is it still my move, or...?" He looked up. Their eyes met.

Tony held his gaze, trying to read all the things that Donovan might not be willing to say from his expression. "We can do whatever you want."

Donovan glanced down, but only briefly. "You wouldn't let me get away with saying that to you."

Tony grinned, thrilled by yet another show of increasing confidence. He reached out and stroked his fingers down Donovan's cheek. "No," he allowed. "I wouldn't, but our positions are slightly different."

This time, when Donovan looked down, it seemed like a less positive gesture.

Tony tucked a knuckle under Donovan's chin and encouraged him to look up again. "I'm not insulting you, sweetheart."

"You're worried I'll freak out and—"

Tony put his hand over Donovan's mouth.

"I'm more experienced than you. I'm far more inclined to boss people about than you are—especially when we're in bed. If I wanted to, I'd find it far easier to ride roughshod over you than you'd find it to push me about. That means different rules apply."

Donovan waited patiently until Tony moved his hand away from his mouth, then he cleared his throat. "The more I think about it, the more surprised I am that you only own one gag."

Tony grinned at him over the top of the toy drawer. "One gag, but two hands—sometimes working without toys is more fun."

"And you can just say you're a dom," Donovan added. "I know the word."

Tony considered Donovan more carefully than ever. Whatever words he might or might not be aware of, he'd never actually applied any labels to them before. "What about sub?" he asked. "Do you know that word, too?"

Donovan nodded. He didn't seem to be the least bit concerned at being referred to that way. They were words that Ryan hadn't tarnished.

"Is that really why you keep checking that I'm into what we're doing?" Donovan asked. "Because I'm a sub and you're a dom?"

Tony stroked his cheek again. "Yes. Even if you'd never met that bastard, I'd still want to be careful with you."

Donovan looked up at him through his lashes. In that moment, Tony knew he'd hit on the perfect thing to say.

"To go back to the original point," Tony said. "If you want to know if I think it would be hot to use it on you—yeah, I do. But do you think it would be?"

Donovan nodded. "I think it could be a..." He paused as if unsure of the right words. "Useful stepping stone." He had that determined look back in his eye.

Tony nodded his understanding. Getting Donovan comfortable with the vibrator would bring them one step closer to being able to have sex and, for better or worse, that was Donovan's main priority. That was the reason why he'd agreed to be Tony's boyfriend and—

Nope. Not thinking about that right now.

Taking the vibrator and handing it to Donovan, Tony

returned the drawer, and the rest of its contents, to the chest. When he turned back, Donovan was staring down at the toy as if it might do something interesting all on its own.

"Tell me what you do want to happen, and what you don't want to happen," Tony said.

* * * * *

Donovan looked down for a moment. Ever since that day he'd asked Tony not to put his hand on the back of his head, Tony had always made a point of checking before they tried something new.

It was Donovan's perfect opening. Now, he just had to get the words out. "I'd like you to trust me to tell you if I'm going to panic and to not be..."

Tony sat down next to him and slid his arm around his shoulder in silent support.

Donovan automatically leaned into him. "Don't be afraid to be a dom with me, at least a little bit?"

"Bossy, I can *definitely* work with that."

Donovan tilted his head back to look up at him. Tony immediately dipped his head and brought their lips together. Donovan went to reach out to him in return, but he still had the vibrator in his hand and he wasn't sure what to do with it. He ended up sitting with his hands in his lap and just letting Tony kiss him. It was almost like being bound.

"You'll tie me up, too?" Donovan whispered, when Tony broke the kiss. It was hard to believe that he could have forgotten to ask when Tony gave him the perfect opportunity.

He always asked and once he did, Tony always said yes, but it wasn't something Tony ever offered off his own bat.

"Not this time."

Donovan pulled back a little, so he could look at Tony properly. "Why not?"

"Because I want your hands free," Tony said, very simply.

Donovan studied him for a few seconds. "Being a dom?" he hazarded.

Tony smiled and pushed Donovan's hair back out of his face. "Maybe a bit. But if you hadn't asked me to be, I'd have still told you I wanted your hands free tonight."

Donovan looked at where the leather cuffs were on the bedside table. "Why?"

"Because I wouldn't be acting like a good boyfriend if I only ever taught you how to have sex while you're tied up." Tony pressed a kiss to his temple. "Wanting the cuffs and needing them are two different things, sweetheart. I don't want you to end up only feeling calm about everything when you're in bondage."

Donovan frowned. The idea of not wearing them wasn't helping his nerves at all. While he could see that needing them wasn't a good thing in the long run, in the short run they were a very effective solution.

"How about, you wear them, but I don't link them together. You'll still feel them around your wrists, but they won't stop you moving about."

Donovan stared at the cuffs.

"I'll tell you exactly where I want your hands every second," Tony offered.

Donovan hesitated. He loved the cuffs. But, he loved Tony telling him what to do, too. And, while he'd had quite a bit of the former, the latter had been much rarer. "Okay." Donovan nodded. Orders. "Yes, I'd like that," he said, more certainly.

Tony brushed their lips together. Taking the vibrator out of Donovan's hand, he tossed it casually on the bed. "Right now, I want your hands to be taking your clothes off. I want you naked."

Donovan nodded in favour of both the idea and the strength in Tony's voice. He reached for the hem of his shirt and pulled it over his head. It didn't take him much longer to have the rest of his clothes off, even with Tony distracting him with teasing touches along the way.

There was no clear intent behind the touches. It seemed more like Tony simply couldn't stand alongside his naked skin without wanting to caress it.

As soon as Donovan was naked, Tony put the cuffs around his wrists. Without the connecting links fastened between them, they were more like substantial pieces of jewellery than bondage.

"Now my clothes."

Donovan looked up at Tony. That was new. He nibbled on his bottom lip. There was something undeniably attractive about the idea.

Sliding his fingertips along the edge of Tony's T-shirt, Donovan gradually pulled the material up and over Tony's head. Almost without thinking about it, he reached out to run his hands over Tony's skin, just like Tony always did when their roles were reversed.

"Sometimes having your hands free can be fun, can't it?" Tony teased.

Donovan nodded as he lowered himself to his knees to help Tony out of his shoes and socks. Tony rested a hand on his shoulder to steady himself. His hand stayed there when Donovan reached for his fly and started to tug his jeans down.

Tony was going commando. That wasn't exactly a rare thing. But it was the first time Donovan found himself on his knees in front of Tony when he freed his erection from behind the denim.

Leaning forward, he wrapped his lips around the tip of Tony's cock. Tony's grip on his shoulder immediately tightened. Donovan looked up at him. Their eyes met. It was different from that angle. In all the times Donovan had gone down on him since that first failed attempt, Tony had never put him on his knees.

Donovan's cock hardened even further as he looked up at Tony. He dipped his head forward, taking more of Tony's shaft between his lips. He could do that more easily now, and he gloried in the taste of his lover on his tongue. With several successful blow jobs to his name and a whole host of good memories to reach for if he got nervous, he was able to relax. There was something almost comforting about having his lips wrapped around Tony's cock. The world was a very simple, very beautiful place.

Tony cleared his throat. "Back up here, sweetheart," he ordered, his voice rough with pleasure.

Donovan reluctantly allowed Tony's cock to slip from between his lips and pulled himself to his feet.

The kiss Tony offered him was sweet. It was obvious that Tony was going out of his way to make it that way, but the sweetness only lasted for a few seconds. As Donovan leaned forward and pressed his naked body against Tony's larger frame, Tony slid his arms around him and gave him the deeper kiss he'd been looking for.

Donovan smiled against his lips. A few seconds later, Tony had kicked off his jeans and was just as naked as Donovan.

"You have some choices," Tony said, as he nudged him onto the bed.

Donovan nodded, even though Tony's back was to him while he got something out of the drawer in the bedside cabinet.

Lube. Donovan looked from the tube in Tony's hand, up to Tony's face.

"Your fingers or mine," Tony said.

"I thought..." Donovan waved a hand toward where the vibrator rested on the bed.

"Fingers first. It'll feel a lot better that way."

Donovan nodded his willingness to trust Tony on that, although he had a feeling it wasn't really going to help with the whole inanimate-object stepping-stone thing.

"Have you ever, when you're by yourself I mean?" Tony asked.

Donovan shook his head. Ryan had sometimes used his

fingers to prepare him a little bit—when he'd been in his more patient moods. It hadn't helped anything feel better.

"Do you actually like the idea of this?" Tony sat on the edge of the bed alongside him. His tone was perfectly easy, as if he would be fine if Donovan said no.

Donovan blinked up at him, taken off guard by the question.

"Some guys just aren't into it," Tony said. "They just top, or they stick to oral. That's fine."

"Do you?" Donovan blurted out. "I mean, have you ever?"

Tony smiled slightly. "Bottomed? Yeah, I've tried it a couple of times. It was nice. You know, it might be a good idea for you to top first. We could do that."

Donovan shook his head.

"Because?" Tony prompted, tracing his fingers up and down Donovan's spine in an absent minded caress.

"I'd rather know what I'm doing first," Donovan said. *If I ever do that, I'd rather be able to copy what you do than what he did.*

"Okay."

Their lips met. Donovan's eyes dropped closed to savour the kiss. When he opened them again, he found himself already lying back on the bed, with Tony lying next to him, propped up by one elbow. That was okay. Donovan was used to the world moving whenever Tony kissed him.

Tony took hold of one of Donovan's hands. Pressing a kiss against the palm, Tony guided Donovan's fingers to rest against his shoulder. He copied the gesture with Donovan's other hand, telling Donovan where he wanted them, just as he promised.

Donovan slid one hand cautiously up to tangle his fingers in Tony's hair, testing to see if that was okay. The move earned him a smile.

When Tony looked down, Donovan followed his gaze and spotted Tony squeezing lube out onto his fingers. Aware that Tony was watching every movement he made very carefully, Donovan shuffled his feet further apart on the mattress, in an effort to make his willingness very clear without having to actually say anything.

The first touch against his hole was so gentle Donovan barely felt it. Tony's fingers moved in slick little circles against him, more a tease than anything else. It couldn't have been less like the way Ryan had touched him. Rather than uncertainty, Donovan felt annoyance bubble up inside him. He squirmed on the bed, trying to push against Tony's fingers and gain a firmer touch from him.

"That's right." The words were spoken under Tony's breath. Donovan wasn't even sure that Tony knew he said them out loud.

Then, all thought of Tony's words vanished from Donovan's mind, because one of Tony's fingers was sliding into him. Donovan felt himself tense. It was impossible to believe that Tony didn't notice that, but his finger kept moving slowly into and out of his hole as if everything was fine, and it was fine. Donovan moved his hands over Tony's shoulders and up into his hair, enjoying not just permission to have his hands on Tony's body, but an actual order to have them there.

Tony gradually worked his finger deeper inside him. Donovan gasped and arched on the bed. His cock had been stiff ever since the toy drawer came out. He hadn't thought he could get any harder. He'd been wrong. That touch sent signals to his cock that surpassed everything else — without any pain mixed in with them, they were a thousand times stronger than anything he'd felt with Ryan.

"Good?" Tony asked.

Donovan blinked up at him. He wanted words — now?

Tony made that same motion with his finger again. Donovan bit his lip to hold back a whimper.

Tony dipped his head to whisper into his ear. "I have a hand free. If I wanted you silent, I'd gag you with it."

Donovan carefully released his tooth-hold on his lip. The same second, Tony repeated that magic little crook of his finger. Donovan moaned. As if in reward for that, Tony dipped his head and brought their lips together.

Tony slid his tongue into Donovan's mouth. A second later, Donovan realised that he was matching the way his tongue moved in his mouth to the way his finger thrust into his arse. Donovan whimpered and tightened his grip on Tony's hair. He had no idea how to move if he wanted to get more of either thing, but he squirmed on the bed and did his best.

There was no rushing. Tony's bedroom couldn't have been more different to the one Donovan had shared with Ryan, and Donovan had so many happy memories in this bed. If Tony would just co-operate a bit more, Donovan was sure it could all be quite magnificent.

"Please," Donovan whispered into his kiss, as Tony stubbornly refused to give him anything more than that one finger rubbing against his prostate.

Begging, he already knew, was a wonderful thing, because it almost always convinced Tony to give him exactly what he wanted. It worked this time, too. Tony slid another finger inside him alongside the first. A moment of discomfort passed, then it was obvious that two fingers meant double the pleasure.

Tony pulled back, breaking the kiss.

Donovan tugged at Tony's hair. Tony smiled down at him, as if he wasn't the least bothered by that, but he obviously wasn't going to be influenced by it either.

"Yes?" Tony asked.

Donovan nodded rapidly. Whatever it was that Tony was offering, in that moment the answer was yes. He couldn't imagine not wanting everything Tony could ever give him. "Yes."

Tony took his fingers away. Donovan frowned, trying to sit up. He hadn't wanted to say yes to stopping!

He looked down just in time to see Tony slick the vibrator with lube.

Donovan stared down at it, watching his every movement. His own hands were still on Tony's body. He tightened his grip on him, unwilling to risk him pulling away and deciding they'd gone far enough for that day.

"Sweetheart?" Tony prompted.

Donovan met Tony's gaze. "Now, please?" And, yes, begging was about to be upgraded to his new favourite hobby of all time, because it once more got him exactly what he needed.

Tony rubbed the tip of the vibrator against Donovan's hole. It felt completely different to Tony's fingers. Donovan wriggled, trying to work out what he needed to do to get the thing inside him.

"Patience," Tony chided, amusement in his voice. But, even as he spoke, he began to work it slowly inside Donovan's hole without requiring any assistance from Donovan.

Yes, it was very different. Not so different it didn't feel wonderful, but at the same time, it didn't coax and crook inside him the way Tony's fingers did. Donovan rocked his hips, trying to get the thing to move in just the right way.

The angle changed slightly. Tony's grip on the toy seemed to alter and—

Donovan was aware of letting out a yell loud enough to be heard through whatever walls were between them and Noah and Colby. But, he didn't have time to be worried or embarrassed about that, because there were suddenly vibrations, lots and lots of vibrations. They were pressing against his prostate, dancing inside him and travelling through his whole body.

He stared up at Tony, and he had to assume that he looked as shocked as hell, because Tony grinned.

It was so far beyond anything Donovan had ever experienced, and as Tony moved the toy inside him, Donovan realised there was only one thing that could make it even more wonderful.

Donovan moved one of his hands to his cock and started to stroke himself at the same rhythm Tony used with the vibrator. Yes. He hadn't thought that his own hand could ever provide him with so much pleasure, but added to the toy it took perfection to a whole new level.

For a few moments, there was perfect bliss. Then fingers wrapped around his wrist, just alongside the cuff, and pulled his hand away from his cock.

Donovan peered up at Tony in confusion. Tony smiled as he guided Donovan's hand back to his shoulder.

"I..." Donovan said, but there were no other words in his head. He didn't know if an apology was necessary. Ryan had hated it if he'd tried to jack himself off while they had sex, but Tony wasn't Ryan and—

"Remember what we said, your hands are going to stay where I want them."

Donovan shook his head, knowing he had to find suitable words to explain the absolute necessity of being able to come that very moment, but unable to bring a single syllable to his lips. Tony would understand if Donovan explained it to him, but—

Tony pulled away.

No, that was even worse! Before Donovan could bring an even more fervent apology to his lips, Tony had moved down the bed and wrapped his lips around Donovan's cock.

Donovan's hands fisted in Tony's hair. All thoughts dissolved. He tossed back his head and screamed as the combination of a hot, wet mouth around his cock and the vibrator moving against his prostate sent so many waves of pleasure bursting through him, he wasn't sure he would survive it.

He came into Tony's mouth, hard and fast. He closed his eyes so tightly stars and fireworks fought for supremacy behind his eyelids in an effort to dazzle him. His whole body trembled. He kept his grip on Tony, anchoring himself to reality and safety when it felt like the whole world had dissolved around him.

He had no idea how long he lay there with his eyes closed, trying to put pieces of his brain back together. When he opened his eyes, the vibrator was gone, but Tony's lips still encircled his softening shaft. It took Donovan several seconds to realise that might have something to do with the way he continued to hold onto Tony's hair tightly enough to make every one of his fingers cramp.

Donovan carefully eased his grip and took his hands away. Should he apologise? Tony was very polite about keeping his hands off the back of his head the way Donovan had asked him to. Should he have automatically done the same? It had never even occurred to him to ask if Tony disliked it as much as he did.

Tony moved up the bed to lie face to face with Donovan. His hair was all messed up—Donovan reached out and clumsily tried to fix that for him.

Tony grinned. "You've got one hell of a grip, sweetheart."

Donovan smiled, sleepy and sated. Any worry he'd felt was brushed away as easily as Tony uttered a few teasing words. Then he remembered something. Damn! "What about you?" he said, sitting up.

Tony chuckled. "I had a free hand, and you're seriously underestimating how hot you just looked if you think I need you to do anything else to get me off."

Donovan felt a blush rush to his cheeks, but since there wasn't anything he needed to do, he felt free to just lie there and stare up at the ceiling.

"Well?" Tony asked, after a few seconds.

Donovan hesitated, checking his first instinct. But no, this was Tony. He didn't need to edit what he said in case Ryan took it the wrong way. "I've come to the conclusion you're weird."

Tony raised an eyebrow at him.

"How the hell can you call anything that feels that good *nice*?" Donovan asked.

Tony smiled. "Good stepping stone?"

Donovan nodded.

"I do have some bad news to break to you though," Tony said. He might have pulled off the serious look if his eyes hadn't been sparkling with humour.

Donovan studied him suspiciously.

Tony whispered in his ear, very softly, as if the secret was powerful enough to bring down empires. "The real ones don't actually vibrate."

Donovan chuckled in spite of himself. He leaned forward and tucked his face into Tony's shoulder. It was on the tip of his tongue to point out that, in Tony's case at least, the real one was also a damn sight bigger than the toy, but he chickened out at the last moment.

Still, while the fact that Tony was bigger than Ryan had been more than a little worrying before, now, as Donovan shifted on the mattress, it seemed rather…interesting.

As Tony switched off the light and welcomed him to snuggle close as they drifted off, Donovan rested his head on Tony's chest.

It wouldn't last. Donovan knew that. He'd never let himself fall so far into his fantasy that he ever forgot that completely. Tony sticking with him and getting him to the point where they could have sex wasn't the same as him and Tony being able to live happily ever after.

But, for now, Donovan pushed all those thoughts aside. The important thing was to concentrate on the fact that, for the first time, he was completely confident that he would, at some point in the near future, be able to have sex with Tony. Whatever else the future might hold, that knowledge was gold dust.

Chapter Nine

Conversations with Cosmos, Donovan had come to realise, had certain advantages over conversations with people who were more...sane. It was quite easy not to be nervous about saying the wrong thing when it was obvious that no verbal contribution was actually required on his part. He just needed to nod and smile at the appropriate points, and that was that.

Donovan glanced across to where Tony was talking to Mike and one of Mike's friends from the weight lifting programme.

Tonight.

Donovan had already made that part of the decision. They were going to have sex tonight. It had been over a month since they started working toward it with the help of that little toy. It was time. He took a deep breath and nodded to whatever Cosmos was saying on the general principle that if he'd been listening he would have probably agreed.

Cosmos laughed. "Did you pick up that habit from Tony?"

Donovan blinked and mentally cursed. "Pardon?"

"He lets his mind wander and ends up agreeing with things he wasn't listening to as well," Cosmos said.

Donovan felt the heat rush to his cheeks at the reminder of just what promise Tony's coach had conned out of him using that trick. "I'm sorry. What did you say?"

Cosmos took a sip of his orange juice, making Donovan wait for a few seconds. Then he chuckled. "Don't worry, darling. You didn't promise to do anything interesting for me. Or promise not to get laid. Tony would have my balls if I tried either trick on you."

Donovan was aware that his blush deepened.

Cosmos laughed, delightedly.

"What are we talking about?" Tony asked, sliding his arm around Donovan's waist as he joined them.

"Donovan picking up your bad habits," Cosmos said, with a smirk.

"Impossible," Tony said, without hesitation. "I don't have any."

Cosmos raised one delicate eyebrow at him. "Want me to count them out for you?"

"No, but I think Mike and Wayne want someone to adjudicate for them. Something about highland strength athletics, I think."

Cosmos thought about that for a second. "Hot men in kilts," he mused. A second later Cosmos went away, with nothing more than an arch look warning Tony that he wasn't letting the matter of bad habits drop permanently.

"What did he say to make you blush?" Tony asked softly, as they found themselves alone in their little bit of the pub.

"It was nothing," Donovan said. A glance at Tony's expression told him that he needed to come up with a better answer than that. He cleared his throat. "I might not have been paying attention to what he was saying to me."

"And?" Tony prompted, setting his drink down so he could loop both his arms around Donovan and interlace his fingers behind Donovan's back.

"Well, I wasn't actually checking my text messages, but I was kind of nodding without having any idea what I was agreeing to. Apparently, I picked up the habit from you." He looked up at Tony and smiled.

Tony chuckled and brushed their lips together. "What did you agree to?"

Donovan thought about it. "I've no idea. Cosmos said it wasn't anything bad."

Another glance up. Tony was studying him carefully. Suddenly, Tony grinned. Donovan hesitated, not sure what had pleased Tony so much.

Tony dipped his head to whisper in his ear. "Cosmos is gay. He just implied that you accidentally did something that gives him the right to collect on an unspecified promise. You're completely calm." He lifted his head. "You do realise that this is a huge thing, right?"

Donovan looked down for a moment as he savoured his success. But, it wasn't really his success. It belonged just as much to Tony as it did to him. "You were right, he's harmless." Donovan cleared his throat. "He's sarcastic and hyper as all hell, but he's nothing like Ryan. No one who drinks here is anything like him."

Tony tightened his hold on Donovan. When their eyes met, it was easy to imagine that Tony actually looked proud of him. The expression gradually faded away as his eyes turned teasing. "So, what were you thinking about that got you so distracted?"

Donovan was powerless to stop the blush returning. "You."

Tony kissed the heated skin along Donovan's cheekbone.

"I think we should have sex tonight," Donovan said.

"You do?" Tony asked.

Donovan nodded. "Yes."

"Because?"

Donovan stared at where his hands were resting on Tony's shoulders. "Because I really want to have sex with you." He forced himself to stop there and not say anything else, not to make excuses or explanations. The answer was complete as it was. He wanted to have sex with Tony— wanted it so badly he could barely breathe through the need to do that.

Tony nodded, as if he really liked that answer.

Donovan took a deep breath. For once, he put aside

good manners. They'd stayed in the pub for as long as Tony wanted every other time they'd been there. Tonight, waiting for Tony to suggest they leave would have been too much like torture.

"Your place?" Donovan suggested.

Tony liked that, too. He brushed their lips together and led him out to his car.

Donovan wasn't sure if the silence was companionable or not. It felt okay to him, but that might have been because a dozen different thoughts were rushing through his head at the same time, making it difficult to remember that the only real sound in the car came from the engine.

At the flat, Donovan went straight back to Tony's bedroom. He was aware that Tony was following behind him. Was he walking faster than usual, or was Tony dawdling?

Donovan stopped alongside the bed. He'd got them from the pub to the bed. That seemed to be quite enough control for him to have taken of the situation.

Tony closed the bedroom door behind him. He smiled when their eyes met, as if he realised that Donovan had come to the end of his move. Tony stroked his cheek. "Tell me what's important," he ordered.

Donovan took a deep breath. Knowing Tony would ask some version of that question had given him plenty of time to work out his answer in advance.

"Face to face—I want to be able to see you. I want us to be able to kiss."

Tony nodded. "I like that idea. What else?"

"I want the cuffs. I don't mind how they're fastened or whatever, but I do want them."

Tony smiled; he seemed to have become a lot more willing to tie him up since Donovan had proved that he remained calm even when he wasn't wearing bondage. Reaching down, he wrapped his hand around one of Donovan's wrists. "Sounds good."

"And..." Donovan took a deep breath, aware that his

next request might not go down quite so well, especially not when they were doing something for the first time. "Be a dom with me?" He looked up and forced himself to meet Tony's eyes, letting him see exactly how important the request was. "Please?"

"There's plenty of time to get kinky about it—"

Donovan took a risk. He reached up and put his free hand over Tony's mouth, the way Tony did so often to him.

Tony's lips moved behind Donovan's hand as he smiled, but he let it happen. In a way Donovan couldn't quite define, it was very definitely something Tony *let* him do, rather than something he did irrespective of Tony's opinion on it.

Donovan swallowed. "I'm not asking just because we both know that's what you prefer. I want it too. But, it seems worth pointing out that, if you're being a dom, you would get to make us go as slow as you want—and keep everything slow until I can't help but beg you to screw me."

Some of the amusement in Tony's eyes faded away, but that was fine, because it was replaced with lust. Tony liked making sure everything was slow. He thrived when he was given control of the details. Donovan was pretty sure that Tony loved hearing him beg, too.

"You being in charge would only make it feel kinky if I was vanilla," Donovan added.

Tony wrapped his hand around Donovan's free wrist and guided his hand gently away from his mouth. "What does it make it if you're not vanilla?" he asked.

"Perfect," Donovan whispered. Tony being in control would make it perfect.

"Dom, at least a bit—from now," Tony agreed.

Donovan felt the last of his nerves fade away. He'd done his part. He'd told Tony all of the important things. In spite of everything he was sure he should be worrying about, he found himself relaxing.

Tony didn't need to relax. He was as calm as he always

was. Nothing ever fazed him.

He kept hold of both Donovan's wrists as he dipped his head for a kiss. It was slow and gentle, and it made pleasure sing through every nerve ending in Donovan's body.

Even after everything they'd done over the months they'd been together, it still baffled Donovan how Tony could manage to do so many other things while simultaneously kissing him senseless.

He must have let go of Donovan's wrists at some point, because their clothes went away and Donovan knew that he'd done very little to make that happen. By the time Donovan was aware of possessing any non-kiss-addled thoughts, he was lying naked on the bed and Tony was wrapping leather cuffs around his wrists.

Tilting his head back, Donovan looked up at the cuffs. Even after all the times he'd worn them, a little shudder of pleasure made its way down his spine at the sight.

Tony grinned when he noticed that. Then, of all the bizarre things to do, he pulled away to kneel naked on the other side of the bed, not touching him at all.

"Tony?"

Tony ran his gaze up and down Donovan's body. "I think it's possible that you're going to regret promising me that we can go as slow as I want," he said, after much consideration.

Donovan swallowed. "I... We will... I mean..."

"We'll have sex?" Tony suggested. "Unless you tell me we've gone far enough at some point, yes, we will."

Donovan nodded.

"But, it's still early," Tony pointed out. "And I have you tied up, and control of the details..."

Donovan tried to take a deep breath. It lodged in his throat. Even when he was completely aware that Tony was holding back and only letting a tiny bit of his dom side out to play, Tony still had the ability to make him lose all power over his own body with a few simple words.

Tony smiled as if he knew what he was doing to Donovan, and he loved knowing it. It seemed supremely unfair to Donovan that Tony could melt his brain when they weren't even touching. He looked at the way they were arranged on the bed. Maybe if he just squirmed a bit, he could lie more diagonally across the bed and his legs would be touching Tony.

Except, that might make Tony move further away. And, Donovan had said that he wanted Tony to be a dom. And —

Donovan took a deep breath and let it out very slowly, trying to slow down his thoughts before they became a complete tangle.

"Sweetheart?" Tony asked. His eyes narrowed as he studied Donovan.

"I'm just trying to work out if it's topping from the bottom if I point out that I'd prefer you to be a dom from less far away."

Tony laughed — an easy, warm sound that invited Donovan to join in.

"You really don't have to worry about topping from the bottom. The only way you'll manage to take control of anything is if I let you, and if I'm letting you do it, it's because I don't have a problem with it."

Donovan looked up at him, wondering if that was why Tony never had seemed pissed off when Donovan made an effort to nudge things in a certain direction, because he knew that he could easily take back all the control whenever he wanted. The idea was almost enough to make Donovan come without a single touch.

"Closer..." Tony mused. Crawling across the bed, he didn't stop until he was looming directly over Donovan. He dipped his head and brought their lips together in a scorching kiss. Supporting himself on his hands, he kept his body up, allowing no contact between them, no matter how much Donovan wriggled and arched his spine.

"Close enough?" Tony teased as he broke the kiss.

Donovan shook his head. "Closer," he said. "Please."

Lifting his head up, Tony smiled down at him in a way that made Donovan wonder if Tony had realised just how quick he was to turn to begging whenever he wanted to get his own way.

Tony lowered his body until skin brushed against skin. Donovan wriggled, spreading his legs further apart to make room for Tony to kneel comfortably between them.

"Close enough?" Tony asked again, dipping his head to brush his lips against Donovan's ear.

Donovan shook his head. "Closer, please." He dipped his voice to a rough little whisper.

Tony pressed a kiss against the skin alongside his ear. "I'll give you a choice, sweetheart. Do you want me to be in control, or do you want me to do as you say the moment you use that tone of voice on me?" He pulled back far enough that they could look each other in the eye without either of them appearing blurry. "Either is fine, but I want you to pick — how much of a dom do you want me to be tonight?"

Donovan blinked up at him. Oh, yeah, Tony knew exactly how quick he was to beg if pleas would let him manipulate the situation...

Did he want Tony's permission to top from the bottom that way? Tony wouldn't have offered if he minded, but at the same time...

"Be a dom," Donovan requested, softly, but with complete confidence that he was making the right decision.

Tony's eyes sparkled with pleasure at that decision.

But not wanting Tony to give in wasn't quite the same as being happy with even the slightest bit of distance existing between them. Being in cuffs wasn't the same as being unable to move those parts of his body that were free.

The temptation was too much. Donovan lifted his feet off the mattress, wrapped his legs around Tony's waist and pulled Tony down flat on top of him.

Tony let out a burst of surprised laughter, obviously

not the least bit bothered by the show of initiative. It was as if Tony had so much confidence in his ability to dominate any time he chose, he found it impossible to feel threatened by Donovan's clumsy attempts to get his own way.

Tony let their bodies remain pressed together as he kissed him again, deeper this time, taking complete possession of his mouth.

Donovan moaned his complete approval against Tony's lips, right up until Tony began to pull away. Disapproving noises made no difference tonight. Tony refused to return and bring their mouths back together the way he usually did when he heard those wordless entreaties.

Kisses against Donovan's neck mollified him slightly. He tipped his head back and welcomed them. Tony reached behind himself and nudged at Donovan's ankles until Donovan relented and released his leg's grip around his waist.

Trailing kisses as he went, Tony moved further down the bed. When he reached one of Donovan's nipples, he circled it with his tongue.

Donovan tried to stay still, although he wasn't sure if that was to encourage Tony to linger there, or if it was in an effort to try to hide just how much he loved what Tony was doing. He bit down on his lip and tried not to moan with need as Tony suckled around the little bud of nerve endings.

When Tony stopped, it was only to move his attention to Donovan's other nipple. Donovan was reasonably sure he was going to draw blood if he bit his lip any harder. But he couldn't worry too much about that because his brain cells were dying very pleasurable deaths by the score, and the pain from his lip was barely a footnote in an essay's worth of pleasure.

He lifted his head from the pillow to stare down at Tony. At the same moment, Tony looked up. He looked so damn pleased with the world. "I love how sensitive you are." He whispered the words against the skin he'd just teased, sending a shiver down Donovan's spine.

Donovan whimpered.

"One day, I'm going to introduce you to some clamps. I'm going to put them here, and here," he said, rubbing his thumbs over each of Donovan's nipples. "Not too tight, not so they'll hurt. Just so they'll make you squirm for me. Then, when I take them off, you're going to be so sensitive—I'll bet I'll be able to make you come just from doing this." He dipped his head and briefly teased one of Donovan's nipples with his lips and tongue once more. "Do you think I could do that?"

Donovan nodded.

"You do?" Tony asked.

"Might do it right now if you're not careful," Donovan managed to grind out.

Tony grinned. "No, not tonight. We have other plans for tonight."

Donovan nodded rapidly.

Tony shuffled back further. He pressed a kiss against Donovan's abs, then another kiss, lower down, within the line of his hips.

When Tony wrapped his lips around the tip of Donovan's cock, Donovan shook his head. "That's not the plan."

"Yes, it is," Tony said, pulling back just far enough to speak.

Donovan shook his head again, but before he could say anything, Tony cut in. "Stage one of the plan," he specified.

Donovan stared down at him.

"You'll be more relaxed after you come."

"I'm not stressed," Donovan said, with complete honesty. "Frustrated, yes, but not stressed."

Tony dipped his head and pressed a kiss against his stomach. "Physically relaxed," he said.

Donovan hesitated, twisting against the bed sheet.

"Trust me," Tony asked—and it was a request. There wasn't even a hint of an order about it. Tony wasn't going to be a dom about that particular detail.

Donovan nodded. Yes. Tony knew what he was doing.

Tony dipped his head. In a few moments it was clear to Donovan that Tony really didn't intend this to be the main event. Every other time he'd gone down on him, Tony had made a point of making things last for as long as Donovan was able to hold back. This was different.

In that moment, Donovan realised that he'd never had a quickie blow job off Tony — the kind where Tony just wanted to make him come fast, hard, and suddenly enough to end up seeing stars. It seemed like mere seconds passed before Donovan was arching off the bed, crying out his bliss as he spilled into Tony's mouth.

He collapsed back on the mattress, keeping his eyes closed because he was pretty sure the whole room would be spinning if he tried to look around him.

"Less frustrated?" Tony asked.

Donovan shook his head, not caring if it was a lie. He might not need to come right then, he might not be physically capable of coming again so soon, but that didn't mean he was going to let Tony off that promise to have sex with him that night.

Even with his eyes closed, Donovan knew Tony was grinning. As Donovan caught his breath, he found himself smiling blindly in response. He'd been telling the truth about how little stress he'd felt, but he couldn't have denied a bit of nerves. There were no nerves now, just that peaceful, happy feeling that could only be found through the perfect combination of Tony, handcuffs, and a recent orgasm.

Taking a slow, deep breath and letting it out as a lazy little sigh, Donovan opened his eyes and peered up at Tony.

"Stage two, now?" he murmured.

Tony stroked a knuckle up and down the centre of Donovan's chest. "Yeah."

Donovan nodded.

Tony kissed him, slow and easy, as if they were both high on afterglow rather than just one of them. A glance down and Donovan confirmed that Tony hadn't actually come.

"Does stage two include lube?" Donovan prompted, trusting Tony not to mind.

"Yes, as it happens, it does." Tony grabbed it from the bedside table. Donovan shuffled his legs apart but Tony shook his head and nudged him to roll onto his side instead.

"I thought..." Donovan said, although his thoughts were travelling so slowly now, he couldn't be entirely sure if he'd explained what he wanted clearly at the start or not. But that was okay, because Tony would understand him needing to explain now instead. Tony was always fine about things like that.

"Face to face?" Tony said.

Donovan nodded. He had said? That was good. He frowned slightly. But if he had explained himself well enough before, then, why...?

"Slow, remember," Tony whispered in his ear as he lay behind him, propped up by one elbow so he could look over Donovan's shoulder. "If you stay in the same position the whole time, you'll end up with cramp when you could really do without it."

Donovan nodded his understanding, although in that particular moment, while his body still felt tingly and sleepy from his orgasm, he mostly just understood that Tony knew what he was doing and everything would be fine.

Slicked fingers slid against his hole and Donovan lethargically shifted positions to make it easier for Tony to do that.

"Relaxed," he remembered. Tony had said that coming would make him a lot more relaxed.

"That's right."

"And nipple clamps," Donovan added, rocking his hips in an effort to make Tony slide his fingers deeper inside him.

"But not tonight," Tony said.

"Another night," Donovan suggested.

"Definitely."

Donovan smiled. He wasn't sure how soon Tony's interest would drift away from him once they started to have sex. With how quickly Tony usually moved from one lover to another, it probably wouldn't be long, but in that moment, Donovan refused to acknowledge any bit of reality that he didn't like. Just for tonight, he would let himself believe in forever. That couldn't get him in trouble if no one knew about it.

"What else?" Donovan asked as one of Tony's fingers worked deeper inside him.

"Sweetheart?"

"What else do you want to do with me another night?" It was less embarrassing to ask the question when he didn't need to make eye contact, but it was surprisingly easy to know what Tony's expression would be like when he answered. Tony never looked serious when he was talking about sex. Sex was always a fun thing when Tony was involved.

"There are so many things I want to do with you," Tony said. "Hundreds of them…"

Donovan shook his head. "Tell me properly?"

Tony carefully worked another finger inside him. Maybe it was having already come once, but it was easier to relax around Tony's fingers now than it had ever been before. Maybe Tony had been right to insist on waiting until tonight, and waiting until after he'd had a blow job. Maybe Tony was right about everything in the world—it seemed quite possible.

"One day, I'd like to spank you," Tony said, carefully.

Donovan's smile broadened—Tony picked the strangest moments to act as if he was still wary of spooking him. "Tony?"

"Yeah?"

"You have a flogger, and a paddle, and a crop, and a thing I don't know the name of. I'm not shocked at the whole—you might like to spank people thing."

Tony chuckled and kissed his neck. "You like the

idea?"

Donovan nodded, rubbing his cheek against the pillow. He'd jacked off thinking about Tony spanking him so often, it was sometimes hard to believe that they hadn't actually done that.

"It's a tawse," Tony said.

"Hm?" Donovan asked.

"The thing you don't know the name of," Tony explained with obvious amusement. "It's called a tawse — it's Scottish. But, we'd only use that if you'd already found out you liked everything else. We'd start off with a bare hand."

"Okay." Donovan was more interested in working out if there was a way of moving his hips and rocking back against Tony's fingers that might encourage him to hurry the hell up.

Digits crooked inside him, rubbing against his prostate. He was already hardening again and wondered if it was worth trying begging even when Tony was being a dom.

"Tony?" he asked.

"Yes, sweetheart?"

Donovan was sure that no one should be able to sound so happy or so amused when they were driving someone else mad with need.

It was no good. Tony's tone of voice made it perfectly clear that begging wasn't going to be of any use right then. Donovan turned his face into the pillow to muffle a particularly desperate little moan.

"That's right," Tony whispered to him. A third finger joined the others playing inside Donovan. "Your turn."

"To what?" Donovan gasped out.

"Tell me something you want us to do another night," Tony ordered.

"Now?" Donovan asked.

"Yep."

"You've got three fingers in my arse. You've already killed off most of my brain cells. You're refusing to do anything according to any sort of sensible time scale. You even sprung stage one on me without anything I'm going to consider sufficient warning. Now you want me to think?" Donovan asked.

"Yep."

Donovan couldn't help but laugh. The sound faded away into a gasp as Tony crooked all three fingers.

"Well?" Tony prompted.

"Everything. I want to do everything with you, one thing at a time, all at once. Whatever you want. But what I want tonight is for you to top me, right now."

"Soon, sweetheart. I promise."

Donovan shook his head. "Now."

Tony kissed the back of his neck.

"Tony?" Donovan said. He was pretty sure the time to make a last ditch attempt at begging had to be now, because if Tony kept thrusting his fingers deep inside him like that for much longer, Donovan was going to lose the power of speech.

"Yes," Tony said. "Now." He took his fingers away and encouraged Donovan to turn onto his back as he deftly rolled a condom down his shaft and slicked the latex with extra lube.

Ryan had never wanted them to be face to face, but Donovan still had plenty of information to work from. He quickly pulled his knees back toward his chest, just like guys did in those oh-so interesting videos on the internet.

Tony leaned over him. For a second, Donovan got the impression that Tony was studying his expression carefully. Then the moment was gone, and Tony was kneeling between his legs, leaning forward to bring their lips together.

Donovan tried to wrap his legs around Tony's waist and pull him closer, like he had before. "Not yet, sweetheart," Tony whispered against his lips.

Before Donovan had time to protest any further delay, he realised that Tony was only talking about his legs. Reaching down between them, Tony guided his cock to Donovan's hole. Donovan bit his lip and fought against the urge to squirm.

Tony met Donovan's eyes. He smiled and rocked his hips ever so slightly; it was more a tease than anything else.

Donovan whimpered. "Please?"

The pressure against Donovan's hole increased as Tony pressed forward and finally began to slide into him.

The breath caught in Donovan's throat.

"That's right," Tony whispered, rocking his hips, lodging himself a little deeper. "Keep looking right at me."

Donovan stared up at him. Their gazes locked, and he became incapable of looking away. He wasn't sure what Tony saw in his gaze, but it seemed to please him.

"Good boy," Tony said, as if to confirm that.

Donovan managed to take a breath.

Tony rocked his hips again, settling a little more of his cock inside Donovan's body. The tip rubbed against Donovan's prostate, making him whimper.

Staying still and letting Tony have complete control over every single detail was hot as a fantasy. In reality, it was impossible. Donovan wriggled his hips in return, trying to get more.

Tony continued to stare down at him. He didn't even seem to need to blink.

There was slow and there was just crazy.

"Please, Tony," Donovan murmured, pulling at his cuffs as the instinct to reach out to Tony tried to completely overtake him.

Tony dipped his head and brought their lips together. Donovan kissed him back. For once, he didn't even try to follow Tony's lead. Donovan needed the kiss to be pure sex, fast and frantic, the kind of kiss that might inspire Tony to screw him the way he really needed him to.

Tony made no attempt to take back control of the kiss, but the way his tongue duelled frantically with Donovan's made no difference to the slow, gradual penetration. Tony was in complete control of every movement he made.

Donovan moaned into the kiss, loving that fact even while it drove him insane.

Dropping his head onto the pillow, Donovan peered up at Tony as he gasped for breath.

"That's right," Tony whispered again. "So right."

Donovan nodded. So right…

Another tiny thrust forward, and Donovan realised that Tony was finally buried in him to the hilt. For what felt like hours they remained frozen in place, just staring at each other.

Donovan swallowed. Above the cuffs, his hands curled into tight fists. The chains rattled again.

"Take them off?" Tony offered.

Donovan shook his head. "Perfect," he reminded him.

Tony's lips twisted into a slow smile. "Yeah," he agreed. "Perfect." He swayed back a fraction and slid home again.

Donovan murmured his pleasure, closing his eyes to relish the sensations.

Tony built up the movement so gradually Donovan barely noticed the changes occurring. All he was aware of was more and more pleasure swirling inside him until he finally realised that Tony was thrusting into him in earnest. Without any information being offered up by his brain, his body had found a way to move that complimented Tony's thrusts and he was rocking up to meet every movement.

He opened his eyes and stared up at Tony, taking in every detail, trying to commit it all to memory so he would be able to savour it for the rest of his life. This—from that moment on, this was what he was going to remember every time he thought about sex. Tony.

Donovan whimpered. His cock was trapped between them, every time either of them moved, the head rubbed against skin, teasing him with a tiny bit of friction, but never for very long. All the real pleasure came from having Tony's cock buried deep in his arse. It was exactly as fantastic as he'd always thought sex should be.

Donovan pressed his head back against the pillow as he arched beneath Tony. "Please."

"Legs," Tony said.

Donovan's brain drew a blank. His body took over. He wrapped his legs around Tony's waist, holding him tightly, pulling him in every time he thrust, exactly the same way he'd wanted to do from the start.

Time had no meaning. Donovan was lost, and he was found. His brain raced to process every sensation, but at the same time, he became incapable of anything like real thoughts.

The angles had changed as he wrapped his legs around Tony. Everything was just that bit more intense, more perfect. As if he'd realised the same thing, Tony sped up, thrusting into him harder and faster.

Donovan was trying to frame the right words to get one of Tony's hands wrapped around his cock to bring him over the edge when any such plea became irrelevant. His orgasm tore through him, harsh enough to rip his soul in half. Donovan was pretty sure he screamed.

Pure bliss couldn't last forever. Donovan gasped, trying to hold onto the moment, even as it slipped from his grasp. Then, as Tony continued to thrust into him, pushing even more pleasure into Donovan's body as he found his own orgasm, the world gradually went away.

* * * * *

"Everything's fine, sweetheart. You just passed out for a few seconds."

Tony watched Donovan blink open his eyes. He peered around the room as if he had no idea where he was, but he didn't seem to be at all worried about that. He smiled when his gaze came to rest on Tony. "Hi."

Tony grinned as relief rushed through him. "Hi."

Donovan arched on the bed. Tony was pretty sure he

was merely stretching out muscles that had just discovered a whole new kind of work out, but he couldn't help but realise that it was a very pretty move, filled with a beautifully sated kind of satisfaction.

Donovan looked at the cuffs, still wrapped around his wrists, but no longer fastened together or trapped on the headboard. He wriggled against the mattress again, lifting his buttocks up off the bed as he sought for a more comfortable position to rest in.

"Sore?" Tony asked, pushing Donovan's hair back out of his eyes.

"Only in a good way," Donovan whispered, blushing. He nibbled on his bottom lip. "I really passed out?"

"Yep."

"Um...I've never done that before."

Tony bit back any inclination to point out that, in his experience, sex was rarely so intense it felt like his entire world had been turned inside out. Maybe with Donovan it would always be like that. As Donovan met his eyes, it seemed quite possible. "In that case, I'm going to take it as a compliment," Tony told him.

Donovan smiled. "Okay."

Tony slid his fingers down Donovan's cheek, the last of his own tension fading away. Apparently, even passing out wasn't going to faze Donovan tonight, or make him uncertain of whose bed he would be in when he came around. He was so high on afterglow, it was hard to believe that was the only thing he was high on.

"So..." Tony prompted after a few seconds.

Donovan seemed to make an effort to think through everything that had happened that night very carefully. "I think I was wrong before, you're not perfect—and you are a complete bastard."

It wasn't easy to take the words seriously when Donovan continued to look up at him with so much pleasure in his eyes—and yes, Tony reminded himself, it was just pleasure that made his eyes sparkle like that. Donovan had never given any hint that he felt anything else for him.

"Oh?" Tony encouraged.

"You should have insisted we do this the first moment we met."

"I should have?"

Donovan nodded with complete certainty. "I didn't know that sex could be like this, but you did. There's no excuse for us not having sex that first second we clapped eyes on each other. All those wasted months..."

Tony smiled down at him. He knew it couldn't have happened that way, and Donovan sure as hell knew it, too. But in that moment, damn it was nice to pretend everything was that simple. No real past, no uncertain future, just the two of them in that bed forever.

"The first time I saw you, you were in the middle of the institute's dining hall," Tony reminded him.

"No excuse," Donovan said stubbornly.

"You'd have blushed beautifully if we had," Tony said, as he imagined Donovan spread out on one of the dining hall tables, completely oblivious to anyone else who might be in the room and watching their every move.

Right on cue, Donovan blushed, just at the idea. He chuckled sleepily. For a few moments he was silent. Tony was half sure he'd drifted off to sleep by the time he blinked open his eyes. "I've come to the conclusion that I'm really going to enjoy being able to have sex."

"Well, you've got some catching up to do. I don't think it would be unreasonable to do a couple of sessions a day until you're brought up to level." Tony was more than happy to help him out with that. The idea of anyone else being involved in the process was like a knife being twisted beneath his ribcage.

"There's the other things you want to try, too," Donovan reminded him. He sounded just a little bit shy now.

Tony idly ran his fingers alongside the cuffs Donovan

still wore. "Yes, all those things too."

When he looked up, Donovan was studying him very carefully. Tony found himself returning his inspection. Donovan dropped his gaze before Tony could get a good read on him.

"Regrets?" Tony asked, bracing himself for the worse."

"Never," Donovan said. He met Tony's eyes for a moment. "Are you trying to tell me that you reg—?"

"Never," Tony echoed.

Donovan smiled slightly. He wanted to say something, Tony could damn near see the words trembling on his lips, but at the last moment, Donovan seemed to stop himself short.

There were no nerves though. Tony was sure about that. If there were nerves, Donovan wouldn't have been able to hide them from him. It seemed more like Donovan just had a lot to think about, and no one could blame him for that.

Tony had wanted to have sex with Donovan with a deep ache that had almost threatened to consume him, but Donovan had been the one who'd needed to prove to himself that he could still enjoy sex even after that bastard had played those mind games with him.

Tony wrapped an arm around Donovan's shoulders and welcomed him to curl close into his side, simply giving him a safe place to rest while he did his thinking. Whatever was going to happen from here was just as much Donovan's decision as everything else had been. All Tony could do was hope.

Chapter Ten

Donovan hesitated as he stepped into the pub.

Tony would already be there—Tony always got there early whenever they were going to meet up. It was something that could be depended upon.

Donovan scanned the crowd and, yes, Tony was there, talking to some of the other guys from Falconer. About to step forward and join their group, Donovan stopped himself short.

Taking a deep breath, he went up to the bar instead. There was nothing to be afraid of. There were a lot of gay and bi men there, but that was okay. They rarely flirted with him since it became common knowledge that he was dating Tony, and that made it much easier to remember that they were all perfectly nice people who had nothing in common with Ryan.

"Coke, please," Donovan said, when the barman turned in his direction. His words were calm and level. His nerves were only a very small factor. He glanced toward Tony.

The sight of him went straight to Donovan's cock. Nothing had changed because they'd had sex—not for Donovan anyway.

He paid for his drink, but he didn't rush away from the bar.

Tony wasn't going to break up with him the day after they had sex for the first time—if only because he'd always made it clear that he wanted to help him see how a good boyfriend treated the man he was dating, as well as help him have sex.

Things weren't going to last forever, but Tony wasn't going to be a bastard about it. He would give him a few days at least. If Donovan made it clear that he didn't have any unrealistic expectations, maybe Tony would give him far longer than that.

Donovan took a gulp of his drink. All he had to do was be calm, and everything would be fine. Tony couldn't read his mind. Tony had no reason to be pissed off with him. Donovan would be calm, and casual about it all, and everything would be fine.

Donovan took another swig of his drink. Tony wasn't Ryan. He couldn't pull thoughts out of his head and use them against him. He didn't know how hard Donovan had fallen for him. Even if he did, Tony wouldn't use it against him. He wasn't Ryan.

"Don?"

Donovan turned around. Tony was just a few steps away. Donovan pinned a smile to his lips and did his damnedest not to look nervous about anything at all. "Hi."

"I didn't see you come in," Tony said. "What are you doing over here?"

Donovan tilted his head back, as if he had no doubt that Tony would want to greet him with a kiss.

The gesture worked. Tony didn't hesitate to kiss him softly on the lips. When he lifted his head, there was a touch of amusement in his eyes, alongside his concern. "The question still stands, sweetheart."

Donovan looked down, wondering if he could get away with lying. He still wasn't sure whether or not to try it by the time Tony had found an empty table and nudged him into sitting down at it.

"Sweetheart?"

"Last night went well," Donovan blurted out.

"Yes, I think it did," Tony said.

Donovan studied his Coke bottle.

"You're not sure you agree?" Tony prompted.

It took Donovan a few seconds to work out what Tony was asking. "It was perfect." He glanced up to check on Tony's expression. "I mean, for me anyway…"

"You're worried that I didn't enjoy myself." It wasn't a question, it was obviously a realisation and one that Tony found confusing.

"You've had a lot more practice than I have, and…"

Tony shook his head. "Just to be very clear, as far as I'm concerned, last night was as close to perfect as sex gets. It's…that kind of chemistry, that sort of intensity; it's not something a guy finds with just anyone, Don." He tucked a knuckle under Donovan's chin and made him look up.

"So you do want to, again?" Donovan asked.

"Yes."

Donovan nodded. That fact allowed him to breathe a little more easily.

"Are you worried that I don't want to have sex with you, or that, because we have once, I'll expect us to have sex every time I click my fingers?"

Donovan stared down at his Coke. Damn it, Tony had that tone in his voice, the one that meant he was going to get to the bottom of a problem no matter how long it took. There was no way Donovan could get out of this conversation now, but he couldn't think of a single thing to say.

"Here's what we're going to do," Tony announced. "We're going to go back to my place so we can talk in private. On the way there, you're going to try to get your thoughts in order. Then, when we get there, you're going to tell me exactly what's making you feel so nervous tonight. Does that plan sound okay to you?"

Donovan nodded, sure that he probably shouldn't feel so relieved at the simple fact that Tony had a plan—any plan, but the fact that it appeared to be Tony's move made everything so much easier.

* * * * *

Tony scrolled through every curse word he knew. Then, when he ran out, he went back to the beginning and went through each and every one, all over again.

He'd known sex wouldn't be a magic wand, that everything wouldn't suddenly turn into sunshine and fairy dust. He'd been very prepared for it to knock Donovan back several steps if it hadn't gone to plan. He hadn't been expecting the fact it went damn near perfectly to throw Donovan for a loop.

Damn it—Donovan had been full of confidence last night. He'd even made bad jokes and thrown pretend insults around—it had been bloody marvellous.

Parking the car, Tony led Donovan up to the flat in silence, not wanting to break Donovan's train of thought if he really was managing to put together a new list of worries.

In the flat, Tony nudged Donovan onto the sofa, sat down next to him and simply waited.

"Did you mean it?" Donovan suddenly asked, as if they were already in the middle of a long and complicated conversation.

"Yes," Tony said, with complete confidence.

Donovan smiled slightly. "You don't even know what I'm asking you about yet."

"If I said it to you, I meant it," Tony said. "But, if you want to tell me what particular thing you're asking about, I can say yes to that specifically."

"What you said last night," Donovan whispered. "About wanting to try out the other things from the drawer on me?"

"Yes—whatever things in there you're up for, anyway." Tony's mind raced as he tried to look at the problem from all possible angles. He kept his words slow and steady through sheer force of will. "That's one of the things making you nervous?"

Donovan shook his head. "I just... That means you want us to keep hooking up?"

Tony's heart rate doubled as he realised that Donovan might be working his way up to saying something far more terrifying than *I'm nervous about…*

Donovan was trying to break up with him. The moment the possibility hit him, every other thought in his head scattered.

Donovan was trying to break up with him. They'd had sex once. Donovan had regained the ability to get laid. Tony had done his job. He was no longer required. Donovan hadn't come up to him in the pub because, as of today, he was more interested in meeting someone else, and —

"Tony?" Donovan asked.

Tony looked up. Donovan was looking more worried than ever. He'd been kept waiting for an answer for too long.

That means you want us to keep hooking up?

"No," Tony said, very seriously. "We've never hooked up. We've dated. We've been dating for over four months."

"Maybe it would be better if, from now on, we just hooked up instead?" Donovan suggested, addressing all his words to the coffee table.

"Why?" At this point, Tony had to consider he was lucky if Donovan couldn't actually hear how fast his heart was racing.

"I think we should see other people."

Now Tony had the opposite problem. His heart missed so many beats, he was half sure it had stopped. It had been the deal, hadn't it? His job was to get Donovan back in the saddle. Donovan had been very clear about that ever since Trentmoore. Nothing else had been offered.

Donovan closed his eyes for a moment. "It worked well, us only dating each other while we were working things out, I'm glad we did that. But, now that we're past that point, I think it would be better if we saw other people."

"Now that you've proved to yourself that you can enjoy sex, you want to screw around?" Tony's voice remained level through sheer determination, but even as he said the words out loud for the first time, he knew they didn't make sense. They didn't fit with anything he knew about Donovan.

An inclination to panic, yes. An inclination to promiscuity, it just wasn't his style. It was one thing to imagine a guy wanting to screw around as soon as he was able to do that without a panic attack. It was another thing to imagine *Donovan* wanting to do that.

"I know you must be desperate to get back to seeing other men by now, and women too. I—"

Tony leaned forward and used his hand to create a firm seal over Donovan's mouth. It was only luck his fingers weren't visibly trembling. "I've never said that."

Donovan blinked at him over the makeshift gag.

Tony held his gaze for several seconds. "For the record, are you talking about us breaking up the moment we've had sex because you really want to screw other guys now that you're sure you can, or because you think that's what I want?" He took his hand away.

Donovan frowned down at the carpet alongside the sofa. "I..."

Tony stroked his fingers through Donovan's hair, not one hundred percent sure whose nerves he was soothing with the gesture.

"I know that you want—"

Tony put his hand back over Donovan's mouth. Donovan completely failed to look surprised at the move. "I'll tell you about what I want afterwards. You just tell me what you want."

Donovan swallowed as Tony freed his mouth. "I want you. I've always wanted you. Being someone you hook up with now and again, that would be great. You do that with some people, don't you?"

"Yeah, I've done that," Tony agreed. "Like a friends with benefits thing." But now he was listening to what Donovan was actually saying, and to the things Donovan wasn't saying, and he wasn't letting what he was afraid of Donovan saying get in the way as much as he had before. "But that's not something I want with you."

Donovan swallowed. "What about friends without benefits?"

"Is that what you want?" Tony asked, gently, as he slid his arm around Donovan's shoulders.

"I want whatever I can get," Donovan said, simply. "I know things can't go on as they have until now, forever. I've never expected that. But, I just thought that, if I could keep something, it had to be worth a shot."

"Why can't things go on as they have?" Tony asked, wondering if he sounded as baffled as he felt. What the hell had he done to make Donovan think that he didn't want things to be exactly like they were for the rest of his life?

"Because you don't want—"

Tony put a fingertip over Donovan's lips. "You talk about what you want, I'll talk about what I want," he reminded him.

"You're not doing much talking," Donovan pointed out, once he was free to speak again.

Tony took a deep breath and ran everything Donovan had said through his mind very carefully. Not just that night, he went right back to that first drink in the pub, circling some things in bright red pen, adding rows of exclamation points after other statements.

I'm not completely delusional. I didn't have some huge fairy tale romance planned for us or anything stupid like that. I just thought we'd have sex, it would be fun, and we'd go our separate ways.

Tony opened his eyes. "Bloody idiot!"

Donovan pulled away.

Tony realised what he'd just said out loud. Shit! "Not you," he rushed out, tugging Donovan back close. "I'm talking about me. I'm the idiot."

"I—"

"He said something to you, didn't he? Ryan said something. He accused you of…" Damn, what would it be? "Of being in love with him, being too romantic, too soppy?

335

Something like that?"

Donovan opened and closed his mouth, but no words came out.

Tony stroked his hair.

Donovan closed his eyes for a moment. "I'm so sorry."

"No, you're not," Tony corrected. "Because you haven't done anything wrong."

"I..."

Tony brushed their lips together. When Donovan invited him in, Tony let the kiss linger until he thought it had soothed Donovan's nerves as much as a kiss could.

"Can you tell me what he said?"

Donovan shook his head. Tony hadn't seen him so close to losing his grip on his nerves for months. He found himself holding Donovan closer, not just to reassure him, but to make sure Donovan didn't give in to the urge to bolt at an unexpected moment.

"Okay. We'll do something else first. You wanted to know how I want things to be between us, right?"

Donovan pulled himself together enough to nod.

Tony pressed a kiss to his temple in praise.

It was obvious that if they were going to have any chance of moving past that point, Tony would have to be the one to make some sort of declaration. But what the hell could he say without scaring the hell out of Donovan? That was the real question.

Getting too serious too quickly had always seemed like the perfect way to make him run for the hills. Tony met Donovan's eyes for a moment. Would he still think making it clear how serious he was about Donovan was a bad thing if Donovan hadn't spouted all that bull about not being delusional—if Donovan hadn't quoted Ryan at him?

Was it Donovan's fears that were making him wary of telling the truth, or his own?

"Okay," Tony said. He could do this. If Donovan could do things that terrified him, so could Tony.

"I want you," Tony said. To his own ear, it sounded as if he was speaking very slowly, weighing each word carefully. "I don't want us to be friends with benefits, or occasional hook up partners, or anything like that."

Donovan seemed to hold his breath as he waited for the rest.

"I want you," Tony repeated. "I want you to be my boyfriend, not just for however long it takes for you to be able to do whatever you want to in bed—forever. I don't want either of us to have sex with anyone else. I don't want either of us to date anyone else. I want us to keep on going as we are, ideally with lots of sex every time we both want it—and with a lot more of whatever kinks we find you're into, as well."

Donovan looked at Tony as if he'd lost his mind. It wasn't an entirely unexpected reaction, but it wasn't helping Tony push past a flurry of uncertainty, embarrassment and gut-wrenching terror.

Tony smiled and hoped he didn't appear anywhere near as petrified as he felt, but there was no way to put the declaration off any longer. "I used to call Colby every kind of idiot for falling for Noah the first moment he saw him, but—"

Donovan pressed a fingertip against Tony's lips. "Please don't say anything else."

Not quite the response Tony had anticipated at that point. He raised an eyebrow. Donovan immediately took his finger away.

"What do you think I'm going to say?" Tony asked.

"I think you're going to say whatever you think will make me feel better about being in love with you." Donovan's eyes opened wide, as if he couldn't quite believe he'd blurted that out.

Tony smiled as he suddenly remembered how to breathe like a regular human being. "What if what I want to say is the truth?"

* * * * *

Donovan shook his head, knowing that it couldn't possibly be the truth. "I—"

"I don't lie to you. I may occasionally not mention being banned from having sex for a few weeks, but I don't lie."

Donovan gawped at Tony. "You're not in love with me." That was the one thing he was sure about.

Tony smiled. He looked so confident, so at ease with the world. "Sorry to keep arguing with you, sweetheart, but I really am. More and more so as I've got to know you better, but at least a little bit since the first time we met."

Donovan shook his head. "You're not. You can't be."

"Why not?"

Donovan closed his eyes. A voice immediately whispered in the back of his mind. It wasn't Tony's voice. It had no place in his head anymore, but it was there.

"Tell me what he said," Tony ordered again.

"He used to accuse me of being in love with him, or thinking he was in love with me." Donovan looked up and forced himself to meet Tony's gaze. "I never did. I thought he was hot. I wanted to have sex with him, but I never loved him, I never even thought I did."

Tony kissed him tenderly on the lips. "Can you give it to me word for word, sweetheart?"

Donovan closed his eyes. He didn't even have to think about it. The words were right there in the very forefront of his mind. *"Don't get above yourself, Donovan. You're not my boyfriend. I'm not in love with you. You're just someone I fuck occasionally. That's all you'll ever be."*

"How often did he say that?" Tony asked.

Donovan forced himself to open his eyes. "A lot."

"Okay."

Donovan glanced in Tony's direction. "Okay?"

"It's fine." Tony nodded. "All we have to do is push those words out of your head and put new ones in their place.

We can do that."

Donovan blinked at him. "We can?"

"You shared a room with him for less than a year?"

Donovan nodded, now completely lost.

"So, you heard him spouting bullshit for a year at most. That means we have time on our side."

"We do?"

"It's just like what he told you about sex. If you hear us saying the complete opposite of what he said, over and over again, year after year, it will eventually drown out everything he said."

Donovan stared at him. *Year after year?*

Tony touched his cheek and coaxed him to look up. "You are my boyfriend. I do love you. I want to have sex with you every chance I get. None of that is ever going to change."

Donovan felt the heat rush to his cheeks. Part of him still wanted to cling to the idea that Tony didn't mean any of it. There was a strange kind of familiar safety in the idea that no one could ever mean it, let alone someone like Tony. But looking into Tony's eyes, it was impossible to doubt him.

Tony meant it. As unfeasible as it seemed, he meant every word of it. And Donovan's throat had closed up so tightly he couldn't get a single word out in return.

"Can I ask you for a favour?" Tony asked suddenly.

Donovan nodded.

Tony's lips quirked, and Donovan knew that they were both thinking about the first time Tony kissed him, but Tony made no move to kiss him again right then.

"Next time you're worried about something to do with us—if you're scared that I want to screw around, or that I'm not completely serious about you, can you try to just tell me that, rather than try to fix it yourself?"

Donovan tried to make sense of the request and failed.

"You see," Tony went on, encouraging Donovan to snuggle into his side. "I'm pretty sure that when you get worried you try to offer me what you think I want. What you actually do is make it sound like you want to break up with me." He took a deep breath. "And that scares the hell out of me."

Donovan frowned. "You don't get scared."

Tony laughed. "I do when the guy I'm in love with makes it sound like he wants to leave me."

Donovan shook his head. "I don't—"

"Just now, you tried to offer me an open relationship, because you thought that was what would actually make us more likely to stay together, right?"

Donovan cautiously nodded his agreement on that.

"You actually made it sound like—*Thank you for tutoring me in sex for the last couple of months, but now that I know I can get laid, I'd much rather go and do that with other guys. You don't mind, do you?*"

Donovan pushed himself away from Tony, jerking up so he could look him in the eye. "You were the one who said about tutoring me in the first place!"

"Because I thought that was the only thing you were interested in," Tony admitted. "After Trentmoore, it sounded like you were only interested in me because I had a reputation for knowing what I'm doing in bed." He shrugged. "You're not the only one whose so far gone he's willing to take whatever he can get."

Tony was still serious. There was a hint of self mockery in his eyes, but he really had thought that was what Donovan was trying to say. He really had been scared. He really had thought that he was in love with someone who didn't love him back.

Tony cleared his throat and straightened slightly in his seat. "Here's the thing, I've been serious about you—about us—for a long time," he said. "I didn't want to throw it at you before you seemed ready for it, but..." He took a deep breath.

Donovan waited.

"This isn't something I'm proud of, and if you ever tell anyone—especially Colby or Noah, I will completely deny it,"

Tony warned. "But I swear that by the time you let me buy you that first drink I was damn near ready to move into the building opposite you and buy my own telescope."

Donovan was surprised into laughing out loud. He put his hand over his mouth, but he was too late.

Tony's lips quirked into another of those self-mocking smiles. "I'm far less creepy in person than that makes me sound, promise."

Donovan chuckled along with him.

"Seriously sweetheart," Tony said, more softly. "I've never made a habit of pestering people who don't give me any sort of encouragement. Anyone else and I'd have shrugged and walked away after the first few times you brushed me off. You had me by the balls long before you managed to say a word to me."

Donovan reached out and stroked his fingers down Tony's cheek. Maybe Tony didn't panic. Maybe he didn't make every emotion he felt obvious to the whole world, but right then Donovan had no doubt that Tony was making a point of letting Donovan in and seeing every vulnerability he had.

Donovan had never seen him look stronger, more dominant or more perfect.

Leaning forward, he brushed their lips together. It didn't take long for Tony to slide his fingers into Donovan's hair, alter the angle and take complete control of the kiss.

Donovan breathed a sigh of relief. As the kiss ended, he dipped his head so their foreheads rested together.

"I do love you, too," Donovan said. "I'm not just saying it, and it's not just because you...because of all that." He waved a hand toward Tony's bedroom in an effort to sum up all they'd done in there without blushing any more than necessary.

"Although 'all that' is a very nice addition," Tony said.

Donovan smiled, but he wasn't going to let Tony brush aside the things he needed to hear after he'd gone to the trouble to say so much to reassure him.

Donovan closed his eyes for a moment. "The only reason I kept going back to the pub, even though I hated other people hitting on me, and even when I was sure I'd never even be able to have a conversation with you without hyperventilating, was because… For a whole year, just being in the same room as you was the highlight of my week."

"I never even caught you looking in my direction."

"A lot of the time I used to sit with my back to you and eavesdrop. Even doing that seemed like taking a huge chance. If I'd known you and your family were so relaxed about the whole 'acting like a stalker' thing, I might have taken more risks…"

Tony laughed and brushed their lips together in a quick, sweet, kiss.

Donovan smiled against his lips. He took a deep breath. "I do love you. I am your boyfriend. I'll never want that to change." He had a strong suspicion that he wasn't the only one who was savouring those words as he said them for the first time. "I'd also really like us to go back to your bedroom right now, so we can have sex and get kinky," Donovan added, with his best approximation of the teasing tone Tony so often used with him.

Tony grinned. Donovan was pretty sure they both knew exactly whose voice Donovan could hear whispering in the dark recesses of his mind right then.

You are my boyfriend. I do love you. I want to have sex with you every chance I get. None of that is ever going to change.

Author's Note.

There's a free short story that catches up with Tony and Donovan as their relationship progresses. It's called Tony's Move and you can find it on my website.

Other books by Kim Dare

Series

Werewolves & Dragons
The Avian Shifters
Kinky Cupid
FIT Guys
Thrown to the Lions
Rawlings Men
Sex Sells
Sun, Sea and Submission
The Whole A-Z
Pack Discipline
G-A-Y Lust Bites
Perfect Timing
Collared
Pushing the Envelope
Kinky Quickies

Stand Alone Titles

With a Kiss
Mistletoe and Submission
His Very Last Chance
The Gift
Secret Service
Blood Slave
In the Heat of the Moment
Elliot's War
Trust, Love, Submit
Whispers
Between Tooth and Paw

Kim Dare has also written a number of free short stories.
You can find these on her website.

About the Author

Kim is a bisexual submissive from Wales (UK). First published in 2008, she has since released over 100 BDSM erotic romance titles ranging from short stories to full length novels. Having worked with a host of fantastic e-publishers, she moved into self publishing in 2013.

While she occasionally enjoys writing other pairings, most of Kim's stories focus on Male/Male relationships. But, no matter what the pairing, from paranormal to contemporary, and from the sweet to the intense, everything she writes will always feature three things - Kink, Love and a Happy Ending.

You can find out more about Kim's books on her website, follow her on twitter, catch up with her blog, and email her directly using the links below.

Website: **www.kimdare.com**
Twitter: **www.twitter.com/KimDareAuthor**
Blog: **www.kimdare.wordpress.com**
E-mail: **kim@kimdare.com**

www.ingramcontent.com/pod-product-compliance
Lightning Source LLC
Chambersburg PA
CBHW020826180626
46814CB00001B/118